CHILDREN OF OUR AGE

CHILDREN
OF OUR
AGE

A.M.
BAKALAR

JANTAR PUBLISHING
LONDON 2017

First published in London, Great Britain in 2017 by
Jantar Publishing Ltd
www.jantarpublishing.com

A.M. Bakalar
Children of Our Age

Cover and book design by Jack Coling

Grateful acknowledgment is made to the producers of the 'Angielski' series, on BBC Radio 4, where
portions of this novel were broadcast in a slightly different form as 'A Woman of Your Dreams'.

A CIP catalogue record for this book is available from the British Library.
ISBN 978-0-9933773-3-4

Printed and bound in the Czech Republic by EUROPRINT a.s.

For Nancy and Maria

We are children of our age,
it's a political age.

All day long, all through the night,
all affairs –
yours, ours, theirs –
are political affairs.

Whether you like it or not,
your genes have a political past,
your skin, a political cast,
your eyes, a political slant.

WISŁAWA SZYMBORSKA

It's always easier to change places
than change lives.

DANY LAFERRIÈRE

PART ONE

FEBRUARY

1

There were other things, less terrible things, the Kulesza brothers were supposed to be doing. Instead, they drove solemnly across the western boroughs to perform their duty, the only reason why they were expected to be there. The Kulesza brothers seldom relished their threatening disposition. They did not fully understand, or try to understand, how they had managed to find themselves in this business. But it was one thing they were good at, and it came so easily to them, like they were born to erase the lives of others.

Their car rolled slowly to the side of the pavement. A lighter's flame illuminated Damian's face. The lid of his left eye covered the eyeball half way from the outer edge, a remnant of a boxing fight gone wrong, but a small price to pay for a hard-won victory.

'Leave it running,' Damian instructed Igor and got out of the car, slamming the door behind him. He rubbed his damaged eye with his index finger, which watered a little whenever he smoked or when he became agitated. The doctor had once told him he could have it repaired, it would take less than a day's stay in the private eye clinic. No doubt it would improve his vision, but Damian liked the scar. It gave him a sombre and fearsome look.

Damian crossed the street in long strides. He was half a head taller than his younger brother, but if Igor wore thick-soled shoes or puffed his chest and straightened his arched back, the difference was almost unnoticeable. The Kulesza brothers had hard bodies moulded by the years of boxing training and street fights back in Poland – their backs, arms and faces were prominently freckled, their heads shaved. They had only fought each other once, during the club 'Gwardia' championships in their home-town Łódź. A draw.

Damian pushed the door open and entered the building. There was no light in the corridor. He swore because he would have to walk up the stairs to the fourth floor. The staircase smelled of cat piss, a nauseating stink of cooked cabbage hung in the air, and other foul smells he could not quite recognise. At the base of the stairs, household waste was strewn everywhere. He heard a door shutting on the floor below and the muffled melody of someone's phone. He stopped in front of door number A12 and listened. A child's cry was audible from next door, then a woman's high-pitched screaming, then silence. He pounded once on the door with a hand curled into a tight fist. He waited; no one came to the door. He hit the door again. This time he heard quick footsteps and a thin voice.

'Open up,' Damian shouted, then released profanities into the air like flickering sparks.

An eye peered through the narrow opening from inside and Damian kicked his way in.

'I didn't expect you tonight,' a man in his early twenties stammered weakly, and backed away inside the apartment. He gingerly massaged the place where the door had bruised his forehead.

Damian slammed the door behind him. 'I didn't know I needed an invitation.'

'No, of course not. Come in, come in.' The man smiled, trying to keep his voice steady. His could feel a painful bruise forming under his searching fingertips.

With his back to the man, Damian examined the room. Small flies buzzed excitedly about the window, butting the pane. An ashtray full of cigarette ends balanced on the arm of the sofa, and there were dark holes burned into the tattered fabric. On the floor were empty cardboard boxes from yesterday's delivery of Chinese food and a half-full bottle of Coke. Damian allowed the ash from his burning cigarette to fall onto the filthy carpet.

'I thought we had a deal?' Damian turned around and stepped forward. 'Imagine my surprise when I was told that you've been messing around again, spending the money you should have brought to me.' He poked the man's chest with his finger, digging into his sternum.

'Who told you?' the man asked anxiously. 'Karol said it was okay. He said it.'

Damian laughed at this poor attempt at lying. 'The question you should be asking now is what I am going to do to you?' Damian cocked his head to one side and rubbed his bald head. His left eye started to water again but he let the tear run onto his stubbled cheek.

'Damian, please. I'll give it all back. I swear.' The man folded his hands in a prayer and touched the fingertips to his lips as he spoke.

Damian smiled, dimples formed in his cheeks. 'I know.'

He took a swing and his clenched fist landed on the man's jaw, breaking it. Blood splattered on the lamp shade standing nearby. More blood flowed from the man's open mouth. Damian's second punch landed in his stomach; the third one met the other side of his jaw. The man fell to the ground, toppling the ashtray on the way and falling into the empty food boxes, sending whatever re-mained of the noodles onto the floor.

'Look what you did.' Damian turned around to find the bath-room and a clean towel. He wiped red beads of blood from his leather jacket then walked back into the room where the man lay unconscious. He threw the towel on his face and it slowly soaked up blood.

Implementing brutality in the name of Karol was the least satisfying part of the job but this time Damian preferred to act on his own, rather than asking his brother to do it. Igor's capacity for cruelty far exceeded Damian's and, tragically, was his life's greatest accomplishment. There was no alternative path to Igor's life other than tireless ferocity. Damian had suggested they took turns. He did not want either of them to grow too familiar with this existence.

Damian stepped over the unconscious body and looked around the place, hoping he could find the money, but after thirty minutes of turning each shelf and cupboard inside out he found nothing. The money was gone.

Out in the street, Damian walked back to the car. Igor watched him through the window. There was some blood under his fingernails, Igor noticed, as Damian lit a fresh cigarette. Damian bit into the filter, balancing the cigarette in his mouth, took a pocketknife and slowly began to clean his fingernails.

Igor waited for Damian to say something.

'He didn't have it,' Damian said. 'Let's go.'

Since he was a child Damian had remembered his mother's instructions to look out for his younger brother, in her severe motherly tone.

When Igor cornered a girl in the classroom during a break, and crushed her body against the burning radiator, so he could finger her barely forming breasts under the school uniform, Damian took the blame. He let their mother scream at him until she was short of breath. 'I told you to take care of him! How many times do I have to tell you? Is it so much to ask?' But she never raised a hand at them, never slapped their cheeks or pulled their ears: that was their father's job. Because the mother refused to physically discipline the boys, the Kulesza brothers never had the sense of their mother's presence in their lives, not in the same way as their father's.

Later, Damian would wait until the school day ended and follow the girl on her way home – they all lived in the same low-rise blocks of flats – then suddenly grab her skinny arm, shake her roughly and loosely, and say, 'If you ever go to the teacher again I will break your arm.' The girl was too scared to breathe. She would start crying, terrified and powerless, because Damian's grip would tighten and leave red marks on her skin for the next few days. 'Your brother is sick. He should go to a doctor,' the girl sobbed, gathering her last shreds of courage. 'There's nothing wrong with my brother. Nothing! You hear me.' The girl's thin ponytails bounced when she broke into a run, lifting her knees high up. The red and yellow plastic reflective lights attached to the back of her schoolbag slapped against each other, so vigorously that one of them fell off and crashed into pieces as it hit the ground.

As early as primary school, Igor struggled with reading and writing. He lacked the energy and patience to understand what was being asked of him. As a consequence, Igor repeated classes five and six; tongue-tied, yet defiant, every time his parents scrutinised his school certificate. That was how he ended up in the same class with Damian, after their parents bribed the head teacher to let Igor study with Damian in the same class. 'It's best if he's not out of his brother's sight,' Zenon Kulesza suggested and pushed an envelope with American dollars across the headmaster's desk. 'They can learn from each other.' And from now on, Igor never had to repeat a single semester, old Kulesza made sure his education was taken care of. Damian solved all the tests for him and did his homework. When Igor stood under a black board in front of the class, he did not even pretend he was trying to answer the teacher's questions, with his pale lips locked into silence, his freckles burning, he knew, thanks to his brother, he did not even need to prove his knowledge because he had the bare minimum. Education, an unnecessary obligation, was the teachers' responsibility, not Igor's. The life he imagined for himself had nothing to do with mathematics, chemistry or history classes.

If there was something wrong with Igor's head, nobody, not even the teachers dared to say anything aloud or report it to the headmaster. Whenever they suspected something, exchanging hushed comments in the teachers' room about Igor's unashamed lack of willingness to learn the periodic table or complaints brought to their attention by anxious parents, they kept those concerns to themselves, because old Kulesza worked for the police. People talked about broken noses and ribs, neighbours beaten up to a pulp because old Kulesza – with other police in tow – had paid them a visit. The teachers and parents were scared, even if they pretended not to be in front of each other. The teachers wanted to help but did not know how, instead they orchestrated scores of lies of how they would treat every incident of Igor's sinister behaviour with full attention and report it to the headmaster's office, or even higher, to the regional teachers' association, if there was no improvement in the boy's behaviour. They also promised to talk to his father. The parents did not believe the teachers. They saw how scared the teachers were themselves when old Kulesza's name was mentioned during parent-teacher meetings, and the obvious absences of the headmaster in all the meetings, so they instructed their children to stay away from Igor. The parents did not know how serious Igor's condition was but they knew he looked more like a man than a boy. It was enough for them to warn their daughters to keep their distance, always find another girl to walk with back home after school.

Sometimes Zenon Kulesza arrived to the school in his police car to pick up the brothers, a blue Fiat 125p, with a white stripe under its windows and a large white inscription *Milicja* against the blue background on both sides. The coughing roar of the engine, as old Kulesza stepped over and over again on the accelerator pedal before switching off the engine, rattled the thin single-pane windows in the school building. When he marched across the empty school corridor, Zenon's leather boots squeaked so loudly on the polished tiled floor that the teachers and students could clearly hear them, even if they sat in the classroom behind closed doors.

The rumour was that their father was the best interrogation officer against the Solidarity-led opposition; that he could smell a lie on you before you had even thought about hiding it from him. At home, the Kulesza brothers knew that it was best to confess before their father touched the buckle of his stiff police belt. Luckily, Zenon's secretive job required him to spend days, even weeks, away from home, locked away in an undisclosed location, until he mercilessly forced statements of dubious truth from his enervated victims. Sometimes the brothers did not see their father for a month or two. Their mother's hoarse voice, tired from shouting at them, would launch a threat as a last resort in a vain attempt to take control, 'Wait till your father gets back home.' And for the first few days, the boys calmed down and dutifully followed their mother's requests: to clean their cluttered room, but soon, with no father in sight, they again did whatever they wanted, ignoring their mother and letting her cry herself to sleep

alone or bury her head in her Harlequin novels for whole after-
noons and evenings.

It was only when Zenon Kulesza was back home that the house
was still; even the mother was speaking in murmurs. The brothers, behind the shut door in the small room they shared, nurtured
their silent anger and burning tears, massaging their aching backs
where their father's buckle landed, planning their future revenge
in hot whispers.

Because Zenon Kulesza was a strong believer that physical
exercise was the best cure for any illness, he decided to send the
boys for boxing lessons. It was the first time the parents had come
close to facing Igor's illness, though they had never actually mentioned the word 'illness', a fixture of contention in any argument
about the brothers. Instead, they referred to it as 'this thing in his
head' (the father) or 'boys growing up' (the mother). If Zenon
suspected that there was something wrong with his son he never
admitted it. Such acknowledgment would expose his failure as
a husband and a father, or worse, he would become a subject of
cruel jokes among his colleagues. Zenon knew exactly what happened to crazy people – locked in an institution, permanently
obliterated from everybody's memory, slowly dying out of sight.
He personally drove the members of the opposition to the psychi-
atric hospitals across the country, to undergo mental reorientation,
but none of the traitors came out alive.

'A good beating is what they need,' Zenon said to his wife, who
often voiced her concerns just before they fell asleep: her failure to
discipline the brothers, Igor's erratic rages, how she was becoming
tired of asking Zenon to do something because she could not take
it any longer. The exchanges between them, in the middle of the
night, often led to the mother blaming the boys' unruly behaviour

on Zenon's frequent absences, until Zenon ordered her to shut up because she was giving him a headache.

And so, three times a week, after school, the mother took the brothers to a boxing club which ran afternoon classes for policemen's children. It was an hour's bus ride from their home to the police training complex, shared with the army.

She usually sat with a book in her hand, on a hard plastic chair, which numbed her buttocks, and waited until the training had finished. There were other mothers, women who always sat at the same table and shared home-made puff pastry cakes with whipped cream. They held themselves back whenever she was around, saving comments about their husbands' overdue promotions for later when they would visit each other's houses with no strangers eavesdropping, or perhaps they were afraid they would say something they should not in front of Zenon's wife. Who knew if she would not repeat what she overheard to her husband? A harmless, inconsequential conversation could easily deliver a deadly and irrevocable sanction. The women did not like Zenon's growing power, closing the way for their own husbands to rise within the police ranks, so they did not invite her to be part of their group. It was safer to keep the distance, loyal to each other. She did not mind sitting on her own. In fact, she looked forward to this hour and a half, sometimes two hours, because at home with two boys there was always something to do. With a book in her hand, she was deaf to grunts and shouts coming out from the gym, letting herself sink into the world of Harlequin romances.

The first time Damian witnessed Igor's forceful thrusts, with his trousers at his ankles and his bomber jacket still on, humming to himself in painful pleasure, was on a train going to southern

Poland, one of the towns on the way to the Tatry mountains. The brothers wanted to test how far they could go without being caught by the ticket collectors, an experiment in teenage courage, something else to do on a school day because they were bored. Who cared which king ruled Poland in the 16th century, or which enemy nations partitioned the country centuries later, erasing their homeland from the map of Europe? Damian left Igor on his own only for a moment, he needed to use the toilet. When Damian came back, he was surprised to find the curtains inside the compartment were drawn, so he walked past the sliding door, unsure which wagon he left his brother in, only to return and open one door after another. Igor briefly turned his face at the sound of the sliding door, without stopping his thrusting movements, and, seeing Damian, only smiled at him, his freckles almost brown. A half-moan, half-sob, escaped the girl's lips. Damian slowly pushed the glassed door with both hands and leaned against it, facing the window dirtied by the streaks of rain. He counted the passing power poles, until Igor was done with the girl, to take his mind off a sensation growing in the pit of his stomach. For a long time Damian tried to deny Igor's sexual obsessions, this thing in Igor's head that took control over his body.

Damian would have liked his brother to warn him, if he wanted to do anything like that in the future, rather than accidently finding him doing it. What if it was somebody else, a stranger, especially in a public place? Whatever Igor did to the women did not scare Damian, he saw it as a natural urge in a man's body; a stupid thing you did when you were young so you did not do it when you were older. What worried Damian more was the reaction of the others, who would surely find a way to separate them, something Damian could not begin to imagine.

The door slid open from the inside and Igor let the girl out. She wobbled on her feet as the train moved, back down the walkway to her compartment, three carriages away.

'I want to help you,' Damian said, as he sat down opposite Igor and leaned forward, propping his elbows on his legs, 'but you need to tell me what you want and when you want it.' The pungent odour of Igor's sweat hung in the air.

Igor only shrugged and mumbled frantically that how he was supposed to know he wanted to have sex, if he did not know himself until it was actually happening?

Damian did not know how to be angry with his brother. He knew Igor could not control himself, so Damian would have to find a way to protect him.

Years later, when Damian stood outside the prison gate, waiting for Igor to emerge after a two-year sentence, he blamed himself for everything; for not taking enough care of his brother like he was supposed to, for failing Igor's trust, for hoping that it was a teenage phase and that it would soon pass. He hoped that Igor would at least give him some kind of indication when his mind conjured smouldering thoughts and desires that pushed his body into action, but Igor did not.

'Mother didn't come?' Igor asked in a quiet voice, after holding Damian in a clumsy embrace. He was bulkier now, after training in the prison gym every day, and worked as a helper in the kitchen where he could eat as much as he wanted.

Damian could not bring himself to tell Igor that old Kulesza forbade their mother from coming, that he had banned her from mentioning Igor's name ever again, so they could not go back to their parents' home together. 'He's not my son,' Zenon Kulesza said fiercely when their mother pleaded for his forgiveness. Igor was still so young and it was not his fault that he was born like that. 'That he is retarded?' Zenon shouted back, shaking at his own powerlessness in the face of Igor's violent actions. He erased Igor's name from his memory, ashamed but defiant that his son's behaviour had nothing to do with Zenon Kulesza's name.

'We'll go to my place,' Damian said, 'and tomorrow I'll take you to the garage. You can work there with me.'

'I don't want to work in a garage.'

'What do you want to do?'

'Nothing.' Igor stared through the car window at the passing poplar trees lined alongside the cracked asphalt road.

'There's a new gym. We can go there after work when I finish.'

Igor twisted his lips into what resembled a smile. 'I want to get rid of this,' he said, pointing to an ink dot on his nose. 'Can you do that?'

There had been so many sleepless nights in Igor's cell immediately after his imprisonment, he was so focused on getting through the nights that he stopped counting the days to the end of his confinement, he had lost track of his life outside. Then, one day, exhausted from the night panic, he let down his guard; the hands of somebody stronger than him nailed him down in the common bathroom, penetrating pain from behind ruptured through his body, and left him unconscious with a broken nose crushed against the tiled wall. After the swelling from his face subsided, a dot emerged on his nose among the freckles. No amount of scrubbing would take it away, until he realised it would be on his face forever, as long as he remained inside. A stubborn ferocity to survive awakened in him, and with that dot, his hostile self had begun to emerge, a forced mark of his monstrosity. Now, free at last, Igor did not need to wear it any longer.

'I want you to use a knife,' Igor said. 'A scar by a knife will look better than this.' Igor rolled his sleeve to show a piece of pinkish skin deformed by cigarette burns.

So he did it. With a steady hand, Damian slowly drew the sharp edge of the knife across his brother's nose, who gripped onto Damian's legs with both hands as he sat on the edge of the bathtub, and Damian on a kitchen stool in front of Igor. Damian wiped the trickling blood with coarse greyish toilet paper. Then he handed Igor a small mirror. Igor turned his face from one side to another to inspect Damian's cut.

2

'Are you telling me you can't do your job?' Karol was staring at the man, his lips puckered into a small beak. He was absently twirling an earphone cable.

Drawing his breath in, the man faltered, 'I was hoping I could... like...'

'Spit it out, will you? I haven't got time for this,' said Karol, with an exasperated roll of his eyes. He was losing patience. Karol did not inspect the houses he rented across London more than once, unless it was absolutely necessary. It was the Kulesza brothers' responsibility; drive the men (and women if there were any) to a specific location, show them around and explain how things were going to work from then on, and wait for Karol to deliver his instructions about the job situation.

The man was shifting his weight from one foot to the other, rubbing his palms against his thighs.

'So you can't do your job.' Karol delivered his verdict with finality in his voice.

'No, this is not what I'm trying to say.' The man was surprised by his own boldness and immediately regretted it.

Karol cut him short, 'I have plenty of qualified people begging me to work for me.'

'I'm sorry. It's just... I thought there would be more money.'

The comment sent Karol into exaggerated laughter, his head tilted backwards, his mouth so wide his fillings were showing. The man, not sure what else to do, joined him, smiling uncertainly. Karol, now serious, locked the man with his gaze and asked, 'Do you know how many people wanted your job? I could have given it to somebody else, but I trusted you when you begged me to take you on. Do you even realise what I had to go through?' Karol mustered a look of fake sympathy. 'I have created this opportunity for you to come to this country but what do I get in return? Ungratefulness and criticism that you're not making enough money. If you want to work for somebody else be my guest. The door is wide open. Go on.' Karol closed his eyes and theatrically extended his arm. He liked to make grand gestures. It took no effort, modulating his voice, eyes feral with emotion, disorientating his listeners by constantly shifting his moods around them.

Throughout the conversation the man avoided looking in the direction of Igor, with his scarred face. He was leaning against the door frame, scratching the tip of his cut nose; an uneven line. Damian stood next to him, biting the nail of his little finger, and every now and then spitting bits onto the floor.

'The Kulesza brothers are going to pick you all up tomorrow morning at six sharp. Unless there's something else you'd like to talk about?'

The man shook his head. His face tightened.

'How's your family? Children all healthy?' Damian interjected, his pale blue eyes cold.

'Yes, they are fine,' the man hastened to reply.

'Good,' Igor said. He had not spoken since he had entered the room. He rarely opened his mouth, and if he did, he used the minimum number of words possible; the man would have preferred it if Igor remained quiet. Cold sweat formed on the man's wrinkled forehead.

Karol waited to let that hint of threat disappear and be forgotten. It never failed to amaze him how the brothers' presence could shift the dynamics in the room, effortless yet with a frightful efficiency, and the most annoying thing to Karol was that they seemed utterly unaware of the impact they generated. He envied them. Then he said, 'If you need anything you can always talk to Damian or Igor.' Karol fumbled in his bag and took out three crumpled purple packets of Silk Cut. 'Before I forget. For you and the others.'

The man failed to catch all the packets and two fell on the floor, which made Igor snigger; Karol shook his head. It was going to be even easier than he imagined.

Damian paused in the doorway, behind Karol and Igor, and said, 'You should clean in here. It stinks.'

On the floor were three yellowed mattresses and plastic bags in the corner of the room. There were no chairs or a table apart from the one in the kitchen area; all the rooms looked the same: empty spaces except for the mattresses on the floors and heaped ashtrays.

Outside, they walked until they reached the nearest coffee shop, close to the entrance to Norbury station.

'Get me a latte with a sprinkle of cinnamon, nutmeg and three spoonfuls of sugar,' Karol said to Damian, sitting down at a small table outside.

'Are you like fucking Italian or something?' Damian asked with a half-smile.

'Just get me what I want,' Karol snapped, raising his voice unnecessarily, which had the opposite effect than he intended, making him sound thin and too strident.

'What about you?' Damian asked his brother.

'A beer. And chips.'

Inside, a West Indian woman hummed to the vibrant tones of music, blasting from a small radio on the shelf above her head. There was a well-built man sitting on a footstool in the corner, the kind of man Damian would happily acknowledge if they were in the gym or in a ring together. He respected the effort it took to build a body so that it showcased its presence. The man fell silent when Damian entered to make his order. Damian stared at the woman's micro braided hair and wondered how much of it was real. The fact she was smiling at him without any apparent reason made him uncomfortable. Damian did not extend niceties to people he did not know, or anybody else for that matter. This new country with its foreign people puzzled him, and once again he felt a heart-breaking longing for home, a place that did not make him feel so dizzy and out of place and inconsequential, unless he was among his own people.

'Would you like ketchup or mayo with your chips?' the woman asked as she placed the paper plate in front of him.

Damian hesitated then asked for both. The first two English words he had learnt and he had recognised because they sounded so similar in his own language.

When he set the beer bottle and a large coffee cup on the table, a thin crust of grime on the sides, Karol was in the middle of a phone conversation while Igor lazily puffed a cigarette, forming circles of smoke. Damian went back inside for the rest of the order. Karol occasionally picked up a chip as he talked, dipping it slowly in ketchup and mayonnaise, before stuffing it into his mouth as he talked.

'Did you hear him?' Karol asked, recalling the conversation in the flat. His tone was alive with disbelief, a well-practised emphasis which ensured others around him paid him the attention he desired. There was a dab of mayonnaise in the corner of his mouth. 'To ask me, me, about more money, as if it never occurred to him that he belongs to me now and it's up to me to decide what to do with his sorry arse.'

Karol knew the type: as soon as the initial fear of living in a foreign country subsided, with a roof over their heads, settling into the schedule of daily work and having learnt how to say thank you in English, they thought they had an idea of how to survive here without his generous protection. He needed to make sure his workers knew their place. He had realised very quickly that maintaining a certain level of uncertainty and fear was a good way for them to garner the respect and gratitude he deserved. Their fate was in his hands. Taking away people's dignity was the easiest and most natural thing he had ever done.

'We'll deal with him,' Damian said, slowly sipping his beer, and watching people as they rushed to the station.

'But nothing dramatic. I need him to be able to work.' Karol's hand hovered over the plate with chips.

Igor cracked his knuckles, unhappy that Karol had unceremoniously helped himself to his food.

'Sure,' Damian said. It occurred to Damian that his brother could crush Karol's fingers with his one hand and he smiled inside at the thought.

Karol knitted his brows at Igor. If it were not for his brother, Karol would never have had anything to do with him. He was never too sure what to expect from Igor, eager to jump at any opportunity to exert physical force. Karol needed him but he needed Damian more, to control his brother. 'I placed another advertisement. Kętrzyn, Bartoszyce, Biskupiec.'

'What about Ełk?' asked Damian.

Karol wiped a glob of ketchup off his chin. 'You think you can do it?'

'Under 120 kilometres from Bartoszyce.'

'I'll add Ełk to the list. This should be enough.'

'Where are you planning to cross the border?' Karol asked. He liked to keep track of the crucial travel points and make sure they did not use the same border crossing more than twice.

'Słubice,' Damian replied. 'Igor will drive. I'm leaving next week to do some work on the ground.' Once Igor arrived, they would have a window of 24 hours to collect everybody and return to Britain.

Karol was not interested in helping people for free. Over the decade of his dealings with fellow Poles, whether back home or in Britain, he had learnt one thing – everybody and everything was for sale.

The advertisements Karol placed in the local papers across Polish towns were short:

Work in London. £200-600 a week. Men and women. Email: info22@wp.pl, or, when he was in a creative mood: *We're looking for honest and hardworking Poles to join our London-based company. No English needed. Accommodation and bus transfers to London provided. Email:poloniusz@plusnet.pl.*

Within 48 hours the email account – depending on which version he had published – would receive enough responses to fill up two buses. But before Karol decided on the final list, it was critical to find out more details about the respondents' personal situations. Usually a simple question about the reasons why a person wanted to come to Britain provided him with the necessary information. He always assumed the persona of a careful listener. Allowing people to tell their life stories, share their unrealistic dreams, gave Karol the leverage he would need later. The second stage was to make sure the level of desperation in the person's voice was sufficient for Karol to push them in the direction he desired. 'I can only offer this job to somebody who really, really needs it,' Karol would say over the phone, in a carefully prepared monologue, deliberately softening his voice, without a trace of impatience or demand. He flooded the listener with an enticing amount of information, just how much their lives would get better if they trusted his expertise. It was only a matter of time before the person would beg him for a job, buoyed by the smooth words falling out of Karol's mouth. And that was exactly what Karol was waiting to hear, loud and clear, because there was one thing he always made sure of – he never forced anybody to do anything against their will. If people were stupid enough to trust in his lies, Karol believed they deserved to suffer the consequences.

Karol knew how to make people trust him. The unemployed were the easiest to seduce, especially after Karol recalled his invented struggles to find a decent job over the years. So he could tell them he knew exactly how it felt, to wake up day after day with a drowning thought – how to make mortgage payments or pay the bills. Sometimes, he added that he was an orphan, or that his mother died when he was five and he was forced to take care of his siblings, or that his father had left their family before Karol was born. People from small towns and villages soon warmed to these fabricated stories, after he added that he was from a small town himself, with no English when he had arrived in Britain. Who else could they trust if not a fellow countryman? After all, they spoke the same language. Fathers with small children heard that he, too, was a father of two little ones, the lights of his life, and that he would do anything for them – he was wholeheartedly convinced they would do the same for their own children. Those who did not want to leave their newly wedded wives were told, of course, they could bring them over when they settled in, but they had to make the first step and take this opportunity he was now offering. To the middle aged and older, unable to compete with the educated young who spoke two or three languages, he explained that they had a bright future, and that, actually, he preferred mature candidates because they were committed in a way younger men were not. And the twenty-year-olds were assured that gaining experience abroad would work wonders on their CVs, not to mention the language skills that would put them in the privileged position when they de-cided to return home. But the most important thing was: make a decision now, because this job was a once-in-a-life-time opportu-nity and the list was practically closed. 'But in your particular case I am willing to make an exception because you have convinced me how much you want this,' he would finish, loudly and emphatically, ready to quash any hint of hesitancy.

And then there were the homeless. The Kulesza brothers lured them in upon Karol's instructions. They were Karol's most foolish victims, so easy to allure that he could send Igor and Damian to do the job for him. Child's play. With their faded, thinning hair and pallid skin, alone in their daily lethargy because nobody noticed them or could imagine a brighter, different future for them. Except Karol. Their desperate circumstances provided the perfect oppor-tunity to dismantle their lives and re-assemble them again to suit his own well-thought-out plans.

When he travelled to Poland, Damian was in charge of these hopeless cases. He towered over their shrunken bodies perched somewhere on a wooden park bench with green, flaky paint. Damian would sit down, close, to ensure he was not repulsed, like some of the women who hastened their steps and pushed prams with loathing washed across their faces. By the second cigarette the men had a future none of their friends would believe was possible, sleeping in abandoned and long-forgotten train stations or in the city's tunnels. A faded memory momentarily awakened – 'Don't trust strangers.' – the mothers used to warn them, at the time when they still had families who cared about them, because they were sweet little children once, before they were spat onto the streets. Was there anything worse that could possibly happen to them? Britain may be unfamiliar and foreign, but it was, nevertheless, a place where somebody wanted them.

Karol had a flip chart installed in his home office, next to the black and white detailed map of Poland which took up over half of the wall. He drew circles in blue around towns and villages where he had placed the advertisements for the first time, in red when they appeared the next year in the same geographical region. Next to the names of the places, he scrupulously noted the numbers of people recruited. The letters 'DK' were added to numbers of the homeless Damian Kulesza had approached.

Milena, Karol's partner, once observed to her friend Ines that she had never seen anybody so obsessed with numbers, charts and spreadsheets, except the accountants in her office.

'He only keeps his laptop on his desk and perhaps one or two pages of the spreadsheet he's currently working on.' Ines said that it was better to have a man who knew how to keep his surroundings neat because it was such a rare virtue. Milena agreed and said, 'The cleaner doesn't have much to do in his office.' But she did not mention to Ines that the door to his office was usually locked when he was not at home and even she did not have a spare key.

That night, acting on Karol's instructions, Igor and Damian returned to the flat where the men they had brought from Poland awaited. Thick cigarette smoke hung in the air above their heads in the kitchen while the men ate sandwiches they had prepared themselves. The bread was unevenly cut; some slices were thicker on one side. Ham and cheese. The sound of swallowing, coughing and spoons, clinking inside glasses, greeted the Kulesza brothers when they arrived.

'You.' Igor pointed at the man they had seen in the morning.

His name was Tadeusz Mysiak but for the Kulesza brothers his name was not worth remembering.

The man looked around at the others gathered at the table but nobody moved. Instead, they kept eating in silence, staring at the plates before them.

When Tadeusz Mysiak stood up, Damian took his seat at the table and helped himself to one of the sandwiches. 'Have you got any beer?' he asked.

One of the men muttered under his breath, 'In the fridge.'

Because Damian did not move, the man stood up to pick up the can of *Tyskie* beer and handed it to Damian. After a few gulps, Damian released a loud burp and tapped his chest with a hand curled into a tight fist.

Mysiak's face was aflame. Grabbing Mysiak by the arm, as soon as the door to the bedroom closed behind them, Igor dragged him to the opposite wall and shoved his head against it. The man's face was twisted in pain, his lips curled around a suppressed moan.

'We're going to Poland soon. We were thinking of visiting your family.'

'Please,' Mysiak whispered.

'What?'

'There's no need.'

'Don't you want to go back to your family?'

'They need me here,' the man gasped on the verge of tears.

Igor's middle finger snapped painfully against the man's ear. 'Then stop complaining and do your job.'

3

The offices of Milena's Travel, Milena's travel agency, were on the first floor. There was no buzzer; the door was always open during the day to allow the customers to freely access the companies located in the building. On the landing was a small table crammed with a selection of Polish magazines and papers published in Britain: *Cooltura, Goniec, Polish Express,* but also monthlies and weeklies, celebrity and gossip magazines shipped from Poland. Milena prided herself on her knowledge on what was happening back home. She liked to have the latest editions of her favourite publications at hand. When a friend visited her, she liked to have a new outfit by some upcoming Polish designer, recently propelled into stardom on Warsaw TV stations and fashion blogs. She had already ordered a new dress and was waiting for its delivery to her house.

The only customers that called or visited Milena's Travel were Poles. Milena spoke English only in an emergency and throughout all the years of living in Britain she only had to use it once or twice. Though she employed people who spoke English, when she was hiring them the knowledge of the language was rarely a priority, and because her English was limited, she could never tell exactly how well they could communicate. Milena's Travel was a Polish company in the heart of London servicing Poles only. Nobody else ever called.

Milena had worked very hard in order to gain the status of the longest standing, and most profitable, Polish travel agency. According to Milena, this success was due to her unwavering vision, patience, and her admirable work ethic. She used almost the same words when she was nominated for the Polish Business

Woman of the Year Award, at a lavish gathering of women at the Polish Embassy on Portland Place. The Ambassador Janusz Kopecki warmly congratulated Milena for her hard work in front of the excited crowd packed into the Chinese Room on the first floor. A buffet of traditional Polish food was served under crystal chandeliers and the string quartet momentarily hushed the loud, female voices. It was not an evening to miss by any woman who ran her own business. But despite Milena's success at creating a bridge for the families between the two countries – the Ambassador's words that brought a controlled but nervous smile to her lips, enough to acknowledge that yes, she deserved this accolade she was now convinced she was about to receive – Milena Sosnowska was not going to be the Polish Business Woman of the Year. Instead, Renata Wawrzynik, the founder of Renata Wawrzynik Foundation devoted to helping homeless Poles in Britain return to their families in Poland, was the indisputable, and unsurprising, winner, much to Milena's well-hidden but unexpected disappointment. Afterwards, late in the night alone and defeated, standing slump-shouldered in front of an open fridge in her spacious and carefully designed kitchen, she devoured two boxes of strawberry jam doughnuts with a gulp from a soft drink straight from the bottle to help her swallow.

Any kind of failure did not sit well with Milena, but nor did it sit too long, and the next day she usually threw herself back into work with more vigour.

And here she was, on Wednesday morning, storming through the front door, across the main corridor straight to her office with immaculately coiffed deep, electric ruby hair. She sat down in front of her desk without taking off her expensive knee-length coat, playing with a long earring in her left ear as she spoke to somebody on her customised mobile phone. She straightened her arm above her head and shook it, clinking the bangle bracelets on her wrist and snapping her fingers at the same time to attract the attention of the women sitting in the room opposite hers.

Six weeks previously, Milena had her manicure and pedicure appointment at the Ines Hair and Beauty Salon established by her friend. By the entrance hung a wooden plate with shiny, metal plaque attached in the centre, inscribed in capital letters: BEAUTY AMBASSADRESS – INES JANIAK, surrounded by a wide selection of framed black and white photographs with the owner and a number of recognisable Polish celebrities. This flourishing display boasted an air of prestige and exclusivity, immediately humbling those who entered the premises and letting them know at once that they were among the select few who had access to this highly sought-after establishment.

Milena was the only customer Ines Janiak attended to personally, leaving the others in the hands of her three skilled employees – two women and one man. It was not that Milena did not trust Kuba – the hairstylist whom Ines lured into her London salon from Manchester, and the main reason why you had to call at least three months in advance to book an appointment – or the two women who boasted equal prestige, Patrycja and Nikola. There were stories that nobody else could hear, fiery gossip and secrets the two women traded. There was a network of connections Milena and Ines maintained, names and phone numbers that swapped hands in the downstairs beautician's room, behind the accordion door, away from any witnesses or prying eyes.

Six weeks ago, it was Ines who told Milena about the wife of the owner of a recently launched money transfer company. She was slowly massaging Milena's toes and applying a lavender and orange cream to her toenails. 'She has just returned from a shopping trip to Madrid,' Ines said, her head bent over Milena's feet, stroking her pale skin, 'they're looking for a new house, a holiday home. You know how cheap the properties are these days over there.' Milena nodded. Later, on the way out, Ines handed Milena a piece of paper with the woman's phone number. Milena thanked her friend and air-kissed her, wary of ruining her make-up with somebody else's lipstick.

The employees in this money transfer company were a potential goldmine for Milena's Travel holiday deals, insurance, translation services, airline and bus tickets. She was going to ask one of the girls in the office to prepare a full package for this new client, and another to stop wearing that hideous pair of jeans which made the wrong impression. Milena could not wait to talk to Karol about this new contact over dinner tonight.

Milena's Travel was her dream, Karol knew, Milena had told him when they first met.

In those days, Karol worked in the sales and marketing department of *Polish Voices*, one of the most established Polish biweekly magazines published in Britain, where Milena later would place advertisements. Milena was a tough and reluctant negotiator when Karol cold-called her, with an offer to meet and talk about the benefits her business could gain from the magazine. It was the early days of the publication, geared towards growing numbers of Polish immigrants. The owner had put pressure on the sales and marketing department to attract the widest attention of Polish-owned businesses. Karol, with his insatiable hunger for success as well as unshakeable confidence in his talent, believed he could be running the magazine one day. He was desperate to prove he was the best salesman. He wanted to carve a position for himself in the paper where he would be indispensable. He would bring a flood of money and new clients.

Milena's Travel was simply another of the companies Karol identified, a small operation, like any other business Karol recorded in his notebook to approach as a potential client.

Karol had a weekly system he implemented in the sales and marketing department, and he made sure every person who worked there followed his lead. Every Monday morning everybody looked through the Yellow Pages or searched the web and noted down company names, names of the owners which they usually found on the Companies House website, and the phone numbers. Any company they could find and preferably run by Poles. Between 11 a.m. and 1 p.m. they made phone calls, relentlessly, one after another, pacing the corridors, sitting on window sills and facing the wall or, those too self-conscious of their voices, locking themselves in a car. If a client was not interested, you moved on to the next phone number, and the next, until you got what you wanted. A lunch break would be followed by another two hours of phone calls until three in the afternoon. Afterwards they updated their diaries with the meetings they had managed to set up.

Karol explained to the team that the purpose of those phone calls was not to sell the advertisement but to set up a meeting, and only then would they talk about the product.

'During the face to face,' Karol said, standing in front of a flip chart where he noted down the number of phone calls and meetings to take place in the coming days, 'you need to talk to them so that they think placing the ad in our magazine is the best and only way to advertise their business. Always, always,' he said with emphasis, and his eyes blazed, 'make sure you tell them what the advertisement is going to do for their business. You need to force them into thinking that without us they will never be successful. Basically, they need to shit themselves.'

The whole team undertook role playing exercises to make sure they said precisely what Karol wanted them to say, not the approximation of the message but his exact words. He distributed a sheet of paper with a heading 'Prospective Clients – telephone survey' and asked them to play the roles of the secretaries, personal assistants and advisors.

'People don't react well if you introduce yourself as a sales person. I would put a phone down myself if somebody began the conversation in this way. No. But if you say you are an adviser, it's different.' Every detail of the potential conversation was scrutinised: tone of voice, 'remember to be enthusiastic and confident,' Karol said, 'don't let your voice betray you.' Karol advised what to wear to the first meeting or what to take, 'don't even think about going to a meeting without business cards or a laptop. It's all about making the right impression. Once you enter the room, place the laptop on a table and your business cards next to it. Make sure you have printed out the presentation before the meeting.'

He made them practise the strength and timbre of their voices, with a hand on the stomach so that they would feel the movement of the diaphragm, and speaking loudly and clearly, in a slightly exaggerated fashion like in a TV or radio commercial. If they deviated from the prescribed phrases, he stopped them and corrected them at once, and asked them to repeat precisely what he had written down. It was a battlefield and there was no room for error.

Karol sometimes took a colleague to a meeting with a client, to show how it was done properly. It was a mesmerising experience to watch him argue his point, wrap the client around his little finger, disperse any doubts, conduct the conversation so that he was always in charge. But there was no forced direction; instead, Karol gently guided the conversation so that the client himself came to the conclusion that what Karol offered was indispensable to the success of his business. And that was exactly what Karol wanted to achieve: for the client to think it was his idea. If the meeting looked like both Karol and the client were having a good time together, occasionally sharing jokes, laughing so hard that tears would stream down their cheeks, this was still serious business to Karol. Sweat ran down on his back, every muscle was tense, his mind had prepared multiple alternative scenarios depending on what the client said, his eyes carefully assessed every twitch of his client's face; spotting tiny signals which provided the invaluable information for Karol as to whether the client's attention was drifting, so Karol at once adjusted his argument. He may have looked relaxed, as if he was having the time of his life, but Karol never missed when a prospective client began to play with a pencil, gaze over his shoulder towards the window, played with their hair, or whatever it was that sent a signal to Karol that he needed to improve his performance. After shaking hands over newly-signed documents, Karol remained silent for a few minutes on the way back to his office, to regain his energy and to gather his thoughts, to replenish the void in his mind created by the trial of such high concentration and stress.

There was not a client Karol could not convince. He could sell anything to anybody. No doubt his performance was the kind his followers in the team aspired towards.

Milena was smiling the patient smile of someone who had heard the sales pitch before. Ordinarily, she would not waste her valuable time on somebody like Karol, but today she felt like she wanted to be noticed. She had been feeling so lonely. This man intrigued her, so confident of himself but with the right amount of respect and understanding for the woman as the owner of her own business, unlike other men she had encountered. She could not resist being flattered by his knowledge about the travel industry, and the small but steadily growing number of competitors (Karol made sure he was well prepared for the meeting). He did a great job in show-ing her not only how the advertising in the magazine was going to raise her company's profile but suggested areas where she could grow. She could not remember meeting anybody so engaged and genuinely attuned to what she was doing, apart from herself, and it felt intoxicating.

'What about translation services, money transfer, or insur-ance? You can monopolise the market before somebody else does, because somebody will. There's money to be made. There are only a handful of Polish travel operators, but you have the flexibility to move fast, a big company like the Polish Airlines LOT is going to take time.' These were the areas that were not part of Milena's Travel services but something she had already begun to consider. After all, she had only set up the company six months ago but she already had a clear idea about where she wanted to take the busi-ness. And sitting here, was a man verbalising her thoughts before she was ready to take action herself. He did not belittle her en-thusiasm because she was a woman who knew what she wanted. 'And if you just don't go about your business as soon as you can, nobody else will.' She did not even mind that he was repeating himself.

It was Karol's perfect sales pitch, he knew. And the more he talked to this woman with flaming hair, the more his mind was whirling with a plan. It suddenly occurred to him that her company really had potential which he could exploit. And there was something more, something he had not expected when he had been preparing himself for this meeting like he always did, thinking he was going to meet yet another Pole in need of direction, a businessman from a small town desperate to make it in the big city.

Milena knew exactly what she wanted. It was she who said: 'Many of those who come here will eventually get better jobs and they will start to make money, money they will want to spend. Not everyone would like to stay here but they will still need to travel between the two countries. This is one of the areas where I see my business.'

The way Milena said it, with an honesty Karol had rarely encountered. No tiptoeing around the subject, no guilt about her intentions, no apologising that perhaps another time, that she was not ready and wanted to see what was going to happen; no.

To her surprise, Milena felt herself falling, falling quickly, for this man who was so sure of himself, so comfortable in her presence and appreciative of her effort to make something of herself as a woman, when other men held it against her. Karol, too, finally felt at peace that he could share a life with somebody likeminded, unashamed of wanting more from life. They almost frightened each other into action. And if he had recognised her, so she recognised him. Their minds were skipping among endless possibilities of a life together.

A few months later he said: 'The magazine is too small for me. I'm going to set up my own marketing agency – New Market Comms.

I've already registered the domain name. I'm thinking global, they are thinking local. Their business model is not right for me.'

Milena suspected this was going to happen, Karol wanting more, it was only a matter of time.

'They are too stubborn, too short-sighted. I have no more patience for them and their petty fights over who is in charge,' he said.

Milena and Karol would, in the next weeks, ease into a lasting relationship.

They agreed it would be best if their businesses ran parallel to each other. Karol used Milena's contacts and offered marketing campaigns across the country while she, in return, had a growing number of faithful clients who did not hesitate to recommend her to their friends and business partners. Poles arrived every week, setting up businesses small and big, bringing over families, cousins, friends, anybody who had even a remote interest in coming to the island, and Milena and Karol had already been here, settled and secure, before anybody had arrived and made even more money.

'They are not like us,' Karol often said about the new wave, already thinking how to tap into this stream of revenue, and in many cases desperation, coming his way.

It was then Karol suggested she moved in with him, to a house he rented, because it lacked a female touch and Milena could transform it into their home. He said they were good together, so why not make each other happy?

If Karol attended evenings planned by Milena, it was only because the people she had invited had enough money to spend – or knew others who ignited his curiosity – enough to appear alongside his glamorous wife. He did not like wasting his time with people he could not use in some way, or who only boasted about their self-importance with nothing to show for it. People that reminded him of a small town, with inflated ambitions that never came true, content with what they owned because they were too scared to risk what they had. Powerful people, influential people, were drawn to each other, compelled to feed on each other's success and admire the unflagging energy that they generated. Karol made no effort to cover his complete absence of interest during the evenings with Milena's friends who, in his eyes, had nothing to inspire him.

Karol comfortably leaned back and stretched his arm across the back of the chair where Milena sat. He looked around the table, observing everybody, in stony-faced amusement. Milena was engrossed in a conversation with a woman sitting opposite. He did not remember her name. Nodding eagerly, the woman was telling a story of her recent meeting with the programming director of BBC Radio. The director was interested in making a feature programme on Polish businessmen in Britain.

With a thumb Karol gently stroked Milena's bare back. Her spicy perfume tickled Karol's throat and nostrils. He extended his legs under the table as far as he could. He was bursting and with his other hand he fumbled for his belt to loosen its grip across his bloated stomach. He was ready for a dessert and he was getting bored of this conversation, and the attention Milena was quietly stealing away from him. He knew he had the electrifying aura of success about him, and whatever Milena did or said could not diminish his belief in his own greatness, so this one night he graciously decided to let her have it. No matter how hard some people tried they could not transform their future. Unlike Karol whose influence and connections were legendary, and it was not only his imposing presence, a charisma he exhibited with his presence whenever he graced one of the evenings Milena organised. He was the king of commanding undivided attention.

A small burp escaped his lips. The guests at the table pretended that nothing happened as they continued their conversation.

'Karol, what do you think?'

He was glancing at his mobile, waiting for the message to be sent. The restaurant had poor reception.

'Sweetheart?' Milena touched his arm.

'About what?' he said, not bothering to look up.

Everybody stared at him. Milena's face reddened, smiling apologetically.

'About Milena appearing on the BBC,' the woman said, her dislike for him clawing at her throat. Karol remembered her name now. Elżbieta. She spoke slowly, with an air of importance, savouring her words.

'Why not?'

'I would do it,' Urszula added in a high-pitched voice that made Karol grimace and he pointedly stuck a small finger in his ear.

'Of course you would,' Karol said with a slightly bemused expression on his face. He only tolerated Urszula because she was one of Milena's friends, more of an acquaintance really, but Milena had insisted on inviting her this evening. Milena's choice of friends baffled Karol – that she would waste her time on somebody like Urszula. She had nothing else to offer apart from her admiration of Milena, and Milena's occasional gracious consent to wear one of Urszula's outfits at one of the many functions to which they were both invited.

Karol brought his eyes back to the other guests. He began to tap the table with the bottom of his mobile phone. He was readying himself to get up and call Damian, on the restaurant's terrace.

Elżbieta, her teeth clenched, making the lines around her mouth more pronounced produced throaty, unhappy noises. She was getting close to forty and it was beginning to show on her neck and face, looking rather unappealing, Karol thought. As he pushed his chair to get up he bumped two of Milena's guests with his elbows; he offered no apology.

Outside, he observed Milena and her guests. Cloaked in darkness, they could not see his face clearly, only the bright display of his phone. Soon they lost themselves in the conversation and forgot about him. Karol noted bursts of laughter and a man's feminine voice accompanied by his lively gesticulation. He must have complimented Milena's hair as he kept touching the ends. Karol knew nothing flattered Milena more than a comment about the appearance she maintained so meticulously. She laughed graciously and promised to send her friend a text message with the phone number for Ines Hair and Beauty Salon. She was also going to send word to Ines, to make sure Ines found space in her busy diary for this new client.

Unlike Milena's friends at the table, Karol worked hard for his success, and from early on he became aware of the inevitable fact that he was destined to achieve great things in life.

When he was younger he took a PKS bus from his village to the nearest city. He always sat at the back where he could observe every passenger: women with their hair tightly wrapped in scarves in fading colours, freshly laid eggs in baskets between their legs covered in thick woollen tights, unshaven men stinking of yesterday's beer. The men often got off half-way through the journey to drop into the nearest shop in the neighbouring villages to buy more beer and to never return home the same day. There were other young people like Karol, dreaming of a better, easier life than that of their parents, but unsure exactly how they were going to become somebody else because nobody had told them that they could.

The journey usually took an hour, sometimes longer, if the bus stopped at every town and village on its way. The driver impatiently waited for the passengers to load their bundles, parcels and suitcases, dragging reluctant and crying children on board. During winter, the less frequented roads were covered by a thick layer of snow. The driver, obscenities lashing in every direction, refused to go any further, forcing the passengers to make their way on foot because the road was too dangerous for him to continue. He was not going to get stuck in the middle of nowhere. There was no heating on the bus, except the radiating heat of bodies, and the hot air blown from the dashboard vent. If you were lucky you could occupy one of the two seats behind the driver. Grinding his teeth and hiding his hands clenched in tight fists in his bomber jacket pockets, Karol always sat at the back, no matter how cold it was, because he liked to think of himself as resilient, under any conditions. Winter or not, he was not going to behave like the rest of the passengers who fought their way to grab the warmest seat behind the driver. Karol did not fight. He took what he wanted.

It was during those arduous trips to the city, and then, later in the market, located behind one of the old disused train stations, that he had acquired his lasting determination to achieve greatness in life. Every Saturday people like Karol flocked to the market in the hope that the city people would buy their produce displayed on plastic tables of various sizes with folding legs. Karol examined carefully, with sharp eyes and an alert mind, everybody's behaviour. He could tell by the tone of customers' voices when they were about to walk away because the trader refused to lower the price, the sparkle in the curious eyes when they savoured the descriptions of his products, all the miniscule signals an inexperienced observer would miss but not somebody like Karol. During those eight long hours, Karol perfected his skills and he soon earned admiration and a reputation among the fellow traders as the best salesman among them. But Karol always wanted more. There was no thrill in selling eggs or plucked chickens, hand woven woollen socks and caftans made by his mother, dried mushrooms from brown paper bags, fresh herbs, or bottles filled with unpasteurised milk to people who visited the market because they could not afford to go to one of the shops and preferred to haggle with the market vendors in the lashing rain. Karol quickly learnt that if he was going to make money, the kind of money that brought unquestionable respect and adoration, and perhaps a little bit of fear, he would have to move on. He craved power, unlimited control – some extraordinary version of himself beyond the ordinary.

Looking at Milena's guests at the table Karol had no doubt he had carved out a life trajectory for himself none of them could possibly imagine. Terrible as he had become, the breathless emotional emptiness he had nurtured since he was a child had made him, in his eyes, a better person.

He dialled Damian's number and listened for a few minutes to Damian's monotonous voice.

Back inside, Karol approached a waitress and asked for the bill. He had lost his appetite for a dessert and was ready to go home. He dismissed the voices around the table to share the cost, and leisurely threw crumpled notes on the table.

4

Angelika was feeling happy, almost giddy, this Saturday morning, because in less than a few hours the whole family would be on a boat trip. She had got up at sunrise to prepare sandwiches for the children. Kamil was the only child of Angelika and Mateusz born in Britain. His Polish was halting, slowly invaded by English. Every night Angelika read fairy tales to Kamil from the books her mother had bought for her grandson back in Poland. And so, the bookcase in Kamil's room was filled with the colourful hard-bound editions of Polish books, the same stories her mother had read to her when Angelika was a child. But even then, Kamil – with his face alight with curiosity at his mother's flowing words – would sometimes interrupt her evening readings, and say in English, 'Mummy, read the one about the birds' radio.'

Angelika's mother-in-law believed that Kamil had turned out this way because he was born in England, that they should have come back after Angelika realised she was pregnant with a second child, not wait until the boy had grown into somebody for whom his other grandmother would become a person from a photo. Angelika's mother-in-law's biggest fear was that they would not understand each other.

But Angelika was not one of those mothers she sometimes observed at the airport, talking to their children in English, then turning to their friends to continue the conversation in Polish. Angelika's mother-in-law feared the longer they stayed abroad the less Kamil would communicate in his mother's tongue, until he forgot it, completely, because this was what was happening to Karolina. Even though she was born in Poland, it was already too late for her. English had taken over and she let Polish slip from her. Piece by piece her Polish acquired a foreign melody, a deeper, guttural tremor, and often English words invaded Polish sentences. Angelika lacked the patience to discipline her daughter. Although Karolina still used Polish with her parents, with everybody else she chose to communicate in English. She saw herself as English and in English

'Time to get up, sweethearts.' Angelika's singing voice filled the children's bedroom. She opened the curtains to let in the sunshine. The birds were chirping so loudly that Karolina, with a moan, buried her head under a pillow and squeezed it with both hands.

'Do I have to go?' Karolina cried.

'All your friends are coming,' Angelika said as she opened the cupboard to take out fresh underwear.

Karolina wanted to say that they were not her friends, all these people from the church were her mother's friends, but stopped herself. There was no point arguing with her mother, especially if she was so infuriatingly cheerful, but she was always in a good mood, drawing everybody around her into her ferocious happiness.

Karolina, her head still under the pillow, asked, 'Is Dad up yet?'

'Breakfast is ready. Hurry up,' said Angelika.

Sister Celestyna of the Our Virgin Lady of the Immaculate Heart Catholic Church, with a measured smile and old fashioned glasses which covered almost half of her face, welcomed all the families at the front gate. It was not the biggest church in Ealing, neither did it have the largest congregation in comparison to the churches established years before, but it was steadily growing with more Polish families settling in the borough. Sister Celestyna was confident the church would soon boast a full house during each service, and not only on Sundays, their busiest day.

Weekend boat trips on the Thames, bi-monthly pilgrimages to Rome to catch a glimpse of the new Pope, and recently, summer camps with intensive daily language classes for the children in the Bieszczady Mountains, had already generated a swelling interest among the congregation. Then, there were weekly and monthly workshops: pottery, marriage and sex education, drawing the scenes from the Bible (for the children aged five to eight and Kamil's favourite).

The truth was, the Our Virgin Lady of the Immaculate Heart Catholic Church had saved Angelika's life, and deep inside she was convinced it was going to save Mateusz's as well, with whatever problems he was not telling her about. She had come to the conclusion that worrying about money did not solve the problem, so there was no point in doing that. The business fluctuated, some months were better than others, this much she had known, and she convinced herself that Mateusz's hard work would be rewarded in the end. He simply needed to have more faith. Just like she was rewarded with the second pregnancy after years of patient prayers, attending the church every Sunday, sometimes during the week for an evening mass, until the time when she had come to terms with the reality that Karolina was going to be the only child, when she had almost lost her hope. Then, unexpectedly, when on her knees, Angelika admitted in front of God that she was grateful for her family, however small, that actually she did not need anything else anymore, that was when she fell pregnant for the second time. Father Niewiadomski said it was a miracle. 'God had a plan for you from the start,' Father Niewiadomski explained to her, after she came to announce what had happened to her, giddy and excited. Father Niewiadomski was the first one to hear the surprising news – Mateusz the second – not because she did not love Mateusz as much as she loved God, but her relationship with God was for eternity. She never held it against Mateusz that his dedication to God was ambiguous at times. Not faithless, but not entirely faithful either. She knew some people needed more time to understand the greatness of belief, and Mateusz was that kind of a person. He needed more time. But whilst she waited for him to discover that penetrating joy she had experienced so many times, Angelika would make sure, in the meantime, her heart and soul forever belonged to God. Her worship was limitless and she was now rewarded with a new life. The waves of her faith swelled inside. It was obvious to her who was responsible for her miraculous conception.

That day Angelika became a woman of violent happiness, a kind of happiness that glued the whole family together but left Mateusz baffled at times. Sometimes, in the face of Angelika's cheerfulness, he seemed lost, shrunken. Like today, when he was sitting on the bus and could not stop thinking how he was going to tell her the truth. He felt he needed to be honest with her, that he was considering closing down his company after all these years, and their lives would be different from now on. But how could he destroy Angelika's bliss? And perhaps, this once, Angelika was right, if he prayed really hard God would listen. He did everything right in his life; he was an honest, devoted husband, did not shy away from the responsibility when Angelika got pregnant with Karolina, though they were so young – teenagers – when it had happened. Any other boy, any of his friends actually, would have left her to deal with the child on her own, but not Mateusz. He was a man of solid principles.

He remembered that summer at the Mietkowskie Lake, when he saw her for the first time, in white shorts with her hair loose, caressed by the wind from the lake, her body tanned, waving at somebody on the boat far away and he wished it was him. Later that evening, he could not believe his luck when his friend took him to that party on the boat, with Angelika, and how he had summoned up his courage after he saw her a few hours later in the evening, arguing with another boy who left her crying on her own and made her a promise, 'I want to make you the happiest person in the world.' He gently wiped away the tears from her face and took her hands and kissed them, one by one. Her hair smelt of campfire smoke and pine needles. Mateusz was surprised when she kissed him back on the lips. It was as if the universe suddenly stopped in awe of his luck. He was stupefied by her response. They made love that night, he kissing every bit of her naked skin softly, and Angelika holding tight onto him like a lifeboat. He knew the only reason she let him kiss her was because she wanted to obliterate the memory of somebody else. He was not the man Angelika wanted but he held her tight anyway, hoping he could become the person she would fall in love with eventually.

When her period was late, and it was obvious Angelika's ongoing morning sickness could no longer be ignored, he never considered this unexpected and unplanned responsibility as a burden. By then Angelika no longer needed to convince herself to be happy, it came with unexpected ferocity the moment she realised she was going to be a mother. She never wanted to hear the other boy's name again. Mateusz delivered his promise and never let her go.

'Are we there yet?' Karolina yawned.

'Almost,' Mateusz said. 'Look! The Houses of Parliament.'

Though he had seen it before, he always had a choking feeling and his heart beat a little bit faster whenever his eyes met the stunning building. He wanted to take Karolina inside, to show her around. 'Just you and me,' Mateusz said. He was feeling excited about the prospect of this trip with his daughter. He had dreamt of visiting the place but he was, unexpectedly, a little bit scared to do so on his own.

'Sure,' mumbled Karolina, and she was back to reshuffling songs. She had already seen the Houses of Parliament during a school trip a few years ago but it seemed Mateusz did not remember. Karolina had learnt her parents' ability to retain and remember what was going on in her existence was affected by her younger brother's miraculous appearance in their lives. She wondered sometimes if they would notice if she disappeared one day? Would it crack her mother's exuberant happiness, just a little bit? Karolina had to make a great effort to fit into this family, even if she seemed not to care. She thought her parents did not try hard enough to assimilate, her mother never learnt English, although her father did but he often sought advice on some phrases and sayings he found too challenging. They insulated themselves from the encompassing foreignness of England by cocooning their lives within the Polish community. And it was so easy. She knew they wanted to return 'home', to Poland, but Karolina did not. Why would she want to leave her home here and live in a foreign country, because that was what Poland was to her, a place where she would not know how to live. Their need to surround themselves with everything Polish did not resemble her reality. Karolina could not wait to live on her own terms.

The wind was so strong as they were climbing the gangway, Mateusz instructed Karolina to hold on to the railing. He watched

Angelika and Kamil out of the corner of his eye, making sure they were all right. But despite the strong wind and looming clouds, Mateusz was enchanted by the weather. There was something cleansing about having the wind in your face and hair.

'Sit closer together,' said Mateusz, as he was taking another photograph of his family with the revolving London Eye in the background. He had already taken at least twenty photos that he wanted to send to his mother. She would have loved this trip; the singing under Sister Celestyna's guidance, the sharing of food among the group, children's faces struck with excitement as they took in the magnificent landmarks of London their parents had only known from numerous postcards or TV. When Mateusz closed his eyes, he could almost feel he was back home in Poland.

Outside the National Maritime Museum they stopped in front of *Nelson's Ship in a Bottle* and Mateusz was startled into silence while Angelika wiped Kamil's runny nose.

'Is there anything left to eat?' Karolina asked, rummaging through a big bag in which Angelika had packed apples and bananas.

'It was a Nigerian artist Yinka Shonibare,' Mateusz pronounced the name with difficulty, 'who designed it. Pretty impressive, guys, don't you think?'

'Mum, there's no fruit left.' Karolina looked disappointed.

'We'll eat something soon,' Angelika replied, impatient. 'How can you be hungry already? We've just had breakfast.'

'A replica of Nelson's flagship HMS Victory,' Mateusz translated the plaque. 'He died during the Battle of Trafalgar in 1805. I bet he never imagined that one day somebody would stick his ship into a bottle.'

'I need to pee,' Kamil said, pulling on Angelika's sleeve.

Karolina turned on her heel and began walking towards the building, Angelika shouted behind her to wait, but she carried on.

A week ago on Monday morning Mateusz realised that he could no longer postpone the firing his two workers, Michał and Wacek. For four months he had been avoiding this day, hoping every week that he would receive a miraculous phone call which would make him believe change was on its way. Despite advertisements for quarter of a page he had placed in Polish weeklies and local papers, there were hardly any phone calls from new clients.

Now, sitting in the van outside the premises on Grafton road, where his company was hired to do the plastering and painting, Mateusz was rehearsing the message he was going to deliver. He mouthed the words and watched people urgently walking on the street, passing by a man sitting on a pavement. For the last two weeks the man had occupied the same spot, a man younger than him, and not a single person stopped. Mateusz sometimes shared his breakfast with the man, a Lithuanian, but it was not the food the man was hungry for but a job. 'Job, please, please?' the Lithuanian asked every time Mateusz approached him. His English was too limited to understand Mateusz's apologies and a suggestion that perhaps he could try a local Job Centre or one of the organisations that helped people like him, but the man would angrily bury himself under his dirtied coat.

There were types of human behaviour Mateusz struggled to comprehend. It seemed to him that the Eastern Europeans who ended up on the streets – recently he had been noticing them even more often than a few years ago when he had arrived in London – exhibited an air of angry righteousness, especially the younger ones. Of the ones Mateusz had approached with food and small change, after they realised he was a Pole, they lapsed into an urgent expectation that he should help them because they all came from the same place. When he tried to explain, full of halted apologies and awkwardness, that he was struggling himself, they grew resentful as if they blamed him for their predicament.

'It's the banks who messed up the economy,' Michał stated, repeating what he was reading in all the Polish papers. He constantly cracked sunflower and pumpkin seeds in his mouth as he spoke, to keep himself busy and counteract the urge to smoke. 'Last job then?'

'There's one more, on Taunton Avenue, but it's only a one bedroom flat,' said Mateusz.

'I knew I should have gone back. Everybody has,' Michał added and packed another handful of seeds into his mouth, making a wet chewing noise.

Wacek was leaning against the doorway, the cigarette turned to ash between his fingers with short, bitten fingernails. He had bought a piece of land near a small seaside resort in northern Poland, not far from Koszalin where he was from. He showed them photographs on his mobile phone where he planned to build a holiday house with easy access to the beach. His dream was to turn the place into a Polish Riviera, for the French, Germans and the British in search of something exotic on the Baltic coast. That was why Mateusz never held it against Wacek when he worked other jobs, after he finished on one of his projects. Most of the men he employed did. Still, Wacek had it all planned until Mateusz announced next month would be their last pay. Wacek needed perhaps one more year to accumulate enough money, and now, he did not know what was going to happen.

'Do you need me for Taunton Avenue?' Wacek asked and flicked the cigarette butt onto the concrete floor. In his mind he had already moved on to the next thing. He did not want to wait any longer now that Mateusz had delivered the bad news that morning.

'I'm not going to keep you if you want to go,' Mateusz said and thought this was the least he could do. 'I will pay you now if you prefer.'

Mateusz was strangely consoled by the ease with which his employees accepted the news, or so it seemed to him. Michał turned on the radio and tuned in to Polish Radio London. The music blared as they prepared to mix fresh paint in plastic buckets.

It was not so straightforward when Mateusz decided to part ways with Bartek, his first business partner. They installed windows together, back in the days when Mateusz was starting up. It made a lot of sense to team up with a window fitter. Once Mateusz smashed the tiles and ripped into the walls exposing the bricks, Bartek worked his magic.

'Look at these old newspapers,' Bartek said, sweating and swearing, as he tore the yellowed, printed paper from around the pipes. 'That's insulation for you. What year does it say? 1989? Jesus and Mary.'

Bartek hid cans of beer in his backpack and sipped the brew throughout a day's work; sometimes he placed an open can under the bathtub or in the cupboards under the sink. 'Want some?' he asked Mateusz once or twice after breakfast. Mateusz always refused.

When Mateusz asked Bartek not to drink on the job, Bartek said with a grin, 'I drank beer before I drank my mother's milk. Helps me to fit the windows straight.'

Few homeowners could resist Bartek's prices, even if he forgot to deliver the certificates after he had installed the windows.

Because the prices were half of the market rates, at least the ones quoted by the English builders, the clients chose to let it go, pleased they were able to save thousands of pounds. So many of their neighbours and friends used Poles.

Mateusz did not ask him about the details, how he managed to get his unbelievably low prices on windows, because he trusted Bartek must have had a good deal with the warehouse where he ordered them.

'Agatka, the one who does the accounts for them? She helps me out,' Bartek vaguely explained.

Mateusz thought it was convenient to have a fellow Pole working in the warehouse, an inside girl, who probably got some money out of it as well, but he did not want to dwell on it. In a way he was pleased because lower prices always attracted new clients, so Mateusz turned a blind eye. He needed every job he could get.

One day Mateusz got a phone call from an old customer. They had worked on her house a few months ago, complaining about the water leaking inside through the gaps between the window frames and the wall. She also had problems with opening the windows and was worried something was not right. He arrived the same afternoon to have a look.

'I tried calling the other man but he's not answering his phone.' She followed Mateusz around the house while he ran his hand down the frames.

'He's probably very busy,' apologised Mateusz. He twisted the plastic handle but he struggled to open the windows himself. The mechanism underneath the frame was stuck and it did not allow him to fully open the window. He stopped pulling on it, afraid he was going to break the mechanism further.

'I've been calling him almost every day for the past week,' the woman was saying, 'and even sent him text messages but never got a reply. At least you answered,' the woman added, relieved.

Mateusz assured her that he would take care of everything and that she should not worry, but he could not help wondering why Bartek was all of a sudden unreachable. Only two days ago Mateusz had spoken to Bartek and he never mentioned any of this, or that there were any issues after the installation.

'They probably require a bit of regulating now that they have been fitted. It happens.'

Bartek's explanations did not make sense to Mateusz. Bartek claimed his mobile phone was stolen or that he had to urgently go back to Poland which was why he did not know about any of the clients complaining.

'I get that you have a personal situation but you could have at least contacted me, used your wife's phone, if yours was stolen?' Mateusz said to Bartek when he arrived at his flat, irritated and losing his patience, and with a niggling thought that Bartek was lying.

'Piss off, what do you want me to say? They should be grateful for getting the job done cheaper than anybody else.' Bartek paused, with an expression that Mateusz would come to know well, a fake surprise that announced he was not going to take responsibility for any of the issues raised by the unhappy clients.

There had been so many times when Mateusz had feared that this would happen, so many situations that forced him to find somebody else to fix the botched work Bartek had done, and now it felt like the consequences of Bartek's unreliability were going to cost Mateusz more than he could ever recover. He had a reputation at stake, a position for the company he had barely started to build.

And then Mateusz began to hear stories, snippets of conversations he overheard from other builders about Bartek stealing windows from the warehouse, taking the money and never finishing the job – or even beating somebody up.

'I'm telling you what I've heard. I know you've been working together,' the man said, chewing gum with his mouth open. He was piling skirting boards onto his trolley, his shirt stuck to his sweaty back. 'That girl – what was her name – Agatka, lost her job.' But the man did not have her phone number to give and Mateusz could not find out more.

Confronting Bartek was not easy. He ignored Mateusz's phone calls. When Mateusz drove to his flat he was never there, his wife gave him evasive answers that she had no idea what Mateusz was talking about and he had better talk to Bartek and, no, she could not tell when he was going to be home because he was on a job. She refused to let Mateusz in and, yes, she could pass on the message that he was looking for him, though Mateusz sensed her reluctance, but she was not going to make any promises because it was between him and her husband. Then she shut the door in his face.

'Leave it,' Angelika said, 'he obviously has something to hide. Forget about him before it's too late.'

Angelika told him that it was for the best and even if he managed to talk to Bartek he would probably lie to Mateusz again, so there was no point trying to find out what was really going on. Eventually Mateusz stopped calling Bartek, who had probably disappeared on a job in some distant zone. But a few months later, unexpectedly, he saw Bartek in one of the local Polish shops in his neighbourhood. Bartek acted as if nothing had happened and, at first, pretended he had not recognised Mateusz. The initial disappointment Mateusz had nurtured for all these months subsided and the only thing he said was, 'Well, I hope it all goes well for you,' and then he left without waiting for Bartek to respond.

That night, after Mateusz got back home with a sombre feeling which had weighed in his heart since the morning meeting with his employees, he could not sleep. Sadness nibbled away in his mind little by little. He tossed in bed, staring into the darkness, until finally he got up, careful not to wake Angelika, and went outside into the garden to feel the fresh cold air on his face. He could not stop thinking about what Michał had said, of going back. Mateusz had missed Poland. The familiar feeling of belonging, the safety brought by the presence of the family and friends he had left behind. Here, he had no feeling of community with the strangers on the streets, the TV and newspapers triggered unease despite his good command of English. He felt at times he was missing something deeper, something that could not be translated or explained with the childhood memories, which were rooted, instead, among the trees with the swirling leaves by the lake in Mietków, where he had been born.

Sometimes he asked Karolina to clarify an idiom he had heard on a bus or a phrase that puzzled him. 'I don't know, Dad,' she would say, impatient, 'it's just the way you say it.' And when he pressed her to give him the Polish equivalent, so he could make the sentence more familiar to help him remember its meaning, she asked him to leave her alone because whatever she said would not be a good enough explanation to him. He searched for words in the dictionary and would read them to her, with a definition and examples of how to use a word or an expression, but she would give him a wounded look and say, 'Why do you even bother asking me if you have your dictionary? Besides, nobody talks like that on the street anyway.' Karolina was the only one in the family who was not puzzled by the English language. Mateusz noticed a change in her behaviour, a silent condescension at his language mistakes or when he was unable to memorise a structure she had repeated to him already a few times. She began to look at him with the same expression of indifference masked by mild interest he had experienced when he had been in the process of learning English. He spoke slowly, unsure of himself, testing his abilities with more complex grammatical structures. Karolina learnt the language without a hint of doubt. She paid little attention to Polish.

If Mateusz spent the first two years in Britain agonising over whether Angelika would find life in London overwhelmingly lonely, Angelika did not. He chose not to share his thoughts with Angelika to protect her from the self-doubt which lodged like a splinter in Mateusz's mind. He worried about Angelika. How would she find her way home, if she spoke no English? Would strangers be kind to her? Who would recognise her face and offer a reassuring smile or a good word? Mateusz worked incredibly hard, weekdays and weekends, to afford a place which would become a cocoon of love and safety, ready for Angelika and Karolina when they finally joined him. He would prefer not to remember how he slept with complete strangers at the squatters' house to save money, or when he was lucky, as a live-in guardian across various properties, with no rent and bills to pay but in a permanent state of uncertainty and dread that the next day he would not be able to claim the same bed as his own. He remembered the mornings in front of the 'Wailing Wall' in Hammersmith. Under the Coca-Cola banner, hand-scribbled advertisements in the newsagent's window: 'Staff wanted. Bad English no problem,' 'Earn up to £500 a day. Massage,' 'Painters for two months. Immediate start,' 'Strong men. Full time,' 'Every day work. Women only,' 'Plasterers, kitchen fitters, electricians.' Grimacing, grunting, fighting, sweating, shouting, mostly men, Mateusz among them, eyes drowned in anguish, hungrily scanning the pieces of paper, noting down the phone numbers to hurry aside to a corner and be the first one to call, before somebody else snatched away the opportunity. Flip-flops in the rain. Polish consonant clusters thrown at each other. Some were ready to kill. Others would walk away. The survival of the fittest, Mateusz thought sourly. A driver who stopped to select three men, boys really, would come back tomorrow. Perhaps then Mateusz would have more luck.

In London, each night as Mateusz drifted into sleep he dreamt of a day when he would wake up to the sound of his daughter's footsteps and laughter, instead of exploding farts and burps.

In Jaworzyna Śląska, Angelika's hometown with a population of barely 10,000, each day Angelika, with a flaming face, stared at a clunky computer screen at her parents' house, waiting for the internet connection to resume.

There were numerous websites inviting Poles living in the UK to unite, make friends, to share the immigrant experience, find work in a bar, rent a flat, submit a short story, have sex, hire a private detective, come to a gig on Sunday, claim money from any accident, meet African singles, apply for a British passport, find a Polish gynaecologist, buy Polish bread, become an Avon consultant, go to Polish church, send a package to Poland – £18 for 30kg! – claim child benefit, buy a Polish umbrella, transfer money UK-PL for £1, learn about Islam, travel to Cyprus with Milena's Travel, watch Polish television in London, order traditional Polish food, lengthen your eyelashes, take dance classes with Piotrek, learn Polish – first lesson free – watch a football game Poland versus Moldavia in a Polish pub, find Arkadiusz with a tattoo on his neck 'ACDC', print business cards at a Polish printing shop, claim a free rabbit in Bristol, order a minicab with a Polish driver, lose weight for only £30, go to a Polish pharmacy, donate money to fund Polish film about humans as fish in Borneo, buy Polish fashion (account suspended), collect five jar tops from Gerber baby food and win 10,000 zloty, send your photo to a Polish model agency, send luggage and people with Zbyszek, enhance your dating skills with 702,243 registered users, claim incapacity benefit, attend a themed Polish ball 'Solidarity' in the Intercontinental Hotel. This was proof to Angelika that living in London was going to be just like living in Jaworzyna Śląska, or even better, and it made her feel safe. There was nothing to be afraid of as long as she could find her fellow countrymen, people who spoke the same language, had the same values, believed in the same God, and all these people had already arrived, like pioneers paving the way for Angelika and her family.

5

She was choking. The overpowering stench of peroxide flooded Angelika's every gasp for air and her scalp was now beginning to burn.

'Darling, come in two hours, or three. I'm doing full head highlights so it's going to take a while and Anita is not in today… She's sick, poor thing,' Dorota was saying, the phone lodged between her shoulder and ear to keep her hands free as she was separating thin streaks of Angelika's hair with a sharp edge of the comb and carefully applying pale blue dye. 'All right, sweetie. I'll see you soon.' Dorota made a kissing sound. 'Bye. Bye, bye.'

Dorota placed the phone on a table, next to two bowls with hair dye, and combs of various sizes. The gardenia candles Dorota lit at the far corner of the room did little to rid the room of the intense mixture of acerbic and sweet odours which saturated the room. Angelika wished Dorota would open the window to let some fresh air, but despite it being the end of February it was cold and damp and the heating was off at Dorota's house. She was dreading the moment when she was going to leave Dorota's house and let the February chill wrap around her, dampening her blow-dried hair.

'God, so busy these days. I've been working every single weekend.'

Angelika smiled at her reflection in the mirror (clouded in the corners, with Dorota's family photographs stuck between the frame and the glass) as words poured from Dorota's shimmering, lip-glossed mouth.

'I'm not complaining but I'd love to have some time off. This month has been madly busy. Madly busy.' Dorota separated each syllable. 'And my feet are killing me.' She stopped applying the dye and rubbed her right calf with the back of her hand.

Angelika thought she could never bear standing for the whole day like Dorota did, in those high-heeled yellow sandals; not even if she was paid good money to do so. How astonishing it was for women to bear the pain of wearing an accessory that twisted their feet into agony, and it seemed to Angelika, that, granted, if it was in different circumstances, a special occasion – a wedding perhaps (though Angelika remembered wearing flats to her wedding) – she could justify the discomfort that came with high-heeled shoes. But Dorota was at home so for whom was she wearing those shoes?

Dorota stole a glance at a small TV mounted on the wall. 'Oh, look! Jesus, isn't he handsome?' Dorota gave a loud sigh, fluttering her eyelashes.

A popular Polish TV series had been running for the last eight years on the Polish television: a priest cum detective. 'The hottest priest in Poland,' Dorota liked to call him.

'If our priest was that sexy I would go to church every day.' Dorota laughed, her breasts wobbling. Then she said to a girl who stood in the corner ripping the kitchen foil. 'Sweetie, can you use the scissors, please? Scissors.' She spoke with exaggerated slow-ness.

The girl nodded. Her face was dotted with acne but she had stunning hair that reached her bottom, and Angelika wished she could have had hair like hers.

'She's from Albania,' Dorota whispered, bending to whisper in Angelika's ear, 'Poor thing. I've been teaching her Polish but she's not really bright. God knows how long it's going to take her to learn it.' Dorota shook her head.

Angelika had got used to Dorota using God's name in almost every sentence. The first time Angelika came to her house to have highlights done, something inside her cringed at the sound of the word. A Polish woman recommended Dorota at Kamil's school as 'the best hairdresser in Hounslow.' Angelika forgave her for mentioning God in every sentence, because her hair had never looked better, and even Mateusz could not stop himself from caressing it. She later added photos of herself on her Facebook page and had fourteen likes from her female friends back in Poland, marvelling at Dorota's work. She posted Dorota's contact details for her London-based female friends. 'Good hairdressers and dentists are for life,' her mother had once told her, and Angelika had just found a perfect match for her hair. Dorota did not mind employing other Eastern European girls, some of whom Angelika suspected were illegal, but, at least when they got back to Albania or Belarus, they could boast experience at a London hair salon. Angelika was thankful for women like Dorota, who managed to do good things for others.

'Do you watch it?' Dorota asked enthusiastically, glancing at the television screen. 'It's really, really good.'

'Mateusz promised to tune to the Polish channel. But he comes back home from work late. I hardly see him because I'm already in bed when he returns.'

'Which company?'

'I think it's called PolTVLand.'

Dorota stopped applying the blue paste onto Angelika's hair, furrowed her brows and bit onto the outer sharp edge of the comb. 'Never heard of them... Hold on, darling.' She walked out to the kitchen to look for the business card she kept in a basket on the window sill. She returned carrying the piece of paper with oily stains, juggling the many gold coloured bangles around her wrist.

'Here.' She tore a page from her notebook and wrote down a mobile number. 'Tell Mateusz to call Kacper. He's the best.'

Angelika half smiled because Mateusz was not going to call Kacper, reluctant to have anything to do with somebody he did not know. She happily left Mateusz to make the decisions on anything to do with technology in their house.

'Luana,' Dorota called out. 'Could you make us some coffee?' She turned to Angelika, 'You take milk?'

Angelika nodded and the folded foil with streaks of her hair inside, which Dorota had not yet pinned, fell onto her forehead, obstructing her vision.

'Are you going to the Beauty Workshop?' Dorota resumed her work. 'You missed the winter edition last year.' She gave Angelika a mock wounded look. 'God, I am dying for some pampering and, of course, I need to go on a new diet. I mean look at me!'

Angelika looked. Dorota dipped her hand in a small dish full of sweets and chocolate bonbons every few minutes. All things considered, she was skinny, had a beautiful smile but very bad teeth. Too skinny and too fake, according to Mateusz. Dorota was proud of her boob job and wore low cut tops with push up bras, which squeezed her breasts into perfect roundness. Angelika hid her body under layers of clothing. Her stomach had never got back to its flatness after giving birth to two children, and there was a cushion of fat around her hips and under her arms. But sometimes, when Angelika discreetly and enviously eyed Dorota's model-like physique, she wished she had a figure like her, close to perfection she knew from the magazines she liked to thumb through in Tesco. Though Mateusz did not mind her softening body, she wondered if it would be enough in ten years' time, outstripped by the engrossing responsibilities of motherhood.

Luana returned, carrying two cups of coffee.

'Oh bless you, darling!' Dorota took a careful sip. 'I needed that.'

'Where is it?' Angelika asked. She could do with some pampering and diet advice, and perhaps even some lessons in make-up. She wore it only on special occasions like when Mateusz took her to dinner in a restaurant, but it happened so rarely she stopped buying cosmetics altogether. The ones she still kept, hardly used, had crumbled or dried out. Her visits to Dorota to have her hair done were the only beauty regime she maintained.

'It's in the new place this year – Holiday Inn Express Hotel near Hammersmith. We can meet outside and go together if you want.' Which was Dorota's way of saying that she did not trust Angelika to show up and wanted to put just a little bit of pressure on her. 'Just a dab of concealer can get rid of that dark circles under your eyes. And there's this fabulous new retinol cream which can work wonders on tired skin.' She sounded like a sales assistant, eager and mesmerised by the sound of her own voice. During a previous visit, she had told Angelika how she was going to expand her business with sales of creams and face masks. Angelika had asked her if she meant Avon, but Dorota preferred Polish producers. 'Only natural ingredients,' Dorota said, and added that Polish cosmetics had a potential, if she could get them into the hands of some high-profile customers of hers. Angelika was not sure which customers she meant; she had never seen any recognisable faces at her house, at least not when she visited.

'Oh, I don't know yet.' Angelika blushed, self-conscious of her weary look and chipped nail polish. 'I will have to check with Mateusz if he can stay with the children that weekend.'

'Excuses. Excuses.' Dorota shook her head, then added, in that semi-reproachful joking manner, that beauty was fleeting and it was not going to last forever, and if God blessed some women with good looks, he was not there to do the upkeep for them.

Angelika winced at the words, but Dorota was right. Reluctantly, she admitted she enjoyed the Beauty Workshops. To her surprise, Angelika rejoiced in the company of women, many of whom, like her, had the same fatigued expression, but also similar curiosity flickering in their eyes. The air was thick with hope as the women pictured their transformation. They strolled among the tables with rows of colour cosmetics, cream samples, leaflets announcing breakthrough medicine at their disposal and piles of business cards. Angelika did not want to miss a single display. There was so much to see, touch and ask. She would manoeuvre among the bodies, squeezing her arm between women standing like columns in front of the tables which generated more interest than others, in order to grab some samples with a whispered apology. 'This shade, would it be right for my skin?' she would ask, and then she would sit relaxed with her eyes closed, letting the consultant's fingers apply the cream onto her skin or with the feathery touch brush a new shade on her eye lids. The proximity to fashion, nutrition, hair and make-up specialists dazed some less confident female participants, but not Angelika. There was something captivating about the minute attention the beauticians and make-up artists devoted to eyebrows, cuticles, split ends, battling tiny wrinkles around the eyes, and with it an overpowering message of a better, sexier, more confident self. DISCOVER YOUR INNER BEAUTY and BECOME THE WOMAN OF YOUR DREAMS was displayed on rollups positioned strategically in each room, where personalised meetings with the masseurs, beauticians and hair stylists were taking place. It made Angelika doubt whether she was enough: whether there

advertisement I placed in *Cooltura* didn't help. And it's so expensive. Too expensive.'

Angelika resumed dicing the vegetables. There was, in Angelika's demeanour, a withdrawal of heart, a knitted-brow look that said: Best to do it now before it's too late. Her job was to take care of the family and the house, and she loved being a mother and a wife, happily leaving Mateusz to take responsibility for everything else. Her domestic role fitted her, even more now that she witnessed lives falling apart in the merciless, almost inhuman, competition. This Western world she existed in here, she could not fully comprehend. Back home it would have been unthinkable to have lives perpetually overshadowed by unemployment or homelessness. Mateusz was right, of course, to let the men go if they wanted to. She knew he would not take this decision lightly but how he could trust people like that, people who blackmailed Mateusz to pay more knowing that he had a family of his own. She had seen him the past few months struggling to come to terms with the rapidly changing reality of his construction business. Still, she was a little bit frightened that this decision had actually come true, now that he was telling her about it, defeated and withdrawn. More than ever she realised he would need her support, to make sure, despite this latest development, their lives would carry on as usual.

No matter what life threw at them she had learnt not to succumb to the daily melancholy, or to let it drag her onto an emotional roller-coaster like it had done to Mateusz. This reaction was likely to be wistful thoughts, sleepless nights, endless hours spent pondering over past decisions, paths he could have taken to avoid the looming disaster. Angelika's friends resented this quality in her, perhaps mistakenly, that she somehow chose the conscious ignorance, for making life look so easy, that nothing could destroy her dream. The painful tightening in the stomach that moved up into the ribcage, then nestled in the chest and squeezed the breath out with an iron grip. She had known the dreaded feeling of fear too well to let it penetrate her body. A dread that so easily turned into a devouring panic brought nothing but devastation. It would have been, of course, so easy to slip into this feeling, if she wanted to, and prove to those who held it against her that she was as defence-less as the rest of them. But did they have any idea what strength it took not to yield to it?

The vegetable salad was ready. Angelika placed the bowl in the middle of the table, then a plate with slices of bread, butter, cold cuts and cheese.

'You are right,' he said suddenly, regaining his good spirits, 'I shouldn't be worrying so much. It's not only us having problems. So many people are in a far worse situation than us.'

Mateusz had always known that Angelika was very special, and for a brief moment the ominous future did not seem so over-whelmingly scary.

'You did the best you could,' she chimed in. 'I'm sure, with your experience, it will only be a matter of time before you find a new project or more trustworthy people to work with. Something will come up, eventually. I'm sure of it.'

Mateusz felt compelled to let her know that no matter what, he had a plan, but he had already deceived her and he did not want to bury himself further.

Perhaps it was not right to conceal this thought from her; no, of course it was not. One lie was enough, even if it was a well-meant one. Still, the guilt ensnared him in its grip. He would have to come clean eventually, tell her it was his idea to dismiss his workers, but for now he remained silent. His heart wrung in shame, that he was not the brave man he thought he was. But he convinced himself his lying was out of love for her. It was enough he was worried about their future so that she did not have to. He would spare her the agonising thoughts.

Later, when he was drying the dishes, when the children were back in their room happy to be released from the duty of helping Angelika to clean up the kitchen after eating, she said: 'It breaks my heart to see you looking so tragic. Have faith. Good things come to good people.'

6

There was an understanding, an unwritten contract, of how things were run and who took responsibility for the daily arrangements. Though their relationship was rooted in their past in Poland, it was in Britain where it was cemented. Karol knew the Kulesza brothers were people who offered no apologies for how they preferred to execute his business decisions. He was not quite sure of – or chose to deliberately ignore – certain facts about their cruel actions, how quickly their behaviour could escalate into violence. Of course, he knew they had a limitless capacity for falling into fierce darkness. Impassioned with a blazing commitment. Madmen. It took a savage, evil-eyed heart and soul to be like the Kulesza brothers. Karol accepted he was nothing like them but he needed their dedication. For he could not do what they were capable of, so easily, it seemed.

The first thing the Kulesza brothers did was to take their passports away, when all the passengers were still exhausted after a 28-hour coach journey, relieved they had finally reached their destination. Though glued to the windows expecting a glimpse of a postcard image, the Tower Bridge or Buckingham Palace or any other building they memorised back at home, they saw instead Mezopotamya shop and Ali's Kebab Centre, a mother clad in a black cloth with three children at a bus stop, African and Asian faces, Middle Eastern faces, but no English ones. What exactly did an English person look like? They did not know. Something else briefly lodged in their stomachs, a flash of anxiety, a fear of overwhelming possibilities, and if they did not stick together here they would dissolve into nothingness.

When they finally arrived at Victoria Coach Station and Igor bellowed through the voice announcement system 'Welcome to London,' some passengers clapped as if they were on an airplane, not on Milena's Travel coach.

Kętrzyn, Bartoszyce, Biskupiec, Ełk, Bydgoszcz, Poznań, Słubice, Leverkusen, Calais, Dover, Maidstone, London.

Bloodshot eyes. Cramps. Sweaty bodies. They had finally made it.

Most passengers disembarked during the 15-minute break. The ones who travelled on Karol's orders were rushed back inside. Their final stop, 'Greenford' was another good hour's drive away.

There was a large terraced house in Greenford Gardens. It had white walls, a double-glazed porch entrance, attached garage, all its windows covered with thick lace curtains. This was the place where four men and two women followed Damian, after Igor stopped at the bus station on Ruislip Road. Igor did not help anybody to unload their luggage. He stayed inside, with his wrists propped on the edge of the steering wheel, an unlit cigarette between his fingers, whilst Damian hurried everybody to pick up their bags and follow him. The Kulesza brothers called it the Greenford House, one of the many drop-off rented accommodations across London for the Poles they transported to Britain. There were others. It was Karol who had named them after neighbourhoods; Hounslow, Barking, Neasden, Bromley, Mitcham. A series of temporary homes for temporary people.

The only thing they would remember about Karol would be his name, his carefully constructed identity, the story of his non-existent life. He skilfully navigated the space between his necessary lies and the half-truths. He believed them himself. Though Karol's lies did not stay close to the truth, they resembled a reality he liked to control, and so the lies moulded into fact. He had developed the most effective method of constructing his multiple identities, appearances of truth for the interest of his victims and, of course, to ensure his own profit. Their purpose was but entirely according to his will. And if, by some strange chance, he tripped up, because he forgot what he had told one person, he blamed the listener through either immediate attack or swift denunciation of his story, but never by admitting it as his own mistake. Karol knew that tendency in people – as long as no one could ever be sure what they really remembered – he blamed the other person, in case somebody pointed out some discrepancy in his version of reality.

Karol arrived in the afternoon with bags full of take away food, crisps and bottles of fizzy drinks, the cheapest food he could find on the way. 'Have you settled in?' he asked with concern in his voice, rounding them all together in one of the rooms. 'I brought food and drinks. Do you want cigarettes? I have them, too.'

They listened tensely to Karol speaking, his chin thrust out, and hands repeatedly emphasising his words. The rapid, unconscious arm movements helped him to concentrate. 'We're going to arrange National Insurance numbers and bank accounts. This is important before you begin working in this country. I will collect your passports so that I can start setting you up as soon as possible. There's no time to waste. I'd like you to begin your work as soon as we have the formalities out of the way.'

'Thank you so much,' one of them said, handing his passport to Karol, 'you're a good person, helping us out.'

Before Karol left he insisted on inspecting bathrooms, to make sure they had enough toilet paper and toiletries, that kitchen had a kettle and supply of teabags, coffee and sugar. He showed them the television in one of the rooms with Polish channels, and there were Polish magazines for them to read, if they got bored sitting in the house, waiting. Of course, they could go for a walk tomorrow, to have a look around the area, but he would rather prefer them to stay inside, for their own safety. On the way out, he made sure he shook each hand and promised to be back as soon as he sorted their paperwork.

'What's with the concern?' Damian asked sharply when they were outside.

'Simple psychology,' Karol said. For all his usefulness, and ruthless loyalty to his business, Damian failed to grasp Karol's strategy which he had so carefully implemented during the past few months. But then, Damian's analytical skills were not the reason why Karol had introduced Damian into this business.

'First you need to make them feel secure. You saw how I brought food and asked them if they felt comfortable? Basic needs always come first. This is how you make them trust you. Then, you find what motivates them, which we already know is the money.'

'Same as us,' Damian interjected and grinned. 'Nothing wrong with that, right?'

How could he possibly explain to Damian that yes, money was evidently the motivating factor behind human behaviour, but more than that, it was the level of power that came first. Damian, like others Karol had come across, was delusional thinking that money was the ultimate motivator. Harnessing the power over people's naïvety, altering their lives at will, controlling people's perception was what really excited Karol. And, naturally, money followed.

Karol lusted for absolute power. There was nothing in him, just this desire, nothing but the insatiable craving to control others. Money was a tangible outcome of Karol's excellence in manipulating people, his exceptional talents. Because it was his sole motivation he could not imagine there was anything else worth fighting for in the world.

'Have I ever told you about the Maslow's Triangle?' asked Karol. Often he had timed his lectures to the pause in their conversations; he did not wonder at the words he used, it was an automatic response, an experience he had lived through the lives of others. This was what he was best at. 'You cannot reach the peak of your capabilities, the self-actualisation, without fulfilling the basic needs, like physiological needs. Food, water, shelter, whatever you need for your own survival.'

'Where did you learn all that?' Damian asked.

'I have a degree in social psychology.'

'From here?' Damian sounded impressed.

Technically, Karol did not have a degree, not in the sense of a diploma he could show to anybody, but he had read so many articles, blogs and even books he found on the internet, it felt like he had consumed all the knowledge available. Who needed a certificate, a stupid piece of paper he would have to pay for, if he could have all the information he could lay his hands on for free?

Karol continued matter-of-factly, ignoring Damian's question. 'Safety comes as the second basic need, meaning a roof over your head, but also employment, which will guarantee a level of personal and family's safety. Love and belonging follows safety. Your relationship with friends and family. But people sometimes disregard safety for the sake of belonging and financial gain. This is the area which is the most interesting to us.' Karol paused to make sure Damian was still listening to him. 'Nobody forced these fools to come here. They have agreed of their own free will. They deserve what is happening to them. Do I have any respect for them? No. Do

I pity them? No. I only provided them with an alternative, but it was ultimately their decision, with the help of some simple psychology, of course. We all want to be respected and valued, otherwise we risk falling into depression, imbalance in our emotional life, deviations in some circumstances when we force people to respect us.' Here, Karol thought of Igor and wondered if his brother's face also came to Damian's mind, because he remained unusually focused on Karol's words, clenching and grinding his teeth as they walked. Perhaps Damian did not understand fully what Karol was saying. Karol did not ask. What he was saying and how, was far more complicated than Damian could ever comprehend, so Karol did not ponder whether Damian would ever be able to threaten his position, take over the business or set up his own and become competition, using these simple tools for human psychology he was describing in such detail. 'To achieve our potential, to become the most that we can be,' Karol continued, quoting one of the lines he remembered he had read somewhere, 'we need to master all the previous steps. Only then will we reach the peak of our personal growth.'

Damian spat onto the pavement. 'Sounds like bullshit.'

If it wasn't for this bullshit you would not be here with me now, Karol thought.

To Damian, indeed, the explanation of human psychology, even in simple terms, was a waste of time because he naively believed it had nothing to do with him; that the only thing that truly mattered, and was enough to make people do what he wanted, was a combination of different levels of fear. Karol knew that.

For eighteen months the Kulesza brothers and Karol experienced whole new levels of fear, in the 2nd Tank Battalion of the 4th Armoured Brigade in Olsztyn, where they had served together in compulsory military service in the Polish Land Forces. In 1996, the Kulesza brothers arrived at the armed forces recruiting station in Łódź. Their lives, like the other men who reached the age of eighteen, were at a perilous edge, about to tip them over into a well of fear and humiliation or onto a path towards becoming adult men.

A group of ten men was waiting in the corridor, some strolling impatiently and clenching their IDs, passports, or certificates that proved they were enrolled in one of the Universities, hoping it was enough to avoid the conscription or at least postpone it. Finally, the door opened and a young soldier, in a crisp army uniform and boots that reflected the light, asked them to enter the interrogation room and take their places behind the white cloth curtain. The young soldier instructed them to take off their clothes, except for underwear, and wait for their names to be called out by the chairman of the conscription commission. Under the young men's feet lay small heaps of shirts, pairs of trousers, jackets, clothes dropped in haste, as there were no chairs or tables provided on which to place them. As they stood waiting, half-naked and embarrassed, goose bumps formed on their skin from the bracing spring wind which blew in powerful gusts through an open window. The wind also carried the distant sound of strong, vibrating male voices, orders echoing off the walls and the thudding of boots.

The chairman bellowed Igor's name to bring him forward, the voice holding surprising force for his age. He was around sixty years old, a sturdy looking man with spiky sandy hair, immaculately groomed and tailored, a man used to giving orders. His chest was inflated and he sat rigidly.

Igor, with red marks on his back and bruises on his calves, did not move, paralysed with sudden anxiety, when the chairman read out his name.

'Recruit Kulesza, we haven't got all day.' The chairman snapped impatiently.

Damian whispered encouraging words behind Igor's back. He could feel Igor's body trembling, afraid to move.

The young men peered curiously from behind the curtain when Igor walked slowly to face the examiners who smirked arrogantly at every single person to appear before them.

Half of the young men hoped for Category D marked in their military cards, which would allow them to stay at home rather than relocate to army barracks for the next eighteen months, but unless they could prove serious health problems or insanity they faced Category A – fit for military service.

The training the Kulesza brothers had begun at their father's police boxing club was broadcast by their chiselled physiques, their muscles prominently visible, much to the satisfaction of the chairman and other senior soldiers stationed behind the long table covered in bottle green cloth. They admired Igor's frame, grunting and nodding their heads in approval, their eyes glided up and down Igor's body.

'Socks?'

Embarrassed, Igor took them off and crumpled the material in his fist. He curled his toes from the chill.

'Have you got any children? Wife? Any health issues?'

'No,' Igor whispered, losing his voice.

'Speak up, recruit Kulesza. We can't hear you.'

Igor swallowed. 'No wife or children.'

'Good.' The chairman made a mark in the documents. 'Interesting. Your father is in the police force?' The chairman leaned to whisper something to another man, then added, 'Your brother, Damian Kulesza, is he here? Ah, yes, of course he's here. Category B-12.' More whispering followed.

Muscles tensed in Damian's neck. 'Your brother?' somebody behind him murmured. 'They didn't take you in last year?'

'I was sick,' Damian interrupted, unwilling to provide more information. Badly sprained ankle in a plaster had earned him a twelve-month break and a chance to serve with his brother who had just turned eighteen.

'They'll probably put you together. If your father is in the police force.'

'What does that have to do with anything?' Damian hissed. If there was anybody Damian would rather keep out of his and Igor's lives that would be their father.

'I'm just saying. They wouldn't like to piss off somebody in the police.'

'Mind your own business,' Damian snapped.

The chairman shuffled through the papers and said to Igor, 'Recruit Igor Kulesza. You can proceed for your medical examination. Next! Recruit Waldemar Rabiński.'

Damian knew from the panic on his brother's face, from the desperate way he was trying to look normal after he had returned from the medical examination, that Damian should have warned him, prepared him, said something. But how could he have known? His medical examination had been a year ago with a different doctor in a different place. His was an accidental experience which Damian obliterated from his memory. Now, patting his brother on the shoulder in an awkward consolation, his throat constricted at a lack of words as he remembered the day the doctor asked him to drop his underwear to his knees. 'Two testicles?' asked the doctor. Damian automatically grabbed at his crotch, to protect himself from the doctor's hands, but the doctor sternly instructed him to remove his hands so he could continue his examination.

He cupped Damian's testicles and said, 'Cough.' Then, he ordered Damian to bend down.

Karol leaned lazily against the railing of the army house in Olsztyn, looking down at the soldiers. They were still smiling, blissfully unaware. Others exchanged comments, as they marched down the corridor. He spat out a match he was playing with. That morning, the future soldiers hardly noticed Karol, with an open army shirt displaying his naked chest with little hair, hiding in the shadows out of sight. Major Cezary Drozd emerged from his office, angered by the commotion and voices in the corridor. Karol quickly buttoned his shirt and ran downstairs.

'Was there a command to talk?' Major Drozd silenced the newly arrived men. 'You are now the 2nd Tank Battalion of the 4th Armoured Brigade. You are going to loyally serve your fatherland. From now on you are following the orders of your superiors. Is that clear?'

'Yes, Major Drozd!' the voices bounced off the walls.

'I don't care if you cry or shit yourself from pain. You are in my battalion now, the best in the country. Consider yourself lucky to have your training here. I expect perfection and loyalty. Your officers will instruct you on your duties.'

'Yes, Major Drozd!' once again the voices echoed.

Later, in their room, Igor and Damian simply announced to the others which bunk beds they wanted, they were the biggest men in their group. The rumour about their father had already spread among the other soldiers. Karol had overheard Major Drozd mention their names during a telephone conversation: the Kulesza brothers, then Zenon Kulesza, secret services, only a few words out of context, but enough for Karol to formulate the possibility of the future he had begun to imagine for himself in the life outside. Such contacts were worth keeping close at hand, in case the right opportunity presented itself.

Before Karol had joined the army, he was nobody. Weak limbed, spotty faced, with a layer of fat already forming around his stomach, his nails bitten, yes, a small town salesman but nothing more. His quick brains and clever ruthlessness matched Major Drozd's and soon gained the major's appreciation, as well as respect among the other soldiers in 2nd Tank Battalion of the 4th Armoured Brigade.

Like some of the other soldiers who had just begun their service, Karol had survived thick leather belt beatings on his bare back in the middle of the night, standing to attention for half a day while wearing full gear and a gasmask filled with his sweat and tears, crawling for two hours in mud, breathing fumes, behind an army truck. He was humbled into submission with variable degrees of compassion. The words engraved in his mind from his early days, when he was a young recruit himself and nothing but 'a stinking, motherfucker tomcat':

I, the cat,
With my tail high up,
Uglier than my own arse,
Stinking like fart gas,
With my neck ready to be slapped,
Or any other body part to be struck,
Respecting the army rules,
Despite the fact I am only a tool,
I am standing here to solemnly swear,
That I will serve my country and my corporal,
Who from now on is like my beloved general,
Respectfully, I hereby offer my services,

Make tea in the middle of the night,
Every task I will perform with delight.

Now, Karol had Major Drozd's ear. His sweet obedient words, yet with a layer of manipulation, became the shield against Karol's own insecurity, a form of necessary survival. He was Major Drozd's eyes and ears. He reported back promptly on what was going on among the soldiers, day and night, behind Major Drozd's back. He began to form an alliance with the Kulesza brothers. He was quick to spot their potential, more physical than anything else. Karol had already realised that their talents had little to do to with their intelligence. And there was something else. This strange, and somehow unhealthy, devotion to one another. Karol considered a weakness, one he could exploit.

A month into their service, the Kulesza brothers were ordered on a 48-hour lock down inside T-55AM 'Merida' tank during exercises at the Orzysz polygon. Igor refused to go inside. He got violently sick which further infuriated Major Drozd. The Major found the toilet where Igor spat and coughed into a toilet bowl and kicked Igor's bare soles.

'Major Drozd, sir,' Damian said behind him, 'my brother is not good in confined spaces.'

Major Drozd's right cheek twitched. 'What did you say?' he asked quietly, offering a chance for Damian to apologise, to realise his mistake, that nothing in their training was optional. But Damian, stubbornly, pleaded further, defending his brother like he did at school or back at home not so long ago.

'Do you think the enemy will care?' Major Drozd spat in Damian's face, his voice rising, punctuated by sudden swearwords Damian did not know existed. 'Get out! Both of you. Right now!'

A punishment followed. Together Igor and Damian stood for two nights in the paralysing January cold. The cold sent uncontrollable muscle spasms down their legs and froze their fingers to their rifles, but they never complained, even if they were close to fainting from frost and hunger. An order was an order. It was Karol, preparing the daily rota in Major Drozd's office, who casually mentioned that perhaps the Kulesza brothers' spirit could be broken if the whole team was to be punished. 'An experiment in loyalty,' Karol added. Bending over the documents, he pretended he was talking to himself. Another idea occurred to Karol: what would happen if they were separated? The brothers were always together, in an unnatural way, without consideration for anybody else except for each other. Their bond seemed more than the devotion of one brother to another, especially Damian, who would attack anybody making fun of Igor's sick mind. Something else, a hint of suspicion planted in Major Drozd's mind: didn't Damian's injury conveniently allow him to postpone his service until his brother Igor came of age? Of course, there was no proof, but nevertheless an interesting thought. Karol was already thinking ahead, spinning scenarios and planning possibilities for the use of the brothers.

A few weeks later, the seeds of suggestion Karol had so patiently planted in Major Drozd's mind resulted in the separation of Damian and Igor.

Raging inside, Damian surrendered to isolation from his brother, which lasted for over a month. Karol had carefully chosen the right moment to approach Damian. He assessed when Damian was the most desperate, not knowing when or if he was going to see his beloved brother again, or what was going on with Igor exactly. Damian was on his knees, scrubbing the stairs and floors in the left of the building. This was how Karol found him, bent with a worn scrubbing brush in both hands on the steps. First, Karol held out a piece of hard, dry sausage, saying, 'From my mother. Take it. I have some cigarettes if you want some.' Damian straightened his back and slowly rubbed his wet hands on his trousers. Damian towering over Karol, they sized each other up, looking deep into each other. Damian looked down at Karol's hands and said, 'Thank you.' After a moment of silence, with Damian hungrily chewing on the meat he could not refuse because he was famished, Karol mentioned that he had heard Igor had tried to commit suicide. Damian shot up from the stairs. He tripped over the bucket, sending dirty water to the bottom of the stairs. 'He's all right, now,' said Karol, 'He's all right.'

'Where is he? I want to see him. Why has nobody said anything to me?'

'Drozd didn't want you to know,' Karol offered.

'I want to see my brother.'

Karol took his time, forcing Damian to hang onto his every word, savouring Damian's pain. He explained to Damian that he had already spoken to Major Drozd, and the good news was that Igor would be released soon from the service and was returning home.

'I know how close you are to your brother and I told Drozd he should have never isolated the two of you. If you ask me, I have no idea where he got this devilish plan to bring your brother to such desperation. Listen, I've been here long enough to see Drozd's ruthlessness but you didn't make it easy for yourselves when you disobeyed his command. He simply wanted to hurt you, and I did tell him it was going to end badly.'

'I'll kill him,' Damian whispered, shaking, 'I swear to God, I will kill him.'

'Listen,' Karol grabbed Damian's shoulder, and peered into his face, arresting Damian's full attention, 'I get it. He's not going to do anything to you now after what happened to Igor. So let it go. Besides, what good would it do? If you kill him, you will never see your brother again. I'll be out soon. I promise I will make sure he's okay. I'll put a word with Drozd to get you a pass so you can spend some time with Igor. All right?' Karol squeezed Damian's shoulder once again, knowing his words had sucked Damian into perfect obedience.

Years later, Damian joked that he and his brother owed Karol their lives. If Karol had not been there for Damian that day he would have ripped Drozd into pieces. Karol kept his word and took care of Igor while Damian was finishing his army service, because nobody wanted to give them a chance when Igor got out of prison, because Karol never saw Igor as a monster and never judged Damian for loving, and defending, his brother against the whole world. Not everybody understood their brotherly bond, not even their parents. But Karol did.

Damian and Igor were forever and happily caged in their blind gratitude to Karol, the one person who offered them a second chance and gave a semblance of significance to their lives.

Karol's plan was so perfectly executed, he often smiled when he recalled his time in the army.

7

'I can have any girl I want. I'm that good,' Karol shouted into his cousin's ear. There was nothing objective about his statement. He liked to hold people's attention with his exaggerated opinions. Karol looked over secretly to see whether Zygmunt was interested or amazed.

'Come on. Let's have a drink.' His eyes carefully surveyed the mass of people in search of a perfect spot by the crowded bar. The most important thing was to be seen among the right people, successful people, people with money, beautiful people who held the air tightly around them, commanding the glamorous attention. Karol liked to think of himself as one of them – people who effortlessly paraded their hypnotising presence.

'A bottle of champagne,' Karol told the barman, and threw notes on the table, leaning with his elbow on the edge. Zygmunt found him intimidating, the kind of man he aspired to become but had not yet figured out how to be; to have that aura of instant respect the moment he entered a room and everybody hung on Karol's each word.

Anywhere Karol took his cousin, Karol effortlessly struck up a conversation with complete strangers. Especially women. He laughed heartily at their jokes, complimented them on little things that their boyfriends, husbands or partners failed to notice, recognised the brands of their handbags or shoes, and made sure the expensive alcohol kept flowing. He strolled into the VIP area, with an air of instant belonging, with women hanging onto him, impressed with his easiness and power of persuasion. In a fluid, intimate gesture, Karol embraced the women closer on both sides, protectively, and they let him do it. 'You know who you remind me of? Danny DeVito. You look just like him,' commented the woman with skin colour of burnt nuts, in between sips of champagne, and in a motherly gesture placed a hand on Karol's cheek. Zygmunt grinned, stupidly, while Karol, stiffened, shifted his shoulders, his face briefly pinched in concentration. 'You'd be surprised what I could do to you.' There was a warning edge to his voice, his fingers playing with his iPhone in his side pocket, almost tempted to prove his point.

Before Zygmunt had a chance to finish his glass of champagne, choking as the bubbles burst in his throat, unused to this sensation, Karol was already dragging two women to the dance floor, boasting of his long-gone dance career on the way, 'a ballroom dancer, the champion of Poland.' In a firm grip he twisted and twirled the women around, carving a space for himself and his accidental dancers on the crowded floor under the DJ's podium. And he was surprisingly agile, but Zygmunt could not exactly recall those days of Karol-the dancing champion. Instead, this image was clouded in some distant memory of Karol's awkward attempts at dancing, out of sync with the music, at weddings and discos at local towns or villages. The recent photos Karol had shown him, of the time spent in the flashy and decadent clubs of Ibiza, Aya Napa, Las Vegas, Berlin, Miami, Tokyo, in every picture surrounded by the stunning, smiling faces, confused Zygmunt. Karol was so insistent on his distinguished dancing career, together with detailed description of the trophies and titles awarded to him, Zygmunt began to doubt his memories of their past together, like it had never existed. Whatever Zygmunt thought he remembered was quickly replaced by Karol's convincing new version of himself. Zygmunt stared at his cousin in wonder.

'Are Igor and Damian joining us?' Zygmunt asked, when Karol got back.

'Igor and Damian? What for?' Karol asked sharply. Sweat glistened on his heated forehead. The shirt clung to his clammy back.

'I don't know.' Zygmunt hesitated, trying to find the right description for the brothers. He was not sure what the connection was between Karol and the two men. 'Aren't they your friends?'

'They work for me. Why would I want them here?' Karol looked away. He did not see the relief on Zygmunt's face. 'Besides,' Karol added, turning to face his cousin, 'it's your night out.'

It did not feel like that to Zygmunt with Karol leading the way and stealing the limelight everywhere they went. He did not mind. He did not know this city or people like Karol.

As he sat silent and stony-eyed, already a little bit tired in a stupid bliss, staring at the writhing bodies on the dance floor in front of him, he wondered how long it would take him to be able to afford Karol's lifestyle.

Two weeks before, Igor had met Zygmunt at Stansted airport, 'Karol sent me,' was all that Igor said, and he remained silent until they stopped in front of a row of flats because Igor had to pick up something on the way. Igor told him to wait in the car.

'Are you hungry?' Igor asked when he returned. He threw a package onto the back seat.

'I could eat.'

They drove for another half an hour before Igor parked the car in front of Malik's Fried Chicken.

'You have any money?'

Zygmunt did not expect this. He did not know how much food cost here. He handed over a twenty-pound note that he had received in the foreign exchange shop back in Poland, an amount that he could use for a week's food shopping, if he was careful. The note disappeared, crumpled in Igor's fist.

Igor grabbed the package from the back seat. He opened the door on his side and said, 'You coming or what?' He walked to a man sitting outside, a glut of muscles. 'My brother, Damian.' Igor said to Zygmunt as a way of explanation and slumped on the seat next to Damian.

'You're Karol's cousin, right? Sit down. First time here?' Damian asked, squinting in the bright sun. 'Girls? Say the word.'

'I don't have much luck with the girls.'

Igor and Damian exchanged a look and laughed.

'What are you, a fag?' Damian asked. 'No wife or girlfriend? No kids? You handicapped or something? Or maybe you have a crooked, small dick? How old are you anyway?'

'Forty-one.' Zygmunt swallowed.

Damian leaned forward to light a cigarette close to his legs, where wind could not get at it, then straightened up and said: 'Get yourself a placard on your neck that says 'I'm shy' and wait on Kilburn High Road outside the Brondes Age bar. In thirty minutes there will be more girls swarming around you than you can count.'

Nothing made sense to Zygmunt; he felt isolated by their foreignness. It took an effort, an act of will, to follow what they were saying, the ease with which they peppered English words, he did not understand, into their speech, as if they had been here forever. It was the same behaviour he would observe in Karol, when Igor finally dropped him at his place, speaking in a knowing, confident tone.

After Karol showed him a small room, no windows, in the basement where he was going to stay from now on, he left him with Milena because he had some business to take care of. Karol said, 'Milena will tell you what to do.' And she did: 'The bucket and cleaning products are in the cupboard in the kitchen. Remember to always use fabric softener, the purple one with white clothes and towels, the white one with wool. I'll give you cash for the shopping. I'll take you to Tesco tomorrow but you will have to walk there because you won't be able to drive our cars. Make sure to always get the receipt and leave the rest on the kitchen counter. You'll clean the windows once a month. The window cleaner, a bottle with green liquid, is in the cupboard over here. Bathrooms and toilets need to be scrubbed twice a week. This bottle is for washing the wooden floors and that one, to clean the tiles. Don't make a mistake because you'll ruin the floor. Then the garden, there's a lot to do so that should keep you busy for the rest of the day. There's a shed where we keep all the garden tools. Dust the furniture every day. Karol has asthma.'

'Karol mentioned something about working with him.' Zygmunt's voice rang with confusion. His eyes jumped around the room, as he tried to remember why he had come here, because he could not recall Karol mentioning anything about working as a cleaner; a woman's job.

'I know nothing about that. If he has an opening, I'm sure he will tell you. This is what you'll be doing for now. We'll see about other jobs later.'

Zygmunt resigned himself to his fate. 'Thank you. I really appreciate all you're doing for me.'

'Good. You can start today. I'm going to the office so you'll be on your own.'

'You need a National Insurance number and a bank account. I've already notified the Job Centre,' Karol said over breakfast. He ate fast, cheeks puffed. He swept his tongue every few seconds around his lips. 'You don't need to worry about anything.' He spoke to Zygmunt with the authority of someone who had done this before, and Zygmunt trusted him. His future was, after all, in Karol's hands. 'We'll go the bank today. I will do the talking. It'll be easier that way. Besides, I've got a British passport,' Karol added.

'A British passport?'

Karol knew that this document, which he happily preferred to use when crossing the Polish border in order to add a little more importance to his status, ignited a feeling of envy in a way his Polish identity did not. It granted him the grounding in Britain that he liked to boast of in front of other Poles. A different kind of presence, which gave an aura of instant respect and separated him from others.

'If you stay here long enough you can apply for one as well.' Karol smiled broadly. He was in a good mood this morning.

'Oh.'

'It would be good if you could make small contributions to the household. Milena has complained. You know what women are like.' Karol gave him a sly look. He knew Zygmunt was slightly unnerved by Milena, by her self-importance, her use of big words about her business, but it was so easy to snap Zygmunt into obedience.

'Of course. Yes,' Zygmunt said without hesitation, but he stirred nervously. Then he asked how much. When Karol told him the amount, in between sips of coffee with his narrowed eyes set on Zygmunt, he panicked. Over forty per cent of the weekly wage Karol paid him.

Every now and then Karol tapped the edge of the fork against the surface of the table. 'It's a good deal,' Karol assured him. He washed down scrambled eggs with a big gulp of coffee and wiped his mouth. 'I'm not asking you to pay for the water bill, gas and electricity, frankly your money is so small it's not going to make any difference. However, you are my family. I'm just trying to help. You would never make that kind of money back home, would you? And from what I know you haven't had a job for a while?' Zygmunt nodded. 'That's settled then. Now, wash the dishes. Milena doesn't like dirty dishes waiting in the sink. Then we go to the bank.'

At the local bank they were welcomed by a young Asian woman who asked Karol if he would feel more comfortable with a Polish speaker, to deal with their request, after he had provided her with his surname. In his heavy accented English, he responded, without the slightest glimmer of unease, that there would be no need for that. He had opened the account for his fellow country-men a number of times, making sure he did not go to the same branch twice in the same month. Hounslow, Southall, Greenford, sometimes as far as Enfield and Loughton. Karol thought that he would have to be more careful next time and make sure there were no Polish speaking staff.

Zygmunt sat silently as Karol interrogated the bank about vari-ous current accounts, charges, loans, then he presented Zygmunt's passport and confirmed his cousin was a resident at his house, for now. 'He speaks no English. I'm helping him today,' he added, foot fidgeting under the table.

'We have Polish-speaking clerks if Mr Szczepański would prefer to do it himself,' the man sitting in front of them worked around the challenging cluster of consonants.

'That won't be necessary. He asked me to do it for him. It's his first time in Britain. He's happy for me to take care of it. You see,' Karol lowered his voice, 'he's mentally challenged.' Karol was careful not to use the word 'retarded'. He remembered when he used it once in a different branch and the woman he was talking to winced. The woman would certainly remember his face, something he did not need.

'I see.' The bank assistant clerk smiled carefully at Zygmunt, then asked Karol if they would like to follow him to a different room where they could feel more comfortable and private.

'We're fine here,' Karol said and thought he needed to find a new scenario in the future. And asked, 'Where does he need to sign?'

When a few days later an envelope addressed to 'Mr Zygmunt Szczepanski' arrived, with additional paperwork and a bank card, Karol said, 'I'll keep it safe for you, together with your passport,' and he took everything to his office, leaving only the bank card in his cousin's hands. Karol assured Zygmunt that if he needed he could use his computer to check his account online, but the security systems were so complex in Britain, it was best if Karol did it. 'In case you block your access. And since the instructions about passwords and codes and the information in the account itself would all be in English it was really of no use to Zygmunt. Karol went on, speaking very fast, 'And when you decide to return home, I would take care of it for you here.'

The last thing Karol needed Zygmunt to do was to come with him to visit the lawyer, 'so that everything is in order,' Karol added and rubbed his hands together.

Agnes McCormick, a Polish-speaking lawyer, with a Polish mother and Irish father, was puffy-faced with dark circles under her eyes. Karol, with a playful twinkle in the eye, joked that Agnes must have partied hard the night before. 'You know that I don't drink. It's all the last minute work you've been sending me,' Agnes explained. An open packet of painkillers lay on the desk, next to a glass of water.

Karol liked doing this to people, giving them short notice, a few hours or sometimes less, if he needed anything. Everybody who worked for or had any dealings with Karol had to be on a perpetual standby, whether he decided to call in the middle of the night or in the early hours of the day. He liked to remind people that business did not take care of itself. Commitment and unconditional devotion to fulfilling his grand vision was what made him successful. People who lacked either had their contracts terminated, without a word of explanation or apology, since Karol believed none was needed in the face of self-evident lack of dedication towards him.

Agnes McCormick laid various documents on the table and, in a raspy voice, explained to Zygmunt why he needed to sign the power of attorney, which would allow Karol to answer any letters on his behalf. 'Since you don't speak English,' or claim tax benefits, 'why do you need to pay more tax than necessary,' contacting the bank, 'the banks here flood customers with letters,' and most importantly for Zygmunt's own safety, 'if anything happens to you, or you have to go to the hospital, without power of attorney Karol will not be able to help you.' And Zygmunt, overwhelmed, hanging onto Agnes McCormick's every word, signed all documents written in English which the attorney slid in his direction.

After all the paperwork had been completed, Karol asked Zygmunt to wait outside because he needed a word with Agnes McCormick in private. He slowly smoothed the hair on his temples and placed his hands on his knees. He waited for Zygmunt to close the door behind him.

'If you ever talk to me like that again, we're going to have a very different conversation.' He looked Agnes McCormick in the eye, regarding her seriously. His sharp voice dominated the room.

'Karol, I'm really sorry. I'm just tired, that's all.' She was placing the documents Zygmunt had signed in a separate folder. She desperately needed to swallow another painkiller, her headache was getting worse, clouding her thoughts.

Karol set both hands on the edge of the desk. 'I don't care if you are tired or not, or whatever is going on in your life. You don't talk to me in this way in front of another person.'

Agnes McCormick stopped, with documents suspended mid-air in her hand. 'He's your cousin. I didn't think it would be an issue.'

'Agnieszka, I don't care.' His eyes glittered. Karol always insisted on using the Polish equivalent of her first name 'Agnes'. After a few attempts she had stopped correcting him. She also made an effort to speak in Polish, though he did not shy away from emphasising his proficiency in the English; he stumbled and pronounced English words with great difficulty. According to Karol his level of English had nothing to do with the number of adjectives or the complexity of sentence structure he used but the number of years he had lived in Britain. He considered the years here the best testament to his foreign language abilities, as though he had automatically acquired the English simply by being surrounded by the sounds of it on a daily basis. It did not matter that he only conversed with his countrymen but, after all, he lived in Britain which according to Karol, by definition, was enough, as it exposed him to the English. 'I learnt English through osmosis,' he often explained.

His clumsy linguistic endeavours, misplaced intonation, in different circumstances may have been the subject of Agnes McCormick's commentary, but she was too wary of her own position to correct him. He once sent her an email, after Agnes McCormick insisted on communicating in English, 'Though my English is good,' he began first by affirming his fluency, which in his own eyes was almost impeccable, and he was not afraid to challenge her, 'yours I would say even very good, I don't see the point of two people from the same country using a foreign tongue.' Karol was not a person she would like to pick a fight with and, more importantly, he paid her good money, considering the business they were doing. She was also afraid of the Kulesza brothers, no doubt, which is why she forced herself to be so unfailingly polite.

Karol took out a bulging envelope from his bag and placed it on Agnes McCormick's desk. 'Here's your money.'

'Really, Karol, I'm sorry. It won't happen again.'

He got to his feet but kept her eyes on hers, commanding her full attention. 'There'll be more paperwork to be done. I'm giving you a heads up, in case you need to clear your schedule for me. Next week, remember. I'll call you.'

As they walked back to the car, Karol leading the way with his body leaning forward, Zygmunt could not stop thanking Karol for his generosity, for sorting out all the legal paperwork on his behalf. He would have had no idea what to do were it not for Karol and Milena's hospitality, and once he learned the language and saved some money he would be able to find himself a job.

'But you've got a job. No?' Karol asked sharply, without slowing down.

Zygmunt cleared his throat. 'I really don't want to be a trouble for you and Milena.'

'You don't like the job I found for you already? You're home all day. Do you have any idea how expensive life is in London?' Karol could barely hide his irritation and he did not like himself for it.

'If I wanted to make more money…'

Karol glanced at his cousin, resentful at being interrupted. 'I'll sort something out for you. But for now I need you in the house. Milena and I need you. And you have not paid the loan I've given you.'

Zygmunt quickened his pace, to catch up with Karol, and make sure he had heard correctly. 'The loan?'

'For your stay in our house, of course. And the solicitor's fee. I've put my own money for you.'

'I wish you'd asked me,' Zygmunt said in a quiet voice, unnerved how much money they were talking about. The forty percent towards household bills, now the solicitor's fee which was bound to be exorbitant, everything in this city seemed so excessive and out of his reach. If a sandwich Igor bought for him with his own money cost twenty pounds, then a loan and a fee would surely be hundred times more.

'I didn't think I needed to, since I was doing it for your own good. But, well, if you want to work somewhere else, try your luck with strangers who are going to abuse your trust. With no language, recommendation letters, experience in this city. Uhm, I don't know but it will be tough but I'm not keeping you. You think you can find a place to stay and a job? You can go whenever you want.' Karol knew what Zygmunt's reaction would be – the same as everybody else's he put in this position where he owned somebody's life before they realised it.

Then, in the pleading tone that so disgusted Karol, Zygmunt almost begged him, over and over again, to give him a chance, that he would do anything, that he was so grateful, his whole family was grateful, for this opportunity to come here, but Karol's attention was already elsewhere. With Zygmunt's bank account and power of attorney signed, he was ready to start applying for benefits and loans in his cousin's name.

8

A boisterous tune from Kismat Radio drowned out Milena's morning greeting. An agile, old man, with a round, excitable face and frantic eyes, was leaning against the counter, his chin propped on his right hand with a fingernail burrowed in a gap between his front teeth. The man glared unhappily at the packages in Milena's arms and he sucked the air through his teeth, emitting a short, sharp sound from his mouth. As she walked past the food shelves, she reached a rack of newspapers and monthlies. Somebody had left one of the magazines open on a page with a young woman, her legs spread wide, her shaved genitals on display, right next to a kids' magazine *Moshi Monsters*. Milena averted her eyes and stopped in front of the post office counter at the back of the shop. She looked up at a clock on the wall. Ten minutes to nine. She was too early.

'Go away. Not open,' the shop owner shouted in quick bursts, slurring the words and waving his arms. 'You wait outside. Now.'

She hated going to GS and SS Khainwar's shop but the post office outlet GS Khainwar ran on the premises was the closest. The Royal Mail office was a fifteen-minute drive and she was still wary of driving on the left hand side, despite having held a British driving licence for several years now. She should have sent Zygmunt, let him deal with this disgusting old man, an immigrant like the rest of them. How could Milena possibly understand GS Khainwar's English if he was not an Englishman?

The shopkeeper got to his feet and moved in her direction. 'Let go of me,' Milena swore in Polish and left the shop. Nobody who knew her would dare lay a finger on her, but here she was nobody special. If only she did not have to post those packages to Poland.

So she waited outside, fuming, her trembling fingers frantically scrolling down to find Karol's mobile phone number. There was no answer. She was upset.

Customers were rushing in and out while she stood, dejected, on the pavement with the parcels at her feet. She glanced at her watch. It was ten minutes past nine, but she did not see the young man going inside who usually sat behind the glass window of the tiny room at the back. She peered through the glass door and realised, to her surprise, there was already a queue forming. How could she have missed him? He must have come in via the back entrance, through GS and SS Khainwar's flat above the shop or perhaps he lived with them, one of those many cousins from India. As soon as she memorised one face, a new one arrived. She picked up the packages and stormed inside, stirring the little bell above the door into an angry shrill.

She wanted to ask him in English why he did not tell her the post office counter had already been open, but she did not know how.

'What? What?' the shopkeeper sputtered in her silent and frustrated face. His lips glistened with saliva. 'You go.'

Milena ignored him and took her spot in the queue behind the last customer, a woman in slacks with a bulky pram in front of her. She was talking loudly to somebody on a mobile phone.

'No mobile phones.' The shopkeeper once again angrily thrust his arm at a sign on the wall. 'No mobile phones.'

'Oh, shut it,' the woman hissed. 'What? You wanna throw me out?' She turned around to a man standing by the magazine rack, leafing delightedly through the latest edition of *Weekend Sport*. 'Mickey. For Christ's sake. Mickey!' the woman snapped her husband into attention.

Mickey, oblivious to what was going on, finally looked up. 'Fucking hell, woman. What's with the shouting?'

Milena shrank back and prayed there would be no fight. She really did not mind somebody bashing GS Khainwar's head but not when she was around. She just wanted to post the packages and leave. She had a doctor's appointment in less than an hour.

'The man says I can't talk, you get me? Cause of a stupid sign.'

With less confidence now GS Khainwar poked at the sign above his head. 'No mobile. All right. I'm the boss.' He ran his fingers through his thinning hair nervously.

'Oi! No... No it fucking ain't alright,' Mickey approached GS Khainwar who shrank behind the counter. He slumped onto a stool so heavily that he was forced to grab onto the edge of a shelf with cigarettes next to him to stop himself falling backwards. 'Fucking bastard. This ain't the airport.'

'That's what I'm talking about. It feels good, yeah, you know. No way to treat customers like that!' The woman looked at Milena with proud eyes, her Mickey now having restored the proper order. Milena smiled weakly, relieved Mickey was not going to bash GS Khainwar's head against the counter this morning.

When Milena finally approached the window, the young Indian man's eyes were set on his iPhone, scrolling through his Facebook and WhatsApp updates. His little finger had an unusually long nail. She placed the first package on the weight and said 'Poland', then waited for the man to tell her the price in between his eyes darting to his mobile phone. Finally, all packages priced and pushed into a sack on the floor, she was ready to go.

The commotion at the shop made her late for her doctor's appointment. She stormed into the house and bumped into

Zygmunt who had just started to wash the kitchen floor, slowly dragging the cloth mop across the surface.

'Hello,' Zygmunt turned around, his wet hands dripping with water, his face sweaty and red. 'I thought you were gone?'

'I only went to the post office,' Milena left marks on the wet floor with her dusty shoes as she walked past him. Zygmunt sighed because he would have to start with the floor all over again.

'I left you some money on the kitchen counter and a list what to get from the shop,' Milena said after she drained the last of her juice. She grabbed the keys and left the house.

On the way to the Wood Green Underground station, with quick steps and at times breaking into a run, she tried Karol's mobile again. Just as she was going to hang up, he answered, impatiently. He was out of breath, because he was in the middle of something (she thought she heard somebody crying in the background). 'Can it wait till I get back home?' he asked. Her words tumbled out; the old shopkeeper, how scared she was and that it was unacceptable to be treated like that. 'Do something,' she finished. 'All right, all right, I will,' Karol placated her.

The terraced house in West Acton, with its white walls and cream leather sofas in the ground floor reception area, was crowded with patients. Some children played in the corner with their own toys, the others sat on their mothers' laps.

'I'm very sorry but your appointment with Doctor Papuziak is delayed,' a receptionist behind the desk politely informed Milena after she had given her name. 'If you could take a seat please. It won't be long.'

Milena sat down, away from the children, and reached for a magazine, one of many displayed on the low table. Leaflets of the

PolMed Surgery advertising a range of their services (urologist, gynaecologist, optician, dentist, GP, psychologist, paediatrician, laboratory) were scattered among the journals and books left by other patients. It was the largest private Polish surgery in London, and though it was relatively expensive Milena had never seen the reception area empty. Years ago, she used to fly back home to visit her gynaecologist and dentist or have her blood tested, but now, since the PolMed Surgery had opened with only Polish doctors and nurses, there was no need for that. She almost felt guilty when she informed her favourite dentist that she had found a doctor closer to her home, and that she did not have to fly anymore between the two countries. 'The prices are almost the same,' she said, as a form of apology, but her dentist was not surprised and told her that she could come back anytime she wanted. She did not. It was so reassuring to be able to talk with a physician in her mother tongue. There was something unsettling when she visited her local GP for the first time. He was from some African country. Both struggled to understand each other so she left empty handed. Then, there was a Somali gynaecologist – Milena froze with apprehension at the sight of a dark-skinned woman in a headscarf. She never went back.

The receptionist called out her name. 'The doctor is ready for you.'

Doctor Krystian Papuziak was one of the founders of the PolMed Surgery, together with his wife, Doctor Iwona Papuziak, a paediatrician. It was their two adult children who ran the surgery now. With a prestigious degree from the London School of Economics, specialisation in sales and marketing, they had been making plans to open three more branches across Britain – Manchester, Southampton and Birmingham – with the largest pockets of Polish immigrants in the country apart from London, the location of the head office.

'Well, looks like we are pregnant,' Doctor Krystian Papuziak said when Milena sat down opposite him. He wasted no time in breaking the news to her.

'What?' she said, helplessly, and bit her lower lip, 'It's impossible. How did this happen?'

Doctor Krystian Papuziak glanced at her over his reading glasses. 'Usually, it takes two to tango. Roughly sixth week. Congratulations.' Then, because she still did not say anything coherent he added, 'You are over thirty years old. In the medical history you have provided, it says you had a miscarriage. We should carefully set up a plan for you to avoid any complications which, of course, are possible. But I can assure you, with the right approach and care, I don't see why you should not become a mother.' There was in his tone a slight accusation, about her lack of joy, as if she was not sufficiently delighted at her luck of this conception, especially at her age. Doctor Krystian Papuziak preferred younger mothers, easier to control and less likely to suffer from complications. He found he was getting impatient with older women and blamed them for putting their careers ahead of family. He did not like this new attitude among women over thirty that they could wait. He had seen women like Milena in his office before, leaving the pregnancy until it was too late, almost impossible, but this patient was lucky and she did not know it.

The crush of emotions she felt when Doctor Krystian Papuziak announced the news was unbearable. Of course she wanted to have children, but until now it was an idea, a thought that sometimes spread through her mind when she saw other people's children, yet not serious enough for her to consider it in its entirety. Happiness mixed with panic rushed through her body, sharp as broken glass. Yes, there was a miscarriage, a few months after she started seeing Karol, and she never told him about it because she decided it was too early to share such an intimate experience. Besides, then they did not live together and it was so much easier to hide their little secrets from each other. Pockets of her life that belonged only to her slowly began to slip away after they had made the decision to live together, their businesses entwined, their relationship taking a new course. She needed to feel important, she had more import-ant plans for the future. No, it was no time to have a baby, not now.

Back in the office she found Damian waiting for her. 'For you.' Damian handed her a small box with a string of faux black pearls. Whenever he travelled back to Poland he remembered to bring something for her.

'They are beautiful.' She thanked him and placed the box on her desk. 'Did you have any problems at the border?' Milena asked. Damian stood with his back to her, staring through the window in her office.

'Igor didn't mention anything.'

Milena looked through some paperwork on her desk, frown-ing. 'I don't like that new guy, Karol's cousin. He's not working hard enough, he's sloppy.'

Damian turned around, he was playing with a match in his mouth. 'There's a woman. I can bring her around if you want. Or do you want me to talk to Karol first?'

'No. I'll talk to him,' she said without looking at him. She kept glancing at the pearls and wondered what to tell Karol.

A knock on the door interrupted their conversation.

'What is it?' Milena asked sharply, startled.

Daria, apologising first, reminded Milena about her meeting with the Polish Airline LOT she had scheduled for today, and wanted to make sure it was still going ahead or whether Milena wanted it rescheduled? Milena nodded and asked Daria to leave.

'You shouldn't be here. You should go.' Milena stood up, preparing to leave.

'I can drop you off,' Damian offered.

Milena hesitated. She had not decided yet if she was going to tell Damian or not. And how much she was going to tell him. 'Don't you have some place to go?'

'Not yet.'

She grabbed her coat. His eyes were dull and there was none of the old hardness in him she observed when he was around Karol.

He drove slowly, carefully, letting other cars go in front of him, emerging from side streets, or stopping for the pedestrians to cross, and it made her feel safe, unlike Karol who sped through the streets, cutting through other drivers and never letting anybody in. Karol honked earnestly at all pedestrians, particularly impatient with older and sluggish people or mothers with small children. There was always jarring music, which made a conversation almost impossible unless she shouted 'Why do you have to rush so much? We're going to have an accident. Please slow down,' she once shouted to Karol. But he laughed at her and asked her what was the point of living if you could not live on your own terms? She wrapped a shawl around her neck and Damian asked her at once if the air conditioning was too cold and turned the temperature up.

Then Karol called. Milena could hear his raised voice, chasing his own words. Damian lied that he was stuck in traffic, without mentioning he was with Milena, and promised he would get to Karol as soon as he could.

'Why didn't you tell him we were together?'

'What for?'

'He would have understood why you were running late.'

'I'll get there when I get there.'

She realised how silly it had been to ask him. Of course he did not have to explain himself to Karol. He would have told Damian not to drive her because it was quicker to take public transport rather than wasting time like that.

Milena drew her breath in. 'I'm pregnant.'

Damian opened his mouth to say something then closed it.

9

Karol was not used to having his conversations cut off in mid-sentence. The deal with the site manager Maciej Borowik was straightforward until now. Karol sent the men and pocketed their wages. Borowik got a cut and cheap labour. No questions asked. Everybody was happy. Karol wondered if he should change the arrangement but it had worked like clockwork. Perhaps Borowik wanted more money, he wondered, but if it was about the money Borowik was not somebody who would be shy about asking.

Karol recalled that incident with one of the older men, his name escaped Karol's memory, so many faces and names not worth remembering. The man who fell from a rooftop. A terrible accident, the health and safety inspector proclaimed; alcohol in the victim's bloodstream. That day Borowik did not show up to work; a family emergency, and he spent the whole day with his daughter in the park. 'I don't want to know,' he said to Karol, early on, and it suited both of them to keep out of each other's ways. It was Karol who would text Borowik the night before, to take a sick leave or call in a family emergency. He did not care what Borowik said as long as he did not show up to work, so he would not witness something accidentally. Basically, he was doing Borowik a favour.

The man was not supposed to die. It was an accident in poor planning. Igor did not mean to push the fifty-year-old all the way from the rooftop of the house, only scare him but it was dark, the man had had a few beers and Igor misjudged the distance. He let the man fall.

'I'm the only family he has here,' Karol explained to the nurse when he visited the dying man at the hospital. He summoned a look of concern on his face. 'They're all praying for his recovery back home. They begged me to visit him. They had no money to travel at such short notice. An awful accident…Tragedy.' To further soften the nurse's heart, he added: 'He's got a two-year-old son…His wife is pregnant with a second.'

'Normally I wouldn't be able to let you in,' the nurse responded, eyeing Damian pacing behind Karol's back, 'but I can see these are extraordinary circumstances. Please follow me.'

Damian guarded the patient's door whilst Karol stood at the man's feet. The man's chest was slowly rising and falling, the machine, which stood next to the bed, pumped air into the man's lungs. After seeing him Karol thought that there was no chance to recover from brain damage like that, with a blunt liver and spleen injury.

'And?' Damian asked with expectation in his voice when Karol joined him in the hospital corridor.

Karol closed his eyes for a minute, his face full of peace and content. 'A carrot. He's not going to come back to construction anytime soon.' Relief and satisfaction rang in Karol's voice. 'But we can still use his National Insurance number and claim child benefits in his name before his death.'

Later, Karol rewarded Borowik with a bulky envelope with notes, 'For the stress,' he said. 'Take your family somewhere nice or buy something for your wife and daughter.'

Whether Borowik could not or did not want to say no to the money the first time, in every other instance that followed, he stopped wondering about his own motives. He would have been stupid to say no. If he was not going to do it, somebody else would, so he may as well.

'You're helping me. I'm helping you,' was Karol's description of what was going on between them. 'You work hard. I respect that. I'd rather you make money than somebody I don't know.'

Borowik had two phones attached to his belt. Both of them rang at the same time when he approached the white van. He nodded at Damian and Igor and asked, 'How many?' Then he glanced at the display to see who the caller was. 'Hold on … Hello? Yes, yes … where the hell are you? I've been waiting for over an hour … Just get your arse here as soon as you can. I've got to go.' Borowik now picked up the second phone, 'Not yet. We're delayed … Out of my control.' He placed the phone in the belt holster. 'Sorry guys, absolutely crazy this morning. I keep telling them: you want to have a break, go outside, sit on the grass. Yesterday, during lunch break, this twenty-year-old was eating a sandwich in the window, and he doesn't even work windows. He figured he had found a good spot for a break. He fell out. He's at the hospital. Lucky bastard. Broken leg. Where's Karol? I thought he'd be with you.'

'He couldn't come today. He said he would call you,' said Damian.

'Anyway, what's the number of people you have brought today?'

'Six.'

'Okay. For how long this time?

'Two weeks.'

'Get them out.' One of Borowik's phones rang. 'Yes, hello?'

Damian got out of the van and walked around it, tapping the body work with his fist. He opened the back door and let the men out.

The men patiently waited for Borowik to finish talking. Then he said, quickly: 'Where is your protective gear? Right. You see that man standing over there? Go and ask him to take you into the warehouse.' Borowik turned to Damian. 'Tell Karol I'll have to charge for the gear. Unless they bring their own next time.' Borowik brought his attention back to the waiting men. 'Once you get your gear, I'll join you to tell you what to do. Any questions?'

'I'm looking for Maciej Borowik, the site manager?' Mateusz asked the men sitting on the pavement. Some were eating sandwiches, others smoked. 'Do you know where I can find him?'

'He's over there,' one of the builders indicated with his hand.

'Thank you.'

Mateusz waited for a forklift to pass by before he continued walking. He looked up at the skeleton of an apartment building, where some men were raising a scaffolding. Those flats were going to be worth a fortune when finished, he thought.

Borowik was on the phone, kicking stones with his foot, words chasing each other as he hurried the conversation. He briefly looked at Mateusz and nodded but there was no recognition in his eyes. He turned his back on Mateusz and paced away, the phone next to his flamed ear. When he finally finished, Borowik picked up the second phone and scrolled through the text messages. 'Yes? How can I help you,' he said, his eyes focused on the screen.

'Borowik. It's me. Mateusz.'

Borowik lifted his head at once. 'Mateusz. Where have you been?' He grabbed Mateusz by his shoulders and pulled him close. The men heartily thumped each other's backs. 'Why didn't you say it was you? Sorry, mate, I didn't recognise you. Have you lost weight or something?'

'Nothing changed with you. On the phone twenty-four-seven.' Mateusz laughed, pleased.

'Come. I've got some coffee. It's really great to see you, you son of a bitch.'

Mateusz followed Borowik to a mobile canteen, not far from where they were standing.

Mateusz's face throbbed with embarrassment as he asked his old friend for a job.

'Don't be ridiculous,' Borowik said. 'Remember when I first came over? Worked for peanuts in some doghouse or whatever this shithole was. With no language, then you showed up. I wouldn't be where I am now without you.' Borowik placed a mug with black coffee in front of Mateusz and sat down. 'It doesn't pay what it used to though,' he warned him.

They both knew what he meant, how hard it had become. 'I don't have a choice.'

'I'm sorry about your company. I heard some rumours but you know what it's like, people talk and people talk. I didn't think much of it. I thought it was temporary, and then you know, one job, then another, life goes on.' One of Borowik's phones danced, buzzing on the table. He glanced at the display then ignored it. 'I should have called but I figured if you needed anything you'd know how to find me. And I was right.'

'I really wish I didn't have to ask you for help.'

'You can start today if you want. I could use a pair of skilled hands. I've got plenty of amateurs.' Borowik looked out through a small window at a group of men walking by.

'More Poles?'

'Poles, Lithuanians, Romanians, Latvians, some basic language, some don't speak English at all. Work hard. Cheap labour. Very cheap.' A phone rang again and Borowik answered this time. 'They've arrived this morning...Uhm...I was expecting to see you but you sent your muscle instead. That's one way of doing business, Karol…' Borowik broke off irritably, 'Listen. Listen. I don't care and I don't want to talk about it right now. I'm in a meeting.' He threw the phone on the table. From what Mateusz remembered, Borowik was not a man who easily got upset. They were silent, each waiting for the other.

'Everything all right?' Mateusz asked finally.

'Yes, yes.' Borowik was distracted, still thinking about the phone call. He jumped up. 'Let's go. I'll show you the site.'

Igor parked and left the engine running. Damian placed a cap on his head and pulled the visor down low over his eyes.

Damian waited for the people walking by to pass through before he pulled a black scarf to cover half of his face. He lifted two bricks from underneath his feet and opened the door. He stopped in front of the glass door to GS and SS Khainwar's sweetshop, swung his arms and with full force threw the bricks against the pane of glass. The woman inside screamed when Damian entered and in one move he shoved the woman aside, sending her towards the shelves with magazines and birthday cards, which all scattered around the floor. GS Khainwar, roused by his wife's wailing, appeared in the entrance leading to their first floor apartment. Seeing what was going on, he instinctively backed away , but Damian's fist was quicker.

SS Khainwar's voice followed Damian as he ran back to the car.

'Go, go, go,' he shouted at Igor.

Igor swerved into one of the side roads and slowly pulled over by the kerb. The street was dark. A few lamp posts were not illuminated. Someone was walking a dog.

'I'll text you when I'm ready,' Damian said and got out of the car. He left the cap, the scarf and a leather jacket on the backseat.

Zygmunt opened the front door. He did not recognise Damian's face at first, partially hidden in the evening shadow. He walked past Zygmunt who stuck his head out to see if Damian's brother was lurking somewhere in the darkness.

'Milena will be glad,' Karol said after Damian briefly summarised the events of the evening, but asked Karol not to tell Milena it was he who had taken care of the shopkeeper. 'She doesn't need to know,' Damian said. If Karol had been paying attention that evening, he would have noticed Damian was embarrassed by his violent actions.

'Are you going to check on the other men?' Karol asked.

'I'm going back home with Igor. Haven't eaten all day.' Damian peered into the kitchen at Milena standing by the cooker, heavy and slow with weariness, stirring the stew. She was wearing the pearls he had given her. It would have been nice to have a home-cooked meal. He and Igor never spent any time in the kitchen (theirs was bare except for two mugs and a large jar of Nescafé Black Gold coffee and the one spoon they shared); always on the go, from one location to another. They knew the taste of every single ready-made meal and had dined in almost every Polish restaurant in every borough. Sometimes the owner would let them into the back of the restaurant, sit them inside the kitchen, out of respect for Karol and out of fear of the Kulesza brothers. The chef was instructed to serve double portions whenever they arrived, to take special care of them, they were to be treated 'like your own family,' in the owner's words. It was the closest they felt to their mother's cooking: the steam rising from enormous pots with boiling water, the aroma of crushed marjoram and cumin seeds, bacon with chopped onion hissing and spitting over the fire, dry pork meat sausages swinging on hooks. If they closed their eyes they could pretend they were back home.

'Can you swing by Agnieszka's office? I need you to deliver passports and NI cards. I want her to start filling out new application forms,' Karol asked. He wanted Damian to leave because his stomach was rumbling. He did not want to invite Damian in because he would also have had to invite Igor and he was not much of a talker.

'Sure,' Damian suppressed a yawn. 'Will she be up at this time?'

'I'll call her to let her know you're coming.'

10

Milena sat in front of a vanity mirror and in circular motions applied a night cream onto her face. There was a sudden flash of pain in her lower abdomen, a grimace crossed her face, and her hand shot down and squeezed her flesh through her nightgown, the other grabbed the edge of the dressing table. Her fingers were slippery on the surface from the cream. But it was just a burst of pain and it disappeared after a few seconds, as if it had never happened. She breathed through her open mouth, her nightgown damp from sweat. Was it the end of life she carried? A prelude to death? She had read about the waves of pain in the first few weeks, as her womb gradually expanded with the growth of the embryo, but she was not sure if it was supposed to be so painful, or so early. Her body suddenly still, but her mind tense, readying itself for the next shard of pain She uncurled her toes.

'Let's go to Paris tomorrow,' Karol said, entering the bedroom, his head was wrapped in a towel and he had a transparent gel face mask on.

Her eyes went over his reddened, plump face, and said, 'What?'

'Paris. Let's go to Paris.'

'When?' Her jaw tightened.

'Tomorrow. Get one of the girls to make a booking.'

She gulped water from the bottle. 'I can't. There's too much to do in the office.' She was trying to remember whether Doctor Papuziak was in the clinic tomorrow.

'But I want to go tomorrow. The weather's perfect. You can go shopping,' he coaxed her, wanting her to submit, to say yes. This lack of enthusiasm was unlike her and she looked apprehensive.

He approached her from behind and placed both hands on her neck and throat, squeezing it slowly. His thumbs gently rubbed the bones in her neck. He leaned forward and stared at her reflection.

'So, what do you say?' Karol's lips were touching her ear. 'We always have so much fun together.'

He tightened his grip around her throat and neck. Her eyes watered. Milena grabbed his hands with hers, trying to push her fingertips between her throat and his hands, to loosen his choking clasp. He watched her closely, his eyes narrowed, glittering with amusement.

He released her neck abruptly and gently kissed her cheek.

'Book the tickets for this evening's Eurostar train,' he said and picked up a TV remote controller. He hopped onto the bed and switched on MTV, writhing female bodies flashed onto the screen.

Milena stared at him, wide-eyed, fighting to control her breathing, rubbing her neck and throat.

The next day, Milena was on her way to the tube station. She noticed the smashed front glass door to the sweetshop had been replaced with a wooden board. She peered curiously inside and GS Khainwar's black and blue eye stared back at her. The collar of his shirt was torn and his dyed hair was not as sleek and shiny as usual. He must have been up all night and had not shaved or washed his face yet. He had a greyish stubble on his cheeks and throat. His chest lost its puffiness as he slumped his shoulders, like he could not stand straight, only his eyes kept their ferocity.

Whoever was responsible for the damage and the state GS Khainwar was in this morning, she could not help but feel relieved and grateful.

'Was it you?' Milena asked Damian a few hours later. He had joined her in a pub on the corner opposite Hammersmith tube station.

'Does it matter?'

'He's a spiteful and rude old man. If he and his wife died to-morrow nobody would cry for them. Nobody.' Milena's words tumbled out quickly, overwhelmed by her emotions.

Damian's gaze wandered over her face, his forehead wrinkled on one side. GS Khainwar was just an ordinary shopkeeper. Milena's reaction seemed excessive. Perhaps it was hormones. She was, after all, pregnant. He wondered if she had told Karol yet, but frankly, it was none of his business so he decided not to bother her with questions.

'This woman you mentioned the other day, when could she start?' Milena asked.

'For cleaning?'

Milena nodded.

'Whenever you're ready.'

'Good.'

'What did Karol say?'

The most important thing was for Karol to believe it was his idea to get rid of his cousin. Milena did not see anything wrong in nudging him in the right direction. He did that to her all the time. She believed he owed it to her. The past few weeks, when she was alone in the house, after deliberately sending Zygmunt to buy butter and milk, which they did not need because the fridge was full but she insisted, or any other unnecessary item they already had, she added Borax to the washing powder. Karol's skin erupted in a rash and blisters. Another time, when she offered to make tea for Karol, she covertly wiped the inside of his mug with bleach, before pouring hot water. She did not have to wait long for Karol to suffer from a bout of agonizing diarrhoea. With Zygmunt, she just needed to find the right time to plant the idea in Karol's head.

'Is everything all right?' Damian's question threw her off balance. 'Do you need any help? You can trust me, you know that?'

Her hand automatically shot to her throat to readjust the scarf covering the bruises. She drank some cold water to calm herself. 'Why do you ask?'

Damian pretended he did not care, that he only wanted to be nice to her, feigning interest about her wellbeing. The truth was that he could not stand the image of Milena hurting, of anybody causing her harm. A good person like her did not deserve to feel pain. But it was clear Milena was on edge today. He hoped she would tell him if there was anything he could do for her.

'Here are the documents Karol wanted me to get ready,' he said instead.

'We're going to Paris tonight,' she said quickly, like the words burnt the insides of her mouth and she needed to rid of them. She added, urgently: 'I must go. I have to do some shopping before we leave tonight. Can you arrange everything this weekend? I'd like to get it over with as soon as possible.'

She was conscious there was very little time left before the 8.01 pm train, and as usual, with these unexpected trips Karol announced at the very last minute, she was left to deal with all travel arrangements herself. She did not want to disappoint him.

In the past, Milena and Karol always had so much fun together, just like he said. He would leave envelopes with plane or train tickets on the kitchen counter, in the bathroom, by her vanity mirror, in one of those places she usually looked at in the mornings. There were handwritten messages on the envelopes, clues about various destinations.

'I never took him for a romantic,' Ines commented after Milena handed her some of the envelopes, the same day she booked an urgent visit to wax her body. Karol liked her skin perfectly smooth, she knew, especially if they were going to spend the time on a crowded beach. 'My Tomek never takes me anywhere.' Ines applied hot wax on Milena's upper thighs.

'Yes, it's very thoughtful of him,' Milena said, trying to smile, to soften the burning feeling on her skin and stave off nausea. But it was a lie Milena told herself, so she did not have to remember all trips they did not take. Trips they had already paid for but Karol decided to cancel at the last minute.

It always began in the same way. A whirlwind of preparations, last-minute trips to various shops for new outfits, rushed phone calls to the office. Sweating, panting, hungry. What about luggage? The passport? She was relieved when she found it, overwhelmed by the mounting number of tasks that needed to be dealt with before they left. So focused was she on Karol's needs she forgot where she had placed her own documents. Money to exchange. Batteries for the camera. Everything left for her to deal with. Her own life and commitments temporarily suspended.

Bulging bags waiting in the corridor. Milena prepared to break into a run the moment Karol would open the front door and announce: 'Let's go'. Excited and ready to forgive this last-minute arrangement, which turned her life upside down, as if it did not matter to Karol, as if her job was something that could be discarded or utilised for his own benefit whenever it suited him.

But when they did not manage to leave, there was no apology, only statements: 'I changed my mind. There's something I need to take care of. What do you want me to do? We'll go another time.'

The usual conversation followed. 'What about the tickets?'

'Don't worry about it.'

'We've already paid for them.'

'I said don't worry about the money.'

Milena was flushed, and under her astonishment surged frustration, that he had known all this time and let her run herself to exhaustion.

Sometimes she wondered if there was something malicious or deliberately wicked in his behaviour, an experiment to test her commitment, a study in human reaction. She doubted her own spirit, devoid of the astonishing spontaneity Karol possessed.

When they did manage to leave, she was everything he wanted her to be. In her olive green dress, her fiery red hair contrasted with her pale, thin skin through you could see the rivulets and streams of blue veins (so easily burnt, did he deliberately choose to go to places where the sun streamed down like hot oil? she wondered). In high-heeled shoes she was a head taller than Karol. How could she not be grateful for his constant attention, his entire time solely devoted to her, unlike back home when he would disappear for days and nights, returning for an hour or two to have dinner with her, only to go out again. She often fell asleep on her own, with Karol joining her in the early hours of the morning.

At any other time Milena would have been thrilled to jump on a train, and in just over two hours later, immerse herself in the glittering lights of the Parisian cafés and restaurants. She wished this time was one of those failed trips she had experienced before. But this time Karol meant it.

Her throat and neck still hurt from Karol's crushing fingers, her eyes were reddened and watering from lack of sleep. Then there was her pregnancy, still kept from him. Thoughts scattered inside her that she needed to gather. One thing at a time. She calmed herself, and looked through the window, but she saw only her own reflection.

Zygmunt lay on the sofa, one hand propped under his head. BBC News was on and he was reciting in whispers the English words after the presenter. He was best at the weather forecast and sports, less so in live reporting from Afghanistan or Gaza. The presenter's voice was so loud that it was a few minutes before he realised that somebody was banging at the backdoor. In his haste to get up, he dropped the remote, tripped, and tumbled over the bucket next to the sofa, toppling it over and spilling dirty water over the floor.

He stared at the pool of water forming on the wooden floorboards, trying to decide whether he should start wiping the floor or answer the door first. Biting his moustache, he moaned 'Oh, no, no, no.' He ran to the nearest bathroom to grab fresh towels, tripped over on the way on the carpet, then threw the towels on the pool of dirty water, hoping it would stop the spill.

'What the hell is going on?' Damian was shouting behind the closed door while Zygmunt, his hands trembling, fought to find the right key to open the door. He dropped the keys a few times. 'Hurry up! Jesus!' Finally, the door opened and Damian pushed him aside. 'Why are you sweating so much? What have you been doing? Watching porn?'

'There was an accident.' Zygmunt stood, helpless, a wet cloth next to his feet.

'What's all this noise?'

Damian marched into the back of the house, searching for the source of the voices.

'Watching television instead of working?' Damian entered the living room and he saw the mess and laughed. 'Oh, man. Milena is going to kill you.'

'I am so sorry. It was an accident. I swear.' Zygmunt was now behind him, trying to go around Damian to remove the heavy towels soaked in water.

'I bet it was. Well, what are you waiting for? Clean it up.' He walked back to the kitchen, chuckling and shaking his head. 'Idiot,' Zygmunt heard behind him. He was on his knees gathering the heavy towels and stuffing them into the bucket.

'Sit down,' Damian instructed Zygmunt after he returned to the kitchen, wiping the sweat from his forehead with the back of his hand. By the table, Igor sat with one arm behind the other chair back and his legs spread wide. Igor showed no interest when Zygmunt entered, apart from a brief glance. Zygmunt placed the heavy bucket on the floor and sat down, wiping his hands on his trousers.

'So this is how it's going to be.' Damian began. 'You're going to pack your bags and we're taking you to a new home. You're going to work at a construction site with the other men. If you do well, you may keep this new job, if not, well, you can go back to the shithole you came from.'

Igor tried to stifle a yawn. One of those powerful jaw-breaking yawns that spilled tears down his cheeks.

'I don't understand,' Zygmunt said, confused. 'Karol didn't mention anything to me.'

'What's there to understand? Now, get your stuff.'

'But…'

'What are you waiting for? Move!'

Zygmunt hesitated, thinking. These men – even if they talked and behaved like criminals, and probably were but he did not know for sure, the kind of people he would stay away from if he had met them in Poland – were also his only chance in Britain.

'Let's have breakfast in the garden,' Karol happily announced, a surge of energy exploding in his body. He jumped out of bed and walked to open the floor-to-ceiling windows in their hotel room. He inhaled deeply and stretched his arms, basking in the rays of sunshine. 'Don't you just love this place? Are you happy? I'm happy.' He glanced at Milena to make sure she was sharing his vision. 'Imagine, you'd be sitting now in your office, if it wasn't for me.'

Milena, still in bed, murmured a response. She could sense the morning wave of nausea and swallowed. She patted the bedside table in search of a glass of water, struggled to sit up, and drank to suppress the urge to vomit.

'Why don't you go downstairs?' she said quickly, her mouth set hard. 'I'll be there in a moment.'

Whistling a tune, Karol went to the bathroom. He left the door ajar and the noise of his urine hitting the toilet bowl filled the room as well as his clumsy attempt at singing.

When he finally left the room, she rushed to the bathroom. The red marks on her throat had faded, nevertheless, she decided to wear a silk scarf around her neck. Paris was where Karol had proposed to her, though it was not the kind of engagement she had had in mind. In a rented car, waiting for the traffic to move, he said, 'We could get married if you want to. How about that?'

Now, as the memory of that day came back to her, she twisted the engagement ring on her finger. She noticed it had lost its lustre and began to search for a disposable toothbrush. The ring looked expensive, with a chunky diamond set in white gold, an object of envy among her staff and other women. Sometimes, she left the ring at home, afraid it could attract unnecessary attention on public transport. It made her feel uncomfortable. Carefully she squeezed a pea-sized squirt of toothpaste onto the toothbrush and gently began to brush the gold. Karol would have to wait for her a little bit longer.

She jumped at the unexpectedly shrill sound of the phone ringing in the room.

She placed the ring on the edge of the sink and wiped her hands on a small towel.

'Hello?'

'Madame Sosnowski?'

'Yes?' she responded in French.

'Monsieur Sosnowski is not well.'

'Oh.'

'We think it's an allergic reaction. He's choking. Please come quick, Madame. He's asking for medication. He said you have it in the room? Madame? Are you there?'

'Yes, yes, I'm coming.'

She placed the handset back on the receiver; her hand clasped at her mouth. Should she take Ventolin or call emergency instead? She fumbled in their suitcases in search of a small travel pouch where she kept all Karol's medications. She found it. She held the pouch tightly, ready to run downstairs to save him, when she stopped half way. She turned around and hid behind the curtain. There he was, down in the hotel garden, bent forward, wheezing, barely conscious. Nervous hotel staff running around him, shouting something in French she could not understand. One of them thrust an arm in the direction of their window. Karol's airways were getting narrower with every second, swelling, the spasms in his lungs forced him into a convulsive cough, desperately trying to push air into his lungs. Suddenly he looked up, his face red, eyes full of mounting panic, opening his mouth like a fish out of water. She stepped back and waited and wondered if he had seen her.

There was a roaring in her ears, blood rushing through her veins. Then she realised her mobile phone was ringing. Answering, she kept staring down at the panic below.

It was Damian calling to tell her about Zygmunt, that everything had been arranged. He wanted to tell her how he found him lying on the sofa watching TV but she cut the conversation short and said she had to go because Karol needed her.

The phone jolted her back into the present and reality came back, quickly and frighteningly, brought to her by voices she could hear. She ran out of the room, clutching the pouch tightly.

Later, back in their hotel room, Karol slapped her, and she did her best not to panic.

'Look what you did! Look! Why did you take so long? If it was any longer I would have died! A few more minutes and I would be dead.' He glared at her, rage in his voice. Milena felt fear, creeping up her spine, but she knew that this was Karol's natural reaction; his feeling that this was the perfect time to blame her, to show that he was still in charge.

'It was your cousin,' she said, finally, through her tears, which came so easily. She had practised.

'What?' he asked sharply. 'What does he have to do with any of this?'

'It all began when your cousin arrived. You knew I was against it. What kind of a man works as a cleaner? But you insisted. The pouch with your inhalers and medication was not where I usually put it. You know I never misplace anything. You know that, sweetheart.'

He looked at her suspiciously. Was she telling the truth? The past few weeks flashed through his mind, the sudden attacks of diarrhoea, the itchiness all over his skin. She was right. It had all begun with Zygmunt in the house. Milena had lived with him long enough to know his allergies. And she had tried to tell him before but he had ignored her complaints about Zygmunt.

'But you don't have to worry about anything,' she added. 'I've spoken to Damian already. I know he's your cousin but you trust people too much. Even your family. You don't really know this man.'

'Why didn't you tell me earlier?' He drew her close and kissed her cheek, red from his slap. 'I'm sorry I wasn't thinking but if you had told me the truth I wouldn't have hurt you. It's just the way I am. Next time just tell me the truth. All right?'

And in that moment, Milena thought she was very lucky.

11

Mateusz began work at the building site at 6.30 am. Angelika offered to get up with him to prepare his breakfast, 'It won't be a problem, really,' she assured him, 'I'll be able to do more housework. There's always piles of clothes to iron.' But he said there was no need for her to rise so early, almost in the middle of the night. 'Don't be silly, sweetheart,' he said and kissed her on the forehead.

But, in the end, Angelika did not insist on changing Mateusz's mind about getting up together. She called it 'The Devil's hour' – three in the morning when she was afraid of meeting a ghost, witch or demon. The words of an exorcist, who had been invited to the church to present three lectures on how to defend your soul from evil, rang in her head. 'The Devil's hour,' the exorcist explained, 'is the time when the evil is most powerful and destructive. With great zeal you should protect your loved ones.' So she prayed harder every evening before going to bed, to make sure that she, the children and Mateusz were protected throughout the night.

The truth was Mateusz loved sitting in darkness. In the stillness of the night he listened to Angelika and the children's breathing, sometimes he approached Kamil's bed, surprised by how much heat a child's body could produce. He would bend down, stroke Kamil's hot forehead, and hover for a minute or two above his head, inhaling his son's smell.

That time was also when Mateusz sometimes bit on his fist and choked down the tears. An image of himself he was ashamed of, even scared to find in himself so much trembling, torn between the truth and lies, obedience and responsibility. He was not a coward but could not help thinking that his deliberate silences about what he had witnessed were in some strange way comforting.

He did not cry every night. Only at the beginning, before he had made the amends with himself about the future, with the consequences he could imagine and those that he could not possibly foresee.

That conversation with Maciej Borowik kept coming back. Mateusz was perpetually dissecting options in his mind. Sometimes he recalled almost every sentence. At other times, it would be a word or expression on Borowik's face, or nothing at all except how drunk they were that night. Images and sounds in and out of focus. Mateusz wondered how much was actually said and how much he invented, because when he asked Borowik about their time together Borowik would respond: 'How am I supposed to remember? You drank less than I did. You should know. If we don't remember maybe it's supposed to be that way.'

It all happened on a Friday night, a few weeks into the job. Borowik was always running around or answering one of his phones that never ceased to ring throughout the day, and Mateusz was exhausted and hungry. He wanted to get back home to Angelika and the children. Since Mateusz had started working at the construction site they promised each other that they would grab a drink one night, but the days all streamed into weeks and before either of them had noticed, two months had gone by.

'What did you think it was? You thought they were doing this out of goodness of their hearts? Helping fellow countrymen.' Borowik's laughter turned to a cough. He wiped the tears which were streaming down his cheeks.

'Why do you do it?' Mateusz asked.

'Don't be ridiculous.' Borowik poured another round of vodka. 'Cheers.'

They raised the small glasses, gulping the burning liquid in one go.

'Ah.' Borowik drew his lips over his teeth and then snapped them open. 'Good stuff.'

'I wonder, sometimes,' Mateusz was turning the tumbler in his hands, 'if we can help. Do something.'

'Who cares what's right and what's wrong. The only thing that matters is your family. That's why we're doing it.'

'What about their families?' Mateusz raised his head.

'I used to think about them. You know, wives and children, but you can't worry about everybody. I'm not the Pope. Sure as hell you don't look like one either.' Borowik chuckled, holding a fist to his lips.

'Have you ever thought about reporting it?'

'Like where? Police?' Borowik's eyes were wide.

Mateusz shook his head slowly. 'I don't know exactly. There must be someone that can help… who can investigate.'

Borowik lapsed into silence, insulted. 'Why?' He looked annoyed. He picked up a bottle of vodka to pour another round. 'This is not your country. These are not your people.' He waved his arm around, still holding the bottle. 'What are you going to say: "Hello. My name is Mateusz. I would like to report some guys dropping off Poles in a van to work every day at a construction site. One of them has a scar on his nose." There's nothing wrong with that. You get me? Besides, you would snitch on your own people? Is that what you would do? Who do you think you are going to help? I don't know about you but I wouldn't be able to live with myself. Besides, do you honestly think these guys would let you do it?' Borowik grew pensive, as if he had remembered something he did not want to, and said, 'You have no idea what they are capable of. That Igor, with a scar on his nose, I wouldn't like him to come near me or my family. My advice? Don't get involved. And don't do anything stupid.' Borowik grabbed Mateusz's shoulder and squeezed it. 'You hear me? It's not worth it. Just forget it.'

Borowik slammed his glass down on the table and poured another round. He put his arms around Mateusz's neck and pulled him closer.

'Listen, you're a great friend, you know how much I owe you.' Borowik kissed Mateusz on his forehead, his hands on his cheeks and shook his face – which Mateusz found very touching. Mateusz wanted to say how much he liked Borowik but he stopped him with a wave of his hand. 'Shhh, let me talk. You don't betray your own. You just don't.' Borowik vigorously shook his head and Mateusz briefly lost focus of his friend's face. 'No matter what you think,' Borowik continued, 'I get it. It can churn your stomach, it can make you sick, but these are not your own people. Here,' Borowik waved his arm again and Mateusz realised that Borowik kept doing that a lot, waving his arms. This time, Borowik almost fell from his seat because the weight of his own arm pulled him backwards. Mateusz grabbed the lapels of Borowik's jacket and pulled him back. He steadied himself and carried on, 'Here, in this country, I mean. You think the English care about us? We do jobs they don't want to do. I am proud of my job. I fucking am.' Borowik gave himself a strong punch in his chest with a fist and Mateusz heard a hollow noise. 'I don't care what the English say but I worked my arse off to get to this point but it wasn't thanks to them. Oh, no.' Borowik shook his head. 'It was thanks to you, Mateusz, you helped me. Like I said before. My country. My blood.'

They drank another round. Inevitably, Mateusz's eyes filled with tears. It happened whenever he drank too much but tonight it was different. He was fully aware of the surroundings, yes the noises around him were muffled and his eyes took longer to focus, but in his mind he could not be clearer about what he needed to do. Fearless and brave, that was what he needed to be. And it took more effort because he would have to stand up for complete strangers, not the people he truly loved which was so much easier, yet he was convinced he would be doing the right thing. He wanted his children to be proud of him. He hoped his actions would inspire them to be good in their lives.

'Our children would never forgive us if they knew.'

Borowik raised his index finger in the air. 'There's nothing to forgive. I have a clear conscience. At least I give them a place to work. What else do you need from me? This is the best I can do.'

Every morning, Mateusz observed the van that stopped in front of the gate to the construction site. The driver stayed behind the wheel with the engine running, the other man with a damaged eye, walked to the back, banging his fist against the backdoor before opening it to let the men out. The driver, his elbow sticking out through the window, smoked a cigarette and watched the back of the van in his side mirror.

'The Kulesza brothers,' Borowik introduced them.

Most times, Mateusz tried not to notice.

Keep your head down, you need this job, he told himself. But his heart was beating in the way it would if something sharp was caught between his ribs. Then, a crushing weight spread from his neck to his shoulders. It was the moment Mateusz realised that something strange was taking place right before his eyes and he had to do something. During his second breakfast break, Mateusz chewed slowly on his ham and tomato sandwich, sipping black coffee from the stainless steel tumbler Angelika had bought for him. A man, in his forties or early fifties, sat down next to Mateusz. The man pulled small stones from the soles of his shoes. He took out a bigger one, tossing it into the air and catching it in his hand.

'You're Polish?' the man asked.

Mateusz nodded.

'Been here long?'

Again, a nod. 'You?'

'A month. Maybe less.' The man took a swing and threw a stone.

'Aren't you with this group that arrives every morning?' Mateusz asked.

'They pick us up from a place…what's it called? Shit, ah, yes, Greenford Gardens.' He pronounced the words carefully, slowly, with a heavy roll of his tongue on 'r'. 'It's good to have a job. I was lucky. When I responded to the advertisement, I wasn't sure what kind of job we were going to do. We were told a few days after we had arrived.' The man picked up some more stones from the ground and turned them between his fingers. There was dirt under his fingernails, the skin was broken in places. 'These guys here, they are good to us. Give us food and cigarettes. I'd like to go back. My little boy is with his mother but there are no jobs where I live. Reszel. Do you know the place?'

Mateusz shook his head.

'Near Olsztyn. Here, have a look.' The man took out a photo from his pocket. A woman was kissing a little boy on his cheek who smiled widely. 'Jacek and this is my wife, Krystyna. She's pregnant again. Have you got any children?'

Mateusz had memorised their names, even if their faces blurred into one; old or young, blue eyed or brown. As long as Mateusz remembered their names they became real, their lives acquired a meaning and he could not ignore their stories. It was not somebody he read about in the paper. So many terrifying, heart-breaking stories you could become numb to a life that was not your own. How much of somebody else's pain could a person take? It was easier to turn a page, switch a channel, follow a link, quickly immerse yourself in a different, more compelling, positive story, the escape at the tip of his fingers.

How badly Mateusz wanted to believe that the man's story did not affect him. But it was so hard. If only it was just this man, and yet, there were others, tricked and trapped by their circumstances.

Afterwards, Angelika floated between anger and compassion, struggling to fully comprehend Mateusz's decision. She felt she was left out.

'I told myself this is not right. I should do something,' Mateusz was saying earnestly.

'I understand all that. But why you?'

'I'm trying to explain it to you that I don't really know why. It didn't feel right.'

'But they are strangers.' Her voice rose but it was pointless. 'What about our family?'

Her words reminded Mateusz about Borowik's words. And the worst thing was he had no explanation, no arguments, because both of them were right, so why did he feel that he could not stop himself, even if his actions could jeopardise the lives of the people he loved?

'You will see,' Angelika added, 'you are going to regret this.'

He would always remember her expression, her looking at him as if he had betrayed their trust and she did not care anymore. As if she were willing her anger at him, not able to see that he could not do otherwise, because he would have betrayed himself by walking away from the people whom he knew had no way of helping themselves. At that moment he was so frightened and full of guilt that he was unable to convince Angelika, simply because he could not tell her the whole truth. And that he would regret his actions, just as she had predicted. Was it an omen of his future heartache? He tried to dismiss Angelika's prophesy as nothing but an ordinary concern. But, still, it did make him a little bit uneasy. Whatever truth he was going to discover in the course of his actions he decided to keep his little suspicion to himself. It was better if Angelika and Borowik did not know anything, he thought. That would be safer.

He refrained from telling Angelika the whole story, how at the beginning the men were as scared as she was now. When he mentioned to them that they could talk to the authorities, because they did not have to work like slaves, they, to his surprise, begged him not report them. They made him promise he would not tell anybody. How would they find a job if they spoke no English? they reasoned. At least they had a job and all of them would eventually return, and after a while they convinced him that it was not so bad. Perhaps they did not get all the money they were promised, or they were not paid on time, but they did get something, and it was still so much more than they would have earned if they had stayed back at home.

Eventually, they began to avoid him. They ignored his questions. They were more scared of Mateusz and what he could do than they were of the Kulesza brothers.

Mateusz's fingers trembled, ice cold at their tips, when he dialled the number. He spoke hotly, impatiently, urging the person to look into the situation he had unwillingly witnessed. Was the reason he could not give his name because he was 'scared,' the person on the other end asked. Yes, a little bit, perhaps, it was just that he felt something was not right and he was sorry that he could not give his name because what if they decided to investigate him? Borowik was right. There was a danger of Mateusz losing his only income, one he so desperately needed.

He provided the address of the construction site and the address where the men slept, Greenford Gardens. He gave the names he knew. The description of the men driving the van and the number plate. This much he could do.

His heartbeat finally slowed down, his fingers stopped trembling. For a short moment after he placed his phone on the table, he had a feeling of unease, but it was soon gone. It was not so bad, he told himself, even shook his head in astonishment at his own exaggerated fear. He smiled. The thought was comforting, as if now he was finally going to sleep peacefully.

Then, one morning, no van arrived. The next day, the same thing. No sign of the men or the Kulesza brothers. A week went by, but nobody came. Mateusz's head turned towards the gate every time there was the roar of a passing car engine.

'Those men that have been working, you know, the ones that always arrive in the van, what happened to them?' Mateusz finally asked Borowik. 'I haven't seen them for a while.'

'I don't know. I guess they've gone back to where they came from.' Borowik shrugged and walked away, a mobile phone to his ear.

Mateusz wondered if their disappearance had something to do with the phone call. Eventually he convinced himself that they really had returned to Poland or, perhaps, they had found another job, after all, the building was almost finished and Borowik had already been redirecting some of the workers to a new site.

12

The fact was Valerie Hall had no evidence that anything was wrong with Zuzanna Madej's child benefit application. She simply wanted to talk to the woman, but Karol made sure the Kulesza brothers and not he accompanied the woman, in case there was compromising evidence which he would be required to explain later. It was best to stay away and send the brothers instead. Karol did not want to be remembered. As far as the benefit fraud investigation officers were concerned he was a phantom, a mysterious man or even more than one, because how would anyone know who or how many people really were behind this whole operation? Besides, he believed it was the authorities, the civil servants, the police, who twisted the reality to fit their needs. He was not stupid. So he sent somebody else.

The Kulesza brothers, a step behind Zuzanna with ashen face and heavy-lidded eyes, entered the room which was bare, except for a table and a few chairs. Igor breathed heavily as the woman halted.

'Please, sit down,' said Valerie Hall with a smile, looking from one nervous face to another.

'Go on. Sit. What are you waiting for?' Damian growled in Polish into the woman's ear.

'We have a translator if you'd prefer to speak in Polish.' Valerie nodded to a man sitting on her right. The man repeated Valerie's words in Polish but Zuzanna only cleared her throat and whispered that she wanted some water.

Damian and Igor sat down on either side of her, their heavy athletic legs so wide apart they were touching her knees, squeezing her between their hard shoulders. Damian moved his left foot close to Zuzanna's and she tensed. She sat straight in the chair, clearing her throat every now and then, which made Valerie wonder whether she had a cold.

'Miss Madej, in your application you stated you have three children. You were born on 4th October, 1988. Is that correct?'

Zuzanna looked at Damian who, with a strained expression, nodded in agreement, even though he did not fully understand what Valerie Hall was saying. But yes, Zuzanna could respond to this question. She waited for the translator and confirmed Valerie's words.

'Thank you. Can I ask you where your children currently reside?'

Again, she looked at Damian and waited for him to give her the sign. This time he waited for the translator to finish before he signalled to Zuzanna.

Karol did not know it was an accident Zuzanna Madej's application found its way into Valerie Hall's hands. She was sorting out the paperwork on various cases (referral forms, copies of interviews, handwritten notes, and photos of her own daughter that somehow found their way among the stack of pages) when she stumbled upon a child benefit application with a residential address in Greenford Gardens. She would not have thought much about it had she not remembered that a colleague had told her about an anonymous phone call made by a man with a noticeable Eastern European accent, tipping the team about a house in Greenford Gardens, where a group of Poles was being kept, forced to work without a day off. The man refused to leave his name or a phone number. When she checked later, she had found a few applications, with the residential address provided in Greenford

Gardens and other locations across southern and eastern boroughs, all in the same handwriting, which she thought was odd.

Now, as Valerie Hall sat facing the three visitors, she wished she could have talked to the woman on her own. Was there a bruise on her wrist? Zuzanna self-consciously kept pulling on her sleeve. She looked very thin and frail, her matted blond hair gathered into a thin ponytail. She kept biting her lower lip nervously.

'My children live with me,' said Zuzanna.

'In Greenford Gardens?'

Zuzanna nodded. She avoided looking straight at Valerie Hall when asked questions, instead, she stared fixedly at the table between them.

'Is the father of your children living with you?'

'No. We're not married. He…' she hesitated and glanced at Damian. A whispered conversation followed between Damian and Zuzanna, words the translator could not exactly make sense of, and he shook his head at Valerie Hall's questioning look. 'He left me. I live on my own,' Zuzanna added.

'Is he back in Poland?'

'Yes,' Zuzanna said with a sharp intake of breath.

'Is anybody else living in the house in Greenford Gardens with you?'

Damian was hunched over, playing with the pack of cigarettes he was holding. He sucked at his mouth in dissatisfaction.

'Can you look at me when I'm talking to you?' Karol said.

'I'm listening.' Damian shot him a brief impatient glance.

'But you are not looking at me. Your attention is somewhere else and this is important. I would appreciate it if you could focus and look at me.'

Damian sighed unhappily and with one hand pushed the packet away from him. He folded his arms on his expansive chest and leaned back in the chair. He knew if he displayed his lack of attention it would quickly cause Karol to be restless and snappish. There would be no end to Karol's persistent scolding. It was one of those moments when Damian disliked Karol – with his childish insistence, almost obsession, for undivided attention when he talked. Karol did that to everybody, it took getting used to, but often Damian did not mind. He accepted Karol's quick, ever-changing moods, without quite trying to understanding them. But today he held it against Karol that he had sent him and Igor to the meeting at the local council, without preparing him for what might happen, without any instructions about how to answer the questions. Most of the time Damian did not mind Karol's meticulously calculated scenarios of how to run the business. This was a regular routine between the two of them; Karol telling him where to go or whom to meet on his behalf and letting Damian act to the best of his knowledge. Damian knew he made people uneasy. And sure it was enough with the Poles.

He reached out to take a cigarette from the packet. 'You know I don't like it when you smoke in my house,' said Karol.

He put the cigarette back into the pack.

After Karol's asthma attack in Paris he had become obsessed with clean air around him, especially in the house. He binned Milena's collection of essential oils without asking her the night they got back home, and all the scented candles she placed in every room. He was terrified it could happen again. He forbade her from using perfume around him, even though, before the incident in Paris, the scents and smells had not bothered him. If he caught a whiff of Milena using any kind of fragrance he complained immediately that he felt nauseous and coughed in an exaggerated fashion, making choking noises, pinching his nostrils and the tip of his nose, as if he was trying to suppress a sneeze.

'Bring the girl, Zuzanna, to our house tomorrow. She's going to work here from now on,' Karol said firmly. He made it sound as if it was his idea, but Damian knew better. 'We should transfer the men to another location. It means we will have to take care of them earlier. I don't like this Valerie Hall sniffing around all of a sudden. Why don't you keep an eye on her and find out more about her as well.'

'Do you want me to follow her?'

'She didn't want to leave and that scared me, because I thought to myself, what was I going to do if she wouldn't leave?' Mrs Kwiatkowska told Karol the next Tuesday. She had partially dyed brownish hair with a half-a-finger growth of almost white hair close to her scalp. Her thin eyebrows rose into arcs painted un-evenly with an eyebrow pencil.

'She was asking about Zuzanna Madej, she also mentioned some other names. What was I supposed to tell her, if I know nothing?'

'Do you remember her name? The woman who came – what was her name?' asked Karol.

'She left her business card. She wanted me to keep it. She said in case I remember something.' Mrs Kwiatkowska dipped her hand into the front pocket of her apron and produced a card with Valerie Hall's name on it. 'I don't want any trouble. I'm an old woman so how am I supposed to remember anything?' She looked at him anxiously.

'There will be no trouble, Mrs Kwiatkowska.' Karol patted her on her wrinkled hand, peppered with brownish age spots. 'I promise.'

Karol followed her inside the house. Mrs Kwiatkowska held a headscarf in her hand which she now placed on her head. She adjusted the headscarf with both hands and pushed unruly wisps of hair under the fabric behind her ears.

'She looked into every room, every room. And I thought it wasn't right for a stranger to walk around somebody else's home and pepper me with questions.'

'What kind of questions?' Karol was nervous, wondering if this old woman had said something that she was not supposed to say. He could not be entirely sure she was telling the truth or that she remembered all details.

Mrs Kwiatkowska stopped in the doorway to the kitchen. The small radio by the window was on. She was fingering a plastic rosary.

'She asked about the mattresses. She said that if there was a young woman with children living here it did not look like a place they should be staying. I told her I lived on my own and it was my grandsons who had visited me not long ago, but now that they had gone I was on my own again.' She kept humming and breathing heavily, opening her mouth and closing.

Karol thought it was clever of Mrs Kwiatkowska to lie like that, about her grandchildren, but he was worried that the condition of the place could raise suspicion. There was litter everywhere, it was unkempt, he had noticed, when he had a look around. Mattresses lay on the floors in each room, with mugs overflowing with brown water and old, brownish cigarette butts next to them. Despite the open windows, the rooms stank of old smoke. There were large muddy footprints on the floor. He would have to send the cleaners to get rid of the rubbish and clean the house so it was habitable again, the kind of house that would not raise suspicions.

Mrs Kwiatkowska had a short and selective memory, quick hands to grab his envelopes filled with money, but he could not expect the old woman to clean. Cleaning the house was not why he paid Mrs Kwiatkowska. He paid her to mind the place whenever he needed it.

Mrs Kwiatkowska glanced at the clock on the kitchen wall. 'I'd better get ready. I'm going to church this evening.'

Karol handed her the usual amount and thanked her for all the information. He could tell, from the look she had given him, the way she held the money in her hand – checking the thickness of the envelope – that she was waiting for more. He opened his wallet and took out more notes.

Now Mrs Kwiatkowska smiled. 'Thank you.'

He moved slowly towards the door, turned around and said, 'And if that woman comes again, please call me at once. I will deal with it.'

'But I know nothing. Why would she come again?'

'I'll send somebody to come and clean tomorrow.'

13

Igor felt sick from wanting women so bad. He did not trust them, but no matter how hard he tried, he could not ignore the persistent ache between his legs. The softness of the female body, the moist smells, penetrated his mind causing him physical pain. That kind of biting pain distorted his thinking.

There was nothing joyous, no innocence of playful encounter, when Igor, hardly able to utter a single word, approached women – the ones he selected to take away that pain inside his head and chest.

'What did you do? What the hell did you do?' Damian shouted and for a moment Igor saw hatred in his brother's eyes. And something else – unforgiving, murderous anger.

'Nothing,' Igor muttered, defensively. 'Nothing. I did nothing.'

'Don't hide from me. You promised you would tell me if you ever wanted to do something. You promised.' Damian punched the wall with his fist. 'Why? Why did you have to do it?' His voice now calm, defeated, as he touched Igor's naked shoulder but Igor flinched and tried to pull away from him. 'It's all right.' Damian took Igor's head in his arms and drew him closer to his chest, placing his chin on top of Igor's head. 'I'm sorry I shouted at you. It's going to be all right. I will take care of it.'

Igor could not explain why he had become so furious, so suddenly. This much Damian knew, that it was not Igor's fault. It was never Igor's fault, but Damian could easily imagine how it all had happened.

'She was sixteen years old,' Damian whispered. Fool! Such a fool Igor was sometimes. Damian wanted to believe Igor was no longer dangerous. He did his best not to fall into panic, but he could not escape the feeling that there was something inhuman about his brother. 'How could you not see?'

Damian thought they had an agreement, the one they made when it had first happened on the train, because Damian would never let Igor go back to prison. Every time it had taken place – Igor easing his desire with a woman – Damian felt a little bit betrayed, as if Igor did not trust him enough to confess his secret urges in time, to prevent him from harming somebody. But to Igor the intensity he experienced, the sudden, uncontrollable impulse that clouded his thinking was too much to bear or to confide to Damian, because it was like acknowledging defeat.

How was he supposed to know the girl was sixteen? And he did not even like the way she looked. In fact, he was repelled by her. Her oversized breasts squashed into a tight top, sweat glistening on her skin. Thighs so fat they rubbed against each other as she walked down the train platform. He spotted her in a carriage, late in the evening, as she sat engrossed in a book, her other hand slowly dipping in and out of a bag of crisps. Her buttock spilled on a second seat. She licked salt from her beefy fingers, one by one, slowly, then pushed her little finger inside her mouth to recover a piece of food lodged somewhere at the back. The fingers left oily stains on the pages. When she finished the first bag of crisps, without looking, she searched for another one.

She almost missed her stop because she struggled to get out of the seat, rushing to gather her belongings, and she smiled apologetically at other commuters, the rolls of fat on her face squeezing her eyes into slits. Nobody minded – that was what shocked Igor. Nobody said anything. They must have felt sorry for her or were too drunk to react. But not Igor. People like her, ugly, obese people, had no right to live. He blamed her for the extra flesh on her face, for her unapologetic, overbearing, body... Igor was so much smaller and thinner but, back in Poland, people still pointed fingers at him. She was everything he despised in himself.

A woman with so much fat would not feel a thing, Igor reasoned as he followed her down the platform. In fact, he was going to do her a favour. A woman with so much fat would hardly find a man to touch her. Who would have? Only a sick person. She would be grateful afterwards.

He walked behind her, turning around from time to time to see if they were being followed, but he was lucky because it was already dark and only a few people were walking on the other side of the road, rushing to get back home. Not this woman, she took her time, chewing on something, again, on the way. But Igor was not stupid. Though he could sense the surge of growing pain between his legs, he waited, patiently, to see where she was going. If there was a place on the way he would do it. He was so close now. And, soon, there it was. A park. You could almost not hear the trains passing or the traffic on the streets. You could not hear a single voice, only somebody's television set but this sound, too, died in the night.

The girl would get what she deserved.

She was so confused at first when Igor lunged at her before the horror set in her mind of what was happening to her. The bag of crisps dropped onto the pavement. His fingers sank into her flesh when he grabbed her by the arm and dragged her into the bushes. Ugly purplish-orange bruises would form on her delicate pale skin. They fell, and he held her with his hand over her wet mouth. She tried to bite his palm but a punch in her face silenced her cries and the girl lost consciousness. Cursing her, hurting her, but she could not hear him anymore. There were no more cries of protest. Igor's let his fury fully unfold, ripping her clothes, her whole body wobbling under his sudden movements.

No words escaped his mouth, only in his mind, he called her ugly names, names lashed her face like urgent flames.

Igor breathed heavily with his teeth clenched, like when he lifted weights in the gym, mind concentrated on his task, on his soon-to-come release.

'You strangled her with your belt,' Damian said slowly, carefully, because he wanted Igor to fully comprehend his actions. 'Do you realise what this means?'

'Yes … I must go back.'

'That's right,' Damian said, stroking Igor's head, 'You must go back. I'll talk to Karol.'

'No,' Igor's face was twisted and the scar over his nose was dark.

'Look at me.' Damian clutched his brother's face in both hands. 'What happened is between you and me. Nobody else will know. I will never betray you. You know that. But you must leave, tonight. You will take a car and drive. It'll be fine. I have figured out what we are going to do. You will go back and take care of our money. Karol will be glad he has somebody on the ground. But you must promise me that it won't happen again. You can't keep doing it. I always told you if you want a girl I will get you a girl.' Damian was tired, so tired now. He was careful not to make Igor feel guilty, or remorseful, he needed to take this precaution against Igor's anger. Igor would move further away from him and Damian would have no control whatsoever over his brother. But no matter what happened you never deserted your family. Damian was not going to be like their father.

What Igor had done was irrevocable but Damian forgave him, even though forgiveness had become a formless idea, almost an instant obligation on Damian's behalf, because there was nobody else left, just the two of them.

14

The lucky ones who managed to return to Poland tried calling Karol's phone, to claim back the money he had promised them. Not once had he returned their calls and soon the calls went directly to voicemail. Later, there would be a message that the number was not in service anymore. It was one of the many pay-as-you-go phones he kept during the time they stayed in Britain, until Karol finally decided to dispose of them, their presence no longer needed here. As soon as Karol got rid of them, their faces and names stopped occupying his mind, their lives departed and their physical presence did not require his immediate, daily attention. Only their personal details were still in use while he claimed benefits and loans in their names.

'There are no jobs anymore so you'd better start arranging your return to Poland. You can stay here until the end of the week but afterwards you will have to leave,' Karol informed the men after Damian drove the whole group to a place in Norbury. It was not a house like the one they'd lived in for the past few weeks in Greenford Gardens. This space, in comparison to the rooms they occupied in Greenford Gardens, was so much smaller, a garage, actually, next to somebody else's house, converted into two rooms with a shared toilet and a small sink they used to wash themselves. Karol deliberately relocated the men to the most uncomfortable and unwelcoming of the locations he rented around London. He figured he was done being accommodating to the men and the time had come to get rid of them once and for all.

Karol handed each man a thin envelope. 'This is your wage for last week's job.'

'What about the previous weeks?' one of the man asked after he counted the money.

'You will get all your money, in cash.' Then Karol explained how lucky they were that he had managed to secure any job for them during the past few weeks because without him they would have ended up on the streets a long time ago. And that he was being generous and honest, unlike other Poles who would have never found them anything and then left them without any help. He was even giving them more money than they were entitled to, because if they had to pay the tax themselves, they would have got even less, but Karol graciously took care of everything. 'Damian will bring the rest of the money by the end of the week, but in the meantime, with what I have given you now, I strongly advise you to book tickets home.' Karol paced the room as he talked with one headphone, the other, dangling from the cord.

This prolonged conversation was taking too much of his valuable time already, and Karol was getting irritated by their moaning and pleading. A few more minutes and they would never let him go.

'Listen,' he stopped in his tracks, and said slowly, feeling his way, 'I didn't want to say anything but you are leaving me no other option. There were complaints about your performance at the construction site. I know you were working very hard, believe me I know, but I cannot ignore the fact that you were not working as hard as I thought you would.' He paused to let them take in what he was about to say, a tactic he had performed so many times before. 'I could, and I am not saying that I would, but I could use disciplinary action against you, so you should appreciate I'm letting this one go. I have all the evidence and all complaints filed against you. I am going to say this one more time. You have until the end of this week to arrange your return and I will forget about the complaints. I believe this is a fair deal.'

Silence fell in the room. The men were too dismayed to say anything, and they realised that they were in fact fortunate because all they wanted was to get the rest of their money, not face a lawsuit in a foreign country. There was nobody they knew apart from Karol and the Kulesza brothers.

'I want you to know that I'm trying to help here. I could arrange your return with one of the travel agencies … And pay with the money I am due to give you, of course. But it's up to you, really,' Karol offered and waited for their reaction. He knew they would eventually agree.

Karol noted the names of the men who agreed to his offer, among them was Zygmunt. He had had no luck so far talking to Karol, face to face, about what had happened in his house and express how sorry he was. He did not believe the Kulesza brothers had passed the numerous apologetic messages to Karol. He never got any response back. When Zygmunt finally managed to come near his cousin he pleaded, 'Please, Karol, I can't go back. I am so sorry about what happened. I left messages for you. How is Milena? I hope she is still not upset with me about the floor?'

Karol stared at his cousin without recognition. His first impulse was to ask Damian to get rid of him. 'After what you've done to us, how could I or Milena possibly trust you?'

Zygmunt grabbed Karol's arm and pulled him closer. 'I beg you. We are a family.'

Karol looked at him coldly, making him let go of his arm. He motioned to Zygmunt with his head to follow him outside.

'You thought I was never going to find out?' Karol said as he poked his finger into Zygmunt's chest.

'I'm sorry, Karol, but I don't know what you are talking about?'

'You don't? Have I not treated you like family? Why? I know, you are jealous of my life here. What have you got to show for yourself?'

There was horror on Zygmunt's face as he covered his mouth with his hand. 'I don't know what you are talking about. Please, believe me,' he said hastily.

'Tell me the truth, right now.'

'I am. I had nothing to do with any of this.' His eyes probed Karol's, seeking some understanding but Karol's eyes were flat and hard.

'See, you are lying again. I cannot trust you anymore. You can't even be a man and take responsibility for your actions.'

'I swear on my mother's name, I had nothing to do with whatever you are accusing me of,' he pleaded, weakly.

'I have nothing else to say to you.' Karol glanced at Damian, leaning against the wall, pretending he was not listening. This was the moment Karol wanted to make sure his authority was duly acknowledged. No time for weakness, not even with his own blood. 'I'm trying to be a better person here but I cannot have you around my family. We are done. I have given you a chance but, clearly, you didn't deserve it.'

All of the men except two decided to go ahead with Karol's offer. Four days later a group was driven in a van by Damian to Victoria coach station where he stopped briefly to let them out. He gave each man a one-way ticket and returned the passports that Karol had been keeping in his house. There was no more money. Damian promised to have it transferred into their bank accounts once they were back in Poland.

'What are you still doing here?' Damian asked the two men sitting on the floor at the back of the van, looking into the rear view mirror. 'You have to leave now. You can't stay here any longer.'

'But we haven't got the money you owe us. You promised.'

'I didn't promise you anything. Now, get out.'

'Your boss did.'

'Why don't you talk to him about it. Now get the fuck out of my van.'

The men, voices hushed, desperately talked to each other, because they had already decided they were not going to leave without what Karol owed them.

Damian, seeing that they were not taking his threat seriously, pulled the hand brake and climbed through the opening between the front seats to the back of the van.

'Like fucking now,' he cried.

There was scuffling as Damian pulled them from the floor. Damian slapped one of them on the head. A quick and painful punch landed on the other man's jaw. He coughed the blood out on the floor, which enraged Damian even more because now he would have to clean it with bleach. He administered his punches and kicks with precision until they begged him to stop, covering their heads with both arms.

The men lay on the floor, covered in blood, ready to agree to anything.

Damian lit a cigarette and assessed the damages he had caused. He planned everything coldly. It was too dangerous to kick them out now, two battered men would surely raise questions among the passers-by, not to mention the police in the streets. He could not throw them out just yet. He was angry with himself that he had lost his temper, but these two had deserved a beating.

He climbed back into the driver's seat and released the hand brake. With steady gear changes, he drove down Buckingham Palace Road and turned onto Vauxhall Bridge Road. He was going to take them to Vauxhall Park.

Damian wished his brother were here with him. It was Igor who usually took care of dumping the men onto the streets, so efficient and unemotional about the whole process. Damian, on the other hand, often allowed his emotions to take control. Where Igor would proceed without a single word, which was often more menacing than any physical harm he could so easily deliver, Damian spat out words accompanied by kicks and blows. Later, Damian dissected the process to himself aloud, winding himself up, fuelling his anger until he slumped, exhausted by his tortured rage, in the seat and stared at the road in front of him. And all for what? Damian could definitely learn self-control from his brother. And so, it was a mystery to Damian that Igor could be so resilient in the face of their daily work but was unable to maintain control over his resentment towards women. Damian already knew that doing this job without Igor was going to weigh him down.

15

'How was Paris?' Ines asked as she massaged Milena's face. She applied a blend of rosewood and geranium cream onto Milena's cheeks and neck, gently pressing Milena's skin.

'Karol had a severe allergic reaction and he decided to come back.'

Ines stopped rubbing her face for a moment. 'Oh my God. Is he okay?'

'It was not life threatening. He will be fine. He is fine,' Milena said with her eyes shut. 'But you know how he gets after each attack. I can't use perfume or candles around the house anymore. Then we found out that it was actually Zygmunt, Karol's cousin, who was also to blame for Karol's bouts of diarrhoea.'

'I don't understand these people.' Ines resumed the massage, gently pulling the skin at the back of Milena's neck. 'You invite them to your home and this is how they repay you. You are such good people, bringing over family and then this.' Ines stopped and wiped her hands on the towel. 'You look tired. I'm going to apply this new lifting mask, to make your skin glow again.'

Milena heard Ines moving around the room.

'We have a new girl. She's helping us. Zuzanna.'

'Any good? I'm looking for somebody to help me around the house. Perhaps you could recommend someone for me.'

Milena kept her eyes closed and wondered whether she should tell Ines what was happening. 'I think Karol is sleeping with her.'

'What?' Ines stopped in her tracks. 'Are you sure?'

Milena opened her eyes, lifting herself to a sitting position. She held onto the towel which covered her naked body, with one hand.

'The way he talks to her, it doesn't seem so. But I have this feeling…you know how they say that a woman always knows. Milena lay back on the bed motioning for Ines to apply the face mask.

Ines sat down at Milena's feet and stared at her. 'You seem very calm about it. What are you going to do? You are going to dismiss her, right?'

Nothing. That was what Milena was going to do about it. Milena felt the coldness of her mask on her face, then a little tingling sensation. 'We are going to have a baby,' Milena finally said to Ines. 'A child needs a father and I want to have a family.'

It was not the first time she had caught Karol with another woman. Milena did not want to know and as long as Karol behaved discreetly, she was not going to do anything. The knowledge left her feeling heavy. Heavy, because things had been going so well recently, the unexpected pregnancy, which she was finally beginning to accept. But at least she knew that with Karol she would never have to worry about money, which was so important to her now that there was going to be a baby. And she was not going to feel so lonely in their big house, especially in the evenings when Karol worked into the early hours of the morning, often disappearing somewhere without a word of explanation except 'Don't wait for me,' thrown at her on his way out. A family would give grounding to their lives, a purpose, which until now she had feared was steering towards an unspecified territory, where nothing would hold them together except their own ambitions. A child would make her life whole and joyful again, would shape her future, would stop her from feeling lonely.

Milena would not have found out so early about Karol's liaison if Zuzanna had not approached her one evening. Milena was on her own, sitting in the living room and going through the latest editions of Polish magazines. She was looking for an idea of what to wear to a party to which she and Karol had been invited.

To hear from another woman that she had slept with her husband, that 'There was nothing I could do to stop him, but you are a woman, you would understand me,' left Milena numb. But she kept on looking at the photographs of actresses and singers, while Zuzanna pleaded for her attention, which Milena deliberately refused to grant her. She left Zuzanna standing in front of her, never lifting her eyes from the pages, never saying a word. She refused to allow herself to be upset, not in her state. Besides, there was nothing she wanted to say to this woman because it was she herself who had arranged for her to get this job, so Milena blamed herself. If she had asked Damian for another man this would have never happened, not in their house. The thought that it was her fault weighed on her shoulders more than Zuzanna's feelings. And what exactly did this woman expect from Milena by telling her?

Then Milena remembered how carefully Karol and Zuzanna avoided each other, when he saw Zuzanna in the kitchen he retreated, hardly asking her to do anything, while Zuzanna almost looked directly at him. And Zuzanna had started breaking things. One day it was a saucer that slipped and crashed onto the kitchen floor, the other day it was a wine glass. Strangely, this clumsiness occurred only when Karol was around. Zuzanna was hardly Karol's type, Milena thought, with her bitten nails and cheap clothes, from a place in Poland she had never even heard of. Milena had had to teach her what wine to serve at dinner and how to fold the towels in the way that Karol liked.

'I preferred it when you lied to me,' Milena said later when confronting Karol, her heart racing, after he admitted, embarrassed, that yes he had slept with Zuzanna, but it meant absolutely nothing. He was drunk and so tired and needed a release from the stress he had been under. He promised that it would never happen again. If Milena wanted to have somebody else, he would arrange for a new person tomorrow.

She knew from the redness spreading across his face, from the hasty way he went down on his knees in front of her, that it was truly something that he felt should not have happened. She could not blame him for weaknesses that he could not control. How many times had she lost control over herself when she shoved doughnuts into her mouth and swallowed them without chewing, and then a few minutes later she was on her knees in the toilet? So, in her heart, she decided to forgive him, but she needed to make sure he was more mindful of his behaviour. Like she was. No witnesses. She did not want to know.

'I preferred it when you lied to me,' Milena repeated.

'I promise, I promise,' he muttered. 'You know how much I love you. You know you are the only one.'

It was at that moment that she decided to place a new responsibility on his shoulders, so that he would also have something to fight for, something greater than himself. She took his head in her hands and said, 'I'm pregnant.' She would always remember his expression, him looking at her in fear, at first, then as if he was about to cry. She had never seen him crying. Karol buried his face in her lap.

The only dilemma was that Milena was not sure whose baby it really was. The calculation Doctor Papuziak made would place the moment of conception at the time when Karol left on a business trip to Poland. She did not remember if she had deliberately decided to sleep with Damian or whether it was an accident of passion, and too much alcohol. One of those evenings when she inspected red marks on her neck in the mirror, the bruises on her delicate skin on her wrists where Karol held her too tight. It was a game he sometimes played with her to see how much pain she could withstand, a game she remembered playing as a child but had never quite liked – twisting and pulling on her forearm. A stupid game. Or when Karol tickled her until it transformed into almost a wrestling match between them. Whatever the reason that night she ended up with Damian, it did not matter anymore. She decided she was going to have the baby whoever the father turned out to be. She still believed Karol would be a good parent, a loving father, this would change him, and Damian had his brother.

16

'What do you mean he needs to go back to Poland?' Karol asked Damian, 'I need you both here now, not there. It doesn't make sense. Whatever he's done, I don't want to know. He's your brother so sort it out.'

Karol had already begun planning to expand the business. He had made a phone call to Krystian Kowalczyk who operated in Merseyside. He was interested in strengthening their cooperation. Krystian could place people in one of his businesses: packaging frozen meat, shellfish gathering or agriculture – the front of his operations. Karol did not tell Damian, or anybody else, at first, because he wanted to give himself enough time to prepare transporting people from various locations in Poland to the Liverpool area, and then after the planning phase ended, he still did not tell Damian because he wanted to give himself more time to think over this new arrangement again. He was not going to get himself involved in operations outside London without being absolutely sure about every detail. But Damian's entirely unexpected and unjustified request, for Igor to return to Poland, took Karol by surprise, and he did not like surprises. He had to stop himself from reminding Damian that he and his brother (and especially Igor) didn't have much of a future without him. Karol had sunk his roots in Britain but the problem was that the brothers were still deciding – dipping their toes in two countries and testing the waters of where life would be worth living. Who knew where their loyalties really lay?

'There's a salad in the fridge,' Milena said as she entered Karol's room. The flat screen television mounted on the wall blasted pop music. Milena could never understand how Karol could possibly work in such noise. 'I cooked chicken breast,' she added, louder. Karol had been on a diet for the past few months and Milena had been leaving food for him, making sure he ate more fruits and vegetables instead of readymade meals or food he would usually grab in town. 'You're working too hard. Why don't you take a break and eat something?'

'Wait a moment,' said Karol and turned to face Milena, giving her an irritated glance. Only now did she notice headphones attached to the iPhone he held in his hand. He pressed a button on the remote controller to mute the TV. 'What is it? I can't talk right now,' he snapped.

'Oh, I'm sorry. I had no idea you were on the phone. There's food in the fridge if you're hungry,' she said quickly.

He did not like it when she sneaked up on him like that, especially when he was conducting one of his delicate conversations that required undivided attention. He had noticed recently that she had been doing it more and more often. He had a feeling when he was in the house that she constantly lurked in the corridors eavesdropping, perhaps even picking up his mobile phone to see who he had been calling. He once found his phone placed at a different angle than he remembered but so far he had no proof. He had never caught her red-handed. Once, he confronted her but she denied, of course, his accusation as paranoid. Perhaps she was right: he was overworked and needed a rest.

'I'll have it later.'

He waited until Milena left the room and closed the door behind her before he resumed the conversation with Krystian Kowalczyk.

A week later, in Liverpool, Krystian picked Karol up at the train station. The rain pummelled them mercilessly as they ran to Krystian's car – barely a few minutes' walk but enough for the sheets of water to drench their trousers and jackets. Inside the car, Krystian switched the heating on, soon the interior was filled with the heavy smell of their damp clothes and a white film blurred the windows. Karol wiped his red and puffy face with a tissue.

'You're not going to buckle up?' asked Krystian. He was wiping the steam from the window with a small yellow sponge.

Karol did not move. 'I have a motion sickness.'

Krystian raised his eyebrows. He resumed wiping the windows.

'I throw up the moment I can feel the seatbelt around my chest,' Karol explained. 'I don't fasten them. Actually, I have a special document from the police that I don't have to wear a seatbelt.'

'For real?' Krystian said, blinking, amused. He had large bulging eyes, widely spaced. When he was small, no children wanted to play with him because they were scared of his appearance. Now, it gave him an air of vulnerability and uniqueness. 'And I thought it was because you're a fat bastard.' Krystian laughed at his own joke. 'No offence,' he added and slapped his protruding belly, 'courtesy of my wife's irresistible cooking. I should have sent her back home to Poland when she was begging me to go back, now if she goes twice a year she's lucky. Ah, women! I should have never got married.' Krystian laughed again.

There was no conversation with Krystian that would not include a joke or mockery. He made fun of his own shortcomings as often as he did of other people's, so nobody held his comments against him, apart from Karol. Karol resented his jovial nature, his mouth was now a thin tight line. Still, he was pleased to see Krystian. His connections to the Gangmaster Licensing Authority and the knowledge of the local market made him an asset in Karol's eyes, and Karol admired him for his contacts.

While Krystian navigated his way across Liverpool, Karol settled into describing, in general terms, the way he ran business between London and various towns in Poland, the numbers of people he could bring over. He said he would provide his own transport and drivers to get people to the Liverpool area. Over and over he would pause, briefly, to let Krystian ask him a question, or express his admiration, but there were none, so he continued.

'You know,' Krystian finally stopped him, 'my wife has made bigos. You like bigos? I bet you do. Everybody loves it. Shitty weather like that, a hearty plate of cabbage and sausages with mash is the best. Then, we have Żubrówka and talk. You are staying overnight, of course? Why didn't you bring Milena with you?'

Karol stiffened. He was not expecting this. 'I was hoping to catch the last train.'

Krystian rolled his eyes. 'You people in London. You're crazy, you know that? Coming all this way and going straight back. You can stay at our place. We have a spare room.' Krystian said it in such a way Karol realised there was not point arguing with him. He remembered that Krystian was at least ten years older than Karol, and it would be disrespectful to refuse his invitation to his house for a home-cooked dinner (Milena would surely object to Karol eating a heavy dish like bigos, but she was not here yet and so he said yes).

Krystian slapped the steering wheel, startling Karol. 'A priest walks down the road next to the police station and notices a dead dog on the road. Angry, he enters the police station and shouts: "You are all sitting here doing nothing and there's a dead dog lying on the street!" One of the police officers says: "And I thought you're the guy who deals with funerals." The police officers burst out laughing. The priest responds: "I came to inform the immediate family."' Krystian chuckled. 'Good, isn't it?'

Iwona, his wife, was not at home when they got back, and Krystian heated a big pot of browned sauerkraut and mash himself. 'Now I even have to cook for myself. What's the point of having a wife, then,' Krystian muttered to himself and shook his head while he stirred the food with a long wooden spoon.

'There's a bottle of Żubrówka in the freezer,' Krystian instructed Karol. 'And the shot glasses are in the cupboard above your head. I'll get the plates and cutlery.'

The shot glasses had intricately hand painted flowers in various hues of blue. There was a stamp on the bottom of each glass with an inscription: BOLESŁAWIEC – HAND MADE IN POLAND.

'Iwona bought them in Kraków,' Krystian said, noticing Karol carefully examining the tumblers. They felt heavy and fragile at the same time in Karol's hand and he thought how beautiful they were. 'Now, let's eat,' said Krystian, rubbing his hands together.

Krystian may have earned his reputation of a comedian thanks to his abundant cheerfulness and powerful way of talking but hospitality was no laughing matter to him. His mother had a saying: 'To receive a guest is to receive God,' and she had taught Krystian and his two sisters the sacred responsibility of welcoming a person into one's home. She was a teacher in December 1981 when the whole family, except their father who stayed back in Poland, was visiting his mother's distant cousin in Uppsala. After the introduction of martial law, his mother made the most difficult decision of her life – she decided not to come back. At first, they stayed in Sweden where his mother worked as a Polish language instructor at Uppsala University (later they moved to Stockholm). But soon she decided to relocate to Britain, one of the strongholds of Polish emigration. Throughout this time, his mother fought tirelessly for their father to join them but he never managed to obtain the permission to leave the country. With the restricted communication between them, the silences extended first into days, then weeks and months, until there was nothing left to say. When Krystian spoke of the past, he recalled his mother crying herself to sleep and making sure the children never witnessed her pain she had experienced because of the separation from their father. But Krystian had always known. He blamed his father for not fighting hard enough for them. His mother's nostalgia for the country she chose to abandon to ensure her children grew up in freedom took a terrifying toll on her life. After she had found out she had been diagnosed with lung cancer, she drank so much that Krystian took turns with his sisters to make sure there was always somebody in the house with her, to stop her from harming herself. Eventually, there was nothing any of them could do.

Krystian's father never joined them in exile; he remarried sometime in the 1990s and had two more children, but Krystian never returned, or wanted to know his half-brothers. He was eleven in 1981. Poland was like a mirage of his mother's memories to him. He spoke Polish with almost no British accent, thanks to his mother who insisted on a perfect command of their mother tongue. The family's first home in Britain was in Newcastle, crammed with Polish books, magazines and circulars. His mother found a job in a local library and hosted weekly gatherings of other exiled Poles. In January 1982, she participated in a protest on the streets of Newcastle against the imposition of martial law in Poland. It was his mother's dedication to teaching her children to love and respect the country they were born in that Krystian remembered vividly. But he never really shared his mother's obsession, unlike his sisters who performed in the dance group 'Kujawy', helped in organising various exhibitions at the Polish House and, later, after his mother's death, returned to Poland while he remained in Britain. Krystian told Karol how he became infatuated with an English girl, Alison Ellsworth, and followed her to Liverpool, which his mother could never understand because deep inside she hoped he would choose a Polish girl. He had dated many girl-friends, Indian, Chinese and even a French one. At this point in the story, Krystian's face broke into a wide smile as he said, 'I think, back then, I drove my mother mad. But she was right, in the end. A Polish wife was the best thing that could have happened to me. But not to my belly.'

Krystian pushed the plates away and made himself comfort-able in the armchair. A burp escaped his lips. 'Pardon me,' he said then pulled out a toothpick from his wallet. He held it out to Karol but he shook his head.

'Here's a good one,' Krystian remembered one of the jokes, the toothpick twirled in his mouth, 'A guy walks across his village, beaming.

"Janek, why are you smiling so much?"

"I am a father! I've got a son."

"Congratulations, man. How's your wife feeling?"

"I don't know. I haven't told her yet".

Krystian had the rare quality of making you immediately at ease, so you almost forgot how quickly his demeanour could change. So did Karol.

Krystian tucked the stick inside his wallet and picked up a cig-arette pack from a coffee table.

'Now,' he dropped the smile from his lips, 'let's hear what it is that you want from me.' Krystian was playing with a lighter, turning in on his leg.

Krystian's transformation, so sudden and unexpected, reminded Karol that he should never allow himself to be distracted in his presence, never to take Krystian's foolishness for granted. In a way, he was impressed the way Krystian commanded attention.

'As I was trying to explain to you earlier,' Karol began, 'I'm thinking of expanding my business and I've been looking for a serious business partner. I have brought over quite a big number of Poles looking for jobs. I rent properties around various locations where I house them. My two drivers, the Kulesza brothers, take them from their houses to their work places.'

Krystian nodded without taking his eyes off his face. 'And what's the turnaround?'

'You mean how long do they work for?'

'Yes.'

'It depends. The problem is that many want to go back and I'm left with no workers, some stay but the job market has changed, as you know, and I've decided to look outside London.'

'How is it going to work for me?' Krystian leaned forward. 'If your people want to go back? I need stable people. You know what I mean?'

Karol did not like to be hurried. All this time he had patiently listened to Krystian's stories and jokes so now he could allow himself to savour his own words. 'The percentage of workers who decide to go back is so small I wouldn't worry about it. The only reason they are leaving, and it is a small percentage, really, is because the jobs they do, finish. Put it this way,' Karol added, 'there's

174

no problem with the workforce I bring over here, however many you need, consider it done. I'm only interested in securing long-term employment for them.'

'And they don't really care about the location or type of work? If you bring them up here rather than London?'

'It's money.' Karol relaxed. He was pleased that Krystian showed such interest. He wanted to impress Krystian and for Krystian to consider him as an equal because he had so much to offer. 'They don't care where they work as long as they have a job.'

Krystian took his time to stab the end of his cigarette against the ashtray, grinding the stub. 'The way I see it,' he said, 'is to have one person, an intermediary. A person with a good command of English would be the best since he would have to talk to the people at my end. Also, somebody intelligent,' he added, thoughtfully. 'If anything goes wrong – and in my experience you can never be careful enough, besides the fact of my connections – I don't want to have anything tying me to this. Have you got somebody you can trust? What about your crew? Do you trust them? And how's their English?'

The Kulesza brothers were perfect for the kind of jobs which Karol used them for in London, but he was not convinced that they would be a fit for the type of operation he had in mind now. Damian, he could trust, but Igor was a different matter, quite apart from this whole crazy idea of sending him back home. Then there was a problem of the language and their appearance. It had to be somebody whose appearance would not raise any doubts, or immediate apprehension, which was hard to say about either of the brothers. Even if he managed to get Damian to smarten up, get rid of his baggy clothes, his level of English, like his brother's, was basic, peppered with phrases they had acquired from hours of playing Grand Theft Auto or Saints Row. Their English was enough to pretend, to dazzle, also to threaten those who had no idea what Damian was saying, with swearwords aimed at others like missiles, but it was of no use to Karol to represent his business. Or to foster trust. Besides, he needed the brothers to carry out their work. It would have to be somebody he could get rid of at any moment, someone who would follow his instructions, a person he could control completely.

At night, Karol struggled to find a comfortable position on his pillow. He still felt dizzy from the alcohol they had drunk that night, but it was a pleasant humming in his head, the kind that usually allowed him to drift easily into sleep. But there was too much excitement in his body with this new venture, he could feel the familiar tingling somewhere in his chest.

He was lying on the sofa, staring at the ceiling, going over the conversation again and again in his head. He had to force himself to close his eyes but still sleep would not come. His mind was too preoccupied with the planning, flashing ahead to conjure up future profits. And Krystian had said something that gnawed at him, that he did not want to have anything or anybody connecting him to what they were about to begin. Karol had thought about it over the years himself, but he had got too comfortable, perhaps because the success and the fact that he had managed to get away with his actions for so long pushed their way to him so easily. As a rule he kept the full extent of his planning vague to everybody, so only the Kulesza brothers or Milena could guess what was he was thinking.

He sat up and, in the darkness of the room, he found his mobile on the floor. It was two in the morning. He knew exactly who he needed to call to find the right person.

17

'It's Karol,' Borowik said with an intake of breath. The words tumbled out very quickly: 'He needs a new person, somebody to help with his other businesses, and also, I told him your English is very good and that he and his wife could use somebody like you.'

Mateusz stared at Borowik's bloodshot eyes. This offer could not have come at a better moment. Still, Mateusz wondered if Borowik had forgotten the words of caution about Karol and the Kulesza brothers during their conversation not long ago. Mateusz clearly remembered Borowik's warning: 'You have no idea what they are capable of,' and now he was encouraging him to work for these people.

Borowik's voice was hoarse. 'If you want the job, it's yours.'

'This is a lot of money,' Mateusz said, carefully, trying to take in everything that Borowik was telling him. Money he needed, desperately – so many bills were still unpaid. Although he was slowly repaying his debts, new bills kept coming.

Borowik was long in answering. 'You said you needed the money, so here's a chance. You know I don't have space at the new site. Not to match that kind of salary.' He was on the point of adding something more but changed his mind. Borowik kept rubbing his finger against the display of one of his mobile phones, as if he was willing it to ring, to rescue him from further conversation with Mateusz. But for the first time, when they talked, in spite of Borowik, both phones were silent.

'Anyway, this is Karol's phone number. He knows you will be calling. And listen, whatever happens, keep me out of it. I don't need to know.'

'I told you good things come to good people,' Angelika said, her eyes lit up, when Mateusz told her about the new job and the money he could make.

Mateusz was unsure what to expect from Karol. He already suspected, perhaps unfairly, that whatever Karol and his two employees were involved in was not entirely legal or honest. But he owed Karol the benefit of the doubt. After all he had never witnessed Karol in the van or around the workers at the construction site. Mariusz did not know for sure what was Karol's knowledge or involvement in the Kulesza brothers' actions.

The other problem Mariusz was considering was that Borowik was far from specific when it came to the exact job description: 'something about answering the phone, marketing or sales, but could also involve travelling, best if you talk to him directly. Easy money if you ask me.'

To make matters more complicated, Mateusz still wondered about the fate of the men who had disappeared. He almost wanted proof that there was something wrong with Karol and his people for whom he was about to work, some evidence, because until now he had only suspicions, hearsay, stories. What exactly was going on? The more time that passed between the sudden disappearance of the workers from the construction site, the less Mateusz was sure about his own thoughts, about what had actually happened. The reality of the past few months was slipping away from his understanding. So far, he only had his own interpretation of events. He could not count on Borowik, who was refusing with a maddening obstinacy to reveal any more details. But then, there was the money. Mateusz knew he could not say no to the money. Such money could easily release them from their suffocating obligations. If he hated himself for considering this offer, he knew that the need to provide for his family, they came first.

Karol's voice, his encouraging and welcoming words which promised so much, floated in the air, into Mateusz's head. He began to doubt his initial judgement, that Karol was hiding something, that he was a leader of some kind of gang who abused people's trust or used them in murky dealings. Especially after Mateusz had met Karol, the very idea suddenly seemed to him ludicrous, an invention of his mind.

'This is my wife's business and tourism is in high demand, especially now with so many Poles travelling back and forth,' Karol explained in a serious tone, as they sat in one of the small offices on King Street. The offices of Karol's marketing company were being refurbished so they could not meet there. 'You know, Milena, my wife,' Karol continued, his voice animated, 'is one of the most successful businesswomen here. You are married, aren't you? Have you got any children?'

Mateusz nodded, impressed with what he was hearing. He had never encountered Poles like Karol and Milena, zealously entrepreneurial and clearly good at what they were doing, committed enough to treat this place as their home and imagine their future in Britain. Mateusz read about people like them, rooted so deeply into this country they did not need to question their right to live here. Whatever they did worked. Now, they were giving him a chance.

'If you want discounted holidays or cheap flight tickets for your family, then this is the place. It's one of the benefits that come with working for us. I like to take care of my employees.'

Mateusz was overwhelmed by this sudden generosity. 'The job is working for your wife? For her company, I mean?'

'You will be working for both of us. Depending on what needs to be done,' Karol clarified, avoiding any specific details. 'There will be travel involved, of course. The contract will be with New Market Comms, my company.'

Listening to Karol, half in admiration, half in reservation, Mateusz was baffled. Perhaps Borowik was wrong about this man. When Karol smiled, his face lit up, making slits of his eyes. His chubby cheeks shook when he talked. But there was sharpness in Karol's eyes, Mateusz noticed, a friendly but business-like demeanour. This man, with his electric presence from the moment Mateusz shook his hand, had been a success, something Mateusz could not say about his own company. He figured maybe he could learn something from Karol, how to do better.

'Can I ask you a question?' Mateusz said. He decided if he was going to get himself involved with Karol, the best thing he could do was to be honest. He also thought that if Karol was a good person, with nothing to hide, he would not be offended by Mateusz's question.

'Sure.'

'As you know, I worked at the construction site where Borowik is a site manager.'

'Ah,' said Karol. 'He spoke highly of you. In fact, I fully trust Borowik's judgement and I am sure you will not disappoint me.'

Karol's comment made it easier for Mateusz to continue, though at the same time this praise made it more awkward for him to ask the question which he had wanted to ask since the beginning of this conversation. The only reason he decided to carry on was to ensure his conscience was clear, to make sure he was not going to make a mistake. 'There were men being driven in a van to the site, and then, one day, they stopped. I think the two men that drove them work for you as well?'

Karol nodded, with a solemn expression, furrowing his forehead, then said: 'The Kulesza brothers.'

'Yes.' Mateusz took a deep breath and went on, 'the men who worked at the site told me stories...they had bruises on their arms. One day the men stopped coming. The only reason I'm asking this is because I've heard some strange stories. I'm confused about what to believe.'

Karol did not respond to this at once. His eyes seemed to peer into and beyond Mateusz. 'I am very glad you have brought this up.' He leaned forward and placed his hands on the table. He summoned a concerned look. 'What you have described has been my worry for some time now. And it is my own fault I did not realise earlier what was going on. Yes, I sometimes help my friends and family in Poland by agreeing to get a job for them here. Igor, the younger brother, is not working for us anymore. I dismissed him. I have zero tolerance for liars and this, my biggest disappointment, is what Igor proved himself to be. But, if I were you, I would not believe everything you hear. I know for a fact some of the men stole building materials from the site. They also stole money from me.' Karol left the last sentence hanging between them.

'I had no idea,' Mateusz said quickly, embarrassed.

'Of course you didn't,' Karol continued, back in control, 'but I am very happy you have asked about this particular situation. It shows me you are a very perceptive person, an intelligent person, qualities I seek in my employees. And let me tell you, you can make really good money working for me, with your command of English, which again, Borowik complimented, you can take our business to a new level. Besides, we need to stick together.'

'I'm not sure I follow.'

'We,' Karol pointed at himself first, then at Mateusz, 'Poles here. If we are not going to look out for each other, who will?' Karol swelled inside at the sound of his own words, carefully selected for this occasion. He knew Mateusz would fall under his spell but he needed a nudge. He pushed a document across the table towards Mateusz.

'Contract of employment.'

Mateusz glanced at the document.

'Perhaps I can take it home to read.'

'I would like you to start tomorrow. But if you feel more comfortable why don't you work for me for some time first, to see how you like it. Ask anybody, I am a man of my word. Why do you think I would spend so much time talking to you, if I wasn't sure about your ability to do what I require? Listen, I know you are the person I need. I don't need a probation period for you. But if it makes you feel better, we can do that. I will need to call my lawyer to draft a new contract. I am not sure how much time or money this will take but you don't need to worry about this. I will sort it out. It will mean I cannot guarantee when you will be able to start your job. One more thing, you should know I had five different candidates for this position, begging to work for me, so I hope you appreciate the vote of confidence I'm giving you.'

Mateusz was embarrassed. He had misjudged Karol by thinking that he had anything to do with the situation of the men at the construction site, and now, Mateusz was on the verge of jeopardising a secure position as a manager and failing Borowik's trust. He was beginning to realise this could be his opportunity at turning his life around and freeing himself from debt. He needed this job and he had no doubt now that Karol could deliver.

Back home, when Mateusz related to Angelika, almost word for word, the conversation he had had with Karol, she could not hide how proud, and relieved, she was at his decision. Mateusz, too, was quite taken by how accommodating Karol had been when it came to his probing questions, which he now thought were out of place. Karol had been very gracious and understanding, Mateusz thought.

'I saw her photos in one of the magazines,' Angelika said.

'Whose?'

'Milena's. His wife.' Angelika blushed.

'I had no idea you knew her.' Mateusz was surprised.

'I don't know her. I read about her. She was in the running for the Polish Business Woman of the Year Award. Sadly, she didn't win, but she was a strong contender. The ceremony was at the Polish Embassy.'

'Oh, really? Perhaps we could go there someday?' Mateusz grabbed Angelika and pulled her close. He wanted to kiss her. He was so pleased he could bring her such good news about the new job. It could not have come at a better time in their lives.

'Don't be silly.' Angelika laughed, flustered, pretending to push him away but, still, he held her tight. 'I'm not a business woman like she is. I admire her for her achievements, that's all.'

'Well, I'm sure when the time is right you will meet her.'

'Oh, no, no. I wouldn't know what to talk to her about. She seems so self-assured. I'm not like that, and you know it.' She covered her mouth with her hand, hiding her smile.

'Oh, yes, yes,' he teased her. 'And you can be very business-like when you want to.' Then, he kissed her, passionately, basking in this fleeting moment of happiness they shared.

18

Of all the holidays, Easter was Angelika's most cherished, the one that brought her the greatest joy. A week and a half before Good Friday she hung a 'to do' list on the fridge door. The corners of the page were held by colourful Yoplait Petit Filous magnets (Kamil was assembling the alphabet and wildlife collection). She had printed the list from one of the Polish websites.

'What is this?' Karolina asked, staring at the list. She was eating an apple and slurped the juice off her fingers.

'I thought we should get ready for Easter.' Angelika's smiling face was full of light.

'But it's not until next week?'

Angelika watched the drops forming at her daughter's feet. 'Karolina, the juice is dripping on the floor.'

'Sorry, Mum.' Karolina picked up a paper towel and wiped the floor.

'I will need your help. There's so much to do and together we can finish in two days.'

'Why me? Kamil can help. And dad.'

'Dad works, you know that. And Kamil is too small. You are a young woman now and I'd like you to help me. One day when you have your own family you'll need to do it as well.'

Karolina let a heavy sigh. With every year she was finding it more difficult to bring herself to participate in all the holidays her mother so eagerly observed, especially the Catholic celebrations. There were so many of them that Karolina struggled to remember when and how long they lasted. She liked that so many of her English friends were nonbelievers. She felt more normal with them than in her own family.

Angelika wished her daughter was more enthusiastic about Easter, like her. She remembered that her mother had never had to ask her for help because Angelika would happily ease her mother's workload. She wondered whether Karolina's reluctance was because they lived in Britain where she was exposed to all this foreign influence, sinking into the culture she could not fully grasp. She was finding it more and more difficult to convince Karolina to do anything at home, as if Karolina were deliberately sabotaging any chance to bring mother and daughter together. Angelika admitted to herself that her way of expressing love and affection to Karolina was to teach her everything her mother had taught her about homemaking and taking care of the needs of other family members.

Angelika put an arm around her daughter and said, 'It'll be fun. We'll paint eggs together, bake Easter Babka, cook white borscht.'

'Will you make poppy seed roll?' Karolina asked, hopefully.

'Of course I will. I can teach you how to make one yourself if you want.'

'Wicked,' Karolina muttered, finishing her apple. 'My favourite.'

'I know,' said Angelika and kissed her cheek. Poppy seed cake was her bargaining chip whenever she wanted Karolina to do anything in the kitchen.

At the Polish grocery shop, Angelika, slowly, went down aisle after aisle, with a list in her hand, placing various items into her shopping basket. Every now and then she crossed out items on the list and then resumed her search, alert to the prices, noting down the figures so that she could find a better deal in a different shop. She stopped in front of the meat section and asked the shop assistant for white sausage, uncooked and unsmoked, and some traditional long cured ham. The shop assistant cut small pieces from various types of meat and handed them to Angelika to try. In a tray lay fat, glistening smoked mackerels and fat, pale orange pieces of salmon. Angelika pointed to the one that she wanted.

'Mum, Mum,' Kamil shouted, running towards her. 'Look.' He was waving a large Easter palm branch.

'Where did you get this from?'

'A lady gave it to me. Outside.' Kamil beamed, pleased he could contribute to the Easter shopping.

'How many times have I told you not to take anything from strangers? Do you hear me? And I told you to stay near me.'

'But, Mum.' Kamil was on the verge of tears. The palm branch was so colourful, full of dry yellow and red flowers, with a ribbon at the bottom. It was covered in a stiff plastic wrap.

Angelika bent closer to Kamil. 'Don't cry. We will go outside in a minute and choose one together, all right?'

Kamil shook his head and wiped his nose on his sleeve.

'Don't go anywhere. I want you to stay with me.'

Angelika turned to the shop assistant and apologised. There was a long queue of mostly women forming behind her and she did not want to keep the other customers waiting. Everybody was in such a hurry.

Outside, there was a table loaded with Easter decorations. Kamil reached out to touch a lamb made of sugar with a red ribbon around its neck and a tiny red flag with a golden cross. Angelika slapped his hand before he managed to grab it. Kamil rubbed his hand.

'I told you not to touch anything.'

The moment she slapped Kamil's hand, Angelika regretted it. It was so unlike her. Easter preparations were becoming such a stressful time, she had already spent more money than she was supposed to, and she was worried what she was going to tell Mateusz. She had noticed he had been preoccupied with the new job and she did not want to become one more thing he would have to worry about. She should not have taken Kamil with her, but Karolina was at school and she could not leave him unattended at home. Mateusz was never home since he had started his new job, so Angelika was left on her own to take care of everything. She could not even count on Karolina who voiced a litany of excuses and spent most of her time reading books in her room. 'For school, Mum, you have no idea how many books I have to read,' she offered by way of explanation after Angelika had asked, once again, to help her clean the house. The last few days of doing everything on her own was taking its toll on Angelika, the expectation of the perfect celebration she had largely imposed on herself. No, she should not have slapped Kamil.

'I'm sorry, honey.' She kissed Kamil on his red hand. 'Which one would you like?'

Kamil pointed at the largest sugar lamb on the table and Angelika nodded to the woman behind the table to wrap it. She also asked the woman for a palm branch and sprigs of boxwood.

Back home, Angelika peeled the onions and laid the brown skins at the bottom of the pot. Kamil watched as she checked each egg for tiny cracks in the shell, before carefully placing seven eggs on top of the onion skins and covering them with water. Angelika sang a gently melodious church song: *Ciebie Bogawysławiamy, Tobie, Panu, wiecznachwała!* This was her favourite part of the holiday, preparing the eggs, exactly the way she had watched her mother prepare them when she was little. After the hardboiled eggs cooled, she sat down at a table and, one by one, meticulously scratched weaving patterns on the shells with a small knife. She sometimes used egg colouring, yellow, red or green, which she could only buy in the Polish grocery shop or which her mother posted, in sachets, to her. She had kept a few wooden eggs she had bought in Poland – with their mesmerising patterns of delicate petals painted in turquoise blue, orange or purple. The wooden eggs were stored in the cupboard and she took them out only for Easter celebrations.

'Would you like to help me prepare the basket?' Angelika asked.

Kamil pulled his sleeves up his arms ready to get to work. Angelika smiled. She was going to manage. She was going to turn this time into a memorable event, even more remarkable than last year.

The heavy, almost choking, fragrance of white lilies hung in the air as Angelika, Mateusz and their two children entered the Our Virgin Lady of the Immaculate Heart Catholic Church in Ealing. The church was packed and almost every bench was occupied. Some older women knelt in the first rows with rosaries in their hands, whispering the prayers through their dried, pale lips. Others solemnly scrutinised the arriving families, mentally giving verdicts on the Easter baskets which they carried. Angelika recognised a few neighbours in the crowd and smiled in acknowledgment as they walked between the pews. She wanted to first show the children the unveiled tableau of Christ's Tomb. This year the arrangement involved a rock, where a life-sized figure of Christ was displayed. Two girl scouts guarded the tomb, wearing metallic grey shirts, black skirts and gravity on their young faces. Kamil wanted to come closer to have a look at the figure placed inside a rock, but there were too many flower pots at the feet of the Easter grave, so he stood on tiptoe, craning his neck to have a better look.

'Okay, buddy.' Mateusz lifted his son in the air.

'Wow,' Kamil said in English. Angelika grabbed his foot and pulled gently to keep him quiet. Displeasure, inflamed by the sound of the English word from a child's mouth, lined a few old women's faces. This church was a haven, a sacred space. Here was no tolerance for polluting Polish – everybody's mother tongue – with English phrases. Nobody wanted to hear foreign exclamations wrapped around the tongues, especially those of the children, so susceptible to novelty.

Angelika handed the basket to Kamil. She gently pushed him forward to place it on the church floor, covered in a blood-red carpet for the blessing. Kamil hesitated. There were so many Easter baskets of various sizes he was not sure where to put theirs. He briefly turned back to Angelika and Mateusz for guidance but it was Karolina who took his other hand and walked with him around the display to help him find a free space.

Angelika felt happy, and strangely proud, knowing that this year her basket really stood out among the others. The cloth, which she had put at the bottom of the basket, underneath pieces of bread, sausage, ham, two hard boiled eggs, salt and other foodstuffs, was hand embroidered. She had worked for two months on this stump work design of butterflies on flowers and a white bunny – the most complex embroidered Easter cloth she had ever undertaken. She wanted other women to acknowledge her efforts. When it came to Angelika's Easter basket, every year, she increased the difficulty and richness of the design, challenging herself to surpass her previous efforts. It was that one day in the year when pride overwhelmed her.

'Very innovative,' Sister Celestyna commented. They did not notice when she approached them but Sister Celestyna knew everybody and everything. She seemed to always know the exact location of every member of the congregation.

Angelika blushed, slightly ashamed of her own swelling pride.

Sister Celestyna bent down to have a closer look, her wide bottom raised in the air and the back of her robe pulled up, revealing white socks.

'You think it's too much?' Angelika whispered into Mateusz's ear, waiting for Sister Celestyna's reaction.

'Even if it is, it's too late to do anything about it, don't you think?' he said, but seeing the horror in her eyes, quickly added, 'It's gorgeous, silly. And she has already said she likes it. I wouldn't worry about it. To me, it's the most beautiful basket in the whole church.'

'You're right, of course, you're right,' she said. 'Kamil, Karolina, come back please.'

The service was about to start and Sister Celestyna, after once again giving Angelika a congratulatory nod, walked away to greet other people.

Father Niewiadomski, stern-faced, emerged in a white robe with golden trim. He stopped in front of the lectern, above his head hung a flag with the face of the late Pope, John Paul II. As always he was glad to see a full church, and with a fervent enthusiasm he began his serious sermon.

'Blessing of the foods is our very old Catholic tradition. It reminds us about the truth expressed by the Saint Apostle Paul with the following words: "Whether you eat or drink, or whatever you do, do all to the glory of God". Eating is a holy activity, that is why we pray before and after we eat. The biggest holiday of all, the resurrection, we celebrate with food. With happiness in our hearts, we will return to our homes and with Jesus Christ we will sit together at the Easter table. We will share the blessed egg, the sign of a new life. Let's ask Jesus Christ, who is always present among those who love him, to bless this food for our homes.'

Father Niewiadomski positioned both hands for prayer and spoke the words of the blessing, making a sign of cross with his right hand. After he had finished, he picked up an aspersorium, inlaid with gold, containing holy water and a straw brush. He stepped down to the baskets placed in rows, turned his head from left to right, waiting for the congregation's attention to reach its peak in absolute admiration of his actions, then raised his hand with a straw brush dipped in the Holy Water and moved around to sprinkle each basket. With every vigorous shake of the brush, drops landed on people's faces.

'Are we going to kiss Jesus, Mum?' whispered Kamil, overwhelmed by the unfolding ceremony in front of his eyes.

'Not today sweetie.' Angelika stroked Kamil's head.

He was very excited when, a day before, she had taken him to a mass. One of the younger priests had held a large wooden cross displaying Christ in a bronze body. The throng of people scrambled to kiss Jesus's feet, a procession of writhing bodies, the annual enactment of devotion to the statue, even by those who did not believe. An altar boy wiped the saliva from the statue's feet with a white cloth after each kiss.

Now, outside the church, more families gathered, holding baskets of various sizes, waiting for their blessings. Angelika reflected that they had been lucky to go first thing in the morning because, at this time, they would probably have had to wait outside like everyone else.

19

It would have been so easy to let everything go, grab whatever food there was and swallow it so quickly she would not even register the taste in her mouth. Milena opened the fridge and, with her eyes unfocused, stared at its contents, breathing in the cold air. It had occurred to her that she had not gorged on food since she had found out she was pregnant, as if her body automatically knew better than her whirling mind, that eating food and then forcing herself to throw it up would be bad for the baby she was carrying. She still craved it, of course, the act of eating more than the food itself, but there was no rushing panic inside her to get rid of the contents of her stomach as quickly as possible, to discharge the feeling of guilt, that she had failed once again to control her weakness. And, for a short while, the pregnancy had saved her. But now, as she stood in front of an open fridge, there was nothing and nobody to stop her anymore, no child to fill each corner of her heart with everlasting love. She picked up whatever was left of the cheese cake and slowly began to push the food in her mouth with her two fingers. The sweet taste mixed with the saltiness of her tears.

Two weeks ago she had lost all hope.

Something was not right; the dull pain which moved from her abdomen to the lower back made her double over. As she had rushed to the toilet, attuned to these signals of pain her body was sending, something warm and wet leaked down the inside of her thighs. Her throat choked with panic.

Sitting on the toilet, bent forward, she dialled the number for PolMed Surgery. She whispered that she needed to see Doctor

Papuziak, but the receptionist informed her that he was in Poland, 'Doctor Papuziak left to spend Easter with his family. Would you like to see another doctor on duty?' She did not. As the bleeding steadily subsided, and the pain shifted into a recognisable territory, a dull, quiet place she could slowly settle in, there was a thought, perhaps it was meant to be, so why fight? Would Doctor Papuziak be able to stop what her body had begun? Would he save her?

And yet, she felt besieged by her own will that had carried her through all these years against all odds. It was not in her nature to fail, or worse, to give up, so she dialled the number again and, this time, requested to see the doctor on duty.

'Our oldest has been attending the Saturday Polish school. He likes it very much. When your baby is old enough you should sign up as well,' said a heavily pregnant woman in the waiting room. Her hands were placed protectively over her protruding belly. 'Łukasz. Can you please stop and sit down.' A boy was running around the table, where a plastic Easter eggs rolled dangerously to the edge, about to fall to the floor. 'Your first?' she asked, turning back to the woman next to her.

'Yes,' said the second woman, 'My husband is British. He doesn't speak Polish, though he can say a few words.' She gave an apologetic smile.

'Oh,' the first woman grimaced. 'As long as you sign them up to a Polish school and keep talking to them at home it will be fine. It must be difficult to have a foreign husband. Where did you meet him? Here?'

'No, in Poland,' she responded and picked up one of the magazines from the floor.

The first woman was not discouraged. 'In Poland?'

Milena thought the woman was asking too many questions. She did not feel like joining in the conversation, to tell her that it was none of her business to probe into somebody's life like that.

'Are you pregnant as well?' The heavily pregnant woman switched her attention to Milena, since there was no answer. 'Oh my God, wait, haven't I seen your photo somewhere? Yes! I think you're the owner of Milena's Travel? Am I right?'

Milena raised her eyebrows. The woman was one of those strangers who thought they knew everything about her because her face was recognisable, somebody who was best avoided.

'No,' Milena said, surprising herself. How easy it was to lie to strangers, though she was not sure what the right answer should be in her condition.

The receptionist interrupted by calling Milena's name. 'The doctor is ready for you.' Milena quickly got up and followed the girl down the corridor. She managed to overhear the woman's loud whisper, 'I was right. That was her.'

There was an anxious silence in the examining room as the doctor stared at the screen during the ultrasound scan. Milena rolled her hands into two tight fists, digging her long nails into her palms, feeling powerless in the face of what was to come – at destiny's mercy. And yet, observing the doctor's face, she had still held onto a sliver of hope that she had been wrong about the meaning of the clotted blood which she had seen at home in the toilet. She lay silently.

The moment the doctor confirmed that she had lost her baby, Milena almost drowned in her sorrow. She had felt such hopelessness, stilled by the inescapable truth, hopelessness she had not imagined she would be capable of surviving. If there was a tiny flicker of hope while she sat in the waiting room, there was nothing now. For, in that place and in that time she had realised how much, in fact, she had wanted to have a baby, and she could not bear that the life she had carried in herself was so suddenly taken away. She would have liked to scream in the doctor's face, that he was wrong, that he had made a mistake, that it could not possibly be happening to her. She had been terrified that she might go crazy with the bitter pain in her chest.

Now, she stared fixedly at the shelves in the fridge, and one by one, slowly, pushed food into her mouth. It felt good, comforting, almost coming back to her old self, forcing herself to forget this heartache.

Never would Karol experience such a profound feeling of self-doubt.

From the day Milena had shared the news with him, the thought of becoming a father had lacerated his heart with astonishing force. A maddening happiness. She tried to warn him that it was an early stage and anything could happen. 'Nothing is going to happen,' he assured her, baffled by her reaction, 'We are lucky, you and I.' He took hold of her shoulders and squeezed her and repeated, 'Everything will be fine. Stop worrying. Everything will be fine.' Though he sensed in her voice a cautionary warning, as though preparing him for possible complications, which still remained a possibility, he could not accept that anything bad could happen to people like them. Karol wholeheartedly believed he was meant to succeed and dismissed Milena's fear as 'hormonal imbalance.'

The next day Karol bought her a Cartier trinity heart bracelet, 'To celebrate our first born.'

After Milena returned from the PolMed Surgery, she took the bracelet off her wrist, and placed it at the bottom of the jewellery box, buried underneath all the other expensive presents Karol had given her. She never wanted to wear the damn thing ever again.

'Why are you not wearing the bracelet?' Karol asked in the evening. He had not noticed Milena's pale face and reddened eyes.

She could not bring herself to answer. She covered her face with her hands and her shoulders shook.

'There is no baby. There's no baby,' she kept repeating, sobbing.

Karol was looking at her, astounded, trying to comprehend what she was trying to tell him, shaken by the spasms, swallowing her words. Finally, there was nothing else to say, and he was left with anger that destiny had robbed him of the one thing he had made himself desire. He would wonder, later, why it could possibly happen to him. He was braver than this.

'You will get pregnant again,' he finally said, irritated, but with a niggling thought that this was one thing he had no command over. This feeling of lack of control brought on wordless rage.

That night disquiet crept into Karol's heart. He waited until Milena cried herself to sleep then rang Damian and asked him to meet him, alone, in Goose Wood Green pub.

Damian arrived when Karol was readying himself to order another pint.

'For the first time, I felt responsible for somebody. She did it to me. I don't even know how to deal with this, with her,' Karol said, a little emotional. 'Everything I've been doing made sense until now. Why me? Why is this happening to me? I don't understand why. Do you know why?'

'No,' said Damian and licked the foam from his beer off his lips.

'I didn't see it coming, you know, didn't think life could be so unfair to me. What have I done to deserve this?'

'How is Milena?' Damian said. 'How is she feeling?'

'I'm the real victim here. Life played its joke on me. I was cheated of being a father. Her baby is dead now, so it can't feel a thing, but I do. I'm still alive.'

Karol turned the glass in his hands, swirling the beer. He did not like the taste of it, he preferred Polish beer but the pub did not have any on sale.

'Do you think what we do makes us guilty? Because I tried to explain to myself that, perhaps, the fact Milena lost our baby is some sort of heavenly revenge. A way God wanted to punish me for my success, to bring me down. Like He was saying you can have anything you want but not this.'

Damian was startled. Karol slurred his words and Damian was not sure he understood whatever cruel truth Karol wanted to tell him.

Karol grabbed Damian's hand across the table. 'Do you believe in God?'

'Well, yeah, don't we all?'

Karol leaned back heavily in his chair.

'I'll get another round,' Damian said, standing up.

There was a tugging discomfort in Karol's neck, a prickling sensation. What if he was right, he thought. That it was all his fault? He never looked back on his life, always moving forward onto the next thing, always wanting more. He did not feel ashamed that he was better than others, that he grabbed opportunities when he saw them. Stupid people deserved whatever happened to them. In the end he believed he was doing them a favour, he was giving them a life lesson in trust. If they were not strong enough to survive it, it was not his responsibility to take care of them endlessly. He was the light and everybody else was a moth. He had quit caring for others a long time ago. With Milena it was different. But the feeling he had for her could be called love.

'What about redemption?' Karol asked when Damian was back. 'I was wondering whether it is some sort of punishment by whoever sits up there in heaven, whether it's possible to change myself. Be a better person for Milena. But whatever I've been doing I was doing for her, for us. How can she not see this?'

For a moment, Damian did not know how to react to this surge of honesty from Karol. His drunken voice, an air of tragic sadness around him, unlike Damian had ever witnessed, was upsetting.

'You mean like confessing your sins? Asking for forgiveness? No matter what a person has done?'

'Yes.' Karol's eyes shone with hope, a tremor in his throat.

'Shit, I don't know, Karol. I don't wake up in the morning thinking about it but … I guess I believe there is a plan for each one of us.'

'You do?'

Karol nodded slowly, then he sank into his thoughts again, his eyes closed, which made Damian think he was asleep.

Those were exactly the same words Karol had heard from his mother when he had brought her over to Britain shortly after she divorced his father, Henryk. She was reluctant to change her life because of the break-up of her marriage which, according to her, 'was going to happen sooner or later because there is a plan for every one of us.' At first, Karol could not understand why his mother believed dissolution of a marriage was something that could be planned in advance. But it was, indeed, how his mother perceived her life and never fought to change it because it was meant to be the way it was. She was, of course, immensely proud of his achievements, her only son, and listened to his stories of his success abroad during his visits back home and regular phone calls, yet she stubbornly refused when he asked her to come and live with him. Until, one day, she told him things were not working out anymore between her and his father and they were going to get a divorce. She was ready to join him. 'But I don't want to be a burden. You and Milena have your own life. Aunt Basia found a job in a hotel in Brighton and I could live with her.'

There was always a bit of confusion in the Sosnowski family as to who was Karol's real father; Henryk or his brother Jan. Karol grew up oblivious to the havoc his mother's behaviour had caused in the family and among the neighbours. She led a modest and quiet life. She worked as a shop assistant at a village small grocery shop. For some who lived in the neighbouring villages, the shop was the only place where they could purchase freshly baked bread, sugar or flour, cigarettes and also locally brewed beer and cheap vodka. She never missed a single mass in the church and had her favourite seat in the first row, on the right hand side, right next to the portrait of Black Madonna which took up half of the wall, its face darkened by the smoke from the candles.

Everybody knew Maria's face so there was no place for her to hide after the stories of her life started spreading. The words which Jan hurled at Henryk in drunken outrage, in front of six other men who occupied the bench outside the farm buildings where they worked. In the silence that followed, crimson-faced Henryk stood up, grabbed Jan by the lapel of his worn jacket and kept pushing him until Jan's legs and back were against the metal reel of the combine harvester. The men shot up from the bench, unsteady on their feet, to stop Henryk from causing further harm to his brother, and pulled on his arms and shoulders from both sides.

'Henryk! Henryk! Let him go,' they shouted.

'Take it back,' spat Henryk through clenched teeth, hot rage in his stomach. 'Take back everything you said.' And he shoved Jan's limp body further against the reel. Jan did not even try to defend himself.

'He's drunk. Look at him. Leave him be.'

Panting heavily, with saliva dampening the corners of his mouth, Henryk opened his work-heavy fists gripping Jan's jacket. Jan steadied himself to a vertical position and slowly smoothed the half torn lapels, then gave a wan smile, which was enough to spark a new wave of fury. Henryk took a swing to hit Jan's jaw but luckily the men managed to pull him back in time. Kicking and spitting, Henryk felt powerless against his friends' firm grasp. If only he could get his hands around Jan's lying throat.

Orange light from the setting sun streamed in through the windows and, from time to time, skylarks' trilling sounds echoed in the fields outside. Maria sat tight-lipped by the window, a bowl of walnuts on the table. She crushed them, one by one, with a brass nutcracker. The room was silent except for the splintering. Every few nuts, Maria popped one into her mouth and slowly chewed. The ones that were shrunken into tight, blackened, dry mass, she threw into a bucket under her legs. It was the moment she cracked another walnut when, after a thunderous slam of the front door, Henryk stormed in. Without a word he strode into Karol's room and dragged the boy back by his arm to the kitchen.

'Is this my son?' said Henryk. His acidic breath reeked of alcohol and his face was awash with crimson.

Karol's eyes welled with heavy tears, frightened of his towering father. His arm hurt as his father shook the terrified boy.

'Answer me!' His face was twisted in ugly anger.

Maria immediately got to her feet, dropping bits of the walnut shells from her apron on the floor, and launched herself at the boy.

Henryk shoved the crying Karol behind his back so suddenly that the boy almost lost his balance.

'What's wrong with you? You're drunk.'

'I asked you a question. Is this my son?'

'Yes, yes, of course he's your son. What's got into you? Please, I'm begging you, leave him alone. Can't you see you're scaring him?' she pleaded.

Maria, without much result, tried to get hold of Karol but Henryk kept blocking her arms. He tossed the boy from one side to another with his other hand, bruising Karol's arm with his grip.

The stab of fear Maria had experienced was so sharp and so abrupt that it filled her eyes with tears. Seeing Henryk so blinded with rage, there was no way she was going to reveal the truth now, or ever, because she was uncertain herself who the father was, Henryk or his brother, Jan. Maria had stopped long ago trying to comprehend her own predicament. It was the middle of the night when it had happened. The heavy curtains were drawn and there was no light from the moon or the stars. The bedroom was so dark she could not see her own hands in front of her face. Semi-conscious Maria barely registered the warm body behind her, hands pulling on her nighty. She gave in. Henryk had a habit of coming back home in the middle of the night, long after she had gone to sleep. She was used to his ways, allowing him to do what he wanted out of marital obligation because she knew that was what was expected of her. What difference did it make now whether it was Henryk or his brother Jan? The baby was healthy and strong and that was the only thing that mattered to Maria.

'Why was Daddy so angry?' Karol asked later, when they were alone in his tiny bedroom, and Maria held him tight in her arms, rocking from side to side to quieten his nerves. Henryk had disappeared, somewhere into the thick night, and Maria was not expecting him until morning.

'Daddy loves you very, very much. He was a little bit upset but not with you. You are a very good boy.' She smoothed his blond hair from his forehead. 'Now, close your eyes and go to sleep.'

Karol vaguely remembered the circumstances of this incident that had happened over 30 years ago but he clearly recalled his mother's half-heartedness. He thought it irritating, his mother yielding to his father's will all these years. It was like she did not care what happened to her or about the quality of her life with a man like his father. It seemed wrong, a waste, that his mother would seem so unconcerned, however badly his father treated her, and she, in return, always defended him in front of Karol. And when she, finally, agreed to come to live closer to Karol and Milena, he did not believe it, at first. Even more shocking was the decision about his parents' divorce. With her usual calm, as though it was meant to be, she made the most surprising decision of her life, and pretended it was meant to be because, as she repeated over and over again, 'there is a plan for each one of us.'

Now, with his heavy head propped on his right hand, Karol rolled his eyes at Damian, because with the last remnants of soberness in his mind and body, he refused to admit there was some kind of preconditioned plan for his life. In a sudden flame of contempt he thought that his mother and Damian could believe whatever they wanted but Karol knew better.

That evening, as he slipped deeper and deeper into all-consuming intoxication, he mourned, angrily, his own helplessness and how inexplicably unfair his life had become.

20

'The priest approaches an old lady in the church and extends his hand with a small plate where people offer money after the mass. The old lady hides the money in her purse. "No offering from you?" the priest asks and the old lady says, "This is for my hairdresser." "Virgin Mary didn't go to a hair salon," he says. "And Jesus did not drive a Mercedes," responds the old lady.'

Funny, was the word Mateusz used to describe Krystian to Angelika. He self-consciously stopped himself from repeating all the jokes Krystian had told. He did not think Angelika would find them amusing, especially the ones about the nuns or the priests.

Mateusz was full of eagerness, darting around to excel in his new job. He was surprised by Krystian's unexpectedly warm welcome, which put him at ease and made him feel as if he had found the right place for himself, like he belonged. He did not mind travelling between London and other cities because, with Karol and Krystian he sensed a bond of familiarity and trust, something he had forgotten could be possible with his fellow countrymen. After all these years in Britain, the distrust that had defined his attitude towards Poles he had worked with had begun to subside. For the first time in a long time, he felt proud. The sense of accomplishment that came from helping others find a home or a job was so rewarding. Angelika kept repeating that she never doubted that there were good people out there and Karol was certainly one of them. Mateusz thought how fortunate they had been. He happily convinced himself that the initial, gnawing fear about Karol and the Kulesza brothers, was a construct of his imagination; everybody deserved a chance, he thought. He even tried to explain it to Borowik whose only response was, 'Whatever, man. But I'm happy it's working out for you.'

This hunger for doing the right thing Mateusz experienced with the arrival of this new job was exhilarating. He wanted so much, with a childlike desperation, for this relationship to work. And it did. His naive stubbornness to have hope against all odds reminded him of Angelika's. It was so effortless to ease himself into this place of comfort, of letting go. He began to imagine, foolishly, that from now on it could only get better. He would wonder, later, how he could have been so sure.

Krystian greeted him with a firm handshake and a pat on his shoulder, his eyes seemed to be constantly sparkling with laughter. He asked about Mateusz's family and how long he had lived here. 'If it doesn't work you move on. No point in wasting your life,' he said to Mateusz, after Mateusz shared his experience of his lost business. Then he thought that these were the words Angelika would have used. Mateusz told Krystian about chasing Bartek to finish his botched jobs, the feeling of being on his own when something went wrong, the unanswered phone calls or, worse, silence at the other end except for somebody's breathing. 'Stay away from the Poles,' said Mateusz, remembering early advice from a stranger.

Back home in Poland, the thought would have not crossed his mind, to be wary of his fellow countrymen, because he would be taken advantage of, if he was not careful. In Britain, he was advised to pretend that he did not understand Polish, if he had heard people speak his mother tongue on the street or on the bus. 'If they could, they would sell their own souls,' Mateusz recalled another warning, then added, 'But I'm glad you guys are different. You give me hope,' to which Krystian nodded, remembering to congratulate Karol on finding the right man for the job.

Later, on the way back to London, Mateusz wondered if he had, perhaps, said too much, whether his honesty would cost him this new assignment. He cursed his openness with Krystian – he usually refrained from sharing his personal life with strangers or fellow workers – then he composed himself, realising that it was too late, anyway, to retract the words.

'This is where you'll drop them off,' said Krystian, pointing to a house on a quiet street in Southport. 'How many people are you bringing in the first round? Seven, if I remember correctly?'

'Yes,' Mateusz confirmed. He had exact instructions from Karol to follow Krystian.

'Make sure there are no people with shellfish allergies. They'll be harvesting clams, cockles and oysters. I don't want to have anybody complaining. Do you know what I mean?' Here, Krystian blew out his cheeks and grabbed his own throat pretending he was choking. He did a cross eye with protruding eyes and Mateusz could not help but smile.

Wherever they went, Krystian spoke English with no trait of a Polish accent. He introduced Mateusz as Matthew, the English version of his name, and that was how they left it from now on. Only when they were alone did Krystian speak to him in Polish. It did not bother Mateusz because Krystian was born here, a native. And he reserved his judgment only for others who tried to pretend they were somebody else.

It felt good to wear a white shirt and cloth trousers to work, even if most of his time was spent behind the wheel, but then Karol had told him from the very beginning that he was now the face of the company and he needed to look good: 'trustworthy and presentable' were the words Karol had used. For the Polish workers he dropped off across Merseyside, he was the long-awaited assurance that they were in good hands.

Once, the van he was driving was stopped by the police. They asked him to open the back door, the standard road check, to see if the papers were in order, where he was driving them, what kind of job they were doing. The police officers handed him and the men in the van leaflets in Polish: MERSEYSIDE EMPLOYMENT LAW – free service.

As soon as Mateusz was on his own he looked through the pages. He felt strangely proud of living in a country where the police treated immigrants with such respect. He wondered if Polish police would go to the lengths of commissioning leaflets in other languages for immigrant workers; Ukrainians, Belarusians, Vietnamese, Chinese or Russians.

He remembered how his mother used to take him to the open air market at the Stadium in Warsaw to buy trousers and shirts from the Vietnamese traders; how impressed he was that they spoke Polish to his mother, haggling about the price, and that their children who went to local schools would speak among each other in perfect Polish. His mother used to say: 'If it weren't for the Chinese and Vietnamese, I don't know where we would go.' After hours of walking around the stalls, staring at the mannequins dressed in pink shorts or bras of all colours displayed on tables along the way, his mother often could not decide what she wanted, fingering items long enough for the stall seller to almost lose patience with her. Later, they would eat in one of the bars serving Vietnamese food.

'It's clever. And it's in Polish. The helpline is in Polish as well. I'm very impressed with this,' Mateusz said, once back home in London.

'What is it?' Karolina took the leaflets from his hands. 'Victims of crime, support and service,' she read aloud. 'Shit, Dad. Where did you get this from?'

'I was handed one of those by the police today.'

'Police?' interrupted Karolina.

'It's a good thing. This is how they take care of the immigrants in Britain so that they can get help.'

'I guess,' Karolina said and put the leaflets back on the table.

'Imagine if you needed help because, for example, your boss wasn't … I don't know, paying you the money you were due to receive. What would you do? Who would you call?' Mateusz liked to give Karolina scenarios, to make her think, as if she was still that five year-old girl he adored so much, not a teenager who no longer needed his lessons or paid him much attention.

'I don't know,' she said, 'what if they are locked up somewhere? Like in a basement and they are not allowed to go out. How would they know there's a place they can call?'

'You are right and, of course, it's impossible to help everybody but a number of people will read that and they can tell the others.'

'You're such an optimist, Dad,' Karolina said. She was ready to go back to her room.

That his daughter turned out to be so different from him or Angelika, already questioning the world around her at such a young age, seemed to Mateusz some kind of wonder, for it was as if she was a stranger, even though she was a miniature of her mother. In her presence, Mateusz felt his heart contract with burning tenderness. He forgave her criticism and that she often called him naïve. They argued, just like when she pointed out his grammar mistakes or pronunciation, accusing him of not making enough effort. 'Mum will never learn but you're just being lazy,' Karolina said.

'She's growing up so quickly,' he said to Angelika, who was busying herself with folding clothes from the laundry basket. There was something on her mind, clearly, as she had been silent all this time, waiting for Karolina to leave the room.

There was the sound of Karolina's door slamming shut, and shortly after that, loud music could be heard.

'She's been impossible. I don't know what to do with her. She's so unhelpful, unfocussed at what's going on in this house.' Angelika was folding socks into balls and throwing them, angrily, into a basket. 'It's because you're never here. She lacks discipline.' Her words were like a small explosion. She stopped suddenly, wishing she had not lost her temper. It was unfair, she knew, but she was angry. 'I'm sorry I shouted. And then there's Kamil's first communion. I need you to help me with this. I can't do it all on my own.' Angelika's hands fell onto her lap, overwhelmed with a vision of coming days.

'I will see if I can take some time off,' said Mateusz, soothingly, trying to figure out how to placate her. 'I know I've been out most of the week.'

She resumed folding the clothes and smoothing the wrinkles. 'Thank you.' She picked up the laundry basket and left the room to sort the clothes into the wardrobe.

Karol was standing with his hands on his hips. He was wearing grey track suit bottoms and a t-shirt when Mateusz arrived and he waved Mateusz inside. He sat down on one of the cream leather sofas and waited for Karol to finish his conversation over the phone, before asking him for Saturday off, to help his wife with his son's first communion.

Karol put a fingernail in between his teeth; a piece of chicken was stuck inside a broken tooth.

'I understand, but this is your personal commitment,' Karol said slowly, carefully sticking the tip of his tongue in the cavity. A light glaze of sweat glistened on his forehead. 'I have a business to run. We've just launched this new operation near Liverpool and I need you there. Once it's up and running, you will be able to take as much time off as you want. But I don't see such an option at this moment. These are the priorities.'

Mateusz had not expected that. He bit the inside of his cheeks to keep quiet. 'I understand but...'

'No, you don't.' Karol's voice lowered, his gaze authoritarian. 'How long have you been on the job? Under a month? You cannot expect me, as your employer, to give you time off in your first weeks of work. You've hardly begun, really. It's between you and your wife. Why don't you schedule it for another time, after it's less busy, but not now.' He pulled the t-shirt over his protruding stomach and scratched his chest. 'Did you take the photos of the house the workers are staying in, as I asked you to?'

The rest of the afternoon Mateusz spent on the move, quarrelling with himself, about what he should do. Clearly, Karol was not going to let him take a day off. If he had lied, which Mateusz wanted to avoid, and pretended he was sick, so that he could be there in the church with his family, Karol would eventually have figured it out. Karol was not stupid. Angelika would never forgive him if he did not show up at his own son's first communion. He would never forgive himself either. One part of him wanted – in fact was desperate – to go back to Karol, to try and convince him that it was only one day, but one day that would mean so much to his family. Family was, always, all that mattered the most to him. But Karol did not let him speak, as usual, and Mateusz was beginning to notice this behaviour. Instead, Karol flooded Mateusz with arguments that, on second thoughts, Mateusz had to admit were valid. Mateusz tried to put himself in Karol's position. After all, he used to be a boss himself, back in the day when he ran his own company. Mateusz did not need to think long to know the answer to the question: what would he do? Why then, did he feel like he was going to be forced to lie now? It seemed deceiving Karol was the only way for Mateusz to spend time with his family. A discontent settled in him, a battle with his thoughts. He had admired Karol for his entrepreneurial spirit and belief in himself, but Mateusz was learning quickly that Karol was somebody devoid of compassion.

'Look at you in your fancy outfit. Looking good.' Borowik approached Mateusz, grabbed him by his shoulders and pulled him close to pat him on his back. The men shook hands. 'I thought you were never coming. New job. More money. And off you go and I don't hear from you for weeks.'

Mateusz was relieved to find Borowik at the construction site.

'Has it been that long already?' asked Mateusz, embarrassed. 'It can't be.' He owed Borowik this job. The least he could do was to stay in touch. Here he was, not merely a friendly visit, but he needed Borowik's advice, to ask if he had done the right thing. But for now he was happy to see Borowik's face.

Mateusz did not need to wait long for Borowik to finish his shift and then they went to a local pub. It was packed with people, hot and loud, so he took off his black jacket and loosened his tie.

He unburdened himself to Borowik, recounting the conversation he had had with Karol, how he was conflicted about what

21

Karol foresaw the opportunity in arranged marriages before anyone else. He learnt quickly that impersonating a woman required a greater confidence, at least at the beginning, when he exchanged the first emails. He had made a mistake of sounding too vague or offering too little information about himself. It was his first post, under the section 'Job Offers' on www.mypolacy.pl, a site which listed job adverts for Poles living in Britain. He was certain someone would eventually say yes. After all, he was offering the thrill of a lifetime; living in a place everybody dreamt about and getting paid, for the small price of getting married.

I'm looking for girls who would like to visit England and make 20,000 PLN. The only thing you need to do is get married. No need to worry about the rest. I will tell you everything you need to know.

He had received a number of queries, but nothing came of them in the end, and he figured that it must have been something about him being a male, showing little concern for what women wanted to hear. Women were more likely to trust another woman, even if she was a complete stranger. So he made sure he mentioned Milena's name; that they were working together.

He preferred to call the respondents. He knew he had a better chance of convincing the girls to enter into the contract if he could hear their voices. He grew impatient and angry when some of them refused to provide him with their phone numbers. He was reluctant to disclose information via email. In his experience, people who asked too many questions were not going to be easy to convince to take the leap.

You arrive in Britain and live with a guy with whom you are going to get married. You get to know each other, some basic information, but there's no obligation to have sex together. He is going to pay for your flight from Poland, food, if you smoke he will pay for your cigarettes, and give you cash for yourself. You can find a job here and make even more money. If you have any questions, give me your phone number and I'll call you.

The first reply came an hour later. The stupid girl signed the email with her name – Justyna, while Karol preferred to leave his emails unsigned:

Where exactly in England? I speak a little bit of English but I've never been to Britain. How long do I have to be married with him? Which country is he from? When will I get paid? Justyna.

Karol replied:

As you see, there's a lot to discuss. Let me call you and explain everything over the phone. It will be a proof to you that I'm real, not pretending to be somebody else. Really, if you give me your phone number, it will speed things up. There's nothing to be afraid of. I'm not going to call you constantly and if you're scared to go on your own you can always find a friend and take her with you;-)

He read the answer once again before he pressed Send; he made a mental note to include the passage about a female friend more often. It would put them at ease.

It took Justyna two days to respond to his email. He almost wrote this one off his list, there were others he was corresponding with, but when he saw her reply he was annoyed. She wrote:

If I come with my friend, somebody will have to pay for it, right? I really would like to get more information via email first, to think this whole arrangement through. Are you in England or in Poland? Justyna.

He quickly typed his response, already deciding that he was not going to waste any more time on somebody indecisive like her:

I'm here in London. I will call you and explain everything. You can both decide whether you want to come together. No problem for both of you to receive the money.

He never got a response after that and wondered where he had made a mistake. Karol began to analyse the process in detail: women found other women more trustworthy, his email address: kzr21@wp.pl did not disclose whether he was a man or a woman. He never signed any of his messages, which also might have spooked her. And so it was, he needed to sound more feminine and more plausible.

The second time he had placed an advertisement he made sure to give himself a female name – Agnieszka Rogal. He changed his tactics. He decided to provide more information and stopped pushing the women for their phone numbers. The most important thing was to make them feel safe, so he was ready to redesign the communication. He was going to give them the answers they wanted to hear.

I'm looking for a girl twenty-two - twenty-eight years old for my Indian friend in London. The girl should know at least basic English, have a passport and be ready to come here as soon as possible. I am interested only in serious offers, from decisive and serious girls. Amount: £6,000 per wedding. My email: agnieszka.rogal@onet.pl and mobile: 07944483811.

It amused Karol how easy it was to make money simply by placing two strangers in each other's paths, without any danger to himself because, after all, it was not his name on the marriage certificate, but the names of the two people joined in matrimony. He only presented them with a way to ease their lives: one – gaining a visa needed to work in the UK, the other – the money. Later, if they wished to divorce, it was their decision.

Finding a person, male or female, from a non-EU country who wanted to marry was not difficult. In fact, there were more volunteers than he could match with Poles who responded to his advertisements. Karol shared the profits with Ganganjyot Chattopadhyay and his brother-in-law Ujagar Ranah, co-owners of GCUR India Communications. Ganganjyot asked Karol if he knew of any Polish women wanting to marry Indians or Africans.

'It's good money, Karol, good money,' he added with a playful sparkle in his eye, leading the way into the Pan Peninsula building in Docklands. They sat by the bar and waited for the concierge to take them upstairs to the Attic Bar.

Inside, after a few drinks, Karol and Ganganjyot stepped out onto a small balcony. Ganganjyot took out a Hofnar cigarillo, and shielding the tip with his both hands from the wind, slowly lit it.

'Let me run the first person, test the waters, and then, we can talk about a bigger number,' Karol said, after Ganganjyot had outlined the process.

Ganganjyot nodded and they shook hands. Since then, every few months, they met in the Attic Bar, sometimes more often if the circumstances had suddenly changed. If they needed to exchange cash, they headed to the balcony, away from witnesses and the noise of the music, the wind scattered their words among the surrounding skyscrapers. There was no shortage of people that went through Ganganjyot's hands; Indian, Bangladeshi, Ghanaian, Nigerian or Pakistani, some had already been working in one of the shops Ganganjyot and Ujagar owned, others came through their families' or friends' networks.

Once, Milena overheard a conversation Karol had with one of her employees, 'If you have a friend, who would like to make extra money, you can always let me know,' he charmed softly. Later, Milena told him that perhaps it was not a good idea to involve women from her office or at least, let her conduct the conversations. 'Are you jealous?' he asked her, laughing, tickled by Milena's reaction. They settled that Milena would pick up the women from the airport or coach station because it made more sense for her to do it, rather than sending the Kulesza brothers, who 'would only scare the poor girls,' Milena argued.

But Milena did not want to be involved in emailing the women or calling them, it was Karol's responsibility.

I'm looking for a girl who would be interested in getting married with an Indian man. He's going to get a visa, you the money, clean cut business arrangement. He lives in northern London and is twenty-six years old, but you will have to live together.

Karol was typing the response to one of the emails he had received to his new account under the name of Agnieszka Rogal.

He will cover your expenses, the upkeep during the length of the con-
tract and the whole arrangement should finish within three to four
months, depending on how good your English is. If you want to work I
can arrange something for you. I will need your birth certificate, and a
copy of your passport. Ask me for whatever you need.

Two hours later, a girl who had responded to Karol's ad which
he had placed on one of the Polish job sites, emailed him a few
questions. She said she had never been in England before (Karol
thought it was always a good beginning, if he managed to attract
somebody who had never travelled here – he could tell them
whatever he wanted about what life was like here) and didn't
speak fluent English. He liked that too – if anything went wrong
he would not have to worry about the girl trying to explain herself
to the police. He prepared his response:

Once you make the decision, he is going to buy you a plane ticket, you
will need to print it and fly. I will pick you up from the airport. I live
10 minutes from his flat, so you can pop in for tea to my place, but seri-
ously I don't see why there should be any problems. You know why you
are travelling over here, and he knows exactly what he is supposed to
do. The first few days may be a bit awkward, you are both strangers. I
know even from my own personal experience and from the experience
of other women, that everybody is a little bit scared at the beginning.
The longer you think about it, the more questions you will have. I don't
know anybody in this country, who is going to help me? What if this
is some kind of massage parlour? You need to remember that he needs
you, so you shouldn't feel ashamed or have issues with taking money
from him. And you will see how nice it is to spend somebody else's
money. As far as divorce is concerned, the minimum and maximum

period at the same time you need to be married is three years. You must live with each other the minimum amount of time of three to four months, until he gets a visa. You can go back to Poland to visit your family any time you want. England is not a desert island – it's only a two-hour flight away.

He tried to imagine what this girl, whose name she had given as Kasia, looked like. He had not asked for a photo, it was too early, and he did not want her to think that her appearance would change anything, though if she wanted a different job and if she was attractive enough, he could arrange a waitress job in one of the Polish restaurants. He stopped asking himself what kind of a woman agrees to enter into an arranged marriage. If it was his daughter, he would beat her to death.

The next day, Kasia emailed him again.

I'm worried about the police, you know, if anything goes wrong. And the money, how do I get the money? My friend is interested as well. Thank you, Kasia.

Yes, the money, this was the one thing that made people hungry with hope. Karol emailed her back:

The risk is always there but if you are prepared then there's nothing to worry about. You will get the money in cash, so there's no electronic trace of the transaction on any accounts. These are small details, really, but the kind of details the Home Office would look for when they make a decision about a visa. You will get half of the amount up front, and the other after he receives his visa. If you'd like to work here I could arrange something in a pharmaceutical factory packaging medications

*and drugs or in a Polish bakery. Amazon needs employees as well; you
sign the contract for the first three months and if you work hard then
they will sign a longer contract with you. Does your friend want to get
married as well?*

He could tell her whatever came into his head. There was no
way this silly girl was going to check anything. And, in the end,
she would do whatever he suggested to make even more money,
on top of what she would receive through the marriage. But he
was steadily getting fed up with the barrage of questions, sending
the emails back and forth, his forehead furrowed, biting his lips in
annoyance. He was beginning to wonder if she was ever going to
make a decision. So, after another email full of questions he decided to send her a firm response, to show that he was committed:

*I want you to make the right decision, if you decide to come here. I am
not forcing anybody to do anything against their will. However, if you
make the decision, I want to be sure you are ready because I like to deal
with responsible and serious people.*

Karol had always been able to sense the birth of a new opportunity, the tingling sensation of enticing yet another person into
his carefully constructed scheme. Kasia was on the verge of making the decision, he could feel it, this sense of expectation, which
came with the next email. But he decided to wait before he called
Ganganjyot, in order to start making appropriate arrangements.
He had done it once, when he thought the person had made the
decision to come to Britain but, who later, without explanation,
stopped responding to his emails or phone calls. Karol, angry at
the woman's silence, was forced to apologise to Ganganjyot for

wasting his time. Karol had learnt from his mistake – assumption was not the same as certainty – only once the plane ticket had been bought, copies of the passport, birth certificate, and even bank account details exchanged, could he start getting ready. But even then, until the girl actually arrived in Britain, there was still the possibility of things not going to plan. Once the girl was on that one-way flight, there was no going back.

'You'll have to send somebody else,' Milena announced, a week later, two days before Kasia was due to land at Gatwick Airport. Kasia was taking the flight in Koszalin, the closest city to her hometown, Rzyszczewko. 'I'm going on a trip with Ines. It's a beauty retreat in Egypt. I told you about it when I booked it.'

'No, you didn't.' Karol's eyes glistened meanly, irritated. 'I would have remembered.'

'It's not my fault you didn't write this down in your diary. Now you know,' she said, 'I'm sorry. Send one of the drivers.' Karol was not sure, if she meant her voice to sound so distant. She looked straight into his eyes but there was no emotion, no movement on her face, or perhaps she was punishing him. After the night she had told him about the baby, they had never again discussed what had happened; how Damian had brought him home so drunk he had to carry him into the house, or the way he had knelt in front her and pounding his chest with his fist, swearing that he would never look at another woman and she asked him, mildly amused, 'Were there others you think I should know about since Zuzanna?'

'I guess I will have to do without you,' Karol finally said, and decided to ask Mateusz or even Agnes McCormick, if he had to. He did not want to stir Milena's fragile emotions, and since the miscarriage, she was reluctant to have sex with him. Was she afraid

22

It took Mateusz a moment to realise that there was no money transferred to his account. He checked the calendar again, Monday, last day of the month and a Bank Holiday. Perhaps, that was the reason why no money had been deposited, but Friday had been a working day, so money should have reached the account on Friday. He unlocked the drawer and searched for the contract he had signed with Karol. The agreement was written in Polish. He looked for the paragraph where the information about his salary was given. He needed to check, perhaps he was mistaken about the exact payment date. He traced the sentences with his index finger. There, he had found it. Page three, paragraph eight stated: *You are entitled to be paid. Your salary will be paid monthly in arrears at the end of each month or not later than on the 1st of the following month.* So there was one more day to wait but there were bills to pay now.

Karol was not answering his phone and the call went straight to voice mail.

'Is everything all right?' Angelika asked, walking into the room.

'Yes, yes,' Mateusz said, distracted. She was looking at him with her head cocked to one side, her hands were red from grating beetroot. She asked, 'What's wrong?'

'It's nothing. I thought I was going to get paid at the end of the month but the money hasn't come through yet. It will probably come tomorrow. It will definitely come tomorrow,' he repeated, as if to convince himself.

'What about the bills?' She sounded very worried now.

'I'll pay them tomorrow, at the latest. After the money is transferred.'

She smoothed her hair off her face with the back of her hand. A subtle change came over her, a kind of silent alertness. 'What if he doesn't? I really would like to pay the bills today. You know how difficult it has been the past few times.'

'I know that,' he raised his voice, losing his patience; the blood pounding behind his eyes. He did not need to be reminded what was at stake here.

Angelika quietly backed out of the room and Mateusz called after her, 'It's because it's a Bank Holiday,' and she replied, 'Why don't you call your boss and ask him?'

Nervousness swirled around his insides. Last time he had spoken to Karol he had asked him for a day off, on account of his son's First Communion. He was still battling with himself what he was going to do, and there was little time left. Now, he would have to ask Karol why there was a delay with his salary. He was ashamed to admit that he was almost grateful Karol's phone was going straight to voicemail. He played and replayed in his mind the conversation and arguments he wanted to use, trying for a balance between the need to pay his bills and a plausible explanation for the delay. He did not want to sound overly troublesome or demanding.

'Don't you trust me?' Karol asked in a wounded voice after Mateusz, speaking slowly and haltingly, called him – searching for the right expressions and words that would not imply that he blamed Karol in any way for this unexpected delay. 'You will get your money. I was there when the accountant was making the transfer. The way I see it, it is probably your bank's fault, you know what they are like.'

Mateusz agreed, of course, it was probably the bank, as though there could be no other explanation.

'Which bank are you with?' asked Karol.

'Barclays.'

'Well, there you go. They are keeping the money. Not my fault then.'

'I didn't say it's yours,' Mateusz defended himself and once again apologised. He was struggling now to find the right arguments. 'When did you say your accountant transferred the money?'

'Last week, I told you.' He had not, but Mateusz did not correct him, either.

'If the accountant transferred the money it should have come to my account straight away.'

'I told you he did it.' Karol's voice took on an edge of impatience. 'I saw him doing it. You will definitely get your money.'

From the corner of his eye, Mateusz noticed that Angelika was now back, standing in the doorway, listening to his conversation. He could see the tension building on her face and was already dreading the conversation they were going to have.

'But I have bills to pay. Your accountant should have transferred the money on time. You must have known it was going to be a Bank Holiday.' There, he had said it, if not for his own peace then for Angelika's.

'I don't like your tone of the voice or your attitude,' Karol spat out his words, unable to control himself any longer. 'I told you, you will get your money. I think you telling me how to conduct my business is out of line.'

After hearing Karol's response, for a brief irrational moment, Mateusz felt his courage going. He wished he had not pushed Karol like that, but this state of anxiety lent him a strange feeling of determination. And he did not want to look weak in front of Angelika.

'I didn't mean it that way,' Mateusz said, turning his back on Angelika, 'I'm sure this is just a misunderstanding. Try to understand my situation.'

'I know exactly what you meant and I don't like it.'

Mateusz had not anticipated that the conversation would be this way. He was ashamed that he had had to ask Karol about the money. Sensing that further argument would bring nothing but Karol's icy counter-arguments, Mateusz choked back his words. He thanked Karol, apologised once again and hung up. He decided against asking him about a pay slip. Perhaps the postman would deliver it tomorrow. He was not sure what exactly had made Karol so annoyed. If it was frankness that Mateusz valued most, especially in business, honesty and loyalty would eventually strengthen their relationship. He thought, wrongly, that Karol would appreciate this.

The next day, with a heavy heart, Mateusz logged into his account. There was no money. He quelled his panic. Instead of calling Karol, he sent him a text message. The response came half an hour later: *Money will be in your account this afternoon.* It was.

A few days later, Mateusz's mobile phone rang just as the whole family was sitting down to Friday dinner. Angelika's face reddened when Mateusz excused himself and left the kitchen to answer the phone.

He heard Karol's voice, 'I need you to pick up somebody from Gatwick Airport arriving at 1.50 pm tomorrow. One of Milena's friends. Her name is Kasia. You will need to drop her off at the address I will text you when we finish. Then, I want you to come back to the office. Damian will go to Liverpool tomorrow instead of you.'

'I didn't know I was supposed to go to Liverpool tomorrow,' said Mateusz, surprised.

'One more thing, as soon as you pick her up, call me.'

'Okay,' Mateusz said, but Karol had already hung up.

Tomorrow was Saturday, the day of Kamil's First Communion.

23

Igor's muscles were aching but it was the kind of pain he enjoyed the most; two hours of pushing himself to his limits. Damian lay on the dumbbell bench, slowly hissing the air out through his rounded mouth every time he lifted his legs up.

'You done?' Damian asked him, without stopping the movement. 'Give me another ten minutes. I'm finishing the sequence.'

'I'll be in the sauna,' said Igor.

Inside the changing room, Igor wrapped a towel around his hips, then he took a few photographs with his mobile phone of his naked torso in the mirror. He admired the prominent stomach muscles, protruding, with a streak of blond hair curling towards his navel, and slapped his belly in satisfaction. He twisted his legs to the side to see his calves, barely any hair visible, he was still not entirely happy with their shape. This was something he was going to work on next week. He cracked a Coke open and took a large greedy gulp, and burped loudly. He sat down on the wooden bench and with one hand scrolled through the photographs. He was going to upload them to www.polak.co.uk, his nickname – IgoRoo1. In fact, the profile picture he had taken of himself a few months ago, also in the gym, had received nine points out of ten in rating from other users. With this new image he was convinced he was easily going to get the maximum ten points. He flicked through the profiles of newly registered users, winced at another profile photo of a baby, head shots of women pouting, smiling, winking, some wearing very little with their deep cleavages prominently featured, others standing outside the entrance to tube stations or pubs, on motorbikes or having their hair coloured. He could imagine them babbling, tossing their hair and laughing loud enough to catch somebody's attention, with that pungent, acrid-smelling odour around them, which came in waves together with the heaviness of their rich breaths. They were women so old they could have been Igor's mother. He wondered, with disgust, why they would want to put up pictures of their wrinkles and sagging skin out there for everybody to see. There were other men with pronounced muscles, like Igor, half naked, with skin so smooth he found it impossible not to admire them.

'You're still here?' Damian said, walking in. His face was red and drenched in sweat. He pressed his right nostril with his index finger and blew into the sink , switched to the other side and blew again. He took off his gym clothes and changed into a towel. 'You shouldn't be drinking this. Have some energy drink instead.' But Igor, unlike Damian, did not have his brother's wholesome dedication to the body building program. Bottles of protein, keratin, nitric oxide and pre and after workout powders lined the kitchen shelves in their small flat, all that muscle growth energy and fat burning fuel. With religious devotion Damian prepared morning cocktails and carried them in plastic bottles to drink throughout the day, his sports bag bulged with performance jars, packets of amino acid capsules and collagen boosters. When Damian was not around with his supplies, Igor lacked the energy to continue his brother's mission.

They were alone in the sauna, the way they liked it. It was the time of the day when the gym was the quietest with only a few other people exercising. Hardly anybody had the time to use sauna after practice, most people had to rush back to work, but not the Kulesza brothers. Today was their day off.

Damian poured more water on the hot stones which gave off a hissing sound, and thick clouds of vapour and steam rose towards the wooden ceiling.

'They've been writing about that girl,' he said, wiping his face and bold head, 'in the papers. About her family, school. What a kind, loving and talented little angel she was.'

Igor snorted. 'Little angel.'

'That's what they called her.'

Igor rested his head against the boards and closed his eyes. 'She deserved what she got. She was fat and ugly.'

Damian ignored Igor's comment. There was no point having this conversation again, some things were best left alone. Igor's strength and lack of empathy sometimes frightened Damian, yet, at the same time, he still thought of himself as the only person who could control Igor's temper. For how long, though? He knew it was not Igor's fault – he was born that way, Damian kept re-minding himself – but there were moments when Igor's actions overwhelmed him, his sense of comprehension, numbed by the scale of Igor's untamed violence. The thing that Damian feared the most was that, one day, he would be unable to hold his brother back. After the incident with the girl, for the first time in a long time, Damian feared this one thought that kept niggling in his mind: wouldn't it be better to find an ultimate solution before Igor caused more damage? A sick mind required unequivocal love and forgiveness, but also mercy. How much love was left, Damian wondered, how much more could he forgive? He knew he had to stop thinking that way, he had to. If he sacrificed his own brother it would be cruel, merciful perhaps, but cruel. Igor's behaviour was becoming a danger, slow and simmering, years in the making, one that Damian was forced to reconsider every time he did something which Damian had to take care of. Damian was suffocating in his thoughts, caught in the web of Igor's actions.

'Hot. Let's take a break,' said Damian.

Sweat was pouring down the sides of Damian's face, the heat inside was getting to the point of being unbearable. Breathing felt like swallowing burning coals.

They stood in silence outside the entrance to the sauna, leaning against the wall. Some gym staff passed along the corridor and said hello. The Kulesza brothers nodded.

Back inside, after they had cooled down enough to return to the sauna room, Damian said, 'I've spoken to Karol.'

'You didn't tell him, did you?' Igor asked, in a low, urgent voice.

'Don't be stupid. He's got something else going on. And he employed a new guy.'

There was something furtive about the way Karol described the new business, giving very little details, almost no names except Krystian's, whom Damian had met only once and had not liked. The many jokes Krystian told during their meeting annoyed Damian and more than once during the time they spent together he had wanted to punch him and wipe that stupid grin from his ugly face.

'I don't think he trusts Mateusz,' Damian continued, 'Between you and me, I'm surprised that Karol put him in charge of the new operation. Karol doesn't even know him, sneaky bastard in some fucking fancy outfit.' Damian laughed. 'Looks like a clown to me.'

'Sounds like weak-arse thinking,' Igor commented.

'Karol has a mind of his own,' Damian said thoughtfully. The memory of that evening after Karol told him about the baby, leaped into Damian's mind. He chose to keep it from Igor, who would not understand.

'It will bite Karol on the arse … Are we going to get rid of the new guy?' Igor asked, hopefully. 'To show him who's in charge?'

'We can't tentatively beat him up. Karol only wants us to keep an eye on him and his family. He's got two kids. Solid guy, you know, wife and children. The way I see it, he has too much to lose to fuck around and mess with Karol.' Damian wished he had that kind of commitment, and Milena's face flashed before his eyes.

'Or us,' Igor added.

'Or us.'

'What's Karol's deal then?'

'Not sure yet. Getting paranoid, I suspect. There's plenty to do here, so I'm not rushing to drive to Liverpool. Let the new guy sweat a bit. And when the right time comes, then we will see.'

They sat for a few minutes in silence, deep in their own thoughts. Igor tried to figure out which photo would be the best to upload to his profile and whether he should send a message to one of the women, the younger looking ones; Damian continuously worried about Igor's return to London. It had been over a month since Damian lost control over Igor, with devastating consequences. The outraged press articles, which had followed the discovery of the girl's body called for swift action and convinced Damian that his decision to get Igor across the border back to Poland a day after the accident had saved Igor's life. Igor needed to wait, in the safety of his home country, until the incident had become one of many unsolved cases without any suspects or leads.

'I'm glad you are here. It's easier to do the job with you here,' Damian said, finally. 'Best if you lie low for a while, though.' Damian wanted to make sure it was safe for Igor to walk the streets. He was confident, almost certain, nobody had seen Igor's face, the police had no witnesses, and the girl was dead. Igor's only responsibility was to keep quiet about that night. It was not going to be a memory he could ever boast about. But Damian could never be entirely sure the police would not hunt Igor down, in the distant future. Eventually, they would be forced to leave this place. It would never be safe here with Igor's freedom perpetually overshadowed by his past.

24

It was Saturday morning, early. Angelika stood behind Kamil in the bathroom facing the mirror. She had her arms wrapped around his small body and her head gently perched on his shoulder. As she smiled, dimples formed in her cheeks. They were singing a hymn together which Kamil had been selected by Sister Celestyna to perform in front of the congregation.

'A huge honour, a really huge honour,' Angelika told Mateusz after she found out and she had at once began practicing, every day, with Kamil.

Kamil, without blinking, his lips pale and dry, followed Angelika's voice. His arms were rigid against his body, his palms perfectly flat on his thighs. Mateusz felt sorry for this little boy who seemed so determined to please his mother. He wanted Kamil to remember this day as a happy event, special of course, because of its significance, but without the stifling anxiety evident in his son's immobile body.

'Hey, champ,' Mateusz called out when they finished singing, 'that was amazing. You could go on "Britain's Got Talent" with your voice.' He ruffled Kamil's hair and drew him closer in a hug.

'Look what you've done to his hair,' said Angelika. 'Now I have to comb it again.'

Mateusz gave his son a loud kiss on his cheek. 'Now, I better leave you guys, because Mum is already going a bit crazy,' he said, with an amused little smile and a wink, which made Kamil laugh and relax a bit.

'Why aren't you wearing your suit? We're leaving in fifteen minutes,' Angelika asked, alarmed.

'I'd better get dressed then.'

'Hurry up,' she called after him and turned to Kamil to adjust his black tie.

Parents and children were gathered outside the Our Virgin Lady of the Immaculate Heart Catholic Church. The girls were wearing white dresses, some had elaborate hair styles with tiny white flowers or butterfly hairpins holding the hair, others had their heads adorned with pearls and swirled flowers headpieces. All the boys were dressed in similar outfits: black trousers and white, long-sleeve shirts with narrow black ties, in line with Sister Celestyna's guidelines.

'Perfect, it's all going to be perfect,' Sister Celestyna repeated, breathlessly. She was in such a state of excitement that she hardly noticed Father Niewiadomski clearing his throat behind them, trying to get through, until he lost patience and pulled on her sleeve. Sister Celestyna's cheeks turned red hot. In her haste to make way for Father Niewiadomski, she took a few steps backwards, reached the edge of the steps and nearly fell, waving both arms in the air in a desperate attempt to keep her balance. Luckily, one of the parents, who was standing nearby, sprang to grab Sister Celestyna, save her from falling and set her neatly back on the step next to Father Niewiadomski, who had been watching her, unamused. He whispered into the nun's ear to gather her wits and to not embarrass him even further in front of everyone.

Father Niewiadomski gave the microphone a few taps with his index finger to check that it was working. He moved his lips closer to it but a young freckled man with long hair tied into a ponytail at the nape of his neck, the audio-visual technician in charge of filming and the sound system, gently pulled the microphone away from Father Niewiadomski's face. 'Not so close,' he advised in a whisper, and the priest nodded.

'My dearest children,' the priest began his sermon and proceeded to explain the significance of this day. He sometimes rose on tiptoes, to emphasise a particular point.

Mateusz kept glancing at his wrist watch. His other hand was hidden in his pocket, holding onto his mobile phone – set to vibrate in case Karol decided to check up on him – to remind him about today's pick up from Gatwick Airport. He was trying to calculate in his mind whether he was going to make it on time with all the traffic. He had already realised he would have to leave soon, if he was going to get to the airport as planned.

'What's going on?' Angelika whispered into his ear. 'You've been checking your watch every five minutes. You're going to miss the whole thing.'

Mateusz, with a ready smile, mumbled an apology and tried to concentrate on Father Niewiadomski's words. He wished the priest would hurry up but Father Niewiadomski, now swaying back and forth on his feet, was talking very slowly, deliberately savouring his words, Mateusz thought, like somebody in love with his own voice.

Mateusz felt his mobile phone vibrating. Discreetly, he took it out of his pocket to see who the caller was. Karol. Thankfully, Angelika did not notice that his attention was elsewhere. He should not have been worried; he should have told Karol the truth – that his son's First Communion was more important than picking somebody up from the airport, and if this was his wife's friend then Karol himself should take care of it. But Mateusz was too anxious, afraid of losing his job. And now he faced an impossible situation because he had not confronted it when he was supposed to; he had not been insistent with Karol when he should have been, the way Angelika would have wanted.

'Are you coming?' he heard Angelika's voice.

The children now slowly made their way into the church.

'I have to make an urgent phone call,' he said. 'I'll be there in a moment. I promise.'

'Can't it wait?' Angelika asked, her eyes wide in surprise.

'It's Karol. I have to take it. I'm so sorry.'

She bit her lip and followed other parents.

'Is Dad not coming with us?' Karolina asked surprised, turning her head to see where Mateusz was going.

'He's coming,' said Angelika flatly.

Karol and two girls stepped towards the altar and knelt down before they all walked closer and stopped on the left. Angelika, with two other mothers, followed. This was the moment Mateusz was supposed to film with his camera, the moment when Karol was going to sing. Angelika prayed that Mateusz was going to show up in a moment but he was nowhere to be seen. Luckily, Karolina had her mobile phone ready to record her brother's performance.

And Kamil's voice was flawless, strong, without hesitation. He remembered the words perfectly. Angelika was so proud, so elated. Listening to Karol, she was surprised by this rush of emotion, which she had not expected.

'Perfect, simply perfect,' Sister Celestyna whispered to herself, breathing heavily, with her hands on her flushed cheeks, an overpowering warmth spreading through her body. Later, she would tell everybody that she could distinctively feel the presence of the Holy Spirit while the children were singing.

After Angelika got back to her seat, she kept turning, nervously, to see if Mateusz was coming through the crowd. Finally, after the longest ten minutes she could remember, he sat down next to her.

'Where were you?' she said, barely managing to hide the annoyance in her voice. 'You missed Kamil singing.'

'Don't worry, Dad,' Karolina said in a loud whisper, smiling. 'I've got it all recorded.' Karolina tried to rescue him but soon fell silent under her mother's stern gaze. Karolina felt sorry for him, that he had chosen somebody like her mother. Karolina did not know yet what she wanted exactly in life but it was not the kind of relationship which her parents had.

'I can't stay,' Mateusz said to Angelika.

'What?'

'I have to go to work.'

'I thought you sorted it out.'

Somebody behind made a sharp, exasperated sound.

'It's an emergency.'

'This,' Angelika indicated with her chin, 'is more important.'

'Please, be quiet,' said a person behind them.

'I'll be back as soon as I can,' he said and got up to leave.

When he arrived at the airport he was late. He had got lost trying to locate the parking lot and he worried that he was not going to find her. The plane had landed over an hour before. But she was there, standing by the newsagent, looking terrified, almost on the verge of tears. She was biting her nails, nervously. At her feet lay a bulky rucksack, the kind he remembered that young people back home in Poland used for climbing mountains. There was another bag on her left shoulder.

'Hello, I'm Mateusz. You must be Kasia. I'm so sorry I'm late. I was stuck in traffic. Can I help you with your luggage?'

At first, she refused to follow him, said she was expecting to be picked up by a woman, giving Milena's name. Eventually, after some convincing, she followed Mateusz to the car. On the way, he offered to buy her a coffee because it could take them over an hour, if not longer, to reach the place where she was staying. After a while she eased into a conversation with him. That was when she mentioned the marriage, nothing specific, but enough for Mateusz to wonder what the precise reason was for her coming to London. The question about the marriage made him suspicious and unsettled him. He only began to think about it afterwards, little by little, thoughts ballooning inside him, stirring his suspicions.

He decided to take a longer route, via the centre of the city, because he felt so bad that she had had to wait for him over an hour. The least he could do was show her around. She pointed at various landmarks – bridges, unusually shaped buildings and iconic cathedrals – and Mateusz, where possible, stopped for a few minutes so she could snap the first photos. After they arrived at the house in Greenford Gardens, an old woman opened the front door. 'Leave the bags in the corridor,' the old woman instructed but she did not invite him in. He did not mind because he was in a hurry. He wanted to go back to the church as soon as possible. He quickly said his goodbyes. Kasia was relieved to find that the woman spoke Polish, and so was Mateusz because he felt, somehow, responsible for this girl. He could hear the old woman saying something sharply to Kasia, after she closed the door behind him, but then the voices were gone as they disappeared inside the house.

On the way back, he got a text message from Karol: *Come to my house. We need to talk.* He did not want to go. He desperately wanted to get back to Angelika and the children and, for a while, he toyed with the idea of ignoring Karol's request. But he standing position. As he did so, a layer of fat on his stomach wobbled under his t-shirt. He walked to the kitchen counter, to the coffee machine. 'You need to do exactly as I tell you. When I tell you. You work for me. And another thing, I heard you were late. Over an hour late.'

'There was traffic. I'm sorry.'

'I pay you to be on time.' Karol said as he turned his head towards Mateusz.

'She mentioned something about a marriage.' Mateusz was curious to find out Karol's reaction and to divert the conversation from himself.

'What marriage?' Karol got back to his seat, carrying a large white mug with the Starbucks logo on it. He owned a significant collection of Starbucks mugs, stored in the kitchen cupboard. Just when he was about to sit down, with his buttocks suspended over the sofa, he asked, 'You want some coffee?'

'No, thank you. I should be going home, really. The girl I picked up, she was talking about an arranged marriage. I thought it was strange.'

'She's Milena's friend,' Karol lied. 'I don't know anything about it. I don't even know this girl.'

'So you know nothing about it?'

'I just told you.' Karol sipped some coffee. It was hot and the liquid burnt his lips. 'Next week I need you to pick up a package from Krystian. You are going to call me when you get it and drive straight back to my house. You understand?'

Mateusz nodded.

'How's your wife? And kids?' Karol stood up again and went to table where his laptop had announced the arrival of a new email with a loud ping.

Mateusz tensed. He was not sure where Karol was going with this sudden change of topic.

'Karol had his First Communion.'

Bending over the screen to check the incoming messages, Karol mumbled, distracted, 'Oh, yeah? How did it go?'

'It was today.'

'Really? But you know,' Karol said, his eyebrows coming closely together when he frowned, 'I told you when you started that this job always comes first. You got the salary in the end as well, didn't you?' And he shot Mateusz that self-satisfied glance, the kind that meant he was right.

Mateusz should have asked Karol, then, about the payslip, now seemed like the perfect opportunity. He almost asked the question, on the way out, fumbling with the car keys in his pocket, trying to gather the courage to just ask, but then he remembered that he had promised himself that he would wait a few more days. It would have been an unnecessary argument if the payslip was going to be delivered on Monday anyway. And Karol seemed hurried, running back and forth between the sofa and the table with his laptop. Towards the end of the conversation he was preoccupied with the emails and text messages only occasionally glancing at Mateusz. Mateusz would almost have felt guilty at taking up Karol's time with this delayed visit to his house, if it had not been for the fact that it was Karol who had requested his presence, and who was relieved when he, Mateusz, finally left.

No post was delivered on Monday or Tuesday. Finally, on Wednesday, new bills arrived, some junk mail along with a local newspaper but no payslip. Mateusz said nothing to Angelika. She was still upset about his disappearance on Saturday and seemed to be avoiding him during the day, busying herself with cleaning, washing the dishes, ironing piles of clothes or cooking and baking. She was already asleep when he went to bed late at night. He let her sulk as long as she needed, it was his fault after all, and patiently waited for her to forgive him. He watched the video Karolina had recorded and congratulated his son on his performance. 'I'm so proud of you,' he said to Kamil, 'So proud,' but when Kamil asked him, in his small voice, why he had not been there, Mateusz's heart almost broke. 'I'm sorry, son, I had to go to work. I'll make up for it, I promise. Would you like to go the Aquarium next Saturday? Just you and me. And we can go to the cinema afterwards. Would you like that?'

Later, Mateusz went into the garden to call the Tax Office. Glancing over his shoulder to make sure he was alone, he dialled the Helpline number. In his other hand he had all the paperwork, his National Insurance number, previous tax statements. He answered all the questions the person at the other end asked, in a friendly voice, which should have instantly put him at ease; but he was nervous and his voice trembled. His heart sank when he heard the woman say: 'I'm very sorry but there's no record of you working for this company. However, it is still early and the employer has time to submit all the documentation. You should have received your payslip where the individual deductions are listed.' He explained that he had not received the payslip, which was the reason why he was calling.

'Mateusz, what are you doing out there?' he heard Angelika behind him and jumped, startled, his heart pounding.

'Can I call you back? I'm sorry I can't talk right now. Good bye,' he said quickly and hung up. He folded the papers he was holding. 'I'm coming,' he called out to her.

The scarf wrapped around her neck was flapping in the wind and she held on to it with one hand, with the other, she caught her hair close to her neck. 'What are you doing out there? Who are you talking to?'

'Something's wrong with the computer. I was talking to the engineer to come and have a look at it,' he lied.

She hesitated, and said, in a throaty whisper, 'I'm sorry I was upset with you. I know we need the money and you're doing the best you can. I shouldn't have been angry with you. Forgive me.'

Angelika's face softened, her eyes glazed with tears. Mateusz immediately felt ashamed of hiding the truth from her, to be the reason this beautiful and loving woman apologised to him while it was him, really, who was to blame. That terrible feeling he had when he hid something from her crushed his chest and he held her in his arms so that she would not see his guilty expression, hiding his face in her flowing hair, so tight. 'I can't breathe,' she whispered with a giggle, and Mateusz released her from his embrace. It was what he loved about her the most – her ability to forgive, to take the blame for something she did not fully comprehend and was not her doing – but if it restored harmony between them, she would be the first one to come forward. But even now, at this very moment, he could not bring himself to tell her the truth about his suspicions, because if he was correct, it would be better if she did not know, no matter how much it terrified him. He smoothed the hair around her cheeks and held her face in his hands. He kissed her on the lips, and put his arm around her shoulder as they walked back indoors.

25

Milena returned from Egypt with a glowing tan. The ends of her hair had acquired a lighter, scintillating shade, brightened by the overwhelming sunshine. She was thinner than Karol remembered, when she had left for the beauty retreat two weeks ago, and more serene, but she seemed oddly distracted with her own thoughts whenever Karol talked to her. Like when he asked her about the trip and whether she had had a good rest, she only replied 'Fine', but refused to elaborate. She told him she had only taken a handful of photos because her days were full of treatments and relaxation; the ones she showed to him were of the pyramids, mosques and sand.

She did not go back to work straight away. Instead she stayed at home, lying on the sofa under a throw in the living room, women's magazines from Poland (*Elle*, *Gala*, *Grazia*, *Viva!*) and cookbooks stacked on the floor: Jamie Oliver, Yotam Ottolenghi and Nigella Lawson. On the coffee table was a pile of letters from three different banks, insurance and private pension companies, and the energy provider, waiting to be opened. She left them for Karol to deal with. Every day she watched cookery programmes on television or on YouTube, and made notes of the recipes in a small red notebook. When she was not around, Karol had a peek through the pages, hoping to find some answers, but the hand-written passages just listed various herbs and spices the names of which he did not recognise, or else detailed boiling and steaming processes of various food stuffs. There were glossy cut-out pictures, too, of food arrangements on plates, which he later recognised from the dishes she served during meals they had together; the same, meticulous structures on the plates – stone bass and pastille, scented with Arabian spices, fennel, white rice and meat jus; squid with sweet potato and lemon salsa; roast venison with chocolate sauce and glazed chestnuts. Karol had expected less elaborate meals. He had got used to steamed fish with a simple salad, the kind of food Milena would prepare for him to help him with his weight loss, and every now and then traditional Polish dishes. Now, he almost dreaded sitting down to such meals. He hoped Milena's newly developed obsession with fine cooking would be a short-term phase soon to be forgotten.

'When are you going back to work?' he asked her one evening, pushing the food around his plate with a fork. He felt guilty about wrecking the meticulous presentation of the dish.

Milena chewed slowly and sipped some red wine before she replied, 'I don't know yet.'

'But you are going back, aren't you?' Karol said, trying not to sound alarmed.

'Yes, of course,' she replied without conviction, 'I'm working.' She meant checking work emails on her laptop and receiving phone calls. She sometimes let the phone ring without answering, Karol shouting from the other room to answer the damned phone because he could not concentrate.

'Good. That's good because I've been worrying.'

'You shouldn't.'

'You haven't been yourself since you got back,' he said. 'I really don't like it. I don't know if this is one of your mood swings or something else. Or if this is about the baby again.'

She placed the knife and fork at the edge of her plate and carefully wiped her mouth with a napkin. She just looked at him, with that glassy smile, without saying anything for a long, still moment, which she knew would annoy him.

'I don't know what to make of all this.' He pointed at the food in front of him. 'Are you angry with me? I've been quite patient, letting you have your way, but what about me?'

Milena stared at him calmly, without the fear she had at times experienced, without the trepidation that something about her presence might cause his violent reaction, but with curiosity. She was giving him the silent treatment she had read about somewhere, she did not remember where, a technique she had employed since she had lost the baby. A technique which unnerved him, she observed, more than trying to shout over the arguments he usually threw at her.

She picked up the half-full bowls and carried them to the sink. Karol dropped the cutlery, which made a loud clink as it hit his plate, tiny grains of red rice bounced up and landed on the table.

'Are you ever going to talk to me?' He shifted in his seat and turned back to her. 'You've been acting strangely, do you realise that? You and your silences.' His mouth twitched and he fidgeted nervously in his chair, tapping his right foot on the floor, rubbing his hands against his thighs. 'Talk to me. Or don't. I don't know how I am supposed to talk to you anymore.'

As she stood, silently, in her brilliant coldness, continuing to ignore Karol's exasperated pleas, a thought flickered through her mind, of the day she had made the decision to leave him.

Milena remembered the overwhelming, crushing feeling of despair in her heart. In Cairo, she and Ines had gone to a mosque – the great mosque of Muhammad Ali Pasha. (Ines had fought with a headscarf which fluttered in the dry wind and the flame from her lighter that the gusts of wind kept blowing out , cursing at the dirt and sand blowing into her nostrils and eyes). Inside, Milena had taken off her shoes and held them in one hand close to her chest.

She had walked in awe under hundreds of globe lamps hanging in a magnificent circular constellation. She thought of a snail's shell when she looked up to admire the light trapped in the bulky glass jars. A group of girls surrounded Ines, students on a trip to the capital, and their female teacher asked in slow English if the girls could have a photo taken with them, 'They have never seen a Western woman,' the teacher added apologetically. Milena walked outside while Ines, gladly, posed for the photographs. More girls arrived, swarming around them with questions: 'Do you speak English?', 'Are you a Muslim?', 'Where are you from?', 'How old are you?'

Outside, Milena had stopped in front of the wall that surrounded the extensive grounds of the mosque and some other buildings on the hill. She admired the vastness of the city under a veil of smoke and pollution. There were no sounds, only children's laughter, no random men relentlessly interrogating her about her marital status or how many children she had. Which was a relief after days of unyielding pursuit, even covering her hair and half of her face did not provide enough protection. Milena and Ines had quickly learned to lie about their lives, husbands, brothers and children; the stories of their fake families expanded every time they were held up on a street or in a shop. The women felt as if they inhabited a contemporary version of Scheherazade: Egyptian men only left them in peace if they were utterly satisfied with their stories.

There was an incident, one of many which Milena and Ines had experienced, outside the entrance to the mosque after they finished their tour. A bearded man had pushed a child into Ines's arms, a boy aged just over a year, and had insisted on taking a photograph because it was going to bring luck to the boy to have a picture with a fair-haired woman. The father snapped a few photos with Ines holding the child, her hair uncovered, then he said something quickly in Arabic to his wife, in a powerful voice, and waved his hand at Milena and Ines to make a space so that his wife could stand between them. He now wanted his wife to have a photo with them as well. Milena and Ines grinned, amused by the frenzy their appearance had caused among the locals, but the mother had a solemn expression, accentuated by the charcoal around her eyes, giving her a sad and tired look.

It was there, under the mosque's mesmerising influence, among women clad in black abayas flowing in the air, with no men in sight that it had occurred to Milena that she could live like that, without anybody, only with herself. Or, at least, with somebody who would love her for who she really was, without trying to change her.

She thought of the poems Damian had given to her, at the airport a few hours before she had boarded the plane. Karol had no time to drop her off so he instructed Damian to act as a driver instead. Nervous, sweaty-palmed, so unlike his usual confident self. Damian had wished her a good journey, and taken out a crumpled envelope from his back pocket, 'For you. I wrote them for you,' he had said.

Ines had just returned from a newsagent, carrying a bunch of cooking and fashion magazines and sandwiches, and found them staring at each other, with the envelope in their hands.

'What's this?' she had asked curiously. 'A love letter?' she joked, tugging Milena's elbow.

'Nothing. It's nothing,' Milena had said quickly. She had hidden the envelope in her handbag. 'It's some cash from Karol, pocket money.'

On the plane Milena had pretended she was asleep. She did not want to answer Ines's questions about Karol or Damian. It was best if Ines forgot what she witnessed at the airport, and she did, as soon as Milena asked her what she was planning to buy in Egypt. Lulled by her friend's voice, Milena drifted off. She wanted to think about Damian, dip into her memories of every moment they had together and try to understand what it all meant, but it was Karol's bloated face which she kept seeing. Ines was still talking when Milena opened her eyes and called the flight attendant to bring her some alcohol, so she could banish those images from her mind.

In Egypt, Milena had immersed herself in its exotic and unfamiliar culture. She would sit in the hotel lobby, watching strangers who approached the reception desk, some wearing the most peculiar garments she had seen. She had tried to picture their daily existence and wondered what it would be like to live their lives. She had imagined never returning to London. In Egypt, her whole English existence, her past in Poland, had been close to being discarded, like a dream or a story from another time she had lived all these years. It was so easy to forget who she was somewhere else. But she was conditioned to remain true to herself, she did not even realise or fully comprehend to what extent. She may have lived uprooted for over a decade, breathing foreign air, but in a self-made cocoon of familiarities she had consciously built around herself, to keep her core intact. If she imagined a different reality for herself it was only momentary, motivated by the circumstances, her identity had been forged before she was even born. In her adult life she was able to negotiate between expectations and reality, and she longed for that feeling of being whole again.

She had decided, then, in a surge of melancholy, that she was going to let go of Karol, let him live his life the way he always wanted.

Milena leaned against the sink and folded her arms on her chest. 'I'm leaving,' she said, finally.

'Leaving where?' Karol did not understand.

'I'm leaving you.'

'Now, wait a moment.' He sprang up from his seat. He placed his hand on her arm but she removed it and treated him with an indifferent look. There was nothing in her eyes, no warmth or trust, only love long gone. 'We can fix it. Just tell me what to do. You want more money? I'm not spending enough time with you?' he was saying, agitated and blinking, trying to understand her announcement.

'I can't do this anymore,' she said, defeated, with a shudder of nausea. She was going to give him the best reason he could understand. It did not matter to her anymore what it was. 'I feel like I'm always waiting. I don't even know if I want to talk about it anymore.'

'We have a life together. You don't throw it away like it means nothing, all these years,' he said, raising his voice, because Milena opened her mouth, as if she was about to interrupt him. But she did not want to explain herself anymore, and she, too, felt that it was not about apologies. She wanted to curtail this conversation. But with Karol there was no way of stopping him. A flood of arguments and heavy attempts to sway her would swell into a torrent of sentences that would push any response back into her mouth, it was a technique he used that she was all too familiar with, and so she let him carry on. Silence, she had found out, was the only tactic that allowed her to deal with his verbal onslaught. She still heard the words but her mind was elsewhere. Eventually, he would tire of his own voice and stop; that much was certain. 'How do you even imagine yourself leaving behind what we have built? I will never let you go. Do you hear me? Never!'

Throughout his monologue she kept standing. If she sat down it would further invite him to persuade her to change her mind and she was very close, so close in fact, for the sake of peace, to letting him do it. Perhaps she had been too quick in speaking her mind, perhaps she should have waited a bit longer, planned her exit more carefully. She still had the remnants of feelings for Karol. Despite the decision she had made, it was not so easy, now, to go through with it. Leaving would break their lives in half, confuse their friends and family back home, the Sisyphean work of untangling everything that made them a whole would become eventually unbearable and too exhausting. Yet, it was not something that could not be undone. She was relieved now that they had never actually got married. He had kept introducing her as his wife, and she had allowed him, the definition had grown on her. They were roles they enjoyed performing, and they had kept it going with whoever entered their lives. They did not even think about correcting others, or each other, it was an almost automatic response whenever they were introduced together. From the beginning, since they had arrived here, it had suited them. It would be unthinkable to carry on this game back home, where everybody knew them; entangled in a thick web of relatives and friends, and there would simply be no need to do so. With time, Milena had started to appreciate their joint act of deception as a form of distraction, especially after Karol had begun to change and was not himself anymore, at least not the person she had fallen in love with.

'What about therapy?' asked Milena, sitting down. If there was the slightest chance for their relationship, she was curious to see how far Karol was willing to go. But she was also offering him a way to salvage his compulsion for control, out of pity, she wanted to find a way to disengage herself from their daily lives.

Karol followed and pulled another chair to sit close to her. She let him cup her cold hands in his.

'Couples' therapy?' Karol hesitated. 'If that's going to make you feel better?'

She shook her head. 'I want you to talk to a therapist so you can sort out your problem … of sleeping with other women.'

Weariness came into his voice. 'And here it is again.'

'You want me to stay with you? I need to be certain that you are taking this relationship seriously, that you really care about us.

She nudged her head slightly in his direction, waiting, prompting him to make a promise.

'Okay, I will do it!'

'I'll stay with Ines, for a few weeks, maybe a month,' she carried on despite Karol already opening his mouth to contradict her. She would not let him. Now that she had his attention, it was her turn to talk. 'So that you and I can have some space, rethink what we feel. And when you are ready, when you and I are ready, then we will talk again.' And then, on impulse, she leaned forward and kissed him fleetingly on the lips, as a token of good will. And to disperse any doubt on his part, in case he wondered if she meant what she said.

Days later, in a therapist's room (it was their first appointment – and the last one Karol would decide once it was finished) he told the woman sitting across from him and discreetly taking notes that he was only doing this because his wife had insisted, but it probably had something to do with her own insecurities. He, on the other hand, despite his high-pressured job was able to focus on the important issues in their relationship. So he had come, as instructed, to satisfy her. To Karol, this conversation, or rather an inquiry into his state of emotions, seemed exhaustingly annoying. He could not escape the feeling that it was a kind of job he could easily do himself, if he put his mind to it. After all, he could say a word or two about the way he coerced people to work for him. If this was not sufficient proof of his thorough understanding of human psychology – that it was better than anyone else's, better than a therapist in the cushioned environment of her office – then there was nothing left to prove. But he had been distracted lately, he admitted it.

'Perhaps it has something to do with her losing the baby. The grief, I guess. I told her that if she wants another baby we can try but she went for holidays. I don't even know exactly where. It was her decision so I let her do it. Frankly, I don't know what she was thinking,' he said calmly, without looking at Milena, 'but then she comes back and says she wants to leave. Can you see what she's do-ing? Like it's my fault that I am here. She asked me for my opinion. But I put up with it because I'm supposed to love her. That's what people do in a relationship, right? They love each other.' He made small frantic hand gestures, his fingers spread wide, directed at the therapist, ferociously focused on delivering the lines expected from him.

'It's not about the baby. That's not what we talked about at home.' Milena flinched at the impact of his confession, eyes burning.

'Let's focus a little bit more on Karol's feelings first,' said the therapist.

The therapist handed a box of tissues to Milena and smiled encouragingly, raising her eyebrows, which formed a thin line above the rim of her glasses. Karol noticed that without the glasses she could be fairly attractive. In different circumstances, he would have offered to buy her a drink and let nature takes its course. Oh, he could definitely welcome more sex since Milena stubbornly withheld it from him. For a man like him with energy raging through his body, sex was like eating, a necessary function. He did not ponder the deeper meaning of physical attraction.

'The way I see it she needs therapy, to deal with whatever she needs to deal with. What do you think?' He reached out to the therapist with his probing question, but it was pointless because the woman only said, 'Why do you think that is? Perhaps there's a reason Milena wanted to try couples' therapy first.'

'I know I don't feel the same way she does. I told her when we met that it was going to be difficult because I have this emptiness inside me. But she did not believe me when I said that. I told her, you do this, you will be sorry, if I can't feel the same way you do.'

Milena tried, unsuccessfully, to catch the therapist's eye. This was not how she remembered his words. Had he really said that to her? But the longer he talked now, the less convinced she was; her memories became more unfocused. She buckled to his tone of authority, his self-assurance maddened her.

'Tell me about your work. How do you think it affects you and your relationship with Milena?'

Milena's decision threw Karol into a perilous place, one more wearying development which jeopardised how he was going to run things, if she truly decided to leave him. He did not think she actually had it in her. What he did not enjoy was that he was now forced to think about this situation, almost continuously, which was becoming exhausting, instead of focusing on sorting out the immediate issues: supplying Krystian with a steady number of new workers or sending the Kulesza brothers to Poland to pick up the men for the jobs he had begun to advertise again in the local papers. And then there were the marriages, something he had only recently got himself involved in. But like any other enterprise he had envisaged, he had to approach it from every angle, predict not just its future success, but also the possibility of failure, though he was not a man to allow this to happen. His calculations were meticulous and thorough. A few years ago an arranged marriage with a Pole was worth £10,000; now, the price oscillated between £5,000 or £6,000. A Romanian national would happily do it for half the price, driving the Polish candidates out of business, and taking away earnings from Karol's pocket. His thoughts fluttered in a permanent cycle of scenarios, long-term designs, constructing the frameworks for the future projects but ignoring the risks. Then there was the issue of manpower. He had spent hours considering the best way to handle the Kulesza brothers, and now his mind was more often occupied with the new people he entered into business with. Like Mateusz, for example, useful and loyal (two qualities Karol appreciated the most) but he also considered Mateusz feebleminded, easy to convince. And what about Mateusz's suspicions about his salary and requests for holidays, when there was so much work to do? His attitude would have to change. Karol could not possibly allow any indifference to his authority. These thoughts fuelled such urgency in Karol's mind, to act at once because there was no time to waste, and that was the moment when he realised that nothing or nobody else mattered but what he wanted. From now on his needs were the priority. Didn't they see how hard he was working, how much he had sac-

and dialled the voicemail. 'Hi, it's me,' he heard Milena's voice, 'just letting you know everything is okay. Talk to you soon.' They communicated now through voice messages, since Milena refused to answer his calls after she had moved out to live with Ines. She called from private numbers, knowing Karol rejected any unidentified calls on principle, so she could always leave a voice message instead of talking to him.

She had moved out shortly after their first session with the therapist. Only for a short while he wondered what made her so upset, and later, he fell into the whirlwind of his daily routine and he stopped trying to analyse her behaviour.

He refused to call or send any text messages or even visit Ines Hair and Beauty Salon. He could have easily stopped by when he drove past three days ago and surely they must have spotted his car so she would have known he was there. But if she wanted silence from him so that she could think over whatever she needed to think over without him, then he was going to deliver. Despite how much he hurt (not once had she asked him how he felt about this stupid arrangement) his life had to go on. He needed to keep his life on track and he could not afford any further interruptions. Always moving forward. Always keeping an eye on the next thing. He was fond of her, almost loved her, yes, that would be the apt description of the feelings he had for her, which he was now slowly beginning to understand now that she was gone – was it some strange after-effect of the therapy? But he had to focus on the daily routine. He had made up his mind. He was sure they would come to an agreement. A weariness he did not have time for settled in the more he thought about the situation.

The lights had changed and somebody behind him angrily blasted their horn. He looked in the rear-view mirror as he pressed

26

They had hands like leather, swollen with fractured nails and grimed with dirt, the coarse skin broken in places, raw with pain; painfully damaged by the mixture of biting seawater, gale and sharp shells. There was no place to hide from the thrashing wind. At night, the men were driven in a truck (scratched body work with muddied sides), to the nearby bay, later, on quad bikes. They spent hours and hours that seemed like forever, bent over the sand, picking shellfish ('Pain like a motherfucker,' one of them said to Mateusz) and the worst thing was that they knew they had to do it day after day. Others had more luck, transported in a minibus to the food processing factory where they worked cutting chicken and turkey thighs, or as packers; their hands grey and blue after ten-hour days of working in refrigeration containers.

Cigarettes trembled between their fingers and no amount of alcohol could kill the cruel coldness that settled deep inside their bones and muscles. The three men talked to Mateusz with a desperate, clutching attention, shouting over each other. One grabbed his arm and pulled himself so close that Mateusz felt the man's warm breath which smelt like seawater on his cheek, 'You tell them, you tell them,' the man's voice rasped, 'we don't want this shit job.' The man stared into Mateusz's face, looking for some flicker of understanding. Most of them did, hope surging in their eyes. Mateusz looked so out of place in his immaculate suit among them. For the first time since he had started this job, guilt burnt within him. One sat on the floor with his back to the wall and his face turned towards the window. Mateusz could swear he was sleeping with his eyes open. He smelt of raw meat, and Mateusz involuntarily kept his distance.

In the kitchen, the sink was piled with dirty dishes, and on the kitchen table stood mugs with dark brown tea rings or coffee residue underneath them, dirty and matte teaspoons inside, an open bag of white sugar, clumped, next to toppled, empty Coke bottles. The surface of the table was sticky with tea and coffee stains, a small pool of some sugary drink glistened in the middle.

They sat Mateusz down at the table, pushing away the mugs and bottles. 'Coffee? Tea?' one of the men asked.

'Tea. Thanks.'

The man opened the cupboard, grunted a swearword, then without turning around said, 'Tea's finished. Coffee?'

'Coffee is also fine. Black is good.'

'It's not that…we're not grateful,' said the tallest man slowly, halted by his stammer. He sat down opposite Mateusz and placed his large hands around the cup with cold tea. The two others gathered behind his chair and nodded as the man continued, 'but we've been working this job now…over a month. We don't go out much. The guy who comes here took us once to Aldi…'

'And Tesco,' a voice from behind offered.

'Not much sightseeing around here. But, hmm, here's the thing, we haven't got paid yet.' Only when the man scratched his stubbled cheek did Mateusz notice that there was something wrong with his two small fingers, curled in a permanent spasm. The man hid the hand on his leg under the table. 'We were supposed to get our money last week but got nothing. We used our own money that we brought here with us, but the food is expensive, and we haven't got much left. Maybe you can talk to the boss at the agency and ask him when we will get paid?'

'You haven't asked them?' questioned Mateusz.

'We don't want to lose our jobs,' said the man with injured fingers. 'And you, you work for the agency, and you've been always nice to us. You could talk to somebody back there.'

'That young fellow with a funny eye took our passports,' the third man added with a hiss. He was missing one front tooth.

A kind of silent alertness came over Mateusz on hearing the man's words, so that his first instinct was to promise them, at once, that he would talk to Krystian and Karol to find out why the money was delayed and what was really going on with their documents. Before he left the house he took some cash out of his wallet. 'You can give it back to me after you get paid,' he added, handing the money to the tall man.

Later, with Krystian, he listened patiently to a new joke, and he forced himself to laugh out of politeness. 'A blonde answers the phone. "Hello?", "Is this three, eight, one, five, four, five, four?", "No, no, yes, no, yes, no, no.",' then waited for Krystian to calm down from his laughter before he said, 'The men at the house told me they haven't got paid.'

'You should check with Karol.' Krystian stared in front of him. 'He takes care of the salaries.'

'And their passports?' Mateusz added.

'How would I know? Karol sorts the paperwork as far as I know.'

Mateusz gazed at Karol, puzzled, trying to make sense of his explanation. Karol had given him a familiar answer; one he had heard before. 'My accountant is taking care of that. And since when,' Karol's eyes narrowed in warning, 'do you think you are in charge of negotiations with the workers? You don't need to concern yourself with matters that don't involve you. This is not what I pay you to do.'

'What do you want me to tell them?' Mateusz asked, uncomfortably, imagining the men's reaction.

'Whatever you said or promised them is not my concern,' said Karol, unexpectedly fierce, glancing at the Kulesza brothers who were standing by the van smoking and pretending not to listen to this conversation. Damian had a hood on, which partially covered his damaged eyelid, while Igor, with his leg propped on the wheel of the van, kept spitting on the pavement at regular intervals.

Days later, Mateusz would ask Karol about the brothers working for him again (he definitely remembered Karol's words that he had dismissed the older brother) but Karol would only say, 'I gave him another chance.' Mateusz felt too weak and tired to challenge Karol's decision.

Back at home, nobody answered when Mateusz walked inside and called out, 'Hello? I'm home.' On the fridge door he found a hand written note, held by one of Karol's alphabet's fridge magnets: *Gone shopping. Meat dumplings in the fridge. Will pick up Kamil from school. Love, Angelika.* He peered inside; the food Angelika had prepared earlier was in a large plastic container with a blue top, but he took out a plate covered in cling film with slices of Polish ham with thin fat edges and made himself two sandwiches instead. He licked his fingers. He could still detect a whiff of Angelika's perfume and noticed a fresh bunch of bright yellow daffodils in a transparent glass vase. He did not remember seeing the flowers the day before, so she must have bought them sometime today while he was in Liverpool.

He made a strong cup of black tea with a slice of lemon and one spoonful of sugar, and carried the mug with the plate of sandwiches to the other room.

In the stillness of the empty house Mateusz heard Gary, their next door neighbour, singing through the wall. A song he recognised, yes, it was a song by Queen. Mateusz had the complete albums by the band, one of his favourite, but only listened to it on headphones as Angelika complained about the noise.

One evening, on his way out with rubbish bags, he bumped into Gary who told Mateusz how back in the day he used to work as an actor ('*Doomwatch*, you know, on BBC 1, a science fiction series, then I was in *The Hanged Man*. Have you had any of those back home in Poland?'). That was why he liked to sing so much, Gary explained. It had been part of his drama and acting training. The third time Gary sang, Mateusz heard Karolina bang against the radiator with her mobile phone in her room, shouting, 'Shut up! Shut up!' until Mateusz explained to her that it was rude to bellow like that at the neighbours.

'He's moaning, Dad. He goes on and on and on. I can't listen to it anymore.' Mateusz admitted that Gary's best singing days may have belonged to the past, and since he had never seen Gary on screen he could not tell how good he really was. He certainly did not recognise Gary's face as somebody famous, not even after Gary dropped the titles of the TV series he took part in, which to Mateusz meant nothing. But Gary was a sick man, Mateusz knew, he had been diagnosed with liver cancer ('Runs in the family.' Gary shrugged with his hands in the pockets. 'My father died from it. So did my two sisters and my mother.') So he let the man sing his heart out. That was the least he could do – Gary had, at best, a year or two of his life left.

Gary lived on his own, unless one of his male friends visited him, but Mateusz and Angelika had never seen anyone coming or going they only heard male voices, and sometimes the sound of their lovemaking. Which made Angelika rigid with unease and she would leave the room at once, uneasy that they lived in a place with such thin walls. If they could hear Gary and his male friends, surely Gary could also hear Mateusz and Angelika. They made love to each other in whispers or to Gary's loud snoring.

Shortly after they moved in, Angelika baked a poppy seed cake and suggested they should offer half to the neighbour. She asked Mateusz to accompany her, to translate what she was going to say. 'In case we need somebody to watch over our house when we go on holidays,' she argued, as to why they should make friends with Gary. It was before they learnt people here were not interested in new friendships or relations with strangers. Even the Poles, who rented rooms a few houses down the street, kept to themselves, and reluctantly joined the conversation when Angelika approached them in the local Polish grocery. 'Back home in Poland, they would never be so rude. What is it about this place that makes them so indifferent to others?' she asked. Gary was the only person who had lived on the street for the past fifteen years, the people who lived on the other side of their house rented. Mateusz and Angelika saw new faces almost every month. Gary would become the only person they could trust if they decided to go away.

Gary was surprised to see two strange people outside his front door, and for a moment he mistook them for Jehovah's witnesses, 'They come here almost every Sunday morning, you'll see for yourselves,' he said, then he thanked them for the cake and added, 'That's very kind of you, very kind, thank you once again. Are you going to stay here for long?' Mateusz added that yes, they were planning to stay here, though they did not yet have a mortgage.

Now, listening to Gary's singing, Mateusz wondered if he should knock on his door, to ask him for his advice. He was sure

Gary would offer an unbiased opinion because, unlike Borowik, despite his best intentions, Gary did not know Poles like he did. He might have known somebody Mateusz could talk to, perhaps even somebody in the police force. Gary had mentioned, once, that one of his old friends was a retired policeman.

Mateusz did not quite grasp the entire complexity of this situation he had found himself in, what it all meant or what he should do. He had come across a few heart-breaking stories about Poles in Britain: the kind that would motivate Angelika to pray, or call her friends from the church to share this burden of someone else's life. And it was, indeed, what made him type in Google search the words 'Poles, work, UK'. He scrolled through links to the articles on an array of Polish websites. Angelika would have known where and what to look for, he thought, as he opened page after page. Unlike Angelika, he had never really had the time to spend hours on the internet, reading through countless blogs, opinion pieces and websites devoted to UK-based Polish communities.

Brother and sister, Fabian K. and Lucyna K., based in Edinburgh, in cooperation with three Roma individuals in Kędzierzyn-Koźle, enticed homeless people, many with alcohol dependence and mental health problems, with a promise of work in the United Kingdom. The homeless were transferred in vans, cars and coaches to the UK where Fabian K. and Lucyna K. arranged for accommodation in rented flats. The suspects registered the individuals in Job Centres and arranged for the National Insurance numbers and bank accounts. Fabian K. and Lucyna K. then applied for a series of benefits and bank loans using the victims' details and IDs. The money was transferred to the bank accounts opened by the gang rather than the victims, many of whom were left destitute on the streets in Britain. Thanks to the UK based

Polonia Foundation, which worked together with the local authori-
ties in Poland, most of the people have now safely returned home to
Poland. The ongoing investigation is being conducted by the District
Prosecutor's Office in Kędzierzyn-Koźle.

Comments followed below the article, some people had added links to other online pieces. 'I can understand illiterate Africans who run away from domestic conflicts and end up trafficked, but I can't imagine in this age that Poles would look for a job with such people,' said one. 'Bloody Gypsies! They invaded Poland and think they rule our country. And what about the Czech Republic? The same problem!' Then there were the ones which Mateusz read with growing dread, 'The streets in Britain, especially London, are the streets of Africans and Asians. Note the disappearing white colour (you can find them washing dishes for the black owners). Modern day slavery.' Another one read: 'It's better to be homeless in London than to die slowly in Polandia. So many organisations over there will feed and dress you. In Polandia people die of cold and nobody cares. Even the weather is better in Britain.' Mateusz wondered how many of the Poles he passed on the streets har-boured similar multiple antipathies and what they really thought about living in Britain. He consoled himself that the anonymous opinions he had read were voiced in Polish on obscure websites only Poles would know how to find. Although often he woke up with the dull ache of homesickness, he reminded himself of his family – and that warm feeling of belonging blanketed his heart's hunger. He was where he was supposed to be, even if it was not his home country of which he was very proud. It pained him to read these ferocious comments but knew that they were best left where he had found them, hidden in the syntax of his mother tongue.

He loved Poland but feared that here in Britain he would be mis-understood, and remembered, for the offences of the others. If he struggled to comprehend his fellow countrymen – many times ashamed and baffled by their actions or words – what interpre-tation of the Polish nation would the outsider have? – except for a handful of exotic tales pushed around and accepted as the ulti-mate translation of his culture. Yes, the comments were best left alone, safely cocooned in their language and foreignness.

He right clicked on one of the links and a lengthy story opened in the new window. The title line read: 'My life in England'. Marian, the author, told the story of his wife, Gabriela, and their son, Mikołaj, in long incoherent paragraphs, but the words that struck Mateusz were written in Bold: House Benefit, Council Benefit, Working Tax Credit, Child Tax Credit, Child Benefit, Healthy Start Coupons, Sure Start Maternity Grant. The more he read, the less he understood. The man gave examples of Gabriela faking injuries, sexual harassment accusations in her part-time job, and – this is what left Mateusz horrified – taking the child away and disappearing from his life.

Mateusz leaned back in his chair and stared at the screen, gnaw-ing at his fingernails nervously, battling his own thoughts. Yes, he had made that phone call a few months ago, but then he had been courageous, buoyed by the feeling of the anonymity because he had not left his name or phone number. He had nothing to lose, no information that could link him to that phone call. He thought of himself as a good man, a man with a moral sense, which did not allow him to ignore somebody else's suffering. Now, he felt like a coward. The previous clarity of mind he had felt, the simplicity of what was right and wrong was no longer so straightforward, be-cause what if he was to blame as well?

27

The Kulesza brothers were at opposite ends of the city.

The ashtray in the car was overflowing with cigarette butts. Igor had forgotten to empty the container and now he kept stubbing another cigarette inside, half-smoked. He swore as the butts fell out and ash landed around the gear stick and on the car mats, on the driver and passenger sides. Rubbing the soles of his shoes on the ash only made it worse. He could almost hear Damian's unhappy voice complaining about how filthy the car was every time he drove it. Igor voicelessly mimicked Damian's words with a rigid jerk of his head. Damian sometimes complained about stiffness in his neck. Often, after a demanding gym session, he would twist and turn his head, starting by lifting his chin up and slowly pressing the vertebrae at the back of his neck until the skin rolled and he felt a crunch. Igor was re-enacting Damian's head movements, catching his expression in the rear-view mirror. He quickly got bored of this game. He belched, scratched his nose and remembered that he needed to get rid of those cigarette butts before Damian noticed them. He rolled down the window and threw a few crumpled cigarettes he had picked up from the floor onto the pavement, in a vain attempt to clean up the mess, just as a nanny was passing by. She was pushing an elaborate blue pram with twin babies. The woman in the cream trench coat said something, he bared his uneven teeth at her and the babies and rolled the window up, ignoring her reprimanding voice.

Igor had parked the car close enough so that he could observe the parents and children leaving the red brick school building. Small Polish flags on strings hung from the roof and fluttered in the wind; a teacher was tying four balloons to the hook by one of the large windows, her long striped skirt fluttering against her legs.

A few metres from the entrance to the school building parents stood guarding the tables with various produce: home-baked cupcakes which some mothers had arranged in small pyramids; hot food in flat, metal containers; sausages next to big red bottles of ketchup; cartons of apple and orange juice and towers of plastic plates, cups and paper napkins. The local Polish bakery – from where a staff member had arrived, dressed in a white outfit and a hat displaying the big, red company logo – had supplied bread and sweets: doughnuts with rose jam and cream, and coconut and poppy seed cookies. The children attacked the tables in groups, they moved with frantic speed and unfocused eyes, grabbing the sweets as they bumped into the tables and bounced back onto the playground. They left the mothers and bakery employee with the havoc of leftover food towers on the verge of toppling over. The parents tried shouting after the children to be more careful and to slow down but the children had already scattered in various directions, swallowed up by their own excitement and the commotion of the day.

The head teacher, who was standing by the front entrance, was announcing the winners of a school poetry competition. Children of various ages had participated in commemoration of 'the greatest Polish authors who wrote for children – Julian Tuwim and Jan Brzechwa.' The head teacher's face was alight with excitement.

'Zosia from class Ia, Inga from class IIc, Dominik and Karolia from class IIIa. And, I also would like to welcome the finalists from classes IV to VIII: Jakub from class IV, Weronika and Olivier from class V, Asia from class VI, Julek from class VII and Kalina from class VIII. Please welcome all the finalists!' The head teacher waited for the children to join her while parents applauded and followed them with the lenses of their cameras. 'And now, each finalist is going to read from the poems they have selected for us today.' The head teacher vigorously clapped and nodded for the youngest child, Zosia from class Ia, to begin.

Igor searched for Kamil but he could not see him. The boy was not among the children gathered around the head teacher or playing in the main courtyard. Neither could Igor find Angelika. Perhaps she was somewhere inside the building, in the toilet, together with the child. For a moment he thought they had already left, but he would certainly have seen them if they had gone through the main gate – he had parked close enough to have a good view of everybody who entered or left the school's premises. There was no way he would have missed them. But it was difficult to see everyone – his view was partially obstructed by a massive slide and bouncy castle. With the children continuously running around Igor could not get a good look at them, especially the ones with their faces painted white, red or yellow, wearing cat's faces, pirates, butterflies, which all made it even more difficult for him to spot Kamil's face among the others.

He glanced at his mobile phone to check the time. His buttocks were beginning to hurt from sitting in the same position. He had stayed in the car for over an hour and he was getting bored of waiting and smoking. He was getting bored of staring at the children and their parents, and their happiness. If he had been a different kind of person, with a normal mind, perhaps if his parents had displayed that kind of joyful attention, perhaps he would have had a chance for happiness. But the warmth and affection he craved was never there. Zenon Kulesza felt disgusted by his son, Igor had quietly discovered over the years. His father preferred to avoid him, rather than allow himself to get to know Igor. Igor was naturally suspicious of his mother's love, that it was not a genuine feeling but a form of compassion towards someone who was damaged. The more his father avoided him, the more his mother sought to console Igor in her forced embraces, but never actually protected him from his father. Igor began to resent his mother for her feeble attempts to atone for Zenon Kulesza's lack of attention. Even when she tried to explain his father's behaviour, Igor did not trust her and was not interested in knowing. And so, he quickly learnt how to conceal his pain and hurt. Igor was not going to give anybody the satisfaction of knowing what he felt, especially his parents. He was full of hatred in the face of happiness, and wanted others to suffer as much as he did, because he knew it was not fair that he was robbed of a chance of being loved so early in his life.

An ice cream van drew up next to Igor's car, white with blue and red stripes; the van then slowly rolled into the school's courtyard. The driver's arm hung out of the window. A melody was playing through the loudspeaker on the van. One of the teachers waved to the driver and indicated where he could park. The children ran towards the van, shrieking in excitement, with their mothers and fathers following, and then Igor finally noticed Angelika chasing a boy with a face painted like Spiderman. On her head rested a pair of oversized yellow, tinted glasses. She held the glasses with her right hand as she ran after Kamil, calling him.

Now that he had finally located them, Igor relaxed and leaned back comfortably in his seat, reaching for another cigarette. He could finally decide what he was going to do. He was not supposed to talk to them, the instructions which Damian had given him were clear, but Igor felt Damian had been deliberately holding him back. Igor did not want to sit idly, now that he was so close to them. He let himself savour this brief moment of stillness in his otherwise humming mind.

Damian phoned Igor. 'Have you seen them?'

'Brats running around and screaming. Some kind of children's festival. Parents and teachers are here, too.'

'She's there with her son then?'

'Yes.'

'Hmm…Come back. Too many witnesses.'

'You sure?' Igor sounded disappointed.

'Yes.'

Igor did not want to rush, the traffic would be unbearable at this time of a day. Wisps of smoke drifted slowly through the open window. It was what directed Karolina to his car, the smoke signals he was sending, she would joke later.

'Can you give me a cigarette?' Karolina asked in English. She startled him when she leaned in through the window. He was so focused on the school and the children that he had not even noticed her silhouette in the rear view mirror.

'What?' he asked in Polish.

'A cigarette?' She said now in Polish and smiled.

He was so surprised to see her that he dropped the pack on the floor. Of course he had recognised her face but there was that moment of astonishment, an involuntary response to her question, so immediate before the features of her face triggered recognition, a split second when he had momentarily lost the ability to think or act.

She took a cigarette from his fingers. She leaned against the car and put one hand into her jacket pocket. He was afraid to say anything so he sat speechless, desperately trying to find a way out of this situation. Perhaps if he did not say anything, she would simply go away. He cursed himself for not noticing her earlier, and pinched the side of his leg, to sharpen his mind into concentration. The pain made him focus and to think quickly about what he was going to do now.

'Polish, right?' Karolina said.

'Uhm.'

'I could have guessed.'

'How?'

'I don't know. You look Polish. Are you waiting for someone?'

'No,' he hesitated. His eyes darted towards the school.

'So you are, like, sitting in your car, watching people?'

'You ask a lot of questions.' Igor was beginning to regain his composure.

'My brother goes to this school.'

'I know,' he responded before he could stop himself.

'You do?'

Igor looked like he was in lot of pain. His brain was buzzing with possible explanations which would not raise suspicion but Karolina leaned into the car and said, 'Aren't you working with my Dad?'

He pinched his thigh harder, clenching the skin.

'Maybe.'

Karolina snorted, an angry teenage response at being lied to. 'I saw you outside our house, sitting in a car, just like this one. I wasn't sure if it was you when I saw you here, but I recognised this car. You are working with my Dad.'

She walked around the car and opened the door from the passenger's side and sat next to him. He was almost afraid to look at her. He could smell her sweat mixed with the cigarette smoke. Her acne-potted face was reddened from the wind.

'So what are you really doing here?'

'Nothing,' he said steadily.

'You are a bit weird, you know that, nice though. Thanks for the cigarette. Don't tell my parents, okay?' She dragged onto the cigarette before she managed to empty her lungs of smoke. Her eyes were watering and she rubbed one with a knuckle of her index finger. She was teaching herself to be tough and smoking helped.

She was the first girl he did not undress mentally. She had an air of false bravado about her, with sadness underneath, just like him. Nobody had ever told Igor that he was nice, not even Damian, even though he loved him. But you could love someone and still think they were not a nice person. You did not have to like somebody to love them.

Dominika Bednarek jumped when Damian touched her arm. She was standing in front of one of her photographs in the small, two-room, Red Window Gallery. An intern was adjusting a framed photograph on the wall with his back to Dominika, saying, 'How is it looking now? Is it straight? Or do you want me to move it a little bit more? I think I'll move it slightly. Now, how is it now?'

'Oh, God!' Dominika said, grasping her throat, 'You scared me. Can I help you?' She smiled and peered with interest into Damian's eyes, noticing that he had a fascinating face, the kind she immediately wanted to photograph, especially his damaged eye.

'Mateusz sent me,' Damian said in Polish. 'You are Dominika?'

'Mateusz?' she looked surprised then she added slowly with her eyes on his face, 'Why? What's wrong?'

'He may not be able to see you anymore.'

Dominika's smile disappeared instantly and a look of surprise mixed with bewilderment settled on her face. She took a step back.

'Dominika? Is everything all right?' the intern asked in English, seeing how pale she had turned.

'But we've been working on this project together for months,' Dominika said. 'It's for his daughter. He can't pull out now.'

'So we have an understanding?' Damian asked and then added in the silence between them, 'Good.' He looked around at the photographs. 'Nice photos.'

Outside, Damian turned and saw her saying something to the intern, who put both hands on her shoulders while Dominika shook her head and briefly turned her head to see Damian standing outside the window. Their eyes met but she quickly turned around and walked into the room where Damian could not see her anymore.

On the way back to the tube station, Damian thought how beautiful Dominika was, and crazy, with her faded pink hair, piercings in her tongue and numerous tiny earrings in both of her earlobes. But there was warmth radiating from her big, honest smile, a childlike curiosity in her face, and she had stunning features; high cheekbones, the bluest eyes he had ever seen and a row of even white teeth. She had a glow about her that made men follow her, in the hope of possessing her. This was not how he had imagined Mateusz's friend, or whatever this was to him.

Two weeks ago Karol had asked Damian to follow Mateusz, 'I have a strange feeling about him,' Karol had said but he had not provided any more details about what exactly was wrong with Mateusz. Damian did not see the point in chasing after somebody like Mateusz, who had the kind of life Damian wanted for himself one day, when he settled down with a family of his own, and he had thought it was Karol's growing paranoia which led to the phone calls waking Damian up in the middle of the night or text messages beeping on his phone at four in the morning, as if Karol never slept. 'Why are you calling me?' Damian would answer, not fully aware of what time it was, semi-conscious, with eyes swimming in and out of focus. 'Something happened?'

'Nothing has happened. I was too busy during the day to talk.'

'I'm sleeping.' Damian was readying himself to get back to sleep.

It happened so often that Damian began to take sleeping pills. It was the only way to ignore Karol's phone calls. Damian knew better than to succumb to Karol's suspicions, the most ridiculous ones about Milena, that she was hiding something from him. To Damian she was a perfect woman, gentle and caring. He observed her behaviour and how she put Karol's needs ahead of hers, with never a word of criticism, at least not in front of Damian. She was the kind of woman with whom he would gladly wake up and fall asleep. Somebody he could devote his whole life to making happy.

But Milena was not the only person Karol doubted. Sometimes, for no reason at all, Karol would lash out at Igor or Damian in anger, as if a light had flared inside Karol. Furious about people lying to him, Karol insisted that Damian always keep him informed about his whereabouts. Karol wanted to know the names of the people Damian was meeting and what was said, always wanting to make sure Damian acted precisely the way Karol wanted him to. Damian did not tell Karol that he thought his idea to follow Mateusz was stupid. Karol was being unreasonable, imagining suspicious schemes, until Damian witnessed with his own eyes that Mateusz, in fact, was hiding something. Karol's imaginary scenarios had turned into reality. Karol was a rigorous thinker, Damian concluded afterwards, even though some would call him cruel.

All morning he followed Mateusz's car: he stopped to do some shopping at Tesco, went into the Co-operative bank very briefly, and there was nothing out of the ordinary about Mateusz running various errands with a list in his hand, which Angelika had handed to him at the door. Until Mateusz went to Bethnal Green. Mateusz stopped the car on a quiet side road and walked towards the front door of a two-storey house, which looked like it had a newly added top floor flat. 'Well, well, not such a good daddy after all,' Damian whistled and murmured to himself, sitting straight up to see better. Mateusz reappeared after around an hour. She was holding a cycling helmet in her hand and she waved at Mateusz with her free hand as he drove away, while Damian waited in his car. She went back into the house and, a few minutes later reappeared, pushing a black sports bike.

Damian quickly got out of the car and approached her on the pebbled driveway as she was climbing onto her bike. The helmet and part of the bike frame were covered in stickers.

'Excuse me?' he said in Polish, 'Do you live here?'

'Hello.' She was pushing the streaks of pink hair under the helmet, the bike propped between her legs. She had toned arms and legs and her breasts were small; she could have passed for a boy with her slim physique. Her body had not yet given birth.

'My wife and I are looking for a flat in this neighbourhood. You wouldn't know if there are any flats for rent here? It looks like a nice place.' Damian smiled and looked up at the windows. 'Have you lived here long? We have a small child and with the park nearby it would be perfect for us.'

'Yes, it's very nice. I live on the top floor but all flats are taken in this building. You might want to try the estate agents.'

'Thank you.'

'Good luck!' she said, cycling away.

'Yeah, thanks,' Damian murmured and returned to the car.

It was close to midnight. Damian was sitting at the kitchen table when Igor returned, eating a sausage and unevenly cut pieces of white bread, like a hungry wolf. He took large gulps from a canned Tyskie beer. The sausages, half uncovered in white paper, lay in a heap in the middle of the table.

'Want some?' Damian lifted an unopened can of beer and held it out towards Igor.

Igor sat down heavily and broke off a piece of sausage.

'Where have you been?' asked Damian, his mouth full of bread as he wiped the beer off his chin, 'I've been waiting for you for hours. Something wrong with your phone?'

'Battery went flat… I saw them,' Igor said, and sunk his teeth into the meat. 'His son looks exactly like his mother. Like a girl, not a boy.'

'You said it.'

Igor gulped more beer. A loud burp shook his chest and shoulders. 'No. I walked into the schoolyard. You know, have a close up look at them.'

'You fucking brain-dead?' Damian spat out the words. He angrily slammed his open hand on the table. 'I told you to come back straight away.' Chewed pieces of food landed in front of him.

'Come down, *bro*.'

'Did she see you?'

Igor hesitated, 'Kind of.'

'What does that mean? What happened?' Damian grabbed Igor's shoulder.

'The boy talked to me. I was standing near the ice cream van and he asked me if I was selling ice cream. Polite little shit. His mother wasn't around, or his sister. I don't think they saw me.' Igor was saying very earnestly, with a shake of his head. 'Seemed very happy.'

'You were not supposed to talk to them.' Damian opened another can of beer. Then after a brief pause added, 'Mateusz is seeing another woman, or at least looks like it. She's some kind of friend, close enough to visit her at her place.'

Igor's mouth stopped chewing. 'Damn, I was beginning to respect this motherfucker. Does Karol know?' he added quickly, glancing at Damian. 'People have no respect for the family any- more.'

'What have you been doing all this time?' Damian gave him a suspicious look, a silent watchfulness coming over him.

'Here and there. Driving around.'

'Do you want to go to the gym tomorrow?'

'Sure.'

'I'll pack the power bars.'

28

With wet hair, half-dressed and unshaven, Karol paced the room, nervously turning his mobile in his hand, plotting the best way to eliminate Mateusz. He did not like what he had heard from Krystian. Mateusz's unhealthy interest in the wellbeing of the men up north and his own financial situation worried Karol. Krystian could not have been clearer when he told Karol to sort this mess out before he did. After their conversation, Krystian had told him another joke, in an effort to defuse the tension between them, but the joke did not sound funny – it sounded more like a threat. But it was evident to Karol what his business partner meant. 'Leave it to me,' he had said a bit too quietly, anxious to finish this.

The main difference between Karol and the rest of the world was that he did not care about anybody but himself. Mateusz, like others he had encountered, were mediocre men, unable to achieve greatness because they were too preoccupied with others. Karol knew his was a solitary existence – there was no room for compassion other than towards oneself. The only reason he respected Krystian was because Krystian seemed like himself, dispassionate and cold in his assessment of any situation. They were naturally drawn towards each other, and if somebody or something stood in their way, they would not hesitate to do the right thing, the thing that was best for them. Others, like Mateusz, chose mediocrity, and life did not reward men like him. Karol knew that he was always going to be alone in his choices, and that was what made him so successful. The simple belief Karol had was that he had been condemned to greatness.

Later, that evening, at the newly opened Polish restaurant *Crispy Bacon* (Poles referred to it by its Polish name *Skwarek*), booming with fiery, watery eyes in the searing heat, the head chef, Tomasz Jaworski, shouted the orders across the kitchen. The commotion was overwhelming: relentless dashing between the stoves, flames blazing under frying pans and pots with steaming water, somebody vigorously pounding freshly boiled potatoes in milk and butter, smells of fried bacon and meat, an explosion of steam. The waitresses wearing dark grey skirts and black shirts, hair tightly gathered at the back of their necks, hurried out of the kitchen with platters of various sizes in their hands.

Karol said to Damian, 'I want you to take Igor and go to Southport and Liverpool, before the next group arrives in London. The men have been complaining about the working conditions and the money. Take care of it. It's bad for business.'

'What about Mateusz?' Damian raised his voice over the noise of the open kitchen. 'Can't he go?'

'Not this time. Besides, you know I can't trust him as much I trust you,' Karol responded. He was contemplating the menu. 'Are you hungry? I haven't ordered anything yet.' Karol caught the eye of one of the waitresses and asked her for another menu for Damian.

Damian concentrated on the pages in front of him. Although he recognised the ingredients, the names did not make sense to him. He glanced around at the plates laid in front of the other customers – nothing he could name or recognised – but the smell was delicious and comfortably familiar. Damian heaved a big, tired sigh and scratched his cheek, pulling it with his mouth open.

'The chef is a Polish Heston Blumenthal.'

'Who?' Damian asked in an effort to think. He had no idea what to make of this place, so very different from any other Polish restaurant he had been to.

Karol waved his hand at him. 'Never mind.'

'Red cabbage ice cream with cumin infusion?' Damian raised an eyebrow. His forehead was gleaming with perspiration.

'Milena read about this place. I'm going to bring her here. She would love it.' And, of course, Karol wanted to meet the chef, puzzled by how Tomasz Jaworski had so quickly managed to establish himself in this city, without Karol knowing. In the London Polish community, Karol was the person whom everybody knew and sought advice from, but he did not remember Tomasz Jaworski ever reaching out to him. It annoyed him. Milena had found out about the restaurant after it had been featured in *Time Out*. Karol had not even been invited to the grand opening. To him, that was disrespectful.

'Has Milena moved back in?' Damian asked casually.

Karol tapped the menu, ignoring the question. 'You should give it a go. Go on, order something.'

'Nah.' Damian shoved the menu on the table and pushed himself back in his chair. 'I need to go back home. Igor's waiting for me.'

Karol had a bouquet of thirty blood-red roses – Chrysler Imperial – delivered to the Ines Hair and Beauty Salon. His car's roaring engine announced his arrival to the customers and staff. He knew they would now be peering through the windows, to see this magnificent car he was so proud of and which he had hand washed in the mornings. He sat inside, pretending he was talking on the phone, an inflated sense of his own worth accentuated by pressing the accelerator from time to time, to ensure everybody heard the powerful engine. There, in the car, taking his time, he savoured this moment. It was also an attitude, a man for whom everybody waited. He opened the glove compartment and stuck his hand inside to grab a handful of parking and speeding tickets he had been given in the past few days, tickets he had refused to pay, which he would throw away on the pavement. The thrill of driving his car, the exaltation he felt whenever he was on the streets of London, unjustifiably and so cruelly curbed by a Nigerian traffic warden who refused to turn a blind eye to his car parked for five minutes in the space reserved for the disabled. Karol's ears burned when he saw the ticket stuck behind the wind screen wiper. The disabled should never be allowed to drive, they were the real danger to the traffic, not he. And why were they given special treatment, taking away the parking space for people like him, people who actually mattered?

On the seat next to him was a box of *Wawel* chocolates, wrapped in dark, golden paper and violet ribbon, which he had bought on the way, from one of the Polish grocery shops. He was going to give it to Ines or whoever was working that day. The flowers were for Milena: a token of goodwill but not an apology. He had waited long enough for her to make up her mind about what she wanted from him, and this situation of living apart was becoming unbearable; laughable even – that the one person Karol had known so intimately was the person he had failed to subject entirely to his will. If he was not convinced about his abilities this melodrama between them would have threatened his self-confidence. He was not going to allow it to continue any longer.

Karol stepped out of the car and threw the crumpled tickets at his feet, pushing them with a tip of his right shoe further off the kerb, under the car where they could no longer be seen. He glanced to the left and right, and jogged up the wide pavement, zigzagging through the pedestrians.

He pushed the front door with too much force. It bounced against the door stop, and he had to hold his hand out to protect himself. He glanced from one face to another but did not utter a greeting since he had already made a loud entrance, only asking, 'Has Milena got my flowers?' An earphone dangled from his right ear and he patted the chocolate box against his thigh. He stepped into the middle of the room, turning his head, expecting an immediate answer.

Ines, her jewellery blazing in the strong sunlight, stood behind the counter next to the front window, staring at a computer screen as she uploaded new appointments to her diary. She was typing slowly and cautiously with her right index finger. Her left hand rested on a page of a thick diary, with various post-it notes stuck between the pages, her nail making a dent in the paper. She was glancing from the diary page to the screen and back to the keyboard, making sure there were no mistakes in the entry.

'Has she received my flowers?' Karol's gaze bore into Ines.

'Hello Karol,' she said in a crisp, cold voice.

He noticed a bouquet in a basket propped by the wall in the far corner of the room. The card in a tiny envelope was still stuck among the flower heads.

'Who placed the bouquet over there?' Karol approached the woman with his chin and stomach forward. He threw the chocolate box onto the table, on top of the hair pins and flat combs, relieved that he could finally rid himself of this present, which nobody here truly deserved.

'Stop harassing my staff. They're not one of your thugs,' Ines warned him and he turned immediately at her insolence.

'I'm asking a simple question and I don't understand why it is so difficult to give me an answer.' There was anger in his narrowed eyes. If Milena had not been best friends with Ines, he would have dealt with this stupid woman a long time ago.

Patrycja and Nikola stood rigid behind the customers' heads, exchanging glances. It was best not to get involved, especially when Karol was around, and today's visit was turning into an unpleasant spat between him and Ines. The worst of it was that it was taking place in front of the customers.

Ines gestured at the stairs down to the beauty treatment rooms. 'Milena is downstairs but I don't think she's ready to talk to you, so perhaps you should leave.'

Karol did not wait for Ines to finish. Of course Ines could not stop him. He knew that if she did not want him to see Milena she would not be telling him where she was.

'You don't need to shout. I could hear you upstairs,' Milena said as he entered. She was holding a small mirror, applying mascara with quick movements. 'Thank you for the roses but there was no need for them,' she added, without stopping what she was doing. Her mouth was slightly open and her head cocked to one side.

'You didn't like them? You haven't even read the note.' He was disappointed. He had gone to so much trouble to find her favourite colour, arrange the delivery (even though it was actually Damian who had given him the idea and he had asked Damian to call the florist) and not a single thank you. As he looked at her stunning face, after not seeing or hearing from her for days, he felt gripped, all of a sudden, by proud possession. In his mind, she still belonged to him.

She stopped twirling the mascara brush and finally met his eyes. 'You promised you would keep seeing the therapist.'

'I did.' He raised his voice in protest. He had not come here to be interrogated and he did not like her urgent questioning.

'Once. You think that is enough?' She shook her head. 'You promised me.'

'Haven't I done enough?'

She stood up from the chair and busied herself with packing eye shadows, powder and blush cases and brushes of various sizes into her make-up bag.

'If you were not going to do it properly why even waste my time?' she said, her mouth dry, fighting with the zip of the bag which had got stuck. She kept pulling on it forcefully. Karol now stood behind her and wrapped his arms around her body and placed his hands on hers, stopping her movements.

'This is ridiculous,' he said into her hair, soaking up the familiar smell. 'Come back home.'

Milena's chest rose and fell rapidly as she wriggled her way out of his embrace and turned around. Karol pulled her face close to kiss her, gently at first, but his excitement was rising and he pressed his body against hers, forcing her to back against the edge of the table. He had always liked to have her underneath him. Now, as she sat down on the edge of the table he towered over her and pulled her hair down, forcing her to tilt back her head to look into his face.

He was surprised that Milena had given herself so willingly. He remembered the last time they had had sex she was less eager. He imagined how she would come back home and he would arrange for a perfect romantic evening, the way she liked it, with a dinner in some fancy restaurant she had read about in one of her cooking magazines – *Crispy Bacon* would surely secure her gratitude for the rest of the evening – and later, when they arrived back home, she would give herself to him, like she used to. The first sex they had after she had withdrawn from him was not supposed to take place on a table in a beautician's room, but he appreciated this sudden intimacy, as if they had lapsed into their old selves again. He did not question her motives.

They were lucky. A few minutes after they finished they heard the footsteps on the stairs. 'Milena, are you all right?' Ines called.

Karol was standing with his back to her, his ears red, fiddling with his trousers' zip.

'Yes,' Milena said breathlessly. Her lips glistened slightly. 'I'll be up in a moment. Everything's fine,' she added in a calmer tone as Ines eyed Karol and Milena with suspicion.

After Ines left the room and they heard her climbing the stairs, Milena asked, 'Are you done?'

There was the sound of a blow drier and loud music upstairs. Somebody had turned up the volume on the radio.

'You can leave, now,' she said, trying to prevent the shrillness that crept into her voice. 'You disgust me.'

'What?' The blow of her words and the loathing in her voice was so unexpected, so unlike her that he took a step back.

'I'm not coming back. It was what you wanted to find out, wasn't it?' Her fists were clenched at her sides.

Karol took a step towards her but she screamed, 'Get out!'

29

Hunger gnawed at his insides. Mateusz took out a plastic container from the fridge and quickly devoured the contents, leaning against the kitchen sink. Angelika had prepared cabbage leaves stuffed with meat and rice for later but he was too hungry to wait for her or to heat the food in a microwave. By the time Angelika returned, the rain had stopped and the streets glistened with water under the last rays of setting sun. Kamil, leaving wet and muddy footsteps on the floor, ran excitedly towards Mateusz, 'Dad! Dad! Look.' He turned his painted face from left to right for Mateusz to see.

'Hey, Spiderman, look at you. Looking great,' said Mateusz, admiring the paint which was now slightly streaked by the rain and beginning to fade, on his son's temples. 'Did you have fun with the other children?'

'Kamil. Take off your shoes this minute!' Angelika set the heavy shopping bags on the floor and the lighter ones on the kitchen counter, and continued, 'There are no clean plates in the house?' She eyed the plastic container in Mateusz's hand, his fork suspended mid-air. 'Karolina!' Angelika called.

'She hasn't come back yet,' Mateusz said. He was uneasy and embarrassed that Angelika had caught him like that. He knew she did not like it when he ate in a rush, standing or without heating the food first, which she said was an unhealthy habit, behaviour he had acquired living in this country where there was never enough time for anything. And now, it was Karolina who had followed in his footsteps, and Angelika, justifiably, blamed him for it.

Angelika glanced at the clock on the wall. 'It's past six. Where is she?' One hand propped on her hip, she dialled Karolina's mobile phone number. 'It's going to voicemail. Where is this girl?'

'Do you need any help?' Mateusz asked. He placed the empty dish in the sink, careful not to topple a tower of mugs and glasses waiting to be washed.

'No, thank you. I'll handle it,' she said, distracted. She took off her scarf and coat and threw them onto one of the chairs.

Mateusz opened his mouth as though he was about to say something, to ask her if she had had a good day because she looked so tense, but caught himself just in time. He was too tired to argue with her, afraid she might complain again about his long working hours and not helping her when she needed, and it was best to leave her alone.

For the second time, Angelika dialled Karolina's number. 'Where is that girl?' she muttered, again, angrily to herself. 'Kamil. What did I tell you? Take off your shoes.'

Mateusz placed his hand on Kamil's shoulder. 'Come on. Let's get you sorted out.'

Five hours later, Angelika, wild-eyed and pale with a trembling hand to her lips, in a trance of anxiety, was frantically listening to Mateusz explaining to the policeman on the phone that their daughter was missing.

'What are they saying?' she urged him to translate, but Mateusz only squeezed her small hand to let him finish the conversation. His palm was slippery.

After he put the phone down he asked her again, 'Are you sure she didn't stay with one of her friends from school?'

'I've called everybody. I told you that already. What did they say? Are they going to look for her? They must start looking for her. Oh, God. Oh, God.' She was on the verge of tears, convulsive prayers whirling in her mind.

Mateusz hugged her shivering body. 'She's probably lost track of time. I'm sure she's fine. They said we should wait, that it's too early for them to act.'

'It's almost midnight!' she cried and Mateusz, as much as he seemed composed for the sake of Angelika, was beginning to feel the tremor of panic building in his heart. An aching twist rose in his chest.

'I'll take the car and drive around the neighbourhood again,' he forced himself to steady his voice. 'They say some of the trains have been cancelled because of signal failure or flooding. Maybe she went to central London.'

'Why would she do that? She never goes to central London. It's too dangerous.'

'Perhaps she went out with her friends.'

'I'll go with you,' Angelika said suddenly, standing up.

'No.' He grabbed her hands. 'Stay at home in case she comes back. Besides, we can't leave Kamil on his own.'

That night, driving around, Mateusz tried to recollect the last words he had exchanged with Karolina, until he remembered, finally, that it was this morning with a half-eaten sandwich in her hand on the way out to school that she had said something about which college she would like to go to. But he could not remember which one. He suppressed a flash of panic and dialled her mobile phone again but, like numerous times in the last hour, it went to voicemail. Mateusz swore, half-mad at Karolina for being so inconsiderate. It was not the first time she had forgotten to charge the battery and that was the most reasonable explanation for her not contacting them. It had to be.

Somebody stepped out from the shadows and Mateusz hit the brakes. He mouthed an apology but the person only swore at him. His head dropped on the steering wheel, exhausted with worry. 'Where are you my little girl?' he whispered to himself, 'Where are you, sweetheart?'

It would be three weeks later, with no new information from the police, that they would decide, in fits of desperation, to visit a clairvoyant. On the way back home from one of the evening prayers in the church, held to pray for Karolina's safe return, Angelika said – so quietly she had to repeat her words because Mateusz was not sure what she was saying – 'Dorota, my hairdresser, told me about Clairvoyant Manuela. We should go and talk to her.'

In the months that followed, Mateusz thought often of that evening when Angelika had suggested talking to a psychic, because it became the beginning of the end of her belief in God. In the church, he observed her numbed by her pain, with no tears left in her, while Father Niewiadomski, squeezing her hand, told her to stay strong and trust in God's guidance.

'Why?' Angelika whispered, her eyes unfocused, her face displaying the great struggle within. 'Why is He doing this to us? Why has He taken our daughter? What use has He got for her apart from inflicting suffering on her and us?' She stopped, terrified of her own words, angry for her lack of the unquestionable trust that had defined her relationship with God all these years. She had no reason to doubt whether what was happening had been pre-ordained by a higher power, so formidable and mysterious. How could she possibly comprehend even the tiniest fraction of its intentions, she: an ordinary human being? She was neither a priest nor a nun, whom Angelika truly believed were blessed with an extraordinary gift of a union with the divine power, a unique connection she revered. They interpreted the words of God. They knew more than she did, so she had blindly trusted their judgment until now.

Father Niewiadomski patiently replied, 'We don't always know God's ways. You must trust in His love for you. Deep in your heart you know that God has the answer, even if we do not always comprehend His ways.'

But Mateusz saw that it was not enough for Angelika and he felt so powerless in the face of her growing pain. Because Angelika stayed silent, her swollen eyes concentrating on the floor, keeping her lips so tight with all the blood drained from them, as if she was too scared to say what she was really thinking, he quickly thanked Father Niewiadomski for the prayer and guided her towards the exit. They left behind the dull voices of men and women praying and singing. The chorus was led by one of the younger priests. But this message of God's greatness, announced in a zealous tone of triumph, held no more meaning to Angelika. It made Mateusz nervous and scared for her.

Outside, Angelika stumbled and he had to hold her up.

'We'll see the clairvoyant.' He tenderly kissed her forehead. 'We'll call her today. All right?'

On the phone, when Mateusz was making the first appointment, Clairvoyant Manuela asked him to bring Karolina's clothes and a recent photo. 'Make sure this is something she has worn recently. I need to be able to connect with her emotionally,' Clairvoyant Manuela explained. 'It could be the pillow cover if all her clothes have been washed,' she added. They brought Karolina's long sleeve blue top which she liked to wear in the house, the one

Angelika held tight to her face every night as she inhaled what remained of her daughter's scent.

It was getting dark outside, the sky was dove-grey when they arrived, and dogs were barking on the empty street. Heads down, pushing against the sudden gusts of wind blowing around the heavy air, that evening they found the clairvoyant's house. Outside, wild untrimmed bushes of lavender blocked the entrance onto the pathway to the house, and Mateusz had to hold the overgrown boughs apart for Angelika to walk through. The fence dividing the property from its neighbouring gardens had collapsed in places. The thick ivy climbed its way around the wooden boards. The wild grass, untrimmed and long, covered what remained of the pathway, its flat, broken stones barely visible in places.

There was movement in one of the windows on the ground floor – a curtain fluttered.

'Mateusz and Angelika?' Clairvoyant Manuela's face, partially hidden, appeared in the crack of the front door, the moment Mateusz raised his hand to knock. 'Come in, please, come in.'

'Can you smell it?' he whispered to Angelika as they followed the clairvoyant inside the house, 'it smells like, it smells like…'

'Backhousia citriodora or lemon myrtle. Queen of the lemon herbs. A healing plant. Aboriginals have used it for centuries,' the woman said without turning, her bare feet clapping on the tiled hallway. Mateusz felt his skin crawl. How she could possibly have heard the question which he had whispered into Angelika's ear? But then, he thought, she was able to see things which others could not. Perhaps she could hear such things as well.

She sat them on a sofa covered with a colourful patchwork throw of reds and yellows and blues. The room was lit by scented candles which stood on the floor, table and window sill, on the wall were darkened patches from the smoke. She asked them if they would like a drink and left them on their own while she went to the kitchen to make a pot of herbal tea.

'It's weird here,' Mateusz said in a hushed tone, looking around at a small Buddha statue sitting on the floor next to the fireplace, ceramic angels with golden wings hanging from the window frame on nylon fishing lines, and various sizes of elaborately painted china elephants lined up on one of the shelves. 'I guess the one thing missing is a black cat,' he continued but Angelika said nothing. She held tight onto Karolina's clothes and a pillow case, and Mateusz did not see her glance once around the room, as if she herself was in a trance.

Clairvoyant Manuela returned to the room and set a bulky china pot on the table, a delicate smell of peppermint spreading through the air. She opened a cabinet and brought out three cups and three tiny silver spoons. She set her hands on the table, each finger adorned with heavy gemstone rings, amethyst and emerald, and followed Mateusz's gaze and said, 'I lived in China in my previous life. Buddha brings peace to this space, and to my soul.' She smiled and there was a glowing radiance around her face. She had streaks of grey hair but her face looked young, free of wrinkles except for lines on her cheeks when her face broke into a smile.

'Oh,' said Mateusz, but he had no idea what she was talking about. Later, on the way back home in the car, after he tried to criticise Clairvoyant Manuela's past lives, Angelika said, 'I don't care if she was a priest in India or a cabaret dancer in her past life. I just want her to find my daughter.'

Mateusz was uncomfortable, reluctant either to give in to this performance of theatricality (head tilted back, finger tips on the temples with elbows wide out, eyes half closed with only the whites visible, all atremble) or join in the belief that Clairvoyant Manuela could actually see where their daughter was.

He remembered his father's sister, how he used to follow her to the outskirts of their hometown, where the gypsies lived, along the dilapidated row of houses, and into a corridor filled with junk leading to a large dark room with no heat, where a wrinkled, yellow-skinned woman sat waiting to tell Aunt Krystyna her future from the cards and the palm of his aunt's hand. Sometimes, the old gypsy woman poured hot wax into a flat dish, gently splashing water onto the surface of the still liquid wax to harden it, then holding the shape in front of her face, proclaiming the name of the next family member to die or what awaited Aunt Krystyna in her years to come. But there were no deaths in the family or lottery winnings and Mateusz was disappointed – the gypsy's performance was so alluring that he almost believed it. Afterwards, Aunt Krystyna always went to church to reconcile the visit to the gypsy, because her belief in wax and palm readings was a back-up plan, in case the real God did not answer her prayers. 'Better to believe in something than in nothing,' she used to say to him.

Aunt Krystyna's limitless faith, either in the gypsy or the priest, and the plain strategy to make sure her life was exactly the way she desired, with a husband and a family of her own, never diminished. But neither did anything come true, not even after years of waiting for the happy life to materialise. Mateusz could never understand that absurdity of a person's hope against all odds, until now.

He stole glances at Angelika, hanging onto the woman's every word, whether it made sense or not, because a lot of what the clairvoyant was saying was a meaningless mutter. Angelika's hand squeezed his hand tighter and tighter. A wan, fleeting smile appeared on her face when Clairvoyant Manuela assured them the girl was still alive, then, only for the smile to disappear instantly when Angelika heard they must hurry because Karolina's life was fading. Only when Clairvoyant Manuela started to give details (in a low voice, so low that they strained not to miss a single word) did Mateusz consider her words seriously.

'She's in a house. No...it's not a house, it's a flat, she's in a flat. Musty smell, dirty floor.' Clairvoyant Manuela's face twisted. She spat as if she had swallowed a fly. Angelika's hand shot to her open mouth to block out scenarios of what Karolina could be enduring. 'A man is with her. There's something wrong with his face. A knife touched his face a long time ago. Wait!' Manuela raised an open palm and the gemstones glittered. 'I can see it now, clearly. Quick! Quick! Give me a piece of paper!' With her eyes half closed, Clairvoyant Manuela snapped her fingers at them.

Angelika fumbled in her handbag for a diary and a pen, while Mateusz frantically looked around the room to find something, anything the woman could write on. With trembling hands, Angelika shoved a torn page into Manuela's hand.

Manuela's forehead was shiny and her face glowed a fierce, hot red; she was in a trance. She breathed heavily as she drew a building, a mosque, surrounding streets, a park, and then circled a house. 'Here.' She tapped her fingernail. 'Here she is. Inside a flat in this house.'

30

Never would the numbness that had so swiftly spread through his body leave his heart entirely, no matter how much time passed. Damian would never forgive himself for taking Igor with him.

He remembered they had arrived in Southport very late in the evening – Damian was annoyed that Karol kept sending them across London to check that the Bromley house was ready for the new people arriving from Poland – and by the time they had finally managed to get onto the motorway it was already getting dark. They parked the van outside the hotel. After they had checked in, Damian and Igor left their room, in search of a place to have a drink and something to eat.

Two hours later they were so drunk they did not mind the shop owner's skin colour when he handed them paper plates with chunky lamb meat and a heap of sauerkraut. They were the only customers in the brightly lit, small kebab shop. As soon as they paid for the food and the warmth spread onto their open palms they left.

'I'm sorry but you can't bring the food inside the pub,' they heard later, with their heads bent down, wolfing their food with plastic forks. 'You can come back when you finish but please leave now.'

'It's cold out there,' said Igor, spitting the food onto his shirt.

'Looking for something?' Damian asked surprised, pointing with his plastic fork at a security guard behind the barman. The man watched them suspiciously, ready for the eruption of trouble, expecting to have to act at any moment if the Kulesza brothers did not comply with the barman's request. The brothers, swearing and grunting obscenities at both men, grabbed their plastic plates and left the pub. They were too hungry, drunk and tired to start a fight, even though, in the past, they would have jumped at the opportunity. They could wait. Southport was a small place and there was nowhere to run. They would get their chance for revenge, they knew. Huddling from the onslaught of the wind in a narrow alley between two buildings, they finished their food standing. They dropped the empty plates, forks and tissues soaked with grease at their feet.

'You okay?' Damian remembered asking, as Igor poked the long nail on his little finger inside his mouth, staring into the darkness towards the sea they could not see.

Something was troubling Igor. He had been quiet in the car all the way here, pensive, smoking one cigarette after another, until Damian had had to tell him to keep the window open because it was so blue he could not see a thing through the windscreen. Igor squeezed his mobile in his hand all the way, kept opening and closing it, as if he wanted to call somebody but kept changing his mind because he didn't want Damian to hear the conversation.

If Damian had not been so drunk, his suspicions about Igor's state of mind that night would have returned. He would have remembered seeing his brother so withdrawn before, and he would have forced him to confess, to know if there was anything he should have been told. There was, in Igor's demeanour, a certain toughness and indifference, and his mood had improved once their stomachs were full, so that Damian simply forgot about Igor's strange behaviour in the car. For once, Damian did not want to waste his time on deciphering Igor's emotions or thoughts, the randomness of Igor's behaviour was tiring enough. Damian was dead with weariness from dealing with the blitz of Karol's ever-changing requests and demands, so that one night he chose to ignore whatever Igor was dealing with.

'Let's drink,' Igor said all of a sudden.

'Yeah.' Damian's head bobbed up and down. 'Let's drink.' He followed Igor back inside the pub and this was the last thing Damian clearly remembered.

The next day Damian woke up with a shattering headache, curled on the bathroom floor, his clothes heavy, soaked and stinking with sweat. He drank water straight from the tap and undressed, swearing and trying to remember what had happened. He felt a bruise on the back of his head, as he splashed his face and head with cold water.

'Igor? Igor, you there? What the hell happened last night?' he was calling to his brother. 'I don't remember shit,' he was saying loudly as he walked back into the room. Was there any aspirin in his bag? He batted a fly from around his head. 'Igor?'

But Damian was alone.

He heard a muffled vibration. His mobile phone in his soiled trouser pocket. Five missed calls. He saw the time. Two o'clock in the afternoon. He blasted curses. They were supposed to have been on their way to meet the men three hours ago. He scrolled through the missed calls. All of them from Karol. He decided to let him wait because, first, he had to find out where Igor was.

He dropped the phone on the pillow and tried to think. He cupped his hands over his heavy eyelids but there was nothing that would make sense. He had to lie down, at least for a few minutes and gather his thoughts.

He lay on the bed, very still, his feet hanging over the edge. He covered his forehead and eyes with his forearms, the light hurt him and his eyes were watering again.

The phone buzzing next to his ear startled him. He must have dozed off for a few minutes.

'Damian?' he heard Karol's voice. 'Why are you not answering your phone?'

Damian cleared his throat. 'Sorry.'

'I've been trying to get in touch with you the past few hours.'

'I know.'

'Listen, Krystian has called me, he talked to his friends at the police station. A body was found this morning. They don't know for sure but it's best if you call Krystian…The man fits Igor's description. It's the scar on his face. But you need to call him as soon as possible and talk to him.'

Suddenly, Damian was quiet, breathing heavily. 'What happened?'

'The man was cut off by the incoming tide.'

'Igor can't swim,' Damian whispered.

'I can't hear you. Speak up.'

And it was right there in front of his eyes: Igor running around the lake, stumbling onto the train tracks of the miniature rail, shouting to Damian, 'Come on!' and Damian, trying to catch his breath as he leaned with his hand on a roofed structure with a rotted bench inside. Later on the dirty sand, Damian was falling down into pools of water and shrieking drunkenly. His mouth was filling with salty air, sand and dirty water. 'Come back, you idiot,' Damian remembered calling after Igor, but it was too dark to see his brother clearly or was it the alcohol? 'Come back. Come back.' The surface under Damian's feet felt unsteady, moving. He fell down again, his clothes wet. 'Wait till your arse gets cold, you'll be back, fuckwit,' he was now muttering to himself because he had no strength anymore to call after Igor. He waited and waited but

Igor never came back and Damian was tired of waiting and the cold. He took one more look in the direction of Igor and decided to return to the hotel.

'Igor can't swim,' Damian kept saying again and again.

31

The day she lost her hope Angelika refused to go church. Except for Karolina – who was not found in the house – all the details on the map matched when the police arrived after she watched Mateusz handing the piece of paper to the detective. As she sat on the white stones in Altab Ali Park, looking at the house that Clairvoyant Manuela's had seen in her vision, she doubted that she would ever be able to trust those who had no answers. She would think about it, hard, and then decide that her faith had reached its limit. Because the loss of her daughter, her first-born child, was unimaginable, it exceeded her capacity of comprehension.

Her mother suggested that they should come back, that Britain was too dangerous, on a brink of becoming the hottest place for terrorist attacks. Her voice was full of painful reproach. 'It was in the papers. A girl was murdered. People are attacked on the streets. Bombs explode on the buses. How can you live like that?'

Angelika said, angry, 'How can you even ask me to leave if my daughter is still here?'

Angelika's mother stunned her by saying, 'What if she is never found? I want her to return home as much as you do, and I know you don't want to hear it, but what if you never find her? You need to think about Kamil.'

'We are not coming back until we find Karolina,' Angelika said, firmly, leaving no room for objection and putting the phone down, unable to continue the conversation.

There was a throbbing pressure behind her eyeballs, her hands were shaking. She wanted to call her mother straight back and apologise, say that she had not meant to speak to her in such an impatient and angry tone. She had never raised her voice at her parents. But she could not erase her mother's words about Kamil. She knew that her mother was ashamed that she had fallen pregnant so soon with Mateusz, and that she had then decided to keep the baby, against her mother's advice. Now, she had this awful thought, a suspicion, that her mother had willed Karolina's disappearance. Her mother had never loved Karolina with the same love she had for Kamil. Kamil occupied her mother's foremost attention. Karolina came distant second, almost as a conditional interest in Angelika's daughter. Sometimes, Angelika was scared by the flood of her mother's endless love for Kamil, because it left nothing for Karolina. This love thing her mother insisted upon astonished Angelika with its intensity, for Angelika, love for her children was not a choice between the two of them.

A mobile phone rang. She recognised the tone. It was Mateusz's phone, which he must have left in the bedroom. She wiped her tears and picked the phone up from the floor. The caller ID showed 'Grzegorz work' and she pressed the answer button.

'It's me.' Angelika heard a woman's voice. 'I need to talk to you.'

'Who is this?'

Silence.

'I'm sorry. Have I got the wrong number?'

'Who is this?' repeated Angelika.

The woman's confidence was now wavering. 'I'm trying to reach Mateusz? I must have dialled the wrong number.'

'I'm his wife. Who is this?'

The woman hung up.

Angelika quickly found the contact and dialled the number. The phone rang but nobody answered. She kept punching the button and waiting but there was still no answer. The call eventually went to voicemail. Whoever the woman was on the other end, she was not going to answer the phone now, and the only thing Angelika wanted was to find out why she had called Mateusz's phone. She began to scroll through the text messages and as she read the conversation between Mateusz and Grzegorz she slowly sat down on the edge of the bed. After she had read all of the messages she placed the phone on the pillow and went to the other room with the computer. She waited, gnawing her fingernails, until the machine started. There was no password. She opened Outlook and scanned the emails but could not find anything that contained the word 'Grzegorz'. She clicked on the Local disk drive and searched through each folder. She did not know what she was looking for, a photograph or a message, anything to prove his innocence, because if there was nothing then perhaps it was nothing. It could have been somebody else with the same name but why would he save a woman's name under a man's? It did not make sense: the fictitious name or the sweet words the woman had used. All the photographs Angelika found were from their holidays back in Poland or on various trips to the English coast, her heart skipped a beat when she saw Karolina's beautiful face, her little girl. Her wrist was numb with cold, the sinews on the back of her right hand now hurt, as she clicked from one folder to another, files, documents and photographs, opening and closing, an avalanche of windows until finally, when she was on the verge of deciding that it was all pointless and it was, in fact, a wrong number, she found what she had been dreading – one photograph: Mateusz standing next to a young woman, behind them a wall of photos. Angelika gasped at how innocent and beautiful the woman looked. And Angelika could tell, from this moment of climaxing fear and frustration, that this woman had a body that could easily become

When she finished, she slowly wiped her hands on a kitchen towel.

'I'm going to take a bath,' Angelika said.

He stood up and embraced her. 'I'm so sorry. I'm so sorry.'

'It's not your fault. It's nobody's fault.'

She wanted to go but he kept holding onto her, with his head close to her neck.

'You left your phone at home today,' she said, and released herself from his embrace. She moved slowly towards the door, tired and wanting to have a bath as soon as possible so she could go to bed, and pretend another day was over.

'Did anyone call me?'

'No.'

'Nobody?'

Angelika opened her mouth to ask him, bluntly, about the woman and that one photograph, but something held her back. She decided it was enough. She could not take anything else happening to them. She was not going to let him provoke a single word from her. If he did, he would unleash all the unspeakable things inside her, words that would bring havoc and destruction and they would be past the point of no return. If he heard her speak her mind, her words would make his betrayal real. Angelika's deliberate silence on the subject of the other woman was the best argument she could come up with. The only real thing she allowed herself to feel was the fear over Karolina's life, nothing else could distract her. The hovering absence of her child was more real to her than Mateusz's betrayal, or what looked like some kind of relationship Angelika didn't know about. So the affair would remain their unspoken secret.

32

Every time Karol placed a fat envelope into Damian's hands, an amount which also included Igor's share, Damian put it aside. The only reason Damian worked so hard and insisted on living a modest and simple life in London was to buy some land back in Poland, so one day he could settle down with his own family and take care of Igor. He had always known he was the only person Igor could rely on, not their father who refused to remember he had two sons. With this land and the big house he was going to build, Damian imagined he would be able to shield Igor from evil eyes and finally find peace for Igor's mind. And so, a year ago he had bought a plot near Jelenia Góra, seventy kilometres from the German border and four from the Czech Republic. After their mother's death, they had no ties to hold them to their family house, at the opposite corner of the country, except for their ageing father.

The last time the Kulesza brothers saw their father was at the funeral. Their mother's coffin was laid open in the cemetery's chapel with Zenon Kulesza, sobbing and choking voicelessly, on his knees with his fingers curled around the edge of the pine coffin surrounded by bouquets and wreaths of fresh flowers. The Kulesza's wreath was an arrangement of red, pink and white gerberas, their mother's favourite flower. The brothers sat on chairs, staring at their mother's yellowish, sunken face, wrinkled and translucent, with the veins exposed like dried leaves. Then Damian stood up and lifted his father by his elbow, 'Sit down, Father, sit down.' When Zenon rose slowly from his knees, propping himself up with one hand on the coffin and with the other on Damian's arm, as though he might otherwise fall at any moment, and he was finally able to sit down – bewildered, grasping Damian and Igor's hands – he stared at the body with no recognition. This death made no sense at all. Seeing his father, so weak and broken, suspended in time and barely breathing, his body shrunken, transforming him into an unrecognisably old man, it was almost impossible to imagine how long his father could live. Damian remembered Igor saying, 'He stinks,' after the ceremony ended, and they stood up, letting their father go first behind the coffin, carried on the shoulders of the funeral home workers.

They heard whispers among the people who had come to witness their mother buried, distant members of the family and relatives they did not recognise: aunts and uncles, cousins and their children. 'Breast cancer', 'She went so quickly.' Somebody else said, with a note of bewilderment in voice, 'Who would have thought she would go first?', like it was supposed to ease their sorrow, that it wasn't their father, with his inglorious past, who should have been the one lying inside the wooden box.

By the hole in the ground, where everybody had gathered, the Kulesza brothers and their father, squinted at the glaring sunshine and waited for the men to place the coffin on wooden pallets before it was lowered to the ground. The priest spoke, in a hypnotic, soothing voice, of a better world and then read a passage from the Bible. They prayed and wondered what life had in store for them now. Damian looked up into the cloudless sky.

It was during the funeral reception, outside the building when the guests told their childhood stories about their mother, drinking Wyborowa vodka from thin glass tumblers, smoking one cigarette after another, that Damian said, 'Let's buy land. We'll build a house for us. Or we can open a gym, you know. We have the money.'

Igor had looked at the distant headstones with plastic flowers and burnt out candles. 'Okay... But you must promise you won't take the old man. He never wanted me in his life so why should I want him in mine?' A slight anger had come into his voice.

Now, Damian was looking through the photographs of a half-finished building with the surrounding grounds barren except for rowan shrubs growing widely, some razed to the ground by the heavy machinery. There were no windows fitted yet, just holes, a heap of grey bricks by the front wall, a shovel propped against the concrete mixer. It had all been Damian's idea, the house and the land, and after the incident with the girl, a perfect place for Igor. Life for life, Damian caught himself thinking. What good was it all now if Igor was not going to see it finished? Damian had not foreseen that death could come at any time.

Damian had not said anything to his father about Igor's death because it would make it legitimate; irrevocable reality. This could wait a day, perhaps longer, but he knew that he would have to start making arrangements to send the body back to Poland. He could not possibly imagine burying Igor in Britain.

Only with Milena did Damian let himself express his doubts about Igor's death. She had arrived unexpectedly at his flat, a week after he had returned from Southport. Perhaps it was the price his brother paid for all the sadness he had brought on others. He was saying this aloud for the first time, as if she was not there, a confession.

'You can't imagine,' he said slowly, 'you can't imagine that every day, every time he was gone somewhere, and I had no idea where he could be because he refused to tell me, I pictured the worst. He is my brother, my little brother, but maybe it's better that way, that he is gone now.'

'Don't say that,' Milena said, shaken by his words. 'You can't think like that.'

But he knew, oh, he knew what a relief it was, even if shadowed by the overwhelming feeling of guilt, that there was no other way, as though life had taken care of something Damian was unable to, because Damian had loved his brother too much. Igor, perpetually on the verge of devouring himself, would no longer linger in his thoughts. Damian could finally stop worrying for them both; it was only himself now.

Two days ago, when he had finally managed to face Karol – after spending several days in his flat, getting maddeningly, stupidly drunk, quietly trying to obliterate his pain – he was getting out of the car on the street where Karol lived, and was startled by Mateusz. At first, Damian did not recognise him: unshaven and with some crazy and baffling look in his eyes. Mateusz said, 'It was him. It was your brother.'

'What are you talking about? Let go of me,' Damian said, leaning against the car with Mateusz's face close to his.

'Your brother took my daughter. Where is she? Tell me!' Mateusz was shouting, his cheeks burning, feeling murder in his heart. 'Where did he take her? What did he do to her?'

'Igor is dead. My brother is dead. He had nothing to do with it. Whatever happened to your daughter it wasn't him.' Damian almost wanted to ask Mateusz, if the fact that his brother was dead would make him happy, if, in fact, it was Igor who was responsible.

'What? No, this can't be true. He knows where she is. The woman said he had a scar on his face. She said it.'

'What woman? Shit, man, pull yourself together. I'm sorry about your daughter. I really am but it wasn't him.'

'How?'

At first Damian did not understand the question.

'My brother was…he was sick. But he's not a murderer.' Damian's eyes narrowed in a warning.

He was not going to let another girl's murder be pinned to Igor. Not after his death when he could not defend himself, which Damian believed was unfair, whatever Igor had or had not done, Damian owed him the benefit of the doubt. But there was something about Mateusz's stubborn certainty that forced a crushing suspicion to creep into Damian. After he returned home, in overwhelming anger, he turned every room upside down, mattresses, cupboards, loose boards in the living room, boxes on the upper shelves.

He found nothing. Nothing that belonged to Igor.

Now, he looked at Milena fighting back the tears, as she assured him that she was going to do everything she could to help him. She told him about a transport company that, 'specialised in,' she stopped herself for a moment, 'that can take his body home.'

'Thank you.' Damian was grateful for this act of kindness and let her stroke his hands. 'I never had a chance to tell you how sorry I am about your baby,' he added quietly.

Thank you,' said Milena, wiping her tears.

There was a document to be issued by the mayor of Łódź, where Igor and Damian had been born, a certificate which Damian had to present at the Consular Section of the Polish Embassy in London that would allow the body to be transported. 'Sanitary permit,' Damian was told by the funeral manager at the transport company, who asked him what kind of coffin he would like. First, the man showed Damian a catalogue with photographs, then he took Damian to a display room. Damian slowly ran his hand over the surface of each coffin before he said, 'Mahogany.'

'You won't be able to display the body,' the funeral manager said apologetically, 'it's the law when transporting the body back to Poland from abroad.'

'It won't be necessary,' Damian said, with his hand still on the casket. Damian, lost in thought, continued to stroke the surface.

Damian was relieved; he would not be able to bear the sight of Igor again, after he had had to identify him. Besides, he did not think his father would endure the ceremony. His father's voice on the phone had been weak, halting, and at first he had pretended he had not heard Damian when he had called to inform him about Igor's accident. Damian had had to repeat himself three times to make sure his father understood what he was saying, and now Damian was not sure whether his father had genuine hearing problems, or whether he was faking it. Igor and his father had not spoken for years, not since his father had banished Igor from family memory. Even at their mother's funeral, his father had not said a single word to Igor. As Damian kept repeating himself over the phone he had wondered if the words telling of Igor's death had any real meaning to his father, whether they caused any stir in his old heart. Igor was his child, after all, a flawed man whose illness was not of his choosing. Damian could not understand, after so many years, why his father would still hold on to his senseless ideas. 'Stupid, stupid old man,' Damian said angrily to himself afterwards.

After viewing the caskets, Damian and the funeral manager returned to the office to go through the required paperwork and estimated costs of transportation.

'Are you sure you wouldn't like a funeral in London?' asked the funeral manager. 'We would be happy to provide a Polish priest.

Many Polish families here feel more comfortable conducting the ceremony in Polish. We'd be happy to take care of any necessary arrangements.'

'No, thank you,' Damian said, 'the funeral will be in Poland.'

If Igor was buried here, who would remember him? Who would visit or light a candle at his grave stone. At least, back in Poland, Damian would be there for him, to remember.

33

No way was Karol going to die now. Even though he was desperately gasping for air, his chest painfully wheezing with every single breath, his eyes watering. He could not remember where Milena kept the inhalers. He was on the verge of phoning her, despite how badly she had treated him the last time they had seen each other at the Ines Hair and Beauty Salon. His body curdled in blind anger at her indifference to the possibility of his death in a few moments, if he did not find his medication. It was all her fault – the dissolution of their relationship – years of building this life together thrown away in a single day, a few minutes of one conversation. Years of living together turned into nothing with a few sentences. He found the inhalers in one of the kitchen drawers, among the cutlery. He banged the front board with his fist as the mechanism inside got stuck on whisks and wooden spoons, sending teaspoons flying onto the floor. He sat down to calm himself, to let the breath come back. This much he knew: that he needed to rest, at least for a few minutes, so he closed his eyes and let the medication begin to work inside his lungs.

Simmering with rage, a conviction lodged in his head, not for the first time, that Milena had done it on purpose: hiding the inhalers at the back of the cutlery tray, so that he would choke to death. Which was, he concluded, proof of Milena's absolute ingratitude towards his providing her with the life she had always wanted. No other woman he had dated in the past could consider herself as lucky as her. He had made sure her life meant something instead of sliding into nothingness. With him, she mattered. He shook his head. He was appalled at her behaviour. Once, he had found the inhalers under the sofa, only because he dropped the TV remote controller on the floor and it had bounced off the table leg, sliding underneath. He had pushed his hand under, catching the edge of some old cut out photographs of recipes from one of the cookery magazines she subscribed to, touching balls of dust and cobwebs. He had had to use the flashlight to see how far the remote controller had slid and, next to it, he had noticed the blue plastic tube, then another one, he had extracted three unused inhalers from under the sofa.

And all this was bad enough. Yet Karol would find it in himself to graciously forgive her, if she returned. Because of Milena, for the first time in his adult life he had considered having children, a real family. A child would love him absolutely. He had so many people depend on him out of fear or obligation; he was ready to embrace another human being on equal terms.

He had once asked his mother, shortly after the divorce between his mother and father was finalised, after she settled in Brighton with Aunt Basia, 'Are you happy?'

His mother and Aunt Basia used to rent a two-bedroom ground floor apartment, and from time to time they sublet a spare bedroom to visitors from Poland, who were looking for cheap accommodation close to the seaside. Karol had offered them both money on more than one occasion, confused that his mother would resort to having strangers in her own place, walking around. His mother and Aunt Basia had responded by telling him that there was nothing wrong or awkward about subletting a room which most of the time stood empty, anyway. They were living like locals now, they had said, adding that it was invigorating to have new, young people around, listening to their stories, showing them the town. Karol, in comparison, issued warnings about living with strangers who could be thieves or something worse. They had no idea what Poles were capable of in a foreign country. Still, Karol would hand envelopes filled with cash to his mother every time he visited them, despite his mother protesting that it was too much and there was no need, to which Karol always said, 'It'll give me peace of mind knowing you have it, for an emergency, if for nothing else. I may not be able to be here for you every time.' It became their ritual: him handing her the envelope, his mother objecting; in the end the money was always accepted.

Later, Karol watched his mother kneeling over some bulky flower pots in the garden and pulling on weeds. Still bent, she asked, 'What about you and Milena?' Karol wiped his face with his hand, sighing heavily, not knowing how to respond. 'She hasn't come back, has she?' He shook his head. His mother now stood facing him, her fingers dirtied by the wet soil, clutching a bunch of weeds in her hand. 'Do you love her?' she asked.

'That's a stupid question,' Karol said, starring fixedly at the pots.

'Sometimes people grow apart, like me and your father.'

Karol pushed his chair back from the table making a loud screeching noise. 'We haven't grown apart. I'm doing everything I can. Everything she has asked me to do.'

'I know. I know you are. Perhaps if your father had loved me as much as you love Milena, we would have stayed married. I don't know. Perhaps it was too late anyway.'

His mother led the way back into the flat, to make fresh coffee and slice the cheese cake Aunt Basia had prepared the day before. Karol ate standing, while his mother told him how Aunt Basia worried about whether she would find the right type of cheese, the type she always bought when she lived in Poland, but there were a few Polish groceries in Brighton where they could buy almost anything now. 'Of course there are Polish shops here,' Karol said with his mouth full.

Just before he left for London, packing small parcels with Aunt Basia's cheese cake, some fresh fruits, his mother leaned through the car window, 'Drive carefully.'

Karol wanted to tell his mother how Milena had lost the baby, how she had moved out and refused to be reasonable, but he did not say any of that because he knew his mother would not understand and he would only make her cry. He needed his mother to believe in the sacrifices she had made for him, so that he could have the life and success he always craved, so that her life would be worthwhile.

His mother adored Milena. On the cabinet in her bedroom in the old house back in Poland she kept framed photographs of Milena and Karol together; later she brought them to Brighton. When they used to visit his mother back in Poland, he would find them, his mother and Milena, giggling and whispering, his mother sharing stories from Karol's childhood with her hand on Milena's forearm or tucking Milena's hair behind her ear. His mother in such high spirits. She refused to be dampened by his father's unpleasant grunts who, after a barely audible 'hello', would retreat to the adjacent room to watch television with the volume turned up to maximum. His mother's face would momentarily display irritation, a tightness of her lips causing tiny wrinkles to form around her mouth, then she would get up briskly to close the door with a frosted window pane, saying something harsh to his father. The sounds would become muffled and they could see a dark silhouette of his father moving around in the other room through the glass. Sometimes, when his mother could not bear his father's behaviour any longer – his opening and closing the door every few minutes demanding that she make him some tea or coffee, when she was going to make something to eat – she would suggest to Milena that they go for a walk, even if it was snowing. Milena, happily, would accompany his mother, leaving Karol on his own with his father. Once, his mother had admitted that though Karol was the love of her life, Milena was like the daughter she had never had. Milena made his mother smile in a way Karol could not remember her having done for a long time, so there was no way he was going to tell her the truth about his failing relationship and all the exhausting weight between them, caused by the loss of the baby, like reality had gone mad. It would break her heart. It was his way of insulating his mother, of preserving the reality of happiness intact, for as long as he could.

'What's going on?' Damian asked, eyeing teaspoons on the kitchen floor, clothes sprawled around on furniture, a shocking mess which was all unlike Karol.

'I was looking for inhalers for my asthma,' Karol said. He began to complain about how he had nearly choked to death, and it would have been Milena's fault entirely because it was she who had hidden the medication so that he could not find it. He was almost sure because it was not the first time he had found his inhalers in strange places. 'But luckily I did. You have no idea what it feels like when your throat closes and you are gasping for air but there's nothing coming in and out … like drowning, I suppose.' Karol was pouring hot water into mugs, oblivious to the expression on Damian's face which his words had caused. 'If I had not found my inhaler in time, and you had arrived a few moments later, you would probably have found me on the floor. God knows what could have happened to me. Can you imagine?' He paused. 'There was a moment when I thought I wasn't going to make it.'

While Karol was talking endlessly about his near-death experience, Damian stood by the window, looking outside onto the street: people rushing into local shops, children chasing a dog, garbage trucks roaring and grumbling down the street. He was too exhausted to be irritated and to tell Karol to shut up and listen to what he had to say for a change.

'Am I boring you?' Karol asked, suddenly aware that Damian was ignoring him. 'Your coffee is ready, by the way.'

'I'm taking his body back home,' Damian responded, softly, under his breath, facing the window. 'I thought you should know, since I won't be here for some time, until I take care of everything.'

Of course, Karol felt sorry for what had happened to Igor, an accident which had thankfully saved Karol for sure, from the trouble of dealing with possible future complications the longer Igor worked for him. But this untimely development was threatening to affect the business which Karol still had to run, no matter what was going on. Nobody had any idea, except Karol, how much effort it required to keep things running, against all odds. Igor's death was a situation beyond his control. He had to make sure that things were going to return to normal as soon as possible. Karol sometimes felt that it was his life story: endless complications the moment he was onto something big. He was a man often unappreciated, scorned even, for holding himself together by mere force of will in the face of countless obstacles. He needed to make sure this one, Igor's death, was not going to slow down his progress in his money-purposed life.

Violently, Karol sneezed. Loose sheets of paper on the table flew everywhere.

'When are you coming back then?' Karol said. With an effort, he managed to suppress another sneeze.

'Shit. What do you want me to say, Karol? I don't know.' A painful twitch ran across Damian's face, his damaged eye red. 'You'll have to do without me until I sort out Igor's burial.'

'I have a business to run. You know how much I need you,' said Karol, sitting bolt upright, hastening to finish, wary of Damian's threatening tone. At times like this he wished that he was a bigger man, taller and more muscular.

Sitting down, Damian asked, his heated tone calming down a bit, 'What's going on with Mateusz? He sprung at me out of the blue on the street outside your place, babbling something about his daughter, accusing Igor of having something to do with it. Do you know anything about it? I don't need to have this hanging over me or over Igor's name.'

'That's why I had my doubts about Mateusz. I thought he was a good guy, reliable and even-tempered, somebody I could trust. This behaviour, lack of self-control, is not good for the business.'

'What are you talking about? His daughter is missing.'

'Exactly. Perhaps I was wrong, yes, I admit I was wrong in employing him if he cannot get a grip of himself. We all have a cross to bear.'

But Damian surprised him by asking, 'Like Milena leaving you?'

'She did not leave me,' Karol said angrily. 'She's coming back. My private life is beside the point here and it doesn't affect my judgment of what needs to be done, of what's the best thing for the business.'

'You and I know I'm not the brain, and I'm okay with that and, so far, I haven't been complaining. We made some good, easy money.' Here, Damian rubbed his thumb, index and middle finger together. 'But without Igor,' Damian halted, gathered his thoughts, it was still difficult for him to talk about his brother, like he was not there standing next to him 'what I'm trying to say is that I don't know what your plans are.' Karol opened his mouth to contradict him once again but Damian raised his hand to stop him. 'I need some time to think about what it all means.'

'You said it yourself, he sprang on you on the street, accusing you and Igor of God knows what. Frankly, I'm not sure what the hell he was thinking. Anyway, coming back to what I was saying, his daughter's disappearance, as terrible a tragedy as it seems, is a good thing.'

Damian held his mug of coffee in mid-air. 'How is it a good thing?'

'Let me explain it to you.' Karol said in a patient voice, like it was Damian who was the retarded one and not that dead brother of his. Karol was beginning, finally, to ease into his argument. Damian's gaze no longer felt uncomfortable to him. 'We can't have somebody like Mateusz associated with us. His behaviour jeopardises everything we have worked so hard for, everything we have built together – you, Igor and I.' Karol made sure he mentioned Igor here. He knew it was important for Damian to feel included, especially his stupid brother. Now that Igor was gone it did not cost Karol anything to raise his status only a little bit more, and it made a good impression on Damian, tying him more to Karol. Karol had realised at once what he was going to say to strengthen his point. 'Do you really want to have Igor's legacy tarnished by unsubstantiated accusations? Whatever happened to Mateusz's daughter, and between you and me,' Karol lowered his voice, 'we don't really know what happened. We don't really know what kind of family this is, everybody has secrets. What if a member of the family had something to do with her disappearance?'

Damian coughed and Karol's eyes narrowed in hungry expectation. What was it that Damian was hiding from him? 'Remember when you asked me to follow him?'

'And you said there was nothing out of the ordinary.' Karol said slowly, probing, encouraging Damian to speak.

'I didn't say anything at the time. I thought it was nothing relevant, but now, with his daughter gone, I don't know. Perhaps it has something to do with it.'

'Whatever it is that you haven't said, I trust your judgment.' Karol thought it was important to make Damian feel at ease, so that he could find out the little secret Damian was so skilfully withholding from him. At the same time, he was boiling inside, his mind raging, that this glut of muscles, this nobody, would conceal information from him, because he believed he was capable of independent thinking, outside Karol's control. How and when it had happened, Karol did not know.

'I saw him with another woman,' Damian said at last.

Karol felt a prickling running up his spine, a kind of spasm whenever he was forced to react to a situation out of his control, a brief moment which called for a surge of quick thinking, a jolt of an immediate response required in such circumstances. He would not let Damian lie to him again, but for now, he needed to pull him back into loyalty.

'You see? Who knows what else he's hiding. He'll have to go. There's no doubt about it, now that you've told me and I thank you for being so honest with me. I knew I could count on you, Damian.'

34

Ever since Karolina's disappearance, Mateusz had not been himself. He refused to discuss their situation with Angelika any further. The aching silences between them cracked only in the presence of Kamil, when they made sure that they seemed happy and loving, as though nothing had changed. A scar in their relationship that no amount of time or patience would heal. The more time that passed, the less hope radiated in Mateusz and Angelika's conversations. If one of them suspected that they were never going to see Karolina again, they never said it aloud. Hope was melting away, like their intimacy. When they slowly returned to making love, almost ashamed that they enjoyed pleasure because they were not supposed to – how could they be happy again if their daughter was missing and they still had no idea what had really happened – it felt wrong. Their love making was quick and rushed; if intimacy united them briefly, as soon as they finished Angelika left the room to check on Kamil while Mateusz pretended to busy himself with the computer in the other room, staring vacantly at the screen. On other nights, Angelika would hide in the bathroom behind the firmly closed door, biting on a towel so that nobody could hear her crying while Mateusz, waiting outside with his hand on the door, did not have enough courage to interrupt her. What was he going to say? That everything was going to be fine? Once, outside the bathroom door he called her name, half-certain, but she became quiet and, after a while, he retreated to the bedroom. He could not bear listening to her choked crying or her silences, the shutting him out of her feelings. Their own happiness seemed so inconsequential, marred, in the face of their loss. He wondered if they would survive this.

When Mateusz met with the police, one more time, he told them his suspicions about Igor, but it all sounded so improbable. When he heard himself say, 'the woman, clairvoyant, saw his face in one of her visions, please can you … is there any way you can follow this lead?' he realised how ridiculous he sounded. At first he was obsessed, trying to find out as much as he could about Igor, until Borowik told him, with a look of pity, 'I'm worried about you. This whole idea about clairvoyant, man, not good. I mean if you were the police would you believe yourself?'

'You think I'm going crazy, don't you?' Mateusz attacked him, tired of explaining himself, first to the police, now to his friend.

'Listen to yourself, that's all I'm saying. If it was my child, I would probably do the same.'

Mateusz said, bitterly, 'But you don't believe me either.'

'Now that he is dead what difference does it make?'

'I want to know the truth. I need to know. Wouldn't you want to know?'

Consumed with sudden irritability whenever people questioned his suspicions about Igor, Mateusz wondered if he was ever going to find out what had happened to Karolina. His rational mind was still trying to wrap itself around the idea of the clairvoyant and her visions. The possibility that Igor had had something to do with his daughter's disappearance was more believable than a psychic's hallucinations. There were times when, with sharp fear gnawing at his insides, he did not want to know, dreading the moment he would have to face the truth. On some unspoken level, a shadow crossed his mind, a dark sense of guilt he was sinking into, that it was his actions, his stupid self-righteousness that had brought this onto his family. His mind ran around in circles, trying to remember tiny details, anything about the days leading up to Karolina's disappearance, trying to find any clues that could direct him to a resolution. He was losing his strength to urge Angelika towards hope. He was angry when she seemed to be moving on, speaking less frequently about their daughter.

One day he saw her packing Karolina's clothes, books, notebooks and CDs into boxes, almost ridding the room of her physical presence. She lashed out at him when he asked her to stop, that Karolina was not dead yet, 'Leave me alone. You think it is easy for me? I cannot look at her room and not imagine the worst. I can't take it any longer.' She forcefully pushed Karolina's clothes into a bulging cardboard box, kneeling on the floor, trying to push down the lid that would not close.

He crouched next to her and held her shaking hands. 'I'm sorry. I'm so sorry. I don't know what else to do.'

'It doesn't mean I've stopped loving her,' said Angelika, not looking at him. 'But I can't ... I just can't ...'

He held her in his arms, knowing that she was right; they could not go on living like that, with this constant, unbearable uncertainty. 'I'll help you finish,' he said and got up to take another box and help her put Karolina's things away.

Karol had texted Mateusz to meet him in the lobby of one of the hotels in Marylebone, one of the places where he sometimes liked to conduct his business. It made the right, overwhelming impression, especially when he had Poles coming to see him who had not lived for long in London or who had rarely ventured into five star hotels like this one.

Mateusz walked into the reception area and looked around, as if from a great distance, he heard Karol say, in his imperious, loud voice, 'We have the most experienced people and you are not going to find a better company. I can guarantee that once you have worked with us you won't go anywhere else.' He saw Karol sprawled comfortably on a large sofa in the corner with a head-phone dangling from his ear. In front of him lay an open laptop on the table, surrounded by loose printed pages stacked on one side. There were more papers and designer magazines on the seat next to him, one or two had slid to the floor at his feet. Damian stood a few steps away from Karol, by the wall, reading messages on his mobile, chewing on a match. After Mateusz's outburst a few days ago on the street when he had made those accusations about Damian's brother, he felt uncomfortable in Damian's presence. Mateusz wanted to say how sorry he was about Igor's death but the words were stuck in his throat. If Igor, in fact, had had anything to do with Karolina's disappearance, at least he was dead now. He knew it was wrong to think that way; nothing was going to bring his daughter back.

Karol raised his chin when he saw Mateusz approach and motioned to him to sit down. Mateusz glanced at Damian but he did not look back at him. A waitress offered Mateusz the menu but he asked only for a glass of water. He was sweaty and tired. Somebody was playing the grand piano in the middle of the room.

Karol said his goodbyes and ended the call. 'How's it going?' he asked Mateusz and poured himself more tea. 'If you ask me I'd say it's really amazing. Every day something new is happening. Business is going great. More than great,' said Karol, brightly.

'We're trying to stay positive for Kamil.' These days speaking about Karolina filled Mateusz with sadness so he kept his sentences short.

'Well, some things are out of our control. You know what teenagers are like. Boyfriends. Running away from home. Anyway, back to the business. There's something I'd like to talk to you about.'

'If it wasn't for you, my daughter would still be here. If I hadn't taken a job with you, this whole situation would not be happening to my family. Did you really think I wasn't going to realise what is really going on?' Mateusz was pointing his finger at Karol who sat up straight, tense. Karol turned his head to look at Damian, in a vain attempt to attract his attention. 'It's your fault. Do you hear me? Your fault!'

Karol glanced around. 'Can you keep your voice down?'

It frightened Mateusz that he was shouting; he rarely did. Only, now that he thought about this aggression, it had begun to manifest itself the day Karolina was gone. Now, he kept going.

Composed, Karol lifted his teacup and slowly drank some tea. He placed his interlaced fingers on the table. 'Are you finished?'

'You knew about Igor. You knew and you didn't do anything.'

'I don't know what you are talking about.' Karol's face was flushed but his voice was controlled. The more Karol remained unmoved, the less Mateusz believed he could force him to admit. But he was not sure anymore what was real and whom to blame.

'It's people like you. You never did anything to stop him.'

'Whatever you think you know, or imagine has happened, has nothing to do with me.'

'It was all your doing.' Mateusz felt weak, defeated. His face was showing strain. He knew he was losing this argument. He had nothing to show to prove that he was right. It was his word against Karol's. 'I know there's no way for me to prove it but I know you lie to all these people who come here. You lied to me. You make promises which you don't keep.'

'I never forced you to come and work for me. It was your decision. Don't blame me for whatever is happening to your family.'

Mateusz wanted to ask Karol how he lived with himself. After his disappointments with fellow Poles in Britain, he now felt strangely connected to these people. They were all together here, in this foreign language, carving a space for themselves, hoping for a better and larger life – nothing too extraordinary except a chance at happiness. They had all come here bracing themselves against others, never their own kind, never the people who spoke the same mother tongue, who had been born in the same country. But these were not foreigners who became their enemies but people like Karol. Mateusz was one of them now, cheated, defeated by his own blindness, because he had trusted Karol. And, deep inside, he was beginning to realise that he could only blame himself. The lawlessness of Karol's actions had little to do with Mateusz. He had chosen to work for Karol despite his suspicions and Borowik's warnings, even though they had not been entirely clear. Mateusz had stupidly believed he could face any challenges. He had never thought that this could happen to him. The belief of doing something worthy, something real, cracked under the inexplicable logic.

Mateusz stood up, his fists clenched, and began walking away. He wanted to get away from this moment, away from Karol. He tasted defeat in his mouth, but half-way to the door he turned around. He wanted to take a final look at Karol's face. He was already talking to somebody on his phone, laughing, like this conversation had never happened, and nothing Mateusz had said changed anything. There was not the slightest regret visible in Karol's demeanour.

Mateusz walked back to where Karol was sitting and stopped in front of him. Karol raised his eyes and said, 'Have you forgotten something?' And it was then that Mateusz threw a punch at Karol's face, with full force, sending the mobile phone flying out of Karol's hand.

Damian took a step forward. Mateusz held Damian's gaze, readying himself for whatever was going to happen at Damian's hands, but Damian only smiled from the corner of his mouth, amused.

Later, on his way back home, Mateusz got an email from Karol saying: *I just received evidence of your misconduct which warrants a disciplinary action. I will come back to you when I have more details. Karol. Director.* Mateusz stared at his phone and read Karol's email a few times to make sure he had understood; the email contained grammar and spelling mistakes, missing words which Mateusz was struggling to decipher. It was not the first time Mateusz had received a communication from Karol which was rushed, in broken sentences, forcing Mateusz to disentangle the meaning from an array of words that often did not make sense. But this email did. The threatening message was clear.

He scrolled through the contacts in his phone, looking for Valerie Hall's number.

'It's Mateusz. I need to see you...Yes, now. It's urgent...Thank you.'

Then he took the stairs to the Underground.

Angelika's nails were bitten down to the skin, the tips of her fingers were red and raw, and Dorota was not happy.

'You could at least let them grow a bit. What am I supposed to do with you, poor thing?' Dorota said with a heavy sigh, her head lowered over Angelika's hands. 'Everybody's asking about Karolina. Some of my clients saw her picture in *Polish Express*.'

Angelika did not like it when people took pity on her because of Karolina, or when they held her in their arms for too long, like Dorota had when she arrived to have her nails done. She wanted to take her mind off everything in her life, do something different. Her daughter was neither dead nor alive, but even if people expressed hope and forced her to keep thinking that everything was going to be fine, she knew that what they really thought was sympathy she did not want. She wished they would stop talking about Karolina or asking how she was coping. How could she cope? A stupid question. She was tired of feeling agitated and strained, trying to keep a brave face in front of strangers or people who pretended that they could understand what she was going through.

Angelika decided to change the subject. 'The new girl you had, she's not working for you anymore?'

'She's gone back home, I think. Or maybe she has found a different job. I don't really know. One day she was here, the next day she didn't show up to work. If she didn't want the job she could at least have had the decency to tell me in advance, not leave me without help. Useless girl.'

They were alone in Dorota's house. Usually there would be other women, waiting for their hair or nails to be taken care of, sometimes with their children, but not today. It was quieter, as well, Dorota turned the volume down on the TV, perhaps she was ashamed of displaying gaiety in Angelika's presence. Angelika wished it would not be so silent; it was easier to drown your thoughts in noise.

When she had woken up this morning, with the blinding sunlight coming into the bedroom, Angelika had thought that she was going to live the rest of her life without regrets. Her thoughts ran towards Karolina most of the time, but now she could talk or think about her without breaking down in tears. At least now she was teaching herself to conceal her sorrow, to remind herself what kind of person she had once been, so full of happiness and promise, before Karolina's disappearance. She needed to become that person again, for Kamil and for the new baby. Angelika was three weeks pregnant.

She was not ready to share her pregnancy with Mateusz. She kept it to herself, waiting for the right moment. She had almost told him yesterday but had stopped herself after he had broken down with bitter anger about Karol, shouting that he was going to make him pay for everything, throwing his hands in the air; aghast at Karol's email which he had read to her.

'I don't know what's worse,' Mateusz had said as he shook his head, waving his mobile phone in the air, 'the fact that he did what he did and refuses to take responsibility or Valerie Hall who apologised to me over and over again that she will not be able to do anything. She said they have no resources at the council. She promised me that she would protect me, protect us, that she would do everything in her power, and I believed her. I gave her all the evidence I could find, I gave her the names, locations, and you know what she said? That she was working on seven cases at the moment which had more chance of standing up in court.'

'I didn't know you were giving her information, working for her?'

'I'm not.'

'I don't understand.'

Mateusz stumbled over his words. 'I called her, a few times, she works on benefit cases. I thought I told you.'

'You didn't.'

'I didn't want to worry you. I don't know why I didn't tell you. I could swear I did. Perhaps I'm losing my mind, just like Borowik said,' he now muttered to himself. 'I have an idea. I'll find Damian. I will make him talk. Or Karol's wife ... what's her name? Milena. Yes, that's what I'm going to do. I swear I will make them pay for everything. I will go to the press.'

'Stop! Stop it!' Angelika broke through his flow of words. 'I can't listen to you anymore. You've got to stop. I don't want you to have anything to do with these people anymore. I don't want you to talk to that council woman. Find another job. Forget about them. I need you to stop whatever this is that you are doing.'

'I thought ...'

'No. This has to stop. We have to move on. If you want this family to survive, to stay together, you have to stop your craziness because I cannot deal with everything that has been happening to us. I need you to take care of Kamil and me. Just find another job, please.'

She was shaking and could not understand how Mateusz could be so blind. He stared at her in horror but she knew her words had sobered him.

'You're scaring me,' Mateusz whispered. 'You've changed.'

'I didn't have a choice.'

She needed him to let go of his rage, like she had done, let this red passion seep away, and live the life they had forged for themselves, for better or worse; a life that was worth fighting for.

That was why she had decided that morning to live her life without regrets, to find in herself that strength she had once possessed. She used to be that person but there was no going back to her old self. She was going to be better, more daring, against whatever life threw at her. And that new life she was carrying was a sign of how fickle and cruel life could be: to take one child and give her another. Mateusz's relationship with the other woman paled in the face of all this, and Angelika was never going to mention it to him. She was going to get through this, to do everything possible to be happy, because happiness, like pain, could cut through life at any time. Being alive meant having the ability to smile through the shadows, and remembering that even the darkest times could dissolve with a breath of unexpected happiness.

And she was going to forgive God.

35

Milena paid the fare and got out of the taxi. She looked up and saw a gigantic colourful mural painted on the side wall of the tenement house. On the way through the city she had seen others on various buildings; flying ships, people falling from the sky, monstrous, alien faces, old and young women, sparrows, rats and other magical creatures – hallucinations of the city's soul. The colours and images dazzled her. So this was the place – Łódź, where Damian and Igor were born, a place she never expected would hypnotise her. She had no doubt that the people who had created these murals had a legitimate claim on their world and it made her wonder about her own life and what kind of claim she could make? But she was here now. She was here to make things right, the way they were supposed to have been from the very beginning.

Kids were shouting on the street. She found the name listed next to the intercom. The button was partially melted; bored teenagers had probably played with lighters and smouldered the plastic. She had to apply more pressure with her finger for the buzzer to work, but there was no response. She pressed it again and again until she finally heard a distorted male voice. 'Can you hear me?' She moved her lips closer to the speaker.

'You're not trying to sell me something?' The voice was tired and scared.

'No. I'm not selling anything. I came to talk to you about Damian.'

'Uh.'

'I'm only in town for a day. Please, I really would like to talk to you.'

'Second floor.'

She heard the electronic ringing and the door opened automatically. The inside of the house was in desperate need of renovation: the staircase was wooden, with the railing chipped in places and wobbled when she held onto it as she climbed the stairs, the high gloss paint had faded and the oil-painted panelling had lost its lustre. Large patches of oil-based paint were missing, revealing brickwork underneath. On the second landing, an old cat with fur sticky with dirt slept on the windowsill, its belly slowly rising and falling.

The front door to old Kulesza's flat was open and Milena gently pushed. The hinges creaked. She noticed a choking smell of moth balls and stale, sweaty air. The smell seemed to suck all oxygen out of the interior. Her eyes darted over the mess: dirty linoleum floor, piles of yellowed, wrinkled newspapers.

'I'm making tea,' she heard the voice from the kitchen and, moving towards it, she saw Zenon Kulesza bent over an aluminium kettle on the gas stove with a lit match in his hand. 'If you'd like some.'

He turned around and shuffled his feet in brown slippers across the kitchen floor which was dirty with dried dark splashes from tea and coffee. His flabby cheeks jiggled with every step.

'You are a beautiful woman.' He sat down heavily, propping his hands on the table. 'Damian never invited any of his girlfriends here. But you are a beautiful woman,' he said again. His face was hardened with wrinkles and his eyes were walled behind thick glasses. She smoothed her hair, uncomfortable with his comment. He had thick grey hair, cut very short, unusual for his age. Milena saw Damian in his face. She looked around to see if there were any photographs of his mother but she did not see any.

'I'd like to say that I'm very sorry for your loss.'

'Yes, hmm, she was the love of my life,' Damian's father said with reluctance in his voice, which bewildered Milena.

'She? I meant Igor.'

'Who?' he asked sternly with an almost unbearable effort.

Milena hesitated. 'Your son, Igor.'

The kettle blasted steam and a sharp whistle sang out, intensifying in volume within seconds.

'Water has boiled,' he said abruptly, over the noise, and pushed back from the table.

'Can I help?'

'No. You stay where you are,' he barked at her in a half-irritated voice. 'I'll do it myself.'

Milena, astonished, stared at his hunched back. She could almost imagine what it must have been for Damian and Igor to have a father like that, with moods changing in the blink of an eye. His lack of acknowledgment saddened her and she wondered if this was the reason Damian never really spoke about his parents.

'Actually,' she said loudly as she turned to lift her handbag from a back of a chair, 'I came to ask if you could tell me where Damian lives now. He did not leave his new address with me. You know, Damian and …' she almost said Igor but stopped herself. 'Damian used to work with my husband, ex-husband actually, so the only address we have is yours. I'm here on business and stopped by, hoping you could help me.'

Zenon turned off the gas knob under the kettle. The singing noise of the whistle died. He walked across the kitchen to a basket with envelopes and old newspapers on the counter. He tore a page and slowly wrote down the address.

'Here.' He extended his hand and took a deep breath, through his nostrils. 'Damian moved as far away as he could from me. You can tell him that when you see him.'

'Thank you.' Milena looked at the address. Jelenia Góra. More than eight hours on a train from here. If she hurried she could still find a connection. She put the piece of paper in her handbag. 'Can I ask you one more question?'

'What is it?' he sounded tired, exhausted by this conversation.

'Did you go to Igor's funeral? Damian was transporting the body from Britain back home. He told me he was going to organise the funeral here. Since he left,' Milena hesitated, 'I haven't heard from him.'

Zenon gritted his teeth. 'Maybe he doesn't want to have anything to do with you. But he doesn't talk much to me either,' he said, addressing the window, as if she was not standing right in front of him. 'No, I did not go to the funeral.'

'I'm sorry to have taken up your time.'

Milena walked out of the kitchen and was just about to press the door handle when he called, 'Are you sure you're not going to have tea with me?' There was a disappointed glint in his eye and she realised he must feel very lonely, deserted by his own children.

'I really should go. Thank you, once again.'

The towering blocks of flats stood close to each other. Large waste wheelie bins between them with open lids emitted a nauseating, sweet, rotting smell. An old woman tended to a tiny patch of ground with yellow flowers, just under the balcony on the ground floor, as Milena zigzagged among the bins and young men who were drinking beer and laughing and whistling loudly as she passed them. Before she could board the train, to find Damian, she needed to see Zygmunt. It would not have been right to come all this way without offering an apology and an explanation for hurting this man. Whatever Milena had done to him, she wanted

Zygmunt to know she had done it because she had had no other choice; that she had acted in self-defence. The only thing she was trying to do was to survive, like everybody else like her who had come to Britain. She hoped he was going to forgive her. She had come back to her own country to make things right. She did not want to allow anything from her life with Karol to haunt her.

'Who are you looking for?' the old woman asked, seeing that Milena was unsure of where to go. She stopped mid-air with a patch of weeds in her calloused hands. Milena had missed that familiarity, where strangers took notice of each other.

Milena gave the old woman Zygmunt's name and said somebody she had known in Britain had asked her to pass on a small parcel for the family. Milena did not want to give the full story to a stranger. To her surprise, the old woman pointed to the entrance to the block of flats on her right. 'A very nice family. Very polite,' the old woman said, 'the children help me with my groceries, not like these.' The old woman's eyes darted towards the young men by the bins. 'But you are not going to find him here,' the old woman added. 'Zygmunt, the husband, he left a long time ago but he has never returned. No jobs here, not in this place, but he has never returned. Nobody knows what happened to him. But you can talk to the wife. She still lives here. Did you see him there? Did you see Zygmunt in Britain?'

'No, I did not see him there,' Milena lied.

'Ah, I'm sure his wife would still like to see you. Such a nice family and such a terrible thing to happen to them. Children growing up without a father.' The old woman shook her head. 'You should go and see her.' But Milena had turned her back on the old woman and was running away. She could not bring herself to talk to Zygmunt's wife.

'What about the package?' the old woman called after her and the young men howled 'What about the package, what about the package, what about the package!' and the old woman muttered, 'Wolves. Stupid pack of wolves you all,' and returned to tending to her small garden.

Milena promised herself, when she returned to London, she would find Karol's cousin. She would bring him back to his family.

At the Łódź Kaliska train station, she had just missed her connection. But there was an overnight train at one in the morning that night, she was told by a cashier at the ticket office, and she would arrive just before nine the next day. She bought a one-way ticket and went outside to find a restaurant where she could have something to eat and wait until the train left. She did not want to stay at the station, afraid of being bothered by the homeless or drug addicts, who often sought a place to sleep in the station late at night.

There were very few passengers on the platform when she finally boarded the train. In her compartment was a woman with a small boy who kept shrieking and beating his mother with his fists, despite his mother's tired pleas to calm down. The woman kept apologising and saying, 'My husband and I wanted to bring him up using the stress-free method. No screaming or slapping. We let him be free most of the time. But sometimes I feel I should give him a solid beating so that he would shut up.' The woman finished with a tired sigh. Milena left the compartment to find the toilet hoping the boy would be asleep by the time she returned. She stopped in the corridor and stared out through the window. She had not actually thought this conversation through.

In the morning, she was woken up by somebody vigorously shaking her arm, 'Tickets,' she heard a stocky, red-cheeked woman in a tight, navy-blue suit and a heavy, worn leather bag on her left arm say.

'Are we already here?' Milena rubbed her sleepy eyes. For one absurd moment she thought she was back in London, then the distinctive smell of the train hit her and at once she remembered where she was.

'No. Another hour. Tickets,' the woman repeated and clicked her tongue.

There was commotion outside the compartment, young men were running down the corridor and chanting loudly. Somebody's fist suddenly banged against the pane of glass door and Milena jumped.

'SOK will take care of them at the next station,' the woman stated, unperturbed.

'SOK?' Milena repeated unsure what the ticket controller meant.

The woman looked at her in a funny way, out of the corner of her eye. 'Train guards?'

'Yes, of course. I'm sorry. I've lived abroad for a long time now.'

'Clearly,' the woman growled as she marked the ticket with a ballpoint pen. She left the door wide open when she exited the compartment and Milena stood up to close it behind her. She did not want anybody else coming in, especially not a pack of wild, young men.

The mother and the child were gone. They must have got off at an earlier station. Milena breathed, relieved; now she could get ready in peace.

An hour later she arrived at Jelenia Góra and joined a queue for a taxi outside the station. She longed for a cup of coffee. For a brief moment she thought it was perhaps too early to show up at Damian's front door but it was her best chance to catch him.

She sank into the back seat of an old Mercedes. The pot-bellied driver kept glancing at her in the rear view mirror. He drove at breakneck speed, with one hand on the wheel with dirtied white fur around it and the other hanging out of the open window. He slammed his hand against the car door. He ignored the potholes in the road. Every time one of the wheels dipped into the cracked asphalt, she had to brace herself with both hands at her sides. The driver grinned, almost taking pleasure in her ordeal.

'Could you roll the window up,' she asked, 'the wind is blowing really hard back here.'

'It's stuck,' the driver said. He turned the radio up because by now, she had ignored all his questions: whether she was one of those who had left or was coming back; most of the passengers were either leaving the country or returning, so which one was she? She had only responded that she had been living in London, for the past few years, to which the driver said that his friend's daughter, another taxi driver, had also moved abroad. 'Maybe you know her. Her name is Ewa Nowak.' Milena did not know her.

The driver parked the car by the side of an empty road. There was no pavement, the asphalt was unevenly laid for the cars, and there was no path for the pedestrians on either side of the road.

'Are you sure it's here?' Milena asked, seeing the empty fields, woodland area and only three houses, one of them half-finished.

'New development,' the driver said, 'it's the address you've given me so unless you have a different one, this is it.'

'Can you wait for me please? I'm not sure. I'm going to check that this is the place.'

The driver grumbled something about a double charge because they were far away from the town centre. Milena handed him additional notes for his trouble and left the car. Her heels sank into the soft soil.

She knocked on the front door, uncertainly, hoping that she had the right address. She turned to check if the taxi was still there. The last thing she wanted was to be stranded in the middle of no-where in front of somebody's house.

When she saw Damian's face she broke into a relieved smile.

'Milena?' He stared at her wide-eyed. 'What are you doing here?'

Later, when Milena made the decision that she would stay, she eased into his presence around her. In the beginning his attention was awkward; she bumped into him outside the bathroom door and he asked quickly if she was hungry. He did not have much food at home but they could drive to a local restaurant or to the city centre.

'Why don't you show me what you have? Perhaps I can cook something,' she offered.

He was right, there was not much food in the house except for potatoes and some cold chicken in the fridge, so she decided to roast them.

There was also no wine so he went to the local shop to get some. She appreciated that he had remembered she liked wine, and he apologised that it was a small shop and they would not have a big selection but she was grateful for whatever he chose.

'Does Karol know you are here?' Damian asked, after he got back.

She was slowly peeling the potatoes and wondered why it had taken him so long to finally ask this question. This whole situa-tion made her laugh, seeing him taking the wine bottles, milk and some fresh cheese out of the shopping bag and arranging them on the kitchen counter in a perfect line. He looked so different here in his kitchen, without that severe intensity on his face she used to see sometimes when he came to the house in London, and she did not remember such fastidiousness with food. She was not sure whether it was only food he was consumed by – behaviour she nevertheless liked, as it could bring them together – or was it a sign of something different, an obsessive quality to his mind.

'I left him. I'm not going back.'

'I'm sorry,' he said almost at once. It did not sound like he was sorry.

'Everybody is leaving him. Me. You.' Milena was now looking at him, leaning sideways with her hip against the sink. 'You're never going back?'

'I paid my debt to Karol. Without Igor there's nothing to keep me there anymore. I want to finish this house. For Igor.'

'I know.' She resumed peeling the potatoes. She did not want to betray emotion on her face. She decided to carry on this charade about Karol for the time being so she asked, 'Does he know that you are not going back?'

'I think he has probably figured it out by now.' Damian laughed, relaxed. 'He tried calling me at the beginning but I didn't answer. Besides, I'm so busy with all the building work, I have no time for chit chat. And at night, well, I'm too exhausted to talk to him even if he wanted to talk. I'm going to open a gym. That's what Igor and I wanted to do from the very beginning.'

Yes, Milena remembered how Karol could spend hours on the phone in the middle of the night, while she would wait for him, hoping he would come to bed, but the business always took priority.

'Strange though,' Damian hesitated.

'What?'

'I didn't think Karol would give up so easily. One day he just stopped calling.'

Milena honestly believed it would be one of the acute asthma attacks that would bring an end to Karol's life. She was the one who made sure his inhalers were stocked, booked his doctor's appointments for a check-up or rushed him to the hospital if he needed assistance. That sudden attack in Paris brought the possibility of his death to her fingertips. At the time she was shocked she even considered his death as an actual option. She was not that kind of person. She would never harm anybody, not intentionally at least, or she liked to believe that about herself. The idea seemed preposterous. And yet. Karol was dead and she could not bring herself to tell Damian the truth. In the end she did not need to do anything. Just before she had left for Poland she came to the house. She did not think Karol would be there. She still had the keys. A plastic take away container lay open on the table. Chicken with noodles was what killed Karol. They argued. Karol, as always, with his mouth full, shouted how disappointed he was, how she wasted his time. Instead of swallowing, so he could carry on his ferocious tirade, he took a breath in. At first Milena thought he would be okay, after she saw him coughing. When his face had gone red, then purplish, his eyes bloodshot, she almost made a move to slap his back. He desperately waved his arms behind his head. She took a step back, instead, and watched him. Until he fell off the chair. The container with chicken and noodles followed. His eyes held so much disbelief and terror in his last moments. Hers mirrored his with a relief it was finally over.

After dinner Milena and Damian sat in the living room. Her cheeks were flushed from the wine and she felt at ease here with him.

'What happened with that girl?' Milena asked quietly. 'There was a man, Mateusz, working for Karol. I never met him. I saw him once in a car with Karol.'

Milena noticed Damian's expression change. He was pensive. 'I really don't know.' Then, after a short while he added, 'But I do know that Karol may have underestimated him.'

'How?'

She noticed his hesitation. Damian gave her a surprised look, which changed into a slow realisation.

It was easy to forget now, with Milena facing him, that not long ago she had belonged to Karol. Though how much had she known exactly, the details of each operation, the scale of the business? He had never seen her visiting the houses in Hounslow, Barking, Neasden, Bromley or Mitcham; had never seen her participate in or, in fact, witness any conversations the three of them had had; never heard her enquire how many men and women they had brought on a given trip. She had only showed interest when they planned coach trips, which did not prove her complicity. It could have been genuine interest in the welfare of the passengers. She was protective about Milena's Travel, making sure the additional human cargo they arranged to transport on one of the coaches did not interfere with day-to-day activities. Business as usual, or, was it supposed to look that way?

'You knew,' he said.

'What difference does it make?' She dismissed him. 'I don't want to go back to the past. I'm here now.'

'Why did you come?' He was not looking at her. He stared at a space on the floor, his eyes narrowed.

She bit the inside of her cheek, weighing the right words in her mind. 'Because you are a good man. I've always known. Karol never really loved me. He only loved himself and I could never compete with that. There was a time when I thought he loved me. It took me some time to understand that there's something wrong with loving a man for so long if he doesn't love you back in the same way. But you do. I know you do.'

'I've done some terrible things. Terrible, awful things.' He shook his head.

She took his face in her hands. 'You are a kind man, a good man. You did what you had to, to keep your brother safe.'

'I want to tell you something. I haven't told anyone yet.' He took her hands in his. 'I was thinking, I would like to get involved with the local government.' He gulped air and waited.

'Like work for them?'

'Yes. I'm sure they have projects or programmes I could try. I have enough money put aside. I'm prepared to work for free,' he said with determination. He wanted to tell her everything, now that she was here, because her presence gave him courage; he would not have to live his life on his own anymore. 'I feel like I can do it. I love this country and these people. This is where I be-long and being out there, a foreigner, seeing how we Poles live and fail abroad, here in my own country, I want to change that. I don't want people to leave. I want them to want to stay, like me, and you. I promise you now, with you at my side, I will do everything right, everything.'

She was looking at him with wonder at his rising passion, the palpable energy of his well-hidden aspirations. She had not sus-pected he had it in him, the qualities of the winner Karol had so easily carried, but not Damian, the underdog. Was it life abroad that had changed him so much? For a brief moment, she saw herself with his eyes, at his side, in this glorious other life.

'Are you going to say something?' Damian asked, uncertainty creeping into his voice. Milena thought she would tell him to learn to hide that vulnerability he had in her presence which she already knew other people could use against him, but she would tell him that later, now was not a good moment for such naked honesty.

'I'm here now,' Milena said, 'I'm not going anywhere.'

EPILOGUE

Karolina saw her black and white picture in a free weekly she had picked up in a Polish grocery, in the Missing Persons section; next to three other faces, one old woman and two young men, disappeared, like her, somewhere on this island. Under the photo was listed the colour of her eyes and her age, along with the date of her disappearance and a message urging whoever might see her to let them know by calling the phone number provided. It made the vanishing real now. She left the shop in haste, leaving the basket filled with produce on the floor in the middle of the shop, afraid that somebody might recognise her. She did not want to be found, not like that. If she was ever going back, it would have to be on her own terms, she had already decided. She could not bear the embarrassment of somebody crying out her name on the street or the police driving her back home, for all the neighbourhood to see. She worried about the possible consequences, and the more days that went by, the more she hesitated about going back, until she had begun to feel okay about never returning.

For a while, Karolina entertained scenarios of apology to her parents, plausible explanations as to why she had gone missing, anything but the truth – that she could no longer live with them, in their perfect lives which had somehow, somewhere, stopped being her own. One day she was having breakfast with her father, witness to her mother's joyful ignorance the next day, the space at the kitchen table where Karolina usually sat was empty.

There was a pleasure in shattering her mother's perfect happiness. Karolina wanted to provoke an honest word from her mother, unclouded by the church's passionate grip. Her father's strange naïveté frustrated Karolina. Her disappearance was an act of revenge for their passivity, because, for them, it was easier to live their lives holding back some essential part of themselves, gliding through days. She wanted her existence to matter.

The only person her disappearance would matter to was Kamil, and he was continuously on her mind. She wished he was older. She could explain to him that the reason she was not at home any longer was not because she did not love him, or that her leaving had had anything to do with him. She came to a reassuring conclusion that her parents would eventually find a way to come to terms with her disappearance. After all, they were adults and adults were supposed to be able to justify whatever was happening in their lives, according to what they wanted to believe in. But Kamil was too young to learn how to lie to himself. Karolina promised herself that one day she would tell him the whole truth and she could only hope that he would forgive her. But she was not going to ask her parents for forgiveness or offer apologies; she had done nothing wrong. Their role was to love her no matter what. Even if what she had done would surely be interpreted as heartbreakingly cruel, she did not care. She chose to stay away because she could not imagine any other way. If they had been a normal family, this would never have happened.

Karolina realised that if she had not had that accidental conversation with Igor a few months ago, perhaps she would have made a different decision. Perhaps she would have never felt so daring as to leave her parents' house, or would at least have devoted more time to imagining what kind of future she could have if she stayed.

They had been sitting in his car, when Igor threw Karolina's question back at her, 'What are you doing here?'

She had blurted out her response so fast that she almost choked on her breath., 'I'm running away.' It made it more real to say it aloud.

Igor nodded. 'I ran away once.'

'What did you do?' Her interest was visibly piqued. She shifted her body in the seat, to face him.

Igor was like an itch on his father's tongue so one day Igor pledged to himself he would show his father how strong he could be. He knew there was something different about him; different from his brother Damian, but neither was willing to admit that Igor suspected his parents were not his real parents. Damian's yes, but not Igor's. That was why his father was always so impatient around him, calling him stupid. He never called Damian stupid, although the brothers had experienced an equal measure of their father's belt. Igor and Damian would stare at each other's reflection in the mirror, to prove that they were alike, but Igor did not believe the reflected image, so he ran.

The day Igor ran away he did not say anything to Damian. He was too ashamed and worried that Damian would try to stop him, and he wanted to do something on his own, something that did not require Damian's help or protection. His mind was fearless with possibilities, so much so that he had howled with laughter, and when his craziness provoked glances from passers-by, he hooted and barked like a dog at them, louder and louder, scaring them. He felt invincible.

He stole bread and a bottle of cheap wine from a shop and ran to the nearest park where he guzzled them down. All of a sudden he felt tired. He did not remember when he fell asleep on the bench. The birds landed nearby to finish off the crumbs. He woke up with a jolt to a dog barking. It was a small black dog, a prager rattler. It bared its tiny teeth and growled in a thin voice. Igor jumped off the bench and kicked it. The dog tumbled onto the grass but quickly raised itself up, back onto its paws, and ran away whining. And then Igor heard a girl's cry. He looked up in the direction of the voice, his eyes unfocused, a girl knelt down cuddling the tiny animal which was trying to hide in her embrace.

'Why did you do that? Stupid, stupid boy,' she shouted at him, upset.

A spasm rippled through his body, his head felt as though it might pop. Stupid, that was what his father called him, in the same repulsed voice. He was infuriated by the girl's cry. He was suffocating and he swallowed hard. He was crying when he jumped at the girl, lighting-quick motion, hurting. Why did they have to call him stupid? They had no right to call him that.

He knew he did something wrong when he heard in court he was going to prison for two years. The only thing he did that day was defend himself against people like his father, people who called him stupid. Igor was hitting his temples with fists when he was walked down the corridor, Damian's voice somewhere at the back of his mind, shouting that he was here and that he would be waiting for him. Which he was two years later, outside the prison gate. But, by then, Igor had become a stranger.

Igor offered Karolina another cigarette. She was still waiting for his answer but he did not want to tell her everything. He did not want to scare her.

'I never went back,' he finally said. He was not going to tell her what to do because he did not know himself.

'I don't want to be around my parents anymore,' Karolina responded. 'They have my brother Kamil though. I don't think they will really miss me.'

'Are you hungry?' Igor asked. He did not want to get dragged into a pointless and tedious conversation about the parents.

'I was going to stay with my friend. It was our idea, you know, to run away. But she changed her mind,' Karolina said in a quiet voice. She was picking her spots nervously because it was now or never to trust Igor with her future rather than her friend who had deserted her at the last minute.

Igor did not know what to do with her but he knew a place, one of the flats near Altab Ali Park that belonged to Karol, where she could stay. The place stood empty, for now.

'I know a place.'

Her eyes radiated hope. 'Really? I only need a few days. My friend and I were going to go up north together, to Edinburgh. Or maybe even further away, like Aberdeen. I have some money,' she added hastily, but he waved away her last comment and started the engine.

'Thanks! You are so nice. Really nice. I'm just so lucky to have found you.'

She was not afraid of him or disgusted. If she was apprehensive she was not showing her fear. The eagerness with which she accepted his help was gratifying to Igor. He was her saviour and it was she who had given him this perspective. It felt so good and he genuinely wanted to help her. He was surprised by the feeling, slightly numb. All he could think was that she was going to stay with him, and he could see her whenever he wanted, at least for a few days or maybe weeks. She would be the first woman in his life who actually wanted to see him. Igor, wanted so badly for her to like him, to pretend he was normal. With her, he could do more than pretend to be normal.

While she was living in the flat at Altab Ali Park, Igor came by in the evenings, sometimes during the day, to bring her hot food in plastic containers, from Polish restaurants, and she ate it, because she did not want to be ungrateful. He would stay and they ate together. Igor had his first hot curry with Karolina, it made his ears turn red which made her laugh in that sweet way she knew he had grown to crave when he was not with her.

Karolina would have stayed longer, and she had almost forgotten that she was supposed to go to Edinburgh, part of her original plan, when one morning she saw her mother sitting in the park outside. Karolina was standing by the window, finishing the last cigarette from a pack Igor had left for her. Her cough had improved and her eyes did not water any longer. Fear mixed with disbelief surged inside her chest. She jolted into the flat to gather her clothes, money Igor had given her, which she had been keeping in a small pouch in her rucksack, and ran back to the window, tripping on the kitchen rug. She breathed so heavily and so closely to the window, that the thin lace curtain became stuck to her lips for a moment, but her mother did not notice her. Perhaps she did not know exactly which flat Karolina was living in. Her mother looked left and right, her gaze followed people on the street, and only now did Karolina realise that they were coming to get her. Karolina pressed her forehead to the window to look down onto the street. There was no time left. They were going to find her and her running away would have been for nothing. She flattened herself against the wall, heart pounding, waiting for the knock on the door.

She did not know how much time had passed. She was too dazed to look at her mobile; she was convinced it was going to happen any moment now. She heard the footsteps and the voices. She stopped breathing. And then, nothing. Everything went quiet, the voices retreated. She took a small step towards the window and saw her mother getting up, a man was talking to her, her mother nodded her head, picked up her handbag from the bench and followed the man to the car. Karolina saw them driving away. She was safe.

'I can't stay here any longer,' she told Igor and described what had happened. 'I'm taking a train up north. I want to leave today.'

'But they didn't find you. You can stay,' he begged, unnerved by her stubbornness. Her rucksack with her belongings was propped against the wall in the corridor. 'Stay until tomorrow,' he pleaded.

'I already bought the ticket. I'm going.'

Igor admired her daring and resourcefulness despite being scared. The ability of this girl, so young and already so tenacious made him jealous of her convictions, made him want to be part of it. He wanted to see her again. She made him happy, which was mystifying to him since she was not his blood, like Damian, the one person he had truly trusted until now.

'I can bring you some more money,' he said finally. 'Later today.'

She waited for the whole afternoon and when it started to get darker outside she picked up her rucksack and, stood, waiting, hoping Igor would show up any minute. She was afraid to stay in the flat on her own now, unsure whether her mother or the people that she had been talking to would return, to check the other flats. Karolina paced the rooms, from one window to the other, but there was no sign of her mother or of Igor. It was the first time Igor had not showed up as promised and Karolina thought the least she could do was wait for him a little bit longer. Unnerving thoughts gripped her, until her mobile phone beeped: a text message from Igor saying: *On my way to Southport. I'm sorry. Work. I'll be back tomorrow. I promise. Wait for me.* And Karolina waited until she fell asleep on the sofa with her phone in her hand but still with her resolute thought that she would leave tomorrow.

Anger was growing in Igor's heart all the way to Southport. He chain-smoked until Damian told him to stop because he could not see a thing through the blue smoke inside the car. For the first time, Igor had finally found a person that could help him escape himself forever, and, instead of staying with Karolina, or, hell, even accompanying her to wherever she wanted to go, he had been forced to go with Damian. He had no emotional capacity to regret his past crimes. He could only look forward. Karolina made him imagine his future. Igor was permanently at the mercy of his brother. Until now, he had possessed no need to envision any other life for himself; Damian had done that for him since he was a child. Events in his life, when he had hurt people, each act more terrible than the last, were nothing more than politics of life, something he had been unwillingly thrown into. He blamed Damian, always at his side, always leading the way and Igor had let him, because it was so painful, at times, to think about what else he could have done. It was easier to let it go and let Damian decide. For Igor, all Damian did was construct well-meant lies but Igor decided it was going to end today. He was the terrible Kulesza family secret, his brother's terror, fear his daily preoccupation. Today Igor was going to recover what was left of himself, lose the fury that had been devouring his mind from within, lose the emptiness that had taken hold of him.

Igor drank with his brother, with a ferocious overabundance of energy that made him dizzy. When he ran towards the sea he was weightless, deaf to Damian's shouts from the beach. The shock of the cold water took his breath away. He turned around and saw Damian's dark silhouette; he was not sure if Damian was still facing him, it was too dark and he was too far away to hear his brother's voice. Igor could hardly focus through the numbing cold and buzzing in his ears. He could now see the future that would begin tomorrow, upon his return to Karolina. He had promised her he would be back. Igor laughed, a crazy shriek in the darkness, at the explosion of clarity in his mind.

Igor could no longer see his brother, but Igor was going to tell Damian that he was ready to leave. Actually, he could not wait to tell Damian. Damian would be glad, Igor was certain, that he could now walk on his own.

He pushed his feet through the water and stumbled, his feet snagged on something, a nylon rope, the waves surged towards him. He fell, water covered his mouth, but he rose to his feet and grabbed the nylon rope with one hand and pushed it away. He took a step, or he thought he did, but he had stepped into a net. He fell to his knees again, pulling in anger, shouting and beating his hands against the waves. With every minute it was less terrifying.

ACKNOWLEDGMENTS

Although inspired by certain people and real events, this novel is product of imagination. I benefited enormously from people who generously shared their stories and knowledge with me.

My deepest gratitude to my publisher Mike Tate for believing in the story, his patience and overwhelming enthusiasm. I am indebted to Jantar's editors, aka The Commissariat, who edited the manuscript and made meticulous comments and corrections. To Jack Coling for a truly stunning cover. I also would like to thank Friends of Jantar who have read the manuscript and extended their support via Mike.

I feel grateful to Susan Curtis, founder of Istros Books, for kindly introducing me to Mike.

My heartfelt thanks to Gosia McKane, founder of Merseyside Polonia, without whom this book would have never been written. During one of our late night conversations she told me about Poles trafficking Poles to Britain for the benefit fraud. I quickly realised this was the story I should have been writing, instead of a novel I almost finished at the time.

In Liverpool, Constable Andrew Billingsley was generous in answering my questions and helped me understand the way traffickers work. He also shared his invaluable knowledge on the tattoos among Polish prisoners. I borrowed the idea for the dot on Igor's nose from our fascinating conversation.

In London, the detective who wished to be named only as Mr Mafia, was a fountain of information on Eastern European traffickers operating across the London boroughs.

Aleksandra Łojek and Mariusz Śmiejek for their wonderful generosity during my visit to Belfast. In particular to Aleksandra for her passionate book recommendations. Karol would have been a poorer character if not for Robert D. Hare's *Without Conscience. The Disturbing World of the Psychopaths Among Us* suggested by Aleksandra.

My gratitude to Sharmila Beezmohun, Agnieszka Dale, Wioletta Greg, Anya Lipska, Magda Raczyńska, Dr Nancy Roberts for their invaluable comments and conversations, sharing the passion of storytelling and encouragement during various phases of writing this novel. Their support has been a tremendous assistance.

As always, Martin Llewellyn gave me a thorough and much needed editorial advice. His patient reading and comments on the early versions of my manuscript have been incredibly helpful.

Mary B Rodgers, a talented author and my dear friend, for her generosity, kindness and inspiration.

Fernando Álvarez-Jiménez for making all my characters better people and helping me to embrace and understand humans in all shapes and forms.

I thank wholeheartedly Liz Hoggard and Jeremy Osborne who have supported me over the years. As well as the Polish Cultural Institute in London.

On the epigraph page, the verses from Wisława Szymborska are from 'Children of our age' translated by Stanisław Barańczak and Claire Cavanagh, *Poems New and Collected* (Houghton Mifflin Harcourt). The verses from Dany Laferrière are from 'Time in books' translated by David Homel, *The Enigma of the Return* (Maclehose Press). My grateful thanks to The Wisława Szymborska Foundation and HMH for kind permission to use the lines from Szymborska's poem as a title.

Finally, my biggest thanks, impossible for me to put into adequate words, to my husband Asher. His wisdom, immense encouragement and much needed criticism inspires me to work harder.

Also available from Jantar Publishing

FOX SEASON AND OTHER SHORT STORIES
by Agnieszka Dale

Agnieszka Dale's characters all want to find greatness, but they realise greatness isn't their thing. But what is? And what is great anyway? In Peek-a-boo, a mother breastfeeds her child via Skype, at work. In Hello Poland, a man reunites with his daughter in a world where democracy has been replaced by user testing. In other short stories, people bow and are bowed to. They feed foxes or go fishing. They kiss the fingers of those they love while counting to ten.

THREE PLASTIC ROOMS
by Petra Hůlová

Translated from the Czech by Alex Zucker

A foul-mouthed Prague prostitute muses on her profession, aging and the nature of materialism. She explains her world view in the scripts and commentaries of her own reality TV series combining the mundane with fetishism, violence, wit and an unvarnished mixture of vulgar and poetic language.

Also available from Jantar Publishing

IN THE NAME OF THE FATHER AND OTHER
STORIES
by Balla

Translated from the Slovak by Julia & Peter Sherwood

Balla is often described as 'the Slovak Kafka' for his depictions of the
absurd and the mundane. *In the Name of the Father* features a nameless
narrator reflecting on his life, looking for someone else to blame for
his failed relationship with his parents and two sons, his serial adultery,
the breakup of his marriage and his wife's descent into madness.

BURYING THE SEASON
by Antonín Bajaja

Translated from the Czech by David Short

An affectionate, multi-layered account of small town life in central
Europe beginning in the early 1930s and ending in the 21st Century.
Adapting scenes from Fellini's *Amarcord*, Bajaja's meandering narrative
weaves humour, tragedy and historical events into a series of compelling
nostalgic anecdotes.

www.jantarpublishing.com

Also available from Jantar Publishing

BLISS WAS IT IN BOHEMIA
by Michal Viewegh

Translated from the Czech by David Short

A wildly comic story about the fate of a Czech family from the 1960s onwards. At turns humorous, ironic and sentimental, an engaging portrait of their attempts to flee from history (meaning the 1968 Soviet invasion of Czechoslovakia) – or at least to ignore it as long as possible… Light-hearted and sophisticated at once, this is a book that reminds us that comedy can tackle large historical subjects successfully.

GRAVELARKS
by Jan Křesadlo

Translated from the Czech by Václav Z J Pinkava

Zderad, a noble misfit, investigates a powerful party figure in 1950s Czechoslovakia. His struggle against blackmail, starvation and betrayal leaves him determined to succeed where others have failed and died. Set in Stalinist era Central Europe, *GraveLarks* is a triumphant intellectual thriller navigating the fragile ambiguity between sado-masochism, black humour, political satire, murder and hope.

www.jantarpublishing.com

ng

T H ... E L

by Jiří Pehe

Translation by Gerald Turner

Foreword by Dr Marketa Goetz-Stankiewicz, FRSC

Three Faces of an Angel is a novel about the twentieth century that begins when time was linear and ended when the notion of progress was less well defined. The Brehmes' story guides the reader through revolution, war, the holocaust, and ultimately exile and return. A novel about what man does to man and whether God intervenes.

KYTICE

CZECH & ENGLISH BILINGUAL EDITION

by Karel Jaromír Erben

Translation and Introduction by Susan Reynolds

Kytice was inspired by Erben's love of Slavonic myth and the folklore surrounding such creatures as the Noonday Witch and the Water Goblin. First published in 1853, these poems, along with Mácha's Máj and Němcová's Babička, are the best loved and most widely read 19th century Czech classics. Published in the expanded 1861 version, the collection has moved generations of artists and composers, including Dvořák, Smetana and Janáček.